ALIEN DAY

ALSO BY RICK WILBER

The Cold Road
Alien Morning

ALIEN DAY

RICK WILBER

TOR

A TOM DOHERTY
ASSOCIATES
BOOK

NEW
YORK

This is a work of fiction. All of the characters, organizations, and events portrayed in this novel are either products of the author's imagination or are used fictitiously.

ALIEN DAY

A Tor Book
Published by Tom Doherty Associates
120 Broadway
New York, NY 10271

www.tor-forge.com

Tor® is a registered trademark of Macmillan Publishing Group, LLC.

The Library of Congress Cataloging-in-Publication Data is available upon request.

ISBN 978-1-250-26024-6 (hardcover)
ISBN 978-1-4299-6529-3 (ebook)

Our books may be purchased in bulk for promotional, educational, or business use. Please contact your local bookseller or the Macmillan Corporate and Premium Sales Department at 1-800-221-7945, extension 5442, or by email at MacmillanSpecialMarkets@macmillan.com.

First Edition: June 2021

Printed in the United States of America

0 9 8 7 6 5 4 3 2 1

This one is for my wife, Robin Wilber, Ph.D. who's been patiently reading and rereading this novel for a long time, steering it in the right direction. Thanks for the guidance.

ALIEN DAY

PROLOGUE

PACING IS EVERYTHING

My breaststroke was steady and purposeful, though I certainly didn't feel that way myself as I swam slowly toward the ship that stood upright ahead of me in the moonlit water of the Gulf of Mexico. This had seemed like a great idea just a few days ago, when Heather and Twoclicks offered it to me, and the adrenaline rush from that last scare at the beach had propelled me past any hesitation. I was going, and that was that. I'd hugged my brother and my girlfriend and my sister's wife back there on the warm midnight sand of Rum Point, and then I'd boldly gone where no one had gone before—and you know how that line goes.

Now, naked and struggling in the water, I was rethinking the whole thing. Sure, brave Peter Holman heads to the stars sounded great, taking me right back to the sci-fi books I read as a kid, both old school and new. Have sweep system, will travel. S'hudon my destination. Twoclicks and friends as an imperative species, trying to impose some ancillary justice. Me? Part of that? Incredible, wonderful, count me in.

But it had all happened so fast that I realized—swimming along, stroke, stroke, stroke—that there were a lot of questions that I hadn't even thought to ask. Food, shelter, clothing . . . sure, the S'hudonni could handle that. But this strange passage held nothing but dangerous unknowns and only a slight chance that I might do something right. Like survive, and find my sister, and get us both back to Earth. And, oh yeah, there was that whole global war thing, coming our way because two princes from a distant world were squabbling over who was in charge of Earth, and I would be on their home planet, documenting it as they settled their differences. See, what could go wrong?

Swimming along to my left was one of those two princes, Twoclicks himself, moving along at my pace just to humor me. The S'hudonni are semi-aquatic and swimming is effortless for them. I wished it were the same for me as I plowed slowly along.

Twoclicks swore he was here on Earth to lift us up to membership in their empire, if we just did the right things at the right times. He could be very persuasive, with both carrots and sticks. He offered endless energy for a power-starved Earth, and medical devices that could cure what ails you and extend life, and trade and tourism with a half dozen other worlds. The amazement of that!

But he also could snap those thin fingers on his frail arms and send his screamships in to fry a military base or level a city, if that's the sort of mood he was in. Just a week ago I'd seen the first of those happen, and didn't want to see the second. There was no arguing with S'hudon.

So it was ironic that Twoclicks reveled in being of good humor. Mr. Charming, that was Twoclicks. He thought himself a man of good cheer, generous and understanding, and he had a hard time understanding why all these simple Earthies didn't agree with him.

A wave crest caught me and I choked and gasped for a second with my mouth full of salt water. Twoclicks giggled at me and said, "Ho, friend Peter!" with that lisp he used as an affectation, a trick to make him seem friendlier to skeptical Earthies. "Iss not to drink the water! Sswim through it!"

Very funny. I didn't try to respond. Instead, I finished clearing my throat and got back to business: stroke, stroke, stroke, steady on into the slight rise and fall of the Gulf swells. At the top of each one, I could see into the distance ahead, and that ship. It didn't look any closer. The current, I supposed, was working against me, pushing me gently down the coast as I tried to head out to sea. It looked like it would be a long night of swimming. I stopped for a few seconds, floating there in the buoyant salt water.

"You're doing fine, Peter," my other companion said to me, and I looked to my right to see her there, well ahead of me, encouraging me forward. Heather, who'd had been in her S'hudonni form back at the beach when they'd met me and I'd waded in, joining her and the porpoisy Twoclicks. Now she looked human, athletic and strong, but male, with a face I vaguely remembered. Maybe the bodyguard back in Ireland, when it all fell apart? Why had she changed? I didn't know.

"Sure," I agreed. "I'm doing fine."

I dug back into it, thinking about how not so long ago I'd made love to this creature, often. In fact, I'd been *in* love with her, him, it. And that love had seemed so real and true to me that I'd fallen for her in spite of everything that shouted no. There'd been some pain and sorrow that came from that as various realities caught up with me.

Time went by, and the more I knew, the less I loved, and so it was that, ultimately, it had been someone else, an Earthie, that I'd said *I love you* to on the beach that lay a half hour's swim behind me. Chloe Cary—yes, *that* Chloe Cary—hadn't responded with more than a slight smile, so I suspect I was wrong about that relationship, too. Story of my life.

I lost sight of Heather as I sank into a trough between waves. When I pushed forward over the next crest, there she was, floating effortlessly with Twoclicks, the two of them a good ten or fifteen meters ahead, looking back together at me, smiling. I smiled, and gave them a slight wave, and then got back to work.

It all seemed preposterous, how I'd come to this. I'd had an ordinary childhood, growing up in a Florida beach town, snorkeling and kayaking and throwing footballs on the beach with my little brother and sister. Dad was a doctor, Mom was a teacher. I went to the local Jesuit high school and played the usual sports and got the usual grades and then went to the usual college to play Division II basketball. I was pretty good at that and got an offer to try out for a second division pro team in Europe and—what do you know?—I made the team, the Dublin Rovers.

Five years I played there, a shooting guard and occasionally at point, hitting my threes and driving the lane and enjoying the hell out of it, just a young man lost in the game, really. I wasn't good enough to play a division higher, nor bad enough to not be useful to the Rovers. I was happy in Dublin and happy in Europe and didn't give the future too much thought, until that career ended with damage to my left knee and suddenly I had to think of something to do for the rest of my life.

I spent my savings to pay for the tech to turn my English degree and my sports background into some modest success as the latest thing, a freelance sweeper, interviewing celebrities and living an active life while my audience sensed every bit of sight, sounds, smells, touch, taste—all of it. For the price of a receiving system and the willingness to encounter my native ads, you could be inside me, looking out, as I hung out with that famous singer backstage, or played catch with that all-star catcher, or hit a few back and forth with that new tennis star, or had a cup of coffee with that Hollywood A-lister.

It paid the bills, though the tech was new and there was a lot of competition for a small, if growing, audience.

And then our friends from S'hudon arrived, and my little corner of the media sphere was of interest to Twoclicks, and that's all it takes these days. He and Heather liked what they saw of me and, *snap,* I had a new job. Just like that, though nothing in my résumé shouted interstellar ambassador. Within a year, I went from driving the lane and dishing it out to my teammates to heading for the home world of mighty S'hudon. Such is fate.

It was dizzying, how it had all happened, but there it was, further proof, for me, that you just never know how it will all turn out and that's why you play the game, and why what happens in the clubhouse stays in the clubhouse, and why when the going gets tough the tough get going. To coin a few phrases.

I kept swimming, looking every now and then at the ship, when I was at the top of a swell, checking to see if it seemed closer. It did, maybe, a little. Or not.

The ship rose above a spidery network of interlacing stilts that held up the main body, bulbous and smooth, porcelain in its sheen, the size of a twenty-story building. Eventually I'd get there, with nothing on me or with me except my internals—useless without their external hardware—the helpmate I'd been with forever, myBob. My upgraded internal sweep system had been installed just weeks ago in Palo Alto by the best neurologists money could buy. Heather and Twoclicks promised me that the hardware was waiting for me on the ship, and I believed them. Mostly.

So I'd be reporting back to the billions on Earth as Twoclicks's wondrous ship took me to fabulous S'hudon, the pulsing power at the heart of the new empire we would all be part of one day soon. Me, Peter Holman, ex-jock turned celebrity journo and now Earth's first emissary to the stars.

So that's how it works sometimes, friends. One minute your knee is ruined and your hoops career is over, the next minute you swim, swim, swim toward that distant ship, and from there to the distant planet that lies at the center of everything.

And then you get to the ship, and you climb a ladder with the help of your alien pals, the one a clumsy porpoise-shaped thing with a goofy smile and an odd sense of humor and the power to destroy Earth, should that strike him as a good idea; the other a handsome guy who is sometimes a plain Jane and sometimes a beautiful temptress and sometimes a creature that looks a lot like a bull shark. And you've made love with that thing, and now you're climbing up, rung by rung, and then you're aboard and you're ready for everything, absolutely everything, to change.

PART ONE

LIFE ON EARTH

Dying isn't hard. It happens all the time. I should know.

—Peter Holman, *Notes from Holmanville*
(S'hudon City and New York:
Trebnet Press, 2035)

1

FIRST EDITIONS

Chloe Cary was adjusting her sweep receiver and waiting for connectivity as she sat with her legs curled beneath her on the comfortable old recliner that occupied a corner of her bedroom. Out the picture window to her right was the Pacific Ocean and above it the dim predawn light of another perfect California day.

Chloe was tired. It had been a long and loving and very private night before Terri left for home at three a.m., going down the back steps to the beach and the short path to the bat-garage, as Chloe called it. The paparazzi hadn't caught on to that back way out yet.

Then, at five, myBetty had dinged Chloe awake. It was Peter, about to broadcast his live sweepcast from the S'hudonni ship! All over the planet, smarties were dinging and sweepsets were blinking and home AIs were announcing that Peter Holman was aboard the luxury yacht of First Envoy Twoclicks and headed toward the S'hudonni home world! His first sweepcast would be airing in five minutes!

Chloe had been there when Peter snuck away from Earth without anyone knowing except a precious few, and he'd been gone now for eight long days without a word. Chloe had been starting to think she wasn't going to hear from him again.

Now, suddenly, here it was. Peter! Live from outer space!

The headset went on over the ears like a pair of headphones, and then you slid the lenses down over the eyes and that brought the smell and taste tabs into place automatically. Clip on the finger pads and then say "Connect." Chloe didn't wear the unit often, so it took a minute or two, but now, with the unit on, she whispered the magic word, and after a few seconds of flickering gray, she joined him.

She'd already missed the famous introduction where Peter opened with "Hello, Earth. I'm on my way to S'hudon and you're coming with me." But just after that, here she was, inside Peter's head as he walked along the narrow corridors of the S'hudonni ship, following the backside of a waddling S'hudonni.

As he walked, Peter was talking about how he was "sending this live, friends, but I'm told we're already halfway to Jupiter, traveling at a steady one g, and so there's about a twenty-minute lag between when I send and when you receive."

Chloe could smell a strange mix of pine trees and a damp, metallic tang, and she could hear a high, distant whine in the background and a slight susurrus of circulating air. She could taste the coffee Peter must have had right before the sweepcast. They were taking good care of him, then, if he had coffee.

Peter reached up to run his fingers through his hair, and Chloe felt the strands between her fingers. A little more than a week ago she'd come awake in Peter's bedroom at the beach house in Florida and had done just that same thing herself, running her fingers through his hair, feeling the salt and grains of sand from the nighttime swim they'd taken before going to bed on his last night on Earth. They'd showered off outside after the swim but had been in too much of a hurry to do a very good job of it. The good-bye sex that followed was pretty damn nice, and Peter's help-mate, myBob, had recorded it all and edited it down for the day it could be sweepcast. That day would be this one, Chloe thought. It would be a great follow-up to whatever he had going on at the moment.

The enjoyment of that last night wasn't feigned. The guy was a real sweetheart, your basic heart of gold, in fact. There were reasons to like him, for sure, beyond all the fame and attendant fortune.

Peter was talking as he walked the narrow corridor: "I'm following a S'hudonni that I call Sergeant Preston. I named her after that movie from a couple of years ago, *Sergeant Preston of the Yukon,* where that Canadian Mountie rescued her dog from an avalanche with the help of a whole First Nations village. I watched it on the plane from Dublin to JFK and, heck, I wound up really liking it. Great scenery, anyway.

"So why name this S'hudonni after her? Well, when I first got into my room on board this ship, the place was so cold I could see my breath and there was frost on the walls. I'm a Florida boy, you know, so that was insane cold. But a few minutes later this S'hudonni showed up to say she'd been assigned to help me, and when I complained about the cold she whistled and clicked to the room's AI and things got warmer fast. So that's her: my own Mountie from S'hudon, rescuing me from a frozen death."

Peter was a little out of breath. "My quarters on this ship have been made to look like my bedroom back home in Florida. I don't know why or how that was done, but the bed seems the same, the wood flooring seems the same, the dresser, the mirror, the big window that looks out to the Gulf of Mexico . . . That's an image, of course, but maybe it's live? I can't tell. Even my bookcases and my collection of old signed first editions are here, most of them from my years in Dublin: Lady Gregory and W. B. Yeats, Walter M. Miller, Ursula K. Le Guin, Joe Haldeman, John Banville and Benjamin Black, Maeve Binchy, Kate O'Brien, Roddy Doyle, Molly Mc-Closkey, and a hundred more. They're all here.

"And these spacious quarters have been added onto the ship, I think, like a kind of blister attached to the hull. Why? How? When? I have no idea."

He stopped for a second to take a breath. "Man, Sergeant Preston is really moving fast for a S'hudonni, so I'm hustling to keep up. We're on our way to dinner with Twoclicks, in his quarters. I suspect that will be interesting, so stay tuned."

He looked around, and so Chloe and hundreds of millions of others were looking, too, as he glanced up the ceiling that was far above his head, seven meters or more, with dim light coming directly from the metal somehow, with a watery kind of soft glow. Then he looked left and right and the corridor was narrow enough to be claustrophobic, dim gray and more dim gray and more of it still, stretching off in front of him, with nothing but that waddling Sergeant Preston ahead of him, hurrying along.

For a few seconds Peter looked down to his feet. The hero on his way to the alien home planet was wearing his regular black running shoes with scuffed toes. Chloe laughed to see that. Something close to a billion or more people were tuned in live to this or would see it later, and she was probably the only one who knew those running shoes were his favorites when he was home. He'd worn them for a run with her on the morning of his last day on Earth, jogging along the narrow pavement of the single road that ran the length of the little barrier island that held his home and a few dozen others.

The island was a narrow two kilometers long, so they'd gotten to the end of it, looked out over the mouth of Tampa Bay, then come back along the hard sand of the beach, down near the waterline, sprinting at the end and turning it into a race. She'd won, but he always had that bad knee as an excuse, so she hadn't poked too much fun at him for the loss.

He loved those shoes, so the S'hudonni must have gone into his house and picked them up, along with everything else, from bed to books. That didn't seem possible, given what had happened there, but he certainly hadn't moved any of it himself. Chloe had been with him the whole morning, from lovemaking to running to a final walkthrough of the old family home as he'd said good-bye. Then they'd all gone out to the beach and watched as he'd stripped, T-shirt and shorts and underwear and flip-flops all casually tossed to the sand before he'd waded out, stark naked, for the long swim to that distant ship, where his future—and Earth's, too—waited for him.

Sergeant Preston, the waddling S'hudonni, turned a corner, and there was a stairway, a steep one that led up into the darkness. "Well, that's interesting," Peter was saying as he watched Sergeant Preston begin to climb. She was surprisingly nimble, given her body shape, those thin arms grabbing the railing and the short legs bending at the knees to go up.

Peter looked up to see the narrow steps leading to an opening that Sergeant Preston had already reached. Chloe could feel the cold metal of the railing and the moisture on it, and she caught that strange smell of pine as Peter followed. He reached the opening and stepped into another corridor, walked down that for fifty or sixty meters, and then did another climb on more metal steps, talking all the while, going on about how the ship had lifted off so effortlessly that Peter almost missed it.

"There was that flat screen on one side of my quarters," he was saying, "and I happened to glance at it as I walked by and, wow, we were already a thousand feet up and rising steadily. I didn't have any of my sweep equipment on yet, so I couldn't record the liftoff. But I can tell you it was amazing. I could see my own house in the distance, and some people who'd been there to see me off."

Chloe smiled at how he sidestepped the whole reality of who'd been at the beach house and what had actually happened. Chloe had been there as Peter's brother, Tom, the murderous bastard, literally burned down the house. Peter must have seen that in the distance, but he didn't want to share that or what it meant, so she'd keep quiet about it, too.

He was going on: "There was no extra g-force on me, just my normal weight, so I could stand there and watch for nearly an hour as we rose through a cloud deck, and then another, and then kept rising, so that I could see the curvature of the Earth and then the darkness of space and, below, an Earth growing smaller as we moved away."

Peter kept climbing, following the good sergeant, twice more up stairs and down long corridors, all the while talking. "I've been on this ship for, what, a week now?" he said, huffing and puffing a bit as he climbed the second set of steps. "It's hard to keep track of time here. The light inside the ship never changes, and Sergeant Preston shows up at all sorts of odd times to take care of my needs, from bringing me food—pretty decent Earth food, so I suspect it's actual food from home, frozen and then heated up here to present it to me—to taking away my dirty clothes and returning them later cleaned and folded. I've been trying to self-regulate, staying awake for sixteen hours and sleeping for eight. But you'd be surprised how hard that is to do."

He reached the top step, turned right to walk through the strangely narrow but tall hatchway, and then looked right and left to see where Sergeant Preston was. He grunted when he saw her, well down the corridor to his left. He took a deep breath, said, "OK, then," and started walking.

"You can tell I'm out of shape. I've been on a few excursions with Sergeant Preston to see various parts of the ship and to meet the crew—and wait until I tell you about the crew!—and that's about the only exercise I've had. I'm going to start doing calisthenics in my room or something. Heck, that might help me get some sleep."

He was walking along at a good clip now, breathing hard, trying to catch up with Sergeant Preston, who was waiting for him at the next hatch. But he added, in a comment that Chloe knew would keep Earth buzzing for weeks, "So, OK, the crew. I should tell you about them. They're not S'hudonni! That surprised the hell out of me. They're cute little creatures, about a meter tall, with a kind of scaly light blue skin, and facial features that look sort of like lizards'. But they walk upright on two legs and have arms and hands with six fingers on each hand and an opposable thumb. Their faces are yellow, and they have yellow dewlaps that flare out to the sides like flower petals from their throat area when they're excited about something. They almost look like walking and talking daffodils, funny as that sounds. And they're smart! They're the ones that run this ship. When I met them, they were busy standing at workstations, a dozen of them or more. There was a lot of chatter going on, quiet hoots mostly, between them, and then indecipherable murmurs and a lot of head nods and flares of those dewlaps.

"One of them, dressed in the same kind of one-piece uniform the others had, but with a lot of stripes and ornaments on it, came over to me to introduce herself as the chief. She—I think it was a female, but who knows—hooted and flared those dewlaps at me, and then when that didn't work, she spoke Spanish! And then what I think was Mandarin. And then English! We were starting a nice chat about who they were, when some of her crew got excited about something, dewlaps flaring all over the place and the hoots getting louder, and she begged off to solve the problem, saying we'd meet again soon and she'd show me around. Then Sergeant Preston came over and dragged me away."

Chloe smiled. This was all tantalizing to Earth's scientists, she was sure. And as if in response to that thought, myBetty dinged with a high-priority message from Abigail Parnell at the Jet Propulsion Laboratory, Peter's friend who had now become friends with Chloe, too.

Chloe lifted the lenses and glanced at the *Call me!* from Abby. "Tell her I'll call as soon as this is over," she said to myBetty, and slid the lenses back down into place.

And there she was, inside Peter again, as he slowly made his way up one more steep staircase with those moist railings and then stepped from the top of that, through one more hatch, and emerged into a room where everything had changed.

Paneled walls, wood flooring, recessed lighting at a reasonable height just above them. No dripping moisture. Chloe and the many millions more with sweep receivers could feel the wonder of this as Peter stepped into the room, looked to his left and then his right, took a few steps over to the side, and ran his hand along the paneled walls.

"Red cedar," his myBob told him, "from Michigan."

"Very nice," Peter said. And then he leaned down to touch the flooring. "myBob?"

"Brazilian cherry," myBob said.

"Twoclicks sure loves his Earthie things," Peter said, and then he looked up to the ceiling, three meters up maybe, not nearly so high as elsewhere, and shook his head to marvel at the long strips of wood that covered that.

He didn't have to ask myBob, who said, "Teak."

Chloe was impressed, but wondered why this spaceship looked like some fancy art gallery in Big Sur.

She got her answer when a door opened at the far side of the room and Sergeant Preston stood there, holding the door open for Peter to walk through, into a long, narrow room that went on for a good fifty meters. Paintings and displays lined both sides, with a few installations hanging from the ceiling. Sergeant Preston shut the door behind her and waddled briskly past Peter to head down the far side of the room to a large double door. Wood, of course, with brass hardware. There she stopped and turned around, arms akimbo, waiting for Peter to get over the awe of the art on display and to come join her.

But Peter was in no hurry. He walked over to stare at the first display, a glass case attached to the paneled wall at eye level, about six inches deep, with a small gold artifact in it. A straight pin with a Celtic cross at the top, encrusted with jewels and intricate swirls and patterns.

"That's the Tara brooch, everyone," he said. "Anyone who's been to Ireland has probably seen it. Is this a reproduction? I guess so. I saw the original in the antiquities museum in Dublin, back when I played for the Rovers. It's Celtic, I think; an early-Christian-era piece of jewelry." Peter hesitated for a second, then added, "myBob tells me it's from the seventh or eighth century, found in the nineteenth century north of Dublin. Very, very famous."

"I wonder . . ." he said, and he walked along to the next piece, a page of manuscript, large swirls of hand-inked text, in Latin, with a green and red serpent that sat atop the right corner of the page and coiled and swirled its way down the side of the page.

"Yes," he said. "Incredible. It must be a facsimile."

Chloe and a billion others could hear myBob say, "The Book of Kells. Eighth century or a little earlier. Very impressive illuminated manuscript."

"I know," said Peter, shaking his head and walking over to the wall. A small painting there showed a stylized dog. "Picasso," Peter whispered to himself and the billion on Earth. "I've seen that one, too, in Barcelona. A kind of practice painting he did while studying Velazquez's *Las Meninas*. He painted a couple of dozen things from that painting."

He hesitated, so myBob added, "Picasso did fifty-eight paintings as part of his study of *Las Meninas*. You saw them in the Picasso Museum in Barcelona, in the Catalan Republic."

There were other items that Chloe recognized as Peter looked at them and myBob filled him in with the details—a life-size clay soldier from China's Terracotta Army, a small three-thousand-year-old jade giraffe that she knew was from that recent find near Rawalpindi, a mummy from Peru's Norte Chico site, and more—much more. And this, she thought, was just the material that could be shown off in one corridor.

Peter was looking at the mummy when something farther down caught his eye and he walked right to it, laughing. Ten paces down the corridor, toward the entrance door, a baseball bat hung vertically on the wall, secured by a small brace at the top that held the handle, letting the barrel of the bat hang down. Peter reached out to touch the bat, and Chloe and the millions of others could feel the smooth wood.

"Look at this," he said. "It's signed by Ted Williams, a very famous baseball player, for those of you who aren't fans. I was there when the curator gave that bat to Twoclicks. We'd attended a game—the Cards and the Red Sox at rickety old Fenway—and Twoclicks had enjoyed himself there, drinking beer and eating hot dogs and making jokes. Afterward, the owner of the Red Sox gave him this bat. It's amazing to see it here again."

Chloe, comfortable in her Malibu home with the Pacific out the window and funny and sweet Terri still lying on the bed, chuckled at Peter and sports. There he was, millions of kilometers away out in space, on the greatest adventure any human had ever been on, and still he was talking sports. A lunkhead, that's what he was. A charming lunkhead. Walk right by all the museum pieces from all over the world and then stop to praise the baseball bat.

The charming lunkhead went on down the hallway. There were inscribed stone markers, small Roman statuettes on pedestals, and the largest piece, a statue that stood by itself, a headless walking man, muscular, striding along.

Finally, at the end of the hallways, next to the door where a very patient Sergeant Preston waited, a huge wooden propeller was upright on the floor. Four large blades came from a central hub, so that the propeller was a good three meters or more in diameter.

"I know this one, too," Peter said, narrating for the sweep as he walked up to it. "I saw it for the first time just a couple of weeks ago, in the West of Ireland. Can that be right? Just a couple of weeks? It seems more like a lifetime. I was with Twoclicks and Heather and a whole caravan of Irish military as we stopped at a pub in a small village in County Clare and bought this from the pub owner. It's one of the propellers from the Vickers Vimy biplane that Alcock and Brown—a couple of British pilots who'd fought in World War I—flew across the Atlantic in 1919, long before Lindbergh made his solo flight. Twoclicks knew about it, and wanted it, so he got it, and now here it is."

He reached out to touch the lacquered wood of the propeller, ran his finger along the curvature of the blade. Chloe could feel the smooth lacquer as his finger moved down and back.

"I helped lift this huge thing into the back of an armored vehicle, a big one," he said. "Heather Newsome, Twoclicks' aide, was there helping, and some Irish guards. God, the thing was heavy."

He stopped for a second, thinking through what to say. "Things were really tense. Twoclicks was trying to make sure no one got hurt, but I know how it looked to you all: the S'hudonni—the two princes, Twoclicks and

Whistle—fighting among themselves, and Earth, all of us, caught in the middle."

He patted the blade, then reached up with both hands to rub his face and take a deep breath. Chloe could feel all that, his facial skin, his fingertips, his lips, the slight tangy odor of lacquer on wood. "I'd chosen my side," Peter said, "and I think I did the right thing. But damn, what an awful day that was."

Chloe knew Peter was thinking now of his sister, Kait, and how she'd died that day, her body rigged with explosives, meant to kill Peter and Heather and set off a war that Whistle would win. But, she thought, he couldn't talk about that. Earthies didn't know the real story, the whole story, and Peter couldn't tell them, not yet.

"There were people shooting at us from the hill that overlooked the pub. It was crazy, chaotic. Bullets flying around, people shooting back at that sniper on the top of the hill, and there we were, trying to get this down from the ceiling in the pub where it'd been for more than a hundred years and somehow muscle it through the pub, out the door, across the open space where mud and dirt was gouged by bullets."

He sighed, shook his head slightly, reached up to touch the propeller blade one more time. Then he shook himself, stood up straighter, and walked toward the wide double-doored entrance ahead of him. Sergeant Preston turned to press a spot on the doors as Peter walked toward her, and then she and Peter stood there as the doors swung in and open and there was Twoclicks, prince of S'hudon, holding out his arms for a hug and shouting, "Friend Peter! Hello! Iss so good to ssee you one more time!"

Twoclicks was dressed for dinner in an Earthie tux. Chloe thought he must have worn it to several state dinners during his European tour, since he looked comfortable wearing it. It was pretty damn funny to see, squat Twoclicks with those small legs and fragile arms, all dressed to the nines. Chloe supposed it looked charming to the many millions who looked through Peter's eyes at the comically askew bow tie and the white shirt with blousy sleeves covering those thin arms and, even funnier, the black slacks that had to start at that wide, wide waist and then narrow down in a hurry to fit over the short, stubby legs.

Chloe's thought was that she was looking at a caricature who didn't realize he was one. Or perhaps he did. Perhaps this was all part of his con job? The funny, cute creature from a distant world? Chloe didn't quite buy it.

She well knew that Peter seemed to actually like Twoclicks, but Chloe couldn't fathom why. Work with him, become famous, see the universe, save the world? Sure, to all of that. But actually like him? No, thanks.

No matter. Behind Twoclicks stood another S'hudonni, taller and thinner. Chloe knew as soon as she saw her through Peter's eyes that it was Heather, though Chloe had only once seen Heather in S'hudonni form, and she'd been in the water then, cruising slowly back and forth, waiting for

Peter to enter the warm Gulf and head toward her ship. Still, there was something about the way she stood, straighter and taller, no bowlegs like the rest of the S'hudonni, a little more shoulder, a bit of a neck, and those eyes—those very serious eyes. She wore a tux, too, and looked much better in it.

Yes, it was Heather, the strangest alien of them all. She was a kind of machine, Peter said, and one with her own agenda. Peter wasn't sure just what that agenda was, but she had the tools to get it done, of that he was convinced. For starters, she could change shapes, be what she needed to be, do what she needed to do. Here, in the ship, she apparently needed to be a smiling S'hudonni, and Twoclicks's tuxedo-clad strong right hand.

There were hugs all around, Twoclicks reaching out to put his arms around Peter first, and then Heather doing the same before they all turned to walk through the small foyer. Heather was in front and Twoclicks was next, holding Peter's hand and pulling him along, as they all walked toward another door. Heather opened it and stepped aside to let Twoclicks and Peter go through first.

Into a pocket palace. Peter said nothing and simply looked all around, but Chloe, seeing it through his eyes and hearing it through his ears as an unattended piano over in the corner played a delicate song she was sure she knew—"'Interlude,' by Ashley Wolmer, written for the coronation of King William," she heard myBetty whisper in her ear—was stunned. The opulence was incredible. This had to be a copy of a room from some palace—Versailles?

"The room is a one-quarter-size replica of the Picture Gallery in Buckingham Palace," said myBetty, thinking the same thing and looking it up for her. "Amazingly well done." And Chloe agreed. Amazing detail: the piano, the banquet table centered in the room, the portraits on the walls.

Finally, Peter said, "Wow," and walked into the middle of the room to stand next to the banquet table and do a full turn. He'd heard from his myBob the same information that Chloe had from myBetty, so he said, for his audience's sake, "It's just like the Picture Gallery in Buckingham Palace. Really stunning."

"Great friend Peter," said Twoclicks, standing just inside the door, "we liked that room when we ssaw it in London, and sso had it copied here. Iss perfect, right?"

Peter turned to face him. "It's really something, Twoclicks. I'll have to say that."

Chloe smiled, hearing that. A facsimile of a room from Buckingham Palace, on a spaceship filled with aliens who were heading home, an uncountable distance away? Yes, it was really something.

And here Chloe sat. She lifted up the lens of the receiving set for a few moments to look around and remind herself that she sat in the lounge chair in her bedroom in Malibu, the souvenirs from her youth and her career—the Annie Oakley doll and the prop six-shooter, the posters, the autographed napkin from Meryl Streep, the sports trophies and medals, the People's Choice runner-up statuette, and more—on top of the dresser.

Her legs were folded underneath her, her girlfriend still asleep on the bed over there, the Pacific out her window, and that predawn sky over it as the stars slowly disappeared and the ocean rollers sweeping in slowly emerged. Perfect surf, she thought, and briefly considered grabbing her board and her wet suit once this was done—a perk of life in Malibu.

And then she tugged the lens back into place and the rest of the gear snapped into place, too. Aliens! That was just crazy, wasn't it? A few months ago, Chloe wouldn't have believed any of this. It would all have been make-believe, CGI and blue and green screens and digital artistry making the aliens look as real as the waves down there. And now, here she was, inside Peter's head and hands and heart as he walked over to Twoclicks, short and stubby, with that constant grin on his porpoise-like face, which Chloe still doubted was quite as free of irony, free of duplicity, as Peter seemed to think.

Which made him all the more frightening, if she thought about it much.

But back to Peter. He was asking about the art, some of it gifts from King William. "Gifts?" Peter asked, and "Yess, giftss, sso wonderful!" the jovial Twoclicks was saying, and yes, gifts, Heather was agreeing from behind him, and gifts, Chloe was thinking, were just what King William needed to make sure that S'hudon had something to repay. That was how it worked, that was the S'hudonni way, as far as she was concerned. She hadn't seen too much of them, really, but what she'd seen she could sum up with her own answer, which was basically, *Don't do me any favors.* Truth was, she didn't much like them, even jovial Twoclicks, who could be murderous when he wasn't trying to be funny.

There were hoots outside the closed double doors to the room. Peter heard them and turned to look at who might be coming in, but the doors were still shut.

Then there were more of those hoots, and the patter of a lot of feet outside in the corridor, and then a pounding at the door.

Peter turned to watch as Heather walked through the foyer to the door and opened it. Sergeant Preston, who'd been outside the door, came through, whistling and clicking a warning. Right behind her was a host of golden daffodils—the crew from belowdecks—tumbling through, falling over themselves in their hurry to get inside, dewlaps flaring in bright yellow. One of them, the first one through, rolled and then scrambled upright to find her footing and ran toward Twoclicks. Half of the others scrambled to their feet and followed, too.

"I think that's the chief I met," said Peter, watching it all.

"Yes, it is, with all those stripes on that uniform," said myBob, as the chief started whistling and clicking furiously at Twoclicks in what sounded like S'hudonni.

"What the hell is going on?" asked Peter, as more hoots came from the front of the room. A whole other group of the crew was there, hooting and waving their arms and clumsily clicking and whistling.

"We're under attack," said myBob.

"No shit," said Peter, as he looked toward that big, beautiful window into the nothing at the far end of the room and noticed a large oblong shape coming into view, torn from its attachment to the main ship, tumbling slowly, bleeding furniture and books, a lot of books.

"Your quarters," said myBob. "Torn away from the hull and heading toward us."

Chloe, sitting in comfort in Malibu, was completely immersed in the scene, but she noticed that Terri was up and had switched on the wall screen to watch it all in HD. Chloe held out her hand and Terri walked over, took the offered hand, then sat on the arm of the chair to watch the flat screen as Chloe stayed with the sweep.

"Fucking hell," said Terri. And Chloe, transfixed, agreed.

The torn blister that had been Peter's quarters tumbled toward them, and then there were deep rumblings from below, and screeching and tearing noises, and a loud, distant, explosion and then the lights flickered, flickered again, and went out. The ship had lost power.

Chloe saw through Peter's eyes and heard through Peter's ears and tasted fear through Peter, too, as they all were suddenly weightless and the blister met the ship just to one side of that wide window, and the billion on Earth watched, or felt, the blister—implacable forms of something metallic against equally implacable forms of something else metallic—tear through the wall and the air begin to rush out the gaps in that hull as the room filled with debris. The window, thank god, held, or the opening would have been twice as wide. The doors were open and the museum room's artwork, adrift, followed the wind as Picasso and van Gogh and the Splendid Splinter and a huge walking man and Alcock and Brown's propeller and much more began sliding toward the tear that led to the void.

The tear was growing, the wind rushing harder. All of this, all of them, were flying out toward the nothing in the dark, and Peter was hanging on to Twoclicks as they floated through the room, as pedestals rose from the walls and ancient urns slowly rolled and swept on toward the far room.

The lights flickered back on, but only dimly, and Chloe was looking through Peter's eyes as Heather floated ahead of them, her thin arms flailing to find purchase, something to hang on to to keep from flying off into the void as she traveled the length of that room, with those daffodils, petals and dewlaps wide in panic and fear, floating alongside her. Beyond them was Sergeant Preston, tumbling slowly end over end, strangely serene. All of this slow tumbling as they headed to oblivion.

The banquet table, a huge rectangle of solid oak hewn from a forest in Maine, had risen free and now slowly turned in the wind as it led the way toward the hole, now the size of a door, rectangular with torn edges all around. The window next to the hole was trembling as everything flowed through that hole, crowding into it, packed so tightly that the flow slowed until, twice while Peter looked at it, with a sudden *whoomph*, the material—the plates and furniture and chairs and artwork—cleared the hole and escaped into the void.

There was no way to know what Peter was thinking, but his actions said he was trying to save them all as they neared the floor. Chloe watched, and the billion watched, as Peter let go of Twoclicks and shoved hard toward the large table, reached it, pushed off the walls, and then, with the table in front of him, headed toward that doorway into space, trying to get there ahead of Heather, ahead of Twoclicks, ahead of Sergeant Preston and all those friendly daffodils.

And he did get there, guiding the table, top first, as it reached the hole and imperfectly covered it, angled so that most of the hole was blocked. Enough. The rush of wind slowed. Heather arrived behind him with a pedestal that, aimed top first, covered the remainder of the gap. The wind ended instantly, but still they all floated there. Saved. Alive.

And then the trembling window next to the patched hole was hit by more debris. The oak bookcase from Peter's quarters, Chloe thought, with books in orbit around it. The books hit first—Doyle and Binchy and Fowler and Yeats and all the rest, slamming into the window, which shivered under the stress, and then the case, sturdy and heavy old oak, which slammed with a deep thud. The window vibrated with a high screeching and tearing noise, and then it gave way at last with a *whoomph* and a loud crack and the shattering of the glass material, and all was lost. The wind briefly howled as they all went tumbling out. The banquet table, Twoclicks, Heather, one daffodil after another, Sergeant Preston heading into the deep cold. And Peter, watching all of them so Chloe and a billion Earthies could see it happen, held up that baseball bat and tried in vain to jab it against the side of the hole as out he went, looking back for a second or two, reaching back to grab the hands of two of the daffodils and hang on to them, trying to save them, before a final *whoomph* sent them all sailing out, Peter holding hands with those two daffodils. And then the sweep went dark and it was over.

For a few seconds, Chloe stayed connected, waiting for the sweep to return, waiting for it all to have been some terrible joke that was being played by that bastard Twoclicks. But it didn't return, and it stayed dark, as her unit began beeping that the connection was gone.

Jesus Christ. She yanked off the unit, careless with the tongue and finger pads, oblivious to the sharp moment of pain as the tongue pad was ripped out of her mouth. My god, she'd just watched Peter Holman die. She'd been inside his head as it happened. She'd felt that terrible wind pulling him to his death. She'd heard the screams of the daffodils as they'd been swept to their deaths. She'd seen the flailing arms of Twoclicks and the strange expressionless face of Sergeant Preston. She'd felt the wood of that bat—that stupid bat!—in her hands. And then darkness.

She was holding the sweep unit in her right hand, she realized. She stood up from the lounger, held the unit in front of her, and looked at it. The hateful thing. Awful thing. She shook it, banged it against the dresser next to the lounger, banged it again, then threw it across the room to clatter against the far wall. She'd never wear that damn thing again.

And then she cried out, yelling, screaming, "No!" and she burst into tears.

2

OFF BOOK

Six long months after she'd watched and felt Peter and his S'hudonni friends sail off into the nothing, Chloe Cary sat in her trailer on the studio lot in Culver City and watched on the old flat screen as the local news streams went nuts. This morning, a S'hudonni ship had settled down into the revitalized Salton Sea, the first S'hudonni ship in many months to land in that spot. The media, new and old, had gone live with the landing, and social media exploded with conjecture: War? Famine? Pestilence? Tourists from that other world? The news streams had hyperventilated over the possibilities, and then had gotten even more excited when Twoclicks emerged from the ship.

There he was, back from the dead, happily taking a dip in the water to celebrate his return to Earth, waving at the spyeyes and flitters and drones that captured every second of his splashy delight at being back on Earth. He'd been in the water for a good ten minutes, then had gone back into his ship, and now, a half hour later, he was waddling down the ship's wide landing platform and then onto the chopper barge, where he climbed aboard an Earthie helicopter and off it went, headed, the journos were sure, to the S'hudonni consulate in Los Angeles.

Her smarty dinged and myBetty said, "Priority call coming in, Chloe."

The studio head? Had she heard the news? Or Priya, maybe? She might have heard the news, too. They had a date tonight, the two stars trying to get the celeb sites interested. You rub mine, as it were, and I'll rub yours. Sure, it was the usual setup, but she actually liked Priya, did Chloe, and that was a rare thing.

But no. "It's Twoclicks, Chloe, on a personal line. Very private. He's midflight in a helicopter."

Well, that was interesting. Just back in town and right away he contacts Chloe Cary? "I'll take it," she told myBetty.

And so there he was on the smarty's screen, all smiles in that bullet-shaped head of his, blue-gray skin, wide gray eyes with that nictitating membrane, no ears or eyebrows to see, but a flat, splayed nose and that wide, wide mouth, always smiling. He was sitting on a broad, comfortable chair that looked more like a couch, with a hole in the back for his dorsal. She could hear the rattle of the copter's engine and the slap of the rotor blades in the background.

All she could see was his upper body and head, but she certainly knew the shape of the rest of him, and his attitude, too: the usual bonhomie. It was as if he'd never left, as if that explosion and all that chaos never happened.

"Dearest friend Chloe! I have returned! The boys are back in town!"

Always the comedian, that Twoclicks. Peter had talked about it all the time. How Twoclicks thought of himself as gregarious and friendly and funny. And he was. Until, Peter always added, he called in the screamships and things got messy. The fun ended when things didn't go his way.

"Hello, Governor-General Twoclicks," Chloe said, using the formal title that Twoclicks had bestowed on himself just before leaving Earth those long months ago.

"Dearest friend Chloe. I was best friend of our dearest friend Peter and sso were you, sso we are on firsst namess, yess?"

Did she even want to be on a first-name basis with Twoclicks? Wasn't that like being on a first-name basis with some Russian oligarch or some Mafia don? Did the benefits of that friendship outweigh the risks?

Well, it wasn't as if she had a choice. So, "Thank you, Twoclicks," she said. "It's wonderful to hear that you're alive. We were all watching through Peter's sweep when that terrible collision cracked open your ship. It was awful."

"Yess," Twoclicks said, and Chloe could see a sad look on his face, a downturn to the sides of that wide, lipless mouth, his eyes half-closing. It was so Earthie a look that Chloe thought surely it was a learned expression, something he'd practiced. "Sso, sso ssad, dear friend Chloe. Sso many died. Tragic."

"Everyone except you died out there?" Chloe had to ask. She wondered, had Twoclicks seen Peter's death, watched as he struggled for air in the vacuum of space? Seen the struggles end and the body tumbling off into the nowhere?

But he wasn't saying. Instead, "Iss much to talk about, dearest friend Chloe. Sso, sso much. And we musst talk face-to-face, in person, live, yess?"

"All right," said Chloe. "Sure. In person, face-to-face, live." And she gave him her best Chloe Cary smile. Obviously she wasn't going to hear the details of Peter's death until Twoclicks was ready. "When would you like to meet?"

"Ssoon! Today!" he said. "Come to my consulate, dearest friend Chloe." And then he hinted, "All will be told. Whole sstory about your besst friend, Peter. He wass great hero! Ssaved my life and those of otherss! Lifeboatss! Chaoss! Courage! Great Earthie! Great sstory!"

Twoclicks sighed. "We will tell all of it to you. Conssulate in thiss evening? Eight o'clocks?"

"Yes, eight o'clocks is perfect Twoclicks," Chloe said. "I'll be there."

"And tell whole world of thiss, dearest friend Chloe! All sshould know of your wonderful Peter's great courage! Detailss soon! News at eight! All the newss that'ss fit to print about your wonderful Peter!"

Ah, Chloe thought. Of course. Heroism and sympathy for S'hudon. What could be better? But, "Yes, Twoclicks, that sounds perfect. I'll let the world know, and then perhaps you can share the details then?"

"Iss wonderful!" Twoclicks said, and then added, "Dinner tonight!"

"Of course," she said again. "It will be wonderful to finally meet you in person."

"Me, too!" he said, with his usual exuberance. "Sso much to ssay. Big changes coming for Earth! We need you! Ssee you then!" And he clicked off.

"Making arrangements right now," myBetty said, without being asked, and then, maybe thirty seconds later, followed with, "Pickup at seven forty, and you'll arrive at eight p.m. And I've canceled your dinner date with Priya. She says she understands completely."

"Thanks," said Chloe. *Big changes?* That was damn ominous. *We need you?* That one was ominous, too. Shit. She didn't need this. Especially today, when she had poor Peter on her mind. Dead and gone for sure now. There'd always been a little wisp of hope that somehow he'd been saved, that some magic S'hudonni tech had protected him or something.

But no. And now, though the truth was that she'd liked him fine but certainly hadn't loved him—or ever really found anyone to truly love in her thirty-four years on Earth—Chloe would tell the world that the love of her life had acted heroically saving the lives of Twoclicks and a bunch of those daffodil characters. Because that's what they needed to hear, all those billions. She would promise to share more details later.

"Schedule a presser for two hours from now, myBetty, at the studio. Let my people know about it first, of course, so they can be there." Her agent, her publicist, the studio head, and all the assorted hangers-on, would be delighted to hear this news. A global audience for Chloe, sharing the news about Peter Holman. They'd all be there for the presser, she was sure.

So, time to work up a little announcement, personal but not too gushy: proud of her true love and looking forward to meeting Twoclicks and sharing their stories of wonderful Peter. She'd want her eyes to glisten with nascent tears for her Peter Holman when she heard the final news of how he died. The poor guy.

3

FULL-COURT PRESS

At the presser; Chloe held back her tears as she talked about what Twoclicks had said about Peter's heroics, and she promised she'd have more details after her dinner with Twoclicks at the consulate. There were questions, a lot of them, all centered around her feelings for Peter and how was she handling the news from Twoclicks and would she be stepping away from *The Family Madderz* for a while to mourn and when would she have more details and why and how and where and all the rest. The answers were she's handling it with deep sadness, and no, the show goes on, and yes, the details would be coming soon, and so on and so forth.

It was all over in thirty minutes, and then Chloe thanked the assembled journos and left the podium, once again at the top of the news cycle, which was great, though she'd been through it often enough now to know how fleeting this kind of fame was.

Still, all the hangers-on were happy, the studio was happy, and then, as she was escorted through the studio lot to the *Family Madderz* set, she found out how happy Twoclicks was, as myBetty hooked her into the call.

"Dearesst friend Chloe!" Twoclicks fairly shouted at her in delight. "Wass perfect! You are perfect!"

"Thank you, Twoclicks," she said.

"You are famouss!" he said, shouting still. "You are very best friend on whole planet!"

She smiled into the smarty as he said that. Then she said, "I'm honored, Twoclicks, to be your friend," though frankly Twoclicks scared the hell out of her. Did anyone want to be a friend of a creature with that much power? Gee, what could possibly go wrong?

Still, it seemed his was in the right place, as they say, so, "And you're our best friend, too, Twoclicks," she said.

"You will be my advissor!" Twoclicks said. "We will talk of everything! I will tell you about dear friend Peter, your true love! And you will give me advices on Earthie things!"

"Great," she said, though she didn't think she was particularly well suited to being an adviser on matters Earthie. Hell, she hadn't even been anywhere outside of the States except for the usual junkets to Europe and a lot of filming in Canada. Did that count? Hardly. Still, it was probably just some ceremonial position, and if there was one thing Chloe could do, it was act the part. So they parted with cheery good-byes.

And then it was back to work, if that was possible. She'd wanted to be off book for this morning's scene as they started work on the last few episodes of *The Family Madderz*.

These last few episodes had to be good. In fact, they had to be great. The whole world would be watching now. The show had started well, more than six months ago, with Chloe in the middle of her relationship with Peter and Twoclicks and the other S'hudonni showing up, waving friendly hands and smiling.

And then, when all hell broke loose with S'hudon's warring brothers and life got a lot trickier as the country—the whole world, in fact—convulsed with riots and worries and strife, there wasn't a lot of attention being paid to *The Family Madderz*, or to Chloe Cary. The numbers crashed.

That turned around when Peter died so heroically. When, after the horror of that live sweep feed from deep space, Chloe had gone into seclusion and mourning for two weeks and then bravely returned because the show must go on, *The Family Madderz* went to number one and stayed there for five good weeks.

And then it slipped, and slipped some more, and the show was only barely renewed, and this second season it had been on a deathwatch, and Chloe's career with it. How soon we forget.

This presser would bring those numbers right back, she was sure. But for how long? Hard to say. There'd be an earthquake or a volcano or a hurricane or an assassination or a plane crash or a new royal baby or whatever in a week or two and she'd fade away again, just like the last time.

Still, even if the numbers were destined to slip, she wanted to go out in style, and she had plenty of opportunities to do that, since she was the action hero in *The Family Madderz*, taking on the bad guys who threatened her on-screen family, turning from suburban mom to sharpshooter and martial artist at a moment's notice—handing the bad guys their hats, as they say. Lots of high kicks, lots of faux karate mixed with some savate. Some sniper work when it was called for, some shaped charges to blow things up from time to time. It didn't make a lick of sense, and perhaps that was part of the problem, but it was Chloe being badass, and she loved that.

One upside to this role was that she was spending an awful lot of time in the gym and at the gun range lately, with the studio paying to bring her up to speed on her combat skills, so it at least looked real when she fired a weapon or sent a foot into the face of the bad guy.

She enjoyed the training. She'd been an athlete all through school, even got the free ride to swim and play soccer at Stanford. The kicking came pretty easy to her, and it was fun shooting at targets.

Her trainer at the range was Reed Stephens, who'd taught half of Hollywood how to fire a gun realistically. He had her buy a SIG Sauer SP2022 at the beginning, because it was lighter weight, with less recoil. But he'd been impressed enough with her skills to start loaning her his P229 nine millimeter so she could get used to the feel of the heavier, sturdier weapon. She liked it.

She suspected Peter had never fired a gun in his life. Throwing baseballs and shooting basketballs, sure, but firing a gun? No. It might have been fun to take him to the range. He'd have enjoyed that.

She thought about how well it had gone with him, those last few days before she'd stood on the beach and watched as the S'hudonni ship lifted quietly up from the shallows of the Gulf of Mexico, hovered there a long, long moment, and then noiselessly shot upward and out of sight, taking Peter Holman with it.

A few days before that singular moment she'd been in L.A., working on season one. It had been weird to think that the aliens had come and were fighting each other for control of vast swaths of Earth and that her boyfriend was involved in all that and the world was in a mess and yet she, Chloe Cary, had been in her trailer in the studio lot, working hard to get off book for her scene with Felipe Monterey, the male lead. He was going to be in trouble. She was going to save him. Again.

"You can't mean that, Freddy!" she'd been saying to Felipe, when her earpiece dinged and myBetty told her that there'd been trouble with Two-clicks in Ireland, and that meant trouble with Peter, and that pretty much ruined the day as Chloe waited to hear from Peter. Was he still alive? What was happening? There was no more contact.

Eventually, Chloe shut myBetty down and got back to work. The show goes on, right? And finally they nailed the scene and then went right in to shoot it, and there was a dizzying twelve takes before that long day ended.

On the drive home, she'd brought myBetty back awake and listened to the first two messages from Peter. He'd been through some shit, for sure, but he was alive and OK, flying across the Atlantic on Twoclicks's jet, try-ing to get home and away from the crazies, though they had to stop first in Bermuda, where they would meet in a neutral corner, as it were, with Whistle's people. Anything to try to calm things down between the two S'hudonni princes, he'd said.

And then, in the kitchen, opening a bottle of Chalk Hill pinot gris from Sonoma and pouring a glass for Yevonne, with whom she had plans for the evening that included some comfort, certainly, but also reading some lines. A lot of lines. She was determined to be ready for tomorrow's scene.

Then a third message had come in. An awful one. Peter's sister, Kait, had been killed in some kind of explosion. A booby trap, he'd said, killing her in order to try and kill Heather and Twoclicks and—oh, by the way—Peter. It hadn't worked, but Kait, poor Kait, was dead.

That had been terrible news. Chloe had called Peter back, but of course all she could do was leave a message. It was horrible. She'd really liked Kait, a sweet girl who'd been through hell, some of it maybe her own fault, but who knew what buried horrors had led her to the needle? Chloe was betting there was something back there, when Kait was young. Something devastating. Something that a girl could need help with and, if she didn't get it, well, then, she was slip-sliding away.

Kait's wife, Sarah, poor Sarah, had gotten the message, too, from Peter. She was shattered by the news, and Chloe told myBetty to change the route. Instead of heading home, she'd headed to Sarah and Kait's house to spend the evening with Sarah, holding her hand, letting her cry, crying some—a lot, even—herself. It was just too damn awful.

Then Chloe had let the studio know that she had to go to Florida for a funeral, and the studio, wanting to save time more than money, flew her and Sarah out there on the studio jet. They were shooting the whole season before releasing it in one burst, of course, so she knew she could attend it if she had to, and she did. Screw the studio. Kait, sweet Kait, was dead.

It was only after they'd gotten there, taking the limo with the human driver from the airport out to the beach and then the ferry across to the island where Peter lived, that they'd heard from Peter the news that Kait was dead and alive, both. It was some kind of alien magic, some kind of device that copied Kait so that one Kait was murdered horribly and the other, the original, was a captive, a hostage, taken back to S'hudon. They couldn't tell anyone or it would screw up any chance to get Kait back, but Peter felt they had to know.

At first, Chloe thought the story was insane and impossible. On the other hand, from Peter's outside deck she could look west and see the alien ship that had landed out in the shallow Gulf of Mexico, just a couple of klicks off the coast. All spidery and fragile looking, upright on its stilted legs, with the egg shape on top. They'd landed, they'd changed Earth—or started to— and so a copied Kait? Easy enough to believe.

Chloe and Peter had made love that night and then again the next morning. It had been an emotional lovemaking, slow and intense, a coupling that they both knew was a way to say good-bye. Peter had agreed to go with Twoclicks and Heather back to the home world, back to S'hudon, to send the news home to Earth about the peace talks between the two aliens and to be there for Kait. He'd find her, he promised Sarah, and he'd bring her home.

But first they had to say good-bye to the ashes of the version of Kait that had died in that explosion. For that, the beach and the Gulf of Mexico. So, after a long, slow day of mourning for the one Kait and apprehension about the other, truer one, they walked over to the beach to say good-bye—to Kait and, for Chloe, to say goodbye to Peter, too.

Peter's brother, Tom, had shown up when they walked on the beach that second night, carrying Kait's ashes. This was the same Tom who'd tried to kill Peter, and now, because of Kait's death, he wanted to say he was sorry.

Chloe found that unbelievable. How could Peter allow the guy anywhere near him?

It was murderous Tom, who held grudges and wanted to get even. But that night, he'd been there to say his own goodbye to Kait as her ashes went into the Gulf—he didn't know the news about her being copied—and then to watch with Sarah and Chloe as Peter did as he'd been instructed by the S'hudonni: stripped down to nothing, waded into the water, and started swimming toward the distant ship.

The last time they'd all seen Peter he'd been in a nice, steady freestyle and there were two shapes, dorsal finned, one on each side of him. Two-clicks and Heather, she was sure.

Chloe and Sarah then walked back up through the dunes to sit on the back deck of Peter's house and watch the ship go. Chloe was pretty emotional about it. She didn't feel any magic with Peter, no love swoon or any of that crap, but she knew that Peter was courageous about it. He hadn't known when he started swimming what precisely lay ahead. Could be glorious and wonderful and amazing. Could be death. Could be misery. They'd both had that in mind when they'd made love that last time, and then again when they'd hugged and kissed on the beach before parting. A nice way to say goodbye.

Then, as the two women watched from the deck, Tom had come up the steps to join them in watching the ship rise slowly from the water. Chloe had thought he was long gone, but he'd walked on down the beach and into the dunes and then she hadn't seen him after that. But here he was, in beat-up light cotton pants and wearing flip-flops and wearing a life preserver—a bulky, old-school, kapok-filled life preserver. She wondered what he had in mind. A swim of his own?

Chloe had smiled at him, heard Sarah say, "Hello, Tom. Come to see it go?"

"The ship?" he'd asked. "Yeah, something like that."

He'd stood there for a moment, then said, "I think it would be best if you two walked away from what's about to happen here."

"I'm sorry?" Chloe had said. *What the hell?* she was thinking. She'd looked over at Sarah, who'd looked back and shrugged her shoulders and started to rise from her chair.

"This is important," Tom had said, and started taking off the life preserver, which wasn't going to preserve any life at all, Chloe realized, as she took a good look at it.

"Tom?" she'd asked.

"Yes, Chloe. Yes, Sarah. I'm going to wipe the slate clean here. Blow all this to hell and walk away, and you'd be smart to get the hell out of here before I do that."

"No," said Sarah.

"Tom, don't do this," said Chloe. "It's your family home, Tom. Why?"

"Peter is gone and he's not coming back, Chloe. Get used to that idea. I'm pretty damn certain about that. I *do* have friends in high places."

He'd smiled, shrugged off the unclasped vest, leaned over to set it against the sliding glass doors that led from the back deck to Peter's bedroom. "I'm done with them, Chloe," he'd said. "Done with them both." He'd stood up, stretched once, rolled his neck to loosen the tension, then said, "Two minutes, girls. You better get moving. This whole house is coming down."

"Oh, my god," said Sarah, and then Chloe had grabbed her by the hand and tugged her along, down the steps that led from the deck down to the sand, and from there out onto the boardwalk to the beach, and from there they were running hard to get away, looking back once or twice to see Tom smoking a cigarette as he, well behind them, strolled leisurely off the boardwalk and onto the beach and then turned to walk the other way, away from them. Chloe had myBetty on 911, but this was an island, and connected by a ferry, and what few police were anywhere near were stationed at the dock, keeping people away from the home of the famous Peter Holman.

Behind them, the ship had started rising, soundless at this distance, no flame or smoke from engines: just a quiet, slow rise. Higher, and higher. If you weren't looking in the right place at the right time, you might not even notice it. Was Peter inside there, looking out, seeing them? Chloe waved, frantic, and Sarah, seeing that, did the same. Maybe there was something the S'hudonni could do, even from there on the ship?

Or not. Chloe and Sarah stopped and looked back, and there in the distance they could see Tom wave toward the ship, still rising, as there was a huge *whoomph* and a concussion that shook the women even at this distance, and then the sound and then the fury and the flame and the smoke, and that was how Tom Holman had said good-bye to his brother and how Chloe Cary had spent her last day in Florida before heading home, Sarah in tow, to Malibu.

Where now she gathered herself, always the professional, and prepared to get on set and get through the long afternoon of shooting scene five, episode twenty-one, season two of *The Family Madderz*, wherein she would rescue her leading man once again and save the day once again and then, when it was a keeper, she'd head to dinner with Twoclicks

That was the plan, to go as quietly as she could, perhaps in the back seat of a nondescript self-drive, making her way to the S'hudonni consulate and dinner with Twoclicks. What did he really have in mind? Nothing more than a nice conversation about Peter and the details of his death? Or perhaps some dread news about Peter that Twoclicks wanted to say face-to-face, privately. Something horrible? Something about Tom, maybe? Or Whistle?

It had to do with her, whatever it was, and that, she told herself, was why she was going.

4

LET'S MAKE A DEAL

She should have known better. There was no way on Earth, as it were, to meet quietly with Twoclicks upon his return. Instead, she showered and changed and prepped at the studio, with full attention paid by Makeup, and then it was straight to dinner in a human-chauffeured limo. Of course.

The paparazzi followed her with their e-bikes and their drones and flittercams and spyeyes. All that whirring and humming right outside the smoked glass of her window in the back seat of the limo, from the time she left the studio's arched entrance, right through the drive down Culver and then a right on Wilshire, past Louis Vuitton and Spago and all the rest of that, all the way past the Children's Museum and the Tar Pits and MacArthur Park and on to Pershing Square and the ornate deco of the S'hudonni consulate, three floors of quiet grandeur.

Twoclicks was back! And Chloe Cary was coming to pay her respects! His very first visitor! Before the governor or the president or the pope or any of the prime ministers with whom he'd hobnobbed before he left for home those many months ago, Chloe Cary came calling. It was the celeb news of the day, or at least of the hour. Chloe Cary, remember her? She'd been the girlfriend of Peter Holman, the sweep star who'd courageously headed out to the alien home world and died trying to save everyone's life during that terrible explosion on the S'hudonni ship. Remember?

Remember! They'd all thought he and Twoclicks and all those crazy alien daffodils had died! And now, it turned out, Twoclicks was alive and well and back in L.A., but Peter Holman? Well, nothing definite, but it looked like he died a hero's death, and now Chloe Cary, his one true love, was visiting Twoclicks. The biggest news of the day! Questions! Lots of questions!

A lot had happened since that explosion in outer space: volcanoes in Mexico and tsunamis in Japan and the Big Melt in Greenland and the collapse of Miami's new seawall and, heck, little San Marino made the World Cup, and so on and so forth, and the girlfriend of the hero from all those months ago hadn't been in the news anymore. Her show was struggling, her career evaporating.

Until now! "Chloe! Chloe! Chloe!" they shouted at her, as she exited the limo with its human driver, who stepped around the limo to open her door. She was back at the top of the cycle, even if her show was being canceled.

And then, when the consulate's door opened and the most powerful being on planet Earth stepped out, they shouted, "Twoclicks! Twoclicks!

Twoclicks!" And he waved at them as he stepped toward Chloe and gave her that warm hug and said, "Dear friend Chloe, we are sso, sso happy to see you!"

Twoclicks was back on Earth! And he hugged Chloe Cary! The air was alive with buzzing and whirring and humming drones and the smaller flittercams and the pricey new spyeyes. Great stuff! Fabulous!

And then the door shut and that was that. Time to save some battery and bring back the cams and sit and relax for a while. And then wait, and wait some more, if that's what it takes.

Inside, Twoclicks took a step back, held Chloe out by her shoulders, and seemed to size her up. Then he smiled hugely and exclaimed, "Jusst like Peter ssaid! You are a wonder!" And he brought her back in for another hug.

It seemed a little creepy, to be honest. She could feel the oddly cold and slick, dark skin of his arms against hers, and as if that weren't weird enough, he then leaned in to kiss her on the left check.

What was the damn protocol here? myBetty wasn't helping at all. Where was her advice when she needed it?

Enough was enough, so Chloe gently pushed him back and extricated herself from those spindly arms, then forced herself to smile and said, "It's a great pleasure to finally meet you personally . . ."

She hesitated, waiting for help from myBetty, who finally spoke up in her ear. "I'm having connectivity problems, Chloe. But he's Governor-General Twoclicks."

Chloe said that, and added, "Peter said so much about you before he left that I feel I know you, but we never did actually meet."

"Governor-General?" Twoclicks said. "We told you! That iss too sserious! Call me Twoclicks! We are great friends! There is much to say and much to do!"

"Well, OK then," said myBetty.

"Sure, Twoclicks," said Chloe, smiling despite how creepy this was getting to be. She did have a lot of questions, starting with what the hell really happened out there. How did Twoclicks survive and not Peter? And was Whistle—Twoclicks's murderous brother—also back? He'd been gone for a long time, too. The answers to these things mattered.

"So," she said. "What happened out there?"

Twoclicks waved the question away. "Firsst things firsst, dear friend Chloe," he said, and he took her by the hand to walk and added, "Sso much to say for one meal, but we will try, dearest friend Chloe. Come, come, and I will tell you all about Peter and our adventuress. Space ssaga! Amazing! Astounding!"

Maybe he really was this goofy a character? Earth's great alien overlord, the self-styled governor-general, was just a clown? A Falstaff? Yes, maybe that. That's sure what Peter had called him: goofy, yes, and charming. But it was good to remember that he could be deadly, too.

Still, her instant assessment was that this guy, this creature, this porpoise-like thing from another world, was an odd one—but damned if he didn't seem honest about it. This didn't seem to be an act he was putting on, some disingenuous performance for poor Peter Holman's favorite Earthie. Two-clicks did really seem to be a flake.

And then the goofy flake turned back around, still holding her hand, and tugged her along into the dining room. Chloe, smiling, bemused, allowed herself to be pulled through one long hallway lined with paintings and then left into a dining room replete with long curtains closed over the windows for privacy, a long table for formal dinners in the middle of the room, and two waiters standing quietly to the side of it. They were small S'hudonni—children, was Chloe's guess—and so were the first S'hudonni children she'd seen. They wore Earthie tuxedos, which made them look a lot like cute penguins. Chloe thought that had to be purposeful.

And there was one other person in the room: a squat, short human, a man. He wore a kind of naval uniform, with plenty of brocade and medals. He was bald and wore a smile on a jowly face. Instantly, Chloe didn't like him.

He held two drinks in his hands, and walked over to hand one to Chloe. "Good evening, Miss Cary. A drink?" he asked. "It's a Sémillon, very nice. Chateau d'Or, 1817. Pricey, certainly, at eight thousand dollars a bottle, but there aren't many bottles left, so this will be a special treat."

What a pretentious prig, Chloe thought, but "Wonderful!" is what Two-clicks said as he waddled over to take his own glass. And then Twoclicks added, "Dearest friend Chloe, pleasse meet my asssisstant, Jorge Abigail D'Angelo Hanratty. He iss one of you!"

No, he's not, thought Chloe, but "Pleased" is what she said as she reached out to shake Hanratty's hand before accepting the other glass of wine. She took a sip. It tasted fine. She wondered what the uniform was all about.

Twoclicks took a long gulp, drained his glass, and held it out for a refill. Then, while Hanratty poured, Twoclicks whistled and clicked something in S'hudonni to the two waiters standing at the wall. They rushed over to pull out the chairs so Twoclicks, Hanratty, and Chloe could sit.

"Much to talk about, dear friend Chloe," Twoclicks said as he eased back into the chair—at the head of the table, of course—that was built for him, with a high chair back that had an open slot for his dorsal. "Sso let us sit and begin! We will eat and drink and talk of your dear friend Peter and his heroicss!"

Chloe sat to Twoclicks's right and Hanratty sat to his left. The waiters refilled their glasses with that pricey wine, and Twoclicks took a sip and said, in a solemn voice, "Terrible, terrible thing, dearest friend Chloe. Dear friend Peter was sso brave, sso very brave, trying to ssave us all." He shook his head, most of his torso moving back and forth as he did so. "But he could not. Out we went, all of uss! No gravity, the air pushing and pushing and ssucking us out into sspace. Armss and legss flying, whistling and clicking and crying and flailing, ourrself and the Harmonicss, their dewlaps flaring, and your brave Peter, all tumbling and floating away. Horrible!"

He paused, looked at Chloe. "Lifeboatss are automatic, dearest friend Chloe, and searching for uss, coming closer and closer, and then filamentss, netss, emerge and surround us and pull us in. Ssaved!"

He turned that bulbous head back and forth slowly. "But not dear friend Peter. We are in lifeboat, ssafe and ssound! We look around, and plenty of Harmonics, ourselves and your Heather, otherss and otherss. But no dearest friend Peter!"

Twoclicks reached across the corner of the banquet table, held his hands out for Chloe to take them. She did, and he said, "Three boatss of life, dearest friend Chloe. Plenty of room for all! Food, sshelter, and clothing. Beacons to hail other sships! Ssafe and ssound!"

Chloe could see where this was going. "But Peter wasn't in one," she said.

Twoclicks's hands were tiny, with four fingers and a long thumb. Like his arms with their two sets of elbow joints, they weren't designed for strength but more for flexibility and to be small enough to fit into the side pouches where the S'hudonni put them when they were swimming.

So she was surprised when his grip on her hands seemed solid and honest as he looked her in the eyes and said, "There was no greatesst friend Peter in any boat of life, dearest friend Chloe."

"You searched?"

"For many hourss, dearest friend Chloe. Hoping for miracle, you know? Some other sship? Some hidden place in lifeboat?"

"But nothing?"

"Yess. But nothing. No dearest friend Peter. No body, either. Nothing."

"And so he's out there somewhere still? His body floating along through space?"

Twoclicks nodded. "Never sseen by us, dearest friend Chloe, but it must be sso. Your true love Peter died trying to ssave us all. And ssaved we were!"

He let go of her hands, reached over to grasp his glass of that expensive wine. He stood, held the glass high, and said, "To Peter, our greatest friend and hero!"

Hanratty stood, too, and raised his glass. Chloe reached out to take her glass in her hand, stood, and raised it, too, and said, "To Peter."

They sat back down, silent for a moment or two, and then Twoclicks said, "Finally, after a ten-day, we sstopped looking, dearest friend Chloe. And then we waited and waited for our rescue sship to find uss and bring uss aboard."

Hanratty nodded in agreement. "It was very crowded and uncomfortable, and it was a number of ten-days, as they say on S'hudon, before a relief ship arrived."

Chloe nodded. So Hanratty had been there? She hadn't seen him as she'd watched Peter's sweepcast. Meanwhile, she'd been served the opening course, fresh figs with glazed walnuts that Twoclicks exclaimed were "All from your California!" She took a bite. They were fine.

And then, as the plates from the first course were being cleared, and after she'd finished that first glass of wine, a S'hudonni waiter, the shortest of them—and Chloe thought it was a she and that she was very young—poured another for her flawlessly, while her partner, a little taller and thinner, brought in another course for the meal.

Escargot and deep-fried mozzarella, which clanged like a church bell to Chloe but only brought an indulgent smile from Hanratty and prompted Twoclicks to say, with his usual exuberance, "I chose the food for uss all, dear friend Chloe. Comfort! To be back on Earth and eating this!" He delicately picked up a mozzarella stick and ate half of it in one bite.

Three more courses, all as odd as the first two, and then, after the chocolate mousse with a demitasse filled with craft beer, Twoclicks sat back in his special chair, the dorsal fin pushing easily through the slot in the back, and said, "And now is time for my request, dear friend Chloe. We are great friends now, yess?"

How does one respond to that, coming from a being so important and so weird and so powerful? She looked at Hanratty, who sat with his hands churched like a steeple. He sniffed. Good grief, this was a test.

"Yes, Twoclicks, I'd like to think we're great friends," she said, and Twoclicks seemed to accept that.

"Good!" he said, looking her in the eye and smiling beatifically. Saint Twoclicks. "We are told that your *The Family Madderz* show iss ends, right?"

"Is it?" Ends? What did that mean? The show was in trouble, sure, but was it really over? Hell, just the news of Peter's death and Twoclicks's return would bring her the global attention to rocket the ratings for a while, wouldn't it?

But she knew the answer to that even as she thought it. Sure, everyone would pay attention for the last two episodes, and the studio would milk that with interviews and special announcements before and after the episodes and all the rest. But then, in three or four weeks, barring some other revelations, the bottom would drop out and it'd be back to normal. So Chloe knew she needed to talk to her agent, like, now. She leaned back in her chair and turned away from the table as she held up a hand to pause the conversation before saying to her helpmate, "myBetty, is this true?"

"Connectivity isn't restored, I'm afraid, Chloe," myBetty said in her ear. "But the news that was posted an hour ago on the studio news site announced that this season will be the last. Two more episodes and that's it."

myBetty paused for a long second and then added, "And I have new messages in the cache for you on this, all of them an hour old or more. Joan

Kadinsky would like to speak to you. As would Clark Perry and Felipe Monterey and Karin Difario. Remember, though, that I am not able to respond at the moment."

Chloe sighed. Kadinsky was the studio head, Perry the showrunner, Felipe her costar, Karin her agent. "So it must be true," she said to myBetty. "I suppose there's some kind of device that blocks signals in this consulate? When you're able, tell them all that I'm in a meeting with Twoclicks and I'll call as soon as I can."

"Done," said myBetty, and then, as Chloe turned back around, Twoclicks, who had been listening in, said, "Thiss cancel of your show iss no problem, dear friend Chloe! We can fix!"

Oh, no, thought Chloe. There'd be a price to pay, for sure, if the cancellation was "fixed" by Twoclicks. The only question was just how awful that price would be. She'd been in plenty of those situations in her fifteen years in the business. She'd had a classic lucky break to start her career, as Annie Oakley, and then a long dry spell when that show ended. That had taught her a couple of hard lessons: it's who you know and it's you scratch mine and I'll scratch yours. Chloe was Hollywood attractive, sure, and loaded with talent. But there were hundreds, maybe thousands, just as good-looking and just as talented, who were looking for work, looking for that next thing, some lucky break, something to use to carve out a career.

It was Peter Holman and the arrival of those S'hudonni ships that had done it for her, she knew, allowing her to claw her way back. And now, after two seasons, that show was going to close?

What the hell would she do if *The Family Madderz* shut down? She was getting old, in her midthirties and working hard to look ten years younger. That had been the whole point of her faux relationship with Peter Holman, back at the start of all this. She'd needed to get her face and her name back out there before it was too late. A mutually beneficial affair with the rising star of the new sweepcast tech seemed to her agent like a good way to make that happen, and his agent agreed, and there you go.

And, wow, had that worked! They'd built a backstory and then she'd flown down to Florida to have dinner with Peter at a little place on the water, moonlight glistening on the calm water of the bay as they'd shared a bottle of wine and cracked open crabs and dipped shrimp into sauce and waded through some fancy mahi-mahi and another bottle of wine. And then, sandals in one hand and her other hand in his, she'd walked with him on the wide, hard sand of the Gulf beach, the setting as perfect as it could be for his sweep system. And then came the first kiss, followed by the lightly edited lovemaking in his bedroom with those big sliding glass doors that led out to the deck and that view of the sea and sky.

All of this was sweeped through his system to his few hundred thousand receivers, and the ironically named penetration numbers climbed fast as word got around on social media: thirty percent, to fifty, to seventy-five . . . to eighty! Great stuff!

Afterward, they'd lain there for a while and then decided on one last stroll on the beach, and that was when they'd seen those strange lights and their patterns, and the hundreds of thousands on the receiving end saw them, too. And so there it was; the S'hudonni had arrived, and Peter Holman and Chloe Cary were right in the middle of it.

Until this moment, she'd thought it had been pure luck that the ships had danced in the sky over their heads that night. Now, looking at the broad porpoisy smile of Twoclicks, she wasn't so sure. It occurred to her that this wasn't going to get better, that it could, in fact, get a whole lot worse. Damn it, damn it, damn it.

She smiled at Twoclicks and Hanratty, thinking about the price she'd have to pay for their generosity. As far as she knew, the S'hudonni weren't interested in sex with Earthies, but she—and everyone else on Earth—could be wrong about that. Or maybe Twoclicks liked to watch, sort of like Earthies at the zoo watching the monkeys mate. Good god, that was probably it. She looked over at Hanratty and his unctuous smile. The bastard. No fucking way. Nothing was worth that.

She was about to lash out about all this when Twoclicks disarmed her with a shocked look on his face and a loud "No! No! Dear friend Chloe, iss nothing like that!"

Had he read her mind? "Jesus," she said, and myBetty picked up on it immediately to whisper in her ear. "I think he must have just sensed your dismay, Chloe." And hell, thought Chloe, even that was worrisome. Twoclicks could read human emotions?

Twoclicks added, "Iss only friendship, dear friend Chloe! We like you! Our dear friend Peter Holman loved you sso! We want to help! Sshould hear any second about that. Right now! Cavalry iss coming!"

Right, thought Chloe, the fucking cavalry. What did that mean? Where did he get this shit? God knows what movies he'd been watching, this weird ruler of all that he surveyed. And, sure, he was doing it out of the goodness of his heart, or hearts, or whatever pumped his blood around. If he had blood. Christ almighty.

"What do you have in mind, Twoclicks? Can I ask that?" Chloe asked.

"Yess!" said Twoclicks, taking that as her agreement to whatever plan he'd conjured up. A trill came from Hanratty's pants. He reached into his pocket, pulled out a small smarty, looked at its screen, handed it without comment to Twoclicks, and said, "Verbal agreement."

"Hanratty has connectivity," myBetty noted in Chloe's ear, as Twoclicks watched and listened to whoever was on the other end, nodded his head, said, "Perfect," and then put his tiny thumb on the screen and pressed.

"Done!" he said to Chloe. And Hanratty added, "Twoclicks has taken over sponsorship of *The Family Madderz*, Chloe. It's a two-year deal, with a contractual obligation that you remain in your lead role."

Just like that? Chloe looked at Hanratty. Yes, that was great news, but coming from him, this happy little announcement somehow seemed ominous and threatening. He already had the price in mind, she was sure, the slimy bastard. Question was, was Twoclicks in on it, too? Maybe. Maybe not.

She turned to look at Twoclicks and said, "That's wonderful, Twoclicks. Thank you." And she managed a smile when he beamed at her and said, "Iss perfect!"

She thought he really meant it, and then myBetty said, "Connectivity is back, but from a new provider. That's odd."

Something to do with being in this consulate, Chloe figured.

"New calls," myBetty said. "Agent, studio, showrunner, and Priya."

Ah, Priya. Patient, kind, wonderful, discreet Priya. Chloe would need her tonight for sure. "Tell Priya midnight and come in the back way, my-Betty," she told her helpmate. Then she added, "And tell the others I'll be calling back in a few minutes, all right?" She paused, thought it through for a second or two. "And let them know I've said yes."

"Done," said myBetty a second later.

Chloe turned back to face Twoclicks and Hanratty. "This is a lot to process," she said, forcing a smile. "But I'm sure we'll work out all the details in short order. I'm very appreciative of what you're doing here."

"Of course you are," said Hanratty, and he reached out with both hands to take Chloe's hands in his. She acted without thinking, allowing him to hold her hands. They were cold and damp. Awful. She gently pulled them free after a second or two, smiled again, and then turned to Twoclicks, who was stepping toward her for a hug. She took the hug.

Two hours later, in her Malibu home perched on its precarious cliff overlooking the Pacific, Chloe slid open the top of the small wooden box that Twoclicks had given her as a parting gift when he'd hugged her on the front lawn of the consulate and sent the paparazzi into a frenzy. Flitters and larger drones and smaller flyeyes and all the other new devices surrounded them, so tightly packed that despite their tiny brains, they occasionally bumped into one another and gave an angry whirr as they restabilized and kept the live feed going of this wondrous day.

"Too much!" Twoclicks had whispered into her ear as they'd hugged before she left. "Here, ssomething for you, dear friend Chloe," he'd said, and reached into a pocket of his jacket and pulled out the wooden box about the size and shape of a deck of cards. "Iss for you! Privacy! Workss great! Stopps all this," and he waved at the flying eyes that buzzed all around them.

"How does it work?" she asked him as she dropped it into her purse.

There'd be a social media frenzy over that, she was sure. Millions would want to know what was in that box? Something from Peter? Something magical from S'hudon? What could it be?

Chloe supposed that was a good thing. Her publicist and the studio and her agent would all be overjoyed about it.

"Eassy!" he said. "Sslide top open, pull out device, and tell it 'Privacy'!"

They'd both waved at the assembled hacks and photogs and a few hundred civilians out there, too, held back by L.A.'s finest, and then she'd climbed back into the limo with its Earthie driver and they'd headed for Malibu.

Now, here, standing at the big living room window that opened up the vista of the Pacific below, waves crashing, dozens of drones and flitters and spyeyes hovering out there in the breeze, keeping an eye on her as she pretended they weren't there, she turned around so her back was to them, just to be mean, and took the box out of her purse.

"Lots of chatter about your turning around to hide this," said myBetty, approvingly. "Your numbers are the best you've had since the day of Peter's explosion." Chloe could see the grooves on one side of the box. She held it with the grooves up, then pushed on the top of the box, trying to slide it off. Nothing. She turned it around and tried it again, and this time it slid right open.

Inside was a small tube, about the size and shape of her lip balm. Keeping her right hand closed around the little tube, she turned around to look out toward the Pacific and, in the foreground, all those flying cams that were keeping an eye on her. Fifty of them, maybe, or even a hundred. She smiled for the camera, put her hand over her mouth so they couldn't read her lips, and said, firmly, "Privacy."

And nothing happened. She'd thought they all might drop from the sky, disabled, their little engines stopped and their whirring propellers stilled. But no, there they were.

Then good news from myBetty: "The video feed has disappeared, Chloe. I'm checking all the sites, and the feed has gone blank on every one of them. That device works! Odd, though," she added. "I'm still linked through this new provider, Trebnet. The one I had at the consulate. Maybe that's so we won't be affected by the privacy device?"

"No doubt," said Chloe, smiling to see that the watching devices were crashing now, some with one another. Two banged into her large window, hitting it hard and then falling to the ground to whirr there, broken; others moved around in small circles on the ground, birds with broken wings. A few, the most expensive ones, the ones with self-guidance, stayed out of the fray and then turned to leave, set for autoreturn to their home base, she guessed.

Chloe walked to the far side of the living room and opened the door to walk outside to the back deck. There, she picked up the two whirring, dying flitters that had hit the glass and tossed them, one by one, out over the cliff edge and down to the beach below, where they could join a few of their brethren.

That done, she went back inside, sat down on the couch with its now clear view out over the blue Pacific, and got busy with myBetty on arranging her meetings for tomorrow. It would be a face-to-face day, for sure, but somewhere in there she had to meet with the cast and crew of *The Family Madderz*, too. That would be one of their happiest meetings in months. And then, by late afternoon, they'd be back on the set, on the show with a future. Yay.

By then it was getting late, so she had myBetty get the kitchen going on a nice dessert. Chocolate and white wine was called for. Between the two of them, Chloe and myBetty, they had the place all set when Priya arrived, walking up the back path from the shoreline garage.

It was a wonderful thing, how Priya liked to stay in just as much as Chloe did. Together, they did away with the chocolate mousse and that bottle of pinot gris from Chalk Hill , and then they made their way to the bedroom and kept that big window open, too, so they could make love before the moon over the ocean while myBetty kept an eye on the cam feeds. Nothing; all quiet on this western front. Not bad. Not bad at all.

Somewhere in there, maybe at the moment of when her pleasure was greatest, Chloe thought about the S'hudonni device and all those blind spy-eyes and flittercams and all the rest. That thing would change the world if anyone else got hold of it. For the moment, though, she was glad that if only one Earthie could have one, that Earthie was her.

5

SILOS

Dr. Thomas Holman, PhD, from Vanderbilt, postdoc work at Berkeley, tenured before he was thirty, one of the top researchers in his field, leaned against the bumper of the old 4x4 Honda hybrid and smoked a very welcome cigarette as the Irregulars set the silos burning. He'd earned the smoke; it had been a very stressful half hour or so. It was fine being in charge, sure, but leadership takes a toll. In some ways, he thought, it had been better when he was on his own, a lone wolf roaming around the fertile Midwest, exacting a price for the fevered embrace that small-town America gave to S'hudon and its profits. Now, with a whole team to lead, life was more complicated.

He thought about what it meant that Twoclicks was back and Peter was probably dead. He had heard the news just two days ago, reading an actual newsprint newspaper in Great Bend, Kansas. Small towns in the middle of nowhere still had weekly newspapers. It was back to the good old days, print papers popping up all over the place to tell the truth about things, now that the S'hudonni controlled the internet. And cell phones? Ha. Totally restricted by S'hudon, so much so that they hardly worked anymore. The age of instant information was over, the disrupters disrupted.

Great Bend was a nice town, bigger than you'd think, circled by smaller towns, and they, in turn, were circled by farms and silos and plenty of wheat and barley and corn. A lot of that was destined for handcrafted whiskey or ale, the products for which S'hudon was paying top dollar and crowing about all the time on Trebnet. Sell your handcrafts to distant worlds! Reach for the stars! Be your own boss! Design your own products!

All of which was lies and propaganda. All of it. You couldn't trust a damn thing on Trebnet.

But this article from the Great Bend *Intelligencer* seemed legit, and then the editorial in the back of the section talked about what good news all this was for Great Bend and for Kansas. A firm hand back on the tiller of the economy, Twoclicks at the helm. S'hudonni leadership bringing the heartland back into profitability. Shame about Peter Holman, but he'd disappeared into the void after saving Earth's new leader as he helped us join this incredible new union of planets. We should all honor this great hero by working with, not against, the S'hudonni, said the *Intelligencer*.

"Crap," said Tom, tossing the newspaper onto the ground. This meant

Whistle's big plan hadn't worked? Peter was dead, but Twoclicks lived on? Bad news, indeed.

Was Peter still really dead? Yeah, it sure sounded like it, confirming what Tom and billions of others had seen in that live sweepcast. The flailing arms and the choking and the nausea and the gasping for air and the fainting and then gone to black. Just like that. And shit, that was too damned bad. But Tom had guessed something like that was likely, back when he'd watched Peter swim away from his girlfriend and dead Kait's widow and Tom himself. He could have killed Peter himself then, and god knows there was enough at stake to make that a good choice. But Tom had been soft, had gone easy on his brother. He'd made sure Peter knew the threat and knew that Tom had let him live, and then Tom had watched Peter swim away, headed toward that ship and the distant stars. And then Tom had burned down the old family home where Peter had been living, had walked away from that past into this new future.

Every time he burned some of these silos, he thought again of how good it had been to bring down that house. Cleansing, that's what it had been. Done with the past; burn it down. Dead now, all of them, all of it: Peter, Kait, Father and Mother, science and sea turtles and research and tenure and all that crap. Gone now. Moving forward, that was the key.

It was more than six months ago that he'd brought the house down, but who was counting? He laughed. It felt like a lifetime ago.

He'd been merciful as that part of his life had come to an end. He had warned them to get away: that actress, Chloe Cary, who was his brother's girlfriend; and that Sarah chick, Kait's wife. He'd given them time to get the hell away before the device went off and sent the house up in flames.

He'd set that vest against the glass, armed it, walked away, and then tapped his temple to set it off. Then he'd walked along the beach and watched the S'hudonni ship as it rose in the distance. His brother was on that ship, probably looking out some porthole right now, seeing his home in flames, watching Tom walk away from the conflagration he'd started. Good, Tom had thought. He hoped like hell that Peter could see all this, could see what Tom had started.

It wasn't long after that, a little more than a week, that Peter had seemed to die on that very S'hudonni ship that Tom had watched rise and rise and rise as the house burned down behind him. An explosion on that ship, the air escaping, all those looted Earth treasures sweeping out into the vacuum, and Peter Holman, the great adventurer, tumbling away to a sad and miserable death.

Tom had even felt bad about that for about five minutes. It was exactly what Whistle's people had promised when they'd first talked to Tom, who'd been living out there in the wilds of Arcadia, Florida, sulking in a trailer park, walking in the woods, feeling sorry for himself.

There'd been a knock on his door. A tall, thin woman and a short, puffy man stood there, and they had some things they wanted to talk about. They felt his pain. They wanted to help. He could change the world, and right some terrible wrongs while he was at it.

It had sounded good to him. Very good, in fact. What Peter had done to him was awful. They were brothers, for Christ's sake, and he'd taken all this from him: the science he loved and yes, the woman he loved, too. His future. Their future. Hell, Earth's future.

All of that had been stolen from him, and then those two had offered him a way to respond, and to save Earth from the horror of Twoclicks at the same time. Join their side, the side of freedom, the side of an Earth that was S'hudon's ally, not its colony. The side of an Earth that would stay independent.

That was a key moment. Choose your poison: Twoclicks or Whistle. Tom wasn't stupid; he could see Whistle's bullshit from a mile off. But Whistle wanted him, seemed to need him, and that gave Tom leverage, something to work with, something that no other Earthie had with these fucking aliens.

So, OK, he chose Whistle. He was all in. And what it all had finally led to was that explosion out there on the way to another world, the ship opening up and Peter and Heather and Twoclicks and everything else spilling out into the nothing. It had proven Whistle's power, if nothing else, and Tom had taken it in stride. The deaths, even that of his brother, were necessary, part of the process of change.

Sure, the supposed death of Twoclicks and Heather and Peter Holman and all those flowery little daffodil aliens hadn't changed things much. Not yet. The S'hudonni Pax led by Twoclicks continued right along, even without Twoclicks himself directly calling the shots. His side was still in control—a few thousand S'hudonni, that was all, and a whole lot of Earthie collaborators in all the self-styled consulates around the planet, pulling all the economic strings in the great grain belts of America and Canada and Russia and India and Europe and South Africa. Want to make a lot of money off your crops? Do what they want. Grow what they want and prepare it while their spyeyes keep an eye on your handiwork, and then sell it to S'hudon and life is good. You give up a few things here and there, sure, but life is good. Sucker born every minute.

And all this, apparently, had really pissed off Whistle, Twoclicks's brother and competitor and the only choice available if someone—some ex-scientist named Tom Holman, for instance—wanted to stop Twoclicks from turning Earth into one large hand-tended private garden of the S'hudonni mercantile empire. Stir up enough shit, as Tom understood it, and Whistle would take over from Twoclicks. And that would be good for Tom Holman and, hell, for the whole fucking planet.

So stirring up shit had become Tom's raison d'être, his passion, the very reason for being alive. And it turned out he was pretty damn good at it.

Now, watching the silos burn, Dr. Tom was continuing to be, he admitted it, a little sentimental. It was a shame, really. None of those young men and women who'd been defending this farm had had to die. He'd offered them the chance to walk away. He had thirty men and women in the Irregulars, all of them veterans of a dozen actions like this as they'd worked their way through the heartland. They were strong, capable, motivated, and well armed.

And against them there'd been ten: six men—boys, really—and the four women. They didn't stand a chance.

Tom hadn't bothered with any of the precious S'hudonni tech he had along, except for the suppressor that blocked their electronic signature, in case they ran into real opposition. If the Irregulars had used the handheld S'hudonni toys, they could have wiped out the farm boys and their sisters in seconds. One moment they'd be standing their ground, the next moment they'd be turned into tiny particles that drifted in the breeze. Tom had seen that demonstrated by Whistle himself.

Instead, humanely, he'd called out to the group that stood there, offered them the chance to leave and not get hurt. He'd given them that chance, but they'd been full of bravado, since all they'd been able to see was Tom and Nikki, both carrying automatic weapons—but, heck, just the two of them.

"Just go away," their leader, an older woman—maybe the mother of some of them—had yelled. "This is our home. This is our work. You can't just burn it down."

"Well," Tom had said, "the thing is, you plan to sell all that wheat at a nice price to that brewery in Salina that will sell its products to the S'hudonni, who'll turn a nice profit on it by selling it to all those daffodil things and the big ducks and the jellyfish and the rest of them on the other six planets. Seems to me that makes you—all of you—collaborators."

Tom had smiled and walked closer. The team was spread out behind him, using the parked trucks and a couple of outbuildings as cover. Nikki, her hair in that signature flat twist that poked out from underneath her baseball cap, walked along with him and stopped to say to the woman, "It don't have to be this way, ma'am. No one's got to get hurt. We'll burn it down this year, and then next year you just grow wheat for flour and bread that you sell to Americans, or Canadians, or even the Mexicans, if you like. Just don't turn it into beer or whiskey for the damn S'hudonni."

The woman held a shotgun. She brought it up to hold it in front of her. "There's ten of us to just the two of you. Why don't you just turn around and leave us alone?"

"I'm afraid that we can't do that, ma'am," said Nikki. "So, this is your last chance. You going to walk away from all this trouble or not?"

"Let's fight 'em," said one boy, holding what looked like a .22. And he raised his gun to his shoulder. So did the woman, and then so did the rest of them. They didn't have S'hudonni tech—no shimmer of an energy wall, no handhelds, no spyeyes, no floaters.

Too bad, Tom thought. And then, "I'm sorry," he said, and he raised his G36 and let loose, while Nikki broke left. The boys and girls started shooting, too, but none of their shots came close.

Tom kept firing for another few seconds as the team lit the place up from behind cover. The battle lasted for perhaps ten seconds, one of the young girls almost making it to cover behind the granary before she went down. The others died where they stood.

It took the team another half hour to get the silos burning, which went up like smokestacks, one of them with a nice dust explosion that they hoped might spread to the other two, but didn't. Still, nice blazes. Lots of smoke. Tom liked that, the smoke signals, letting everyone in this part of Kansas—Salina was just over the horizon—see what happens to collaborators. Then they walked into the stubble of the harvested field and used the drip torches to get that burning. It wasn't as successful; the stubble was too damp from the recent rains, and stubble was always a problem. Better to fire a field right before harvest, when it really burned.

Still, a job well done. No one came to try to stop them or to put the fires out. In this day and age, you were on your own in rural America. So they took their time getting it done and stopped for a while to admire the silos, once they had them going, drinking some Flying Monkeys ale from the kitchen of the farmhouse. That was the microbrew that started with this farm's crops and, mostly, wound up in Downtone or Harmony, two of the planets in the S'hudonni Empire.

Tom finished his cigarette, then waved to the team by circling his hand over his head. Time to move on. They climbed back into their trucks and hit the road. The next place to visit was in Missouri. A few small farms on the way, one a week or so, and then eventually, in a month or two, as his little army kept growing, Tom had his eyes on that brewery in St. Louis that took the grains from those farms and others and turned it into St. Louis Toasted Ale. The beer was handcrafted all the way, so it employed a couple of hundred people, if you counted the farmworkers—and then that ale was sold directly to the S'hudonni, putting money and power into Twoclicks's tiny pockets.

The brewery was urban, so there was more risk in getting it done; the cities had those militarized police forces to keep the peace. But that was all right, too. It would be a nice little challenge for the Irregulars. They would get it done, even if they had to take out half the neighborhood to do it. They had the S'hudonni devices for that, so maybe they'd finally get to use them.

If Whistle had those suppressors working, and could control Trebnet like he said he could, it wouldn't matter what signature those explosive devices sent out.

Tom looked at the silos. One of them collapsed inward as he watched, the top portion crumbling into the bottom with a roar and sparks flying everywhere and lots of pretty flames.

So Peter was dead. That's what Twoclicks was claiming. Tom didn't know if he believed that or not, but it seemed likely. That was certainly how it had looked as Peter's sweepcast showed that explosion. Tom had a sweep receiver, sure, and he'd been watching through Peter's eyes as that hole sucked the life out of their ship, and the art, and that stupid fucking baseball bat, and then Peter and Twoclicks and Heather and a host of tumbling daffodils. Tom chuckled and shook his head. That was so Peter, to focus on a baseball bat as his life tumbled away into the nothing. A jock, for sure, right to the end.

Maybe. There'd been no confirmation about Peter's death, and now, with the surprise of Twoclicks being alive . . . well, who knew?

But while Peter might or might not be dead, Twoclicks and his S'hudonni certainly weren't, so soon enough they'd be back at it full-time, flitting around in their ships, making their deals and their promises. Now, really, was the time to strike. Put a dent in those S'hudonni plans, slow down the embrace of S'hudon's goodies by all these greedy people willing to make money at the hands of the new empire. If he couldn't stop the great wheels of mercantile colonialism from turning and churning, he could at least throw a few sticks and stones into the spokes. Fuck you, Twoclicks and all your Earthie pals. Fuck you, dead Peter and live Chloe Cary, stream star, and all the rest of them. Burn, baby.

6

ARTS AND CRAFTS

Seven weeks later they were in St. Louis on a warm late summer night. They'd come a careful and disguised hundred kilometers to get there, five or six of them each in one of their vans or the two big gas-eating SUVs or their one old Humvee, painted pink and with flowers on it—just retro hippies on a road trip, smoking Missouri's legal dope and listening to the Dead. They'd taken separate routes, and now, in an hour or so—about ten thirty, depending on what time the Cardinals game ended—they'd meet outside the two-story Kenny's Artisanal Brewhouse and bring the whole thing down while a hundred employees and a few hundred thirsty baseball fans watched it and learned.

Kenny's had a brewery in back and a two-story beer hall in front, with a second-floor balcony that overlooked the first floor's tables and twin bars. Hanging from the balcony were pennants and jerseys and caps from the Cardinals. Kenny's Artisanal Brewhouse was doing so well in selling all the handcrafted ales to S'hudon that they'd started up a separate line of Irish red ales—Redbird—for Cardinals fans. After every home game, those fans packed the place.

Whistle—or more properly, Whistle's people—had sent Tom the instructions via the new encrypted system on Trebnet, the only cloud available now, in this new world of S'hudonni business as usual. It would be a breeze, Whistle promised. He'd made sure there wouldn't be any interference from Twoclicks and his screamships, for starters; and he would block all the communications channels the city's militarized police might have, too, so no one would be able to call in reinforcements. A few private security guards was all they'd face.

They all had their various parking sites mapped out, in a city full of alleys that would give them easy exit to roads heading south, once the action was over, everybody taking their own route south to meet at noon the next day, downriver, in a park outside Kimmswick, Missouri.

Tom parked the hippie Hummer at the end of an alley a few blocks from the site, and he and his little team of five slung their backpacks on and grabbed their small duffel bags by the straps and walked casually through the dark streets and alleys to the empty two-story warehouse building that Angie and Mikey, their two scouts, had picked out the week before. It was one block away from the brewhouse, just one of a dozen such abandoned buildings in that older part of tired old St. Louis.

The arrival of S'hudon, with its free wireless tech that replaced all the clouds that had been shut down and its promises of free energy and rapid transit and medcot technology for those who were righteous in their support of the new kids in town, had energized some parts of the world and had wiped out others. The Midwest was doing all right, but only by selling out completely to the new landlords. So St. Louis was staying alive now as a transport hub and a market town for all those Midwest crops that were being hand tended to become Earthie ales and wines and bourbons. The warehouses and abandoned factories of the city's south side were remnants of an earlier age, when furniture and shoes and dog food and mass-produced beer had kept the economy humming.

Tom and the others were first to get to the warehouse, but the rest of the Irregulars weren't far behind. As Tom walked in, he could read the faded decades-old letters over the door: Globe-Democrat Printing Services. So this had been a printing plant.

In a half hour they all were there, unpacking and getting it ready. There was no power in the warehouse, and St. Louis was hot and humid in the summer, so they sweated in the thin light from their flashlights. There were streaks of mottled mold on the wall and rust on the old printing presses that sat there idle, waiting for the glory days to return, when print newspapers showed up in your driveway every morning and were read and trusted by hundreds of thousands of readers. Now, here, it was hard to breathe in the heat and the mold of the long-abandoned building.

Tom looked at his watch. "Time to go, Irregulars," he said. "We all have our assignments. Nikki's team clears the building but keeps them around to watch. Dieter's team watches for any militias headed this this way. My team sets the charges."

There were a lot of nods and some fist bumps and people adjusting straps and checking their weapons one more time. This was new, this kind of action in a city, and Tom could tell they were nervous. But they'd be good once they got going, he was sure of it. And fifteen or twenty minutes was all it would take.

For Tom and his team, it would be in and out, a lot of shouting and pushing but, with any luck, no casualties as they cleared the main room and set the charges and then ushered everyone outside, the brewers and the keg washers and bottlers and fermenters and stockers and all the rest, to stand with the Cardinals fans and watch the place go out of business for good.

The Irregulars themselves would watch for five more minutes or so to make sure the job was truly done, and then off they'd go, heading downstate. Job done, and with some well-earned respect that might get the word out, mouth to mouth, about what happened to businesses that cozied up to Twoclicks and his tulip-crazed Earthies.

Tom walked around and hugged a few of his Irregulars here and there, including Nikki, who said, "Let's take some scalps," and grinned at him.

Then Tom and his team—Mikey, Tionna, Carl, Angie, Danny, and Aarav—left first, going out a side door that led to an alleyway that angled around to a loading dock to the brewery. They only had to go a hundred meters or so across an alley, and then a side street, and then around to the back of the brewery. As they crossed the side street, Tom looked back once to see if other shadowy figures were coming out quietly and carefully and heading toward their positions. They were. He turned back to lead his team.

Tionna was their best at lock picking, so she went first, once they'd all reached the wide alley at the back entrance. There was a loading dock there, but no trucks around. Three wide overhead doors opened onto the dock. Next to them, on the left, was a regular door, metal, locked.

It took Tionna all of fifteen seconds to tweak open the doorknob lock, and the dead bolt wasn't thrown, so they waltzed right in and gathered inside in a long, dark corridor. Tom had a pen flashlight and he clicked that on. In the thin light they could see the corridor stretch off into the distance.

So Mikey was right when she'd said it would be a breeze getting in. She'd stood in this very spot a week before, when the rest of the Irregulars were a couple of hundred kilometers away or more, in Central Missouri, burning corn. She'd been there during the day and the door had been unlocked. There'd been two trucks pulled up the loading dock, and a half dozen people loading wooden barrels of ale into the trucks. S'hudon had a landing site across the river in Illinois, at old Scott Air Force Base.

The base had been closed for a decade, so the locals had been delighted, months ago, to welcome S'hudon to the air base, a couple of freighters a week landing, loading up for a day or two with all manner of Earthie products—but much of it that handcrafted beer and wine and bourbon and all the rest from all over the heartland—before lifting quietly from the base to head off to one of the Six. Hundreds of Earthies worked at the base now, loading and unloading and running things. Tom heard they made good money.

Mikey, in her fifties at least, was a small woman with graying hair and a lot of confidence. Bold as brass, she'd walked up the steps to the loading dock, pulled open that door, and walked right in like she owned the place. No one had stopped her. Then she'd gone into the brewery proper, waved to a few people and smiled, and they'd all waved back or nodded at her. She'd ended up at the bar at the far end of the building. It was invaluable intelligence, really, and Tom made a mental note to tell her later what a good job she'd done.

Tom took the lead as they walked down the corridor a good thirty meters, ignoring the doors on either side that led to old office or storage space—unused now, Mikey had said. Tom was sure she was right.

He got to the far door, waving away a few mosquitoes but keeping it quiet as he did it, shooing them away from where they hovered right in front of his face, so close he could hear the whine. Damn things. The whole team had been plagued by mosquitoes and gnats all along the way. Maybe it had something to do with how rarely they were able to bathe. A quick rinse in a river or stream was often the best they could do.

He opened the door, expecting to see a dozen or more people standing around, tending to the brewing tanks. But no one was home. The big expanse of the room was dimly lit, just some old fluorescents over in the corner keeping it from being in total darkness.

This didn't seem right. But the tanks looked functional and Tom could hear the hum of the pumps, even though no one was around. He walked in a few more steps, looked around. No one. Walked in a few more and turned to wave the others in. Hell, he thought, they'd be able to place the charges and be out of here in five or ten minutes. They were lucky.

Or not.

He heard the *whoomph* of an explosion from the far side of the room. Muffled, maybe in the next room beyond this one. What the hell? The only explosions should have been in this very room, from Tom's team.

Crap. Something had gone wrong, and Tom had a decision to make: back out , right now, before they were trapped in here, or get the charges placed in a hurry and then go through there, into the next room. That's where the big bar was, and it would be loaded with people. Nikki and her team might be in a fight there right now.

As if to make his point, there was gunfire, rapid, someone with automatic weapons, and then a rattling of more of that, probably return fire.

Tom waved his arm high, turned to face his team, pointed toward the brewing tanks, and said in a whisper, "Get those charges placed and then we'll get out of here. Hurry!"

Four of his team—Aarav, Carl, Angie, and Danny—ran toward the tall tanks, slipping off their backpacks while they were at it.

That left Mikey and Tionna. This would be the first real fight either one of them had been in. They'd burned some fields and torched some silos, but no one had been shooting at them while they did it. This was different.

But both of them had their weapons ready, good solid G38s, German, dependable, supplied by Whistle's people. And both of them looked ready. No fear in those eyes.

Tom looked right at them and said, "We're going through that door and help Nikki and the others, all right?"

They both nodded.

The other four were out of sight, setting the backpacks underneath the tanks, the shaped charges facing up, something they'd been practicing all week.

The tanks had angled bottoms, starting from a narrow bottom valve and widening rapidly from there. The charges would blow the bottom out of the tanks and probably collapse them. Replacing them wouldn't take long, Tom knew, but the message would have been sent.

He could see the others hustling back to the group, shucking the straps on their G38s to pull them off their backs and carry them in front, ready to use.

There was a blast and a white glare from back behind them, not one of the shaped charges but someone else's explosive, back at the door they'd come through to get into this room. A flash grenade and then *whoomph*, and another blinding white flare, two of them.

Tom turned away, raised his hand to get his team behind him, and then ran to the door that led into the bar area and away from the flash grenades. He yanked it open and led the way into chaos.

The first floor could hold several hundred people. That large crowd was why the Irregulars were here, to show off their firepower and their cause in front of hundreds as they ushered them all outside before the brewery tanks blew.

Instead, with those flash grenades behind them and who knew how much militia tossing them in, the only way for Tom and his team was forward, through the smoke and the explosions and the rattle of gunfire.

Tom ran, leaning down as low as he could while still scrambling forward, rounding the end of the bar and hiding behind that for a second before bullets ripped through it and nearly got him. So, OK, run through this room and get outside, that seemed like the best option. Hell, there was so much blinding smoke and noise and gunfire that he couldn't see where any of the other Irregulars were, anyway.

So he turned once to see if his team were there behind him, and they were—lying on the floor or, a couple of them, in crouches. There was too much noise and chaos for him to yell instructions, so he pointed toward where the front door should be and waved at them to follow as he started to dodge and dance through the hail of bullets and yet another explosion, this one off to the side.

Three different times he could hear bullets thunking into the wood of tables or chairs near him, and twice he heard exclamations of pain behind him as he stumbled along, variously running in a crouch or crawling on all fours or, a couple of times, moving along on his elbows, trying to stay as flat as he could on the floor.

Eventually—it seemed like hours later but couldn't have been more than a minute or two—he could see an open door ahead of him. He was on all fours at the time, but there was a jumble of tables and chairs all around him, so he risked rising to a crouch and then rising again to run flat out for that door.

And he made it, stumbling through the door into the thin light of streetlamps and the muzzle flash from guns being fired from both his right and his left.

"Boss!" he heard someone yell, and he looked to the left to see Nikki there, crouched behind a concrete barrier along with a few other Irregulars. Thank god.

"Get your ass over here!" she yelled at him, and he did that, back in a crouch, scrambling along as bullets whizzed by and slapped off the pavement around him. Jesus Christ.

But then he was there. Alive. And Nikki and the others were there, too. A lot of them, he could see now, maybe a dozen. Thank god.

"Where's the rest?" Nikki asked him, as he sat there next to her, glad to be alive.

"Right behind me," he said, but she looked at him and shook her head, so he turned around to look cautiously over the top of the concrete and there was no one there, no one coming, just one body halfway out the door. He couldn't tell who it was.

"Boss," Nikki asked, incredulous, "you the only one to make it?"

Was he? What a disaster. "We were ambushed, Nikki," he said. "Shooters behind us, shooters fucking all around. We just had to get out of there."

"Damn. Glad you made it out. What a mess," she said.

He shook his head. "They were right behind me, Nikki. We were crawling out of there." But as he said that he remembered hearing—who was it, Mikey?—crying out in pain. And then that terrible sound of a bullet thunking into meat and an *oomph* noise from Tionna. Who else? Did they all die back there? Were any still alive?

He turned away from Nikki and looked around the concrete barrier to see the body at the door. Was that Mikey right there? Jesus.

"Boss," Nikki said. "We got to get out of here. And now. Did you get those charges laid?"

"Yeah," he said. But were they still there? He didn't know, but he guessed that the militia—or whoever the hell it was . . . Maybe SWAT cops? Did St. Louis still have those? Whoever they were, he guessed they had come in behind him and had cleared his team out by now.

"Boss," Nikki said. "Dieter has the detonator."

"Tell him to push it!"

She shook her head. "That's him out there, Boss. By the door. He went in to make sure you guys were clear, and then he'd hit the button."

"Fucking hell," Tom said. What the hell else could go wrong?

"Boss," Nikki said, "get your ass out of here. Get everyone's ass out of here." She stared at him, said more slowly, "Everyone, Boss."

She put her G38 down, scooted past him on all fours, turned to face him, and said, one more time, "Everyone, Boss. We'll meet up in Kimmswick. See you there."

And then she got into a crouch, peeked over the concrete to take a look. There was a lull in the shooting, so maybe the cops thought it was over. She took a breath, didn't look over to Tom at all, then sprinted for the door where Dieter lay. Near him somewhere, maybe, was the detonator.

Tom watched her go, then turned around to see what was left of the Irregulars behind cover, looking at him, waiting for his orders. He waved at them, shouted, "Get out of here! Go now! You know where to meet." And then he ran.

7

THE BIG MUDDY

Things were different now. They'd started the fight in St. Louis with thirty-six Irregulars, all of them good soldiers, fighting for what was right. And now, gathered here on the north bank of the Meramec River where it emptied into the Mississippi, there were six, and two of them were walking wounded.

Jesus Christ. A lot of good people were dead, a few others were captured, and others, Tom was guessing, had headed for the hills and weren't coming back. In short, the whole movement was in deep shit. And all because they'd thought it would be a surprise and it turned out the city police—which might as well have been a military unit, given their equipment—were ready for them and executed a perfect ambush.

Nikki, brave and crazy Nikki, had saved the day with that foolish run across the front parking lot to reach the detonator held in dead Dieter's hand. A round from the fifty-caliber mounted on top of the police ARV had ripped half of Dieter's head from his shoulders before he could press the trigger.

Nikki had been winged twice, once in the left arm and then again in the left hip. She'd be fine, but if she'd been a fraction of a second slower getting to Dieter's body and pressing the button, she'd be dead. Somehow she'd made it, diving the last ten meters in a long facedown dive and sliding across the lot to reach the trigger. She grabbed it, pressed it, and thank god the charges were still in place and went off with a nice healthy blast that probably took out a few of the cops but, more important, threw out a huge cloud of dust and smoke that gave the remnants of the Irregulars a chance to get out of that death trap and make an escape. The rowdy crowd of Cardinals fans was long gone by then, running like hell to get away from the bullets flying everywhere, and mixing in with them as they ran helped a few of the Irregulars make their getaway.

Tom had been surprised, and damn happy, to see Nikki running toward him through the fleeing crowd. She'd kept her head down in the smoke and flame and then had gotten away, coated in dust. Together, the two of them had scrambled through alleys, back to the van, and piled in with the others. One fucking van with six fucking Irregulars—the name sounded like horseshit now, pretentious and foolish—and that was it, apparently.

And then it had been back roads in the dark and the suppressor keeping any tech from finding them and a good four hours of lights-off craziness before they finally made it to the muddy north bank of the Meramec, just a quarter mile or so west of the Big Muddy herself, the Mississippi River. They were in a small riverside park—a few picnic tables and rusty grills, a battered swing set with one swing still attached, a basketball pole with a tilted backboard and a rim hanging down over the cracked concrete pavement. That was it.

They'd been waiting here for an hour and no one else had made it, so it was time to get moving. They didn't want to be here when the sun came up, and you could see dawn breaking out over the Mississippi already. Time to fucking go.

Tom was sitting on a wooden picnic table, his feet on the bench seats, his back to the other remaining Irregulars, who stood or sat quietly to watch the proceedings.

He heard a rustling and looked to see Nikki coming over. She sat down next to him.

"We've been talking, Boss," Nikki said. "There ain't no easy way to say this. The guys asked me to tell you they're done with it. They want to go home."

Tom nodded. He'd been expecting this. And who the hell could blame them? "I get it, Nikki. That was hell. I couldn't ask anyone to go through anything like that again. Ever."

He pulled a Camel out of the pack in his pocket. Lit it. Blew out some smoke. Every now and then a quick smoke was just the ticket. Then he stood up, walked over to the van, Nikki by his side.

There, he took a drag on the cigarette and then looked at them, the survivors, and said, "We lost today, Irregulars, and I won't ask any more of you than you've already given."

He took another drag, blew out the smoke, flicked the cigarette off toward the muddy riverbank. "So we should split up and go our separate ways. Keep your heads down, go somewhere quiet. I don't think they'll come after you. Hell, no one knows who you are, really. I'm the only one they'll be after."

There were head nods, some shuffling feet. These guys weren't going to get sentimental about this. They wanted out. And now.

Tom walked over to the van and opened the back door. He pulled up the mat in the back, reached down into the well where the spare was, pulled up a duffle bag, and tossed it onto the ground. "This is yours. Came to me by way of that last meeting with fucking S'hudon a couple of months ago. I'm tired of toting it around. Get in there and split it up."

He turned to look at Nikki. "Can you handle that, Nikki? Just give it out to the all of you equally? I don't know how much there is, but it ought to help everyone get started somewhere else, somewhere far away from fucking here."

Nikki came over, kicked at it, then reached down to zip the top open.

Bills, mostly hundreds, were wrapped up in loose bundles. "That's a lot of money, Boss. You sure?"

"Sure I'm sure," Tom said, thinking about what was next. Back to Florida maybe? Back to the swamps and the woods in the Everglades maybe? Or just get down to Louisiana and swamp it there? That'd be easy enough from here. He could just Huck Finn it down the Big Muddy.

He walked over and started shaking hands, gave Nikki a good hug on top of that, and then turned to walk toward the Mississippi. "I'm going down the river, guys. Find a small boat or a raft and just drift, you know?"

They nodded. They knew.

Then he turned his back to the Irregulars and walked toward the river. In ten minutes he was alone, working through the woods that ran right to the river's edge. There, in a clearing, he looked around. Nothing. And he couldn't fucking swim to Louisiana, that was for sure.

There was a crack of branches being stepped on behind him. He ducked down and cautiously looked back into the darkness of the woods.

Nikki came into the moonlit clearing. "Hey, Boss," she said. "I know where there's a boat."

She walked across the clearing and stood in front of him. They were about the same height, so it was eye to eye. "I figure you can't make it on your own, Boss. And I'm guessing we still got things to do, right?"

Tom didn't agree with all that, but it would be good, really good, to have her along. And sure, maybe—yes, there'd be things to do. They hugged. They got started.

PART TWO

AN IMPORTANCE

Chloe Cary was about the ugliest intelligent creature the ducks of Downtone had ever seen, but they watched her adventures avidly as she traveled a fascinating Earth with cute little Treble and sampled those rare wares.

—Peter Holman, *Notes from Holmanville*
(S'hudon City and New York:
Trebnet Press, 2035)

8

TREBLE IN PARADISE

ONE YEAR LATER

The months had gone by with the usual list of California calamities: fires in the hills, earthquakes in the Bay Area, drought everywhere, and Chloe hard at work starting and finishing the second season of *The Family Madderz*, with booming ratings early on that had plateaued by midseason and were once again sagging badly by season's end. What to do? What to do?

Chloe thanked myBetty for the wake-up song, "Not Yet Not You," from Sally Golightly, and then patted Anjou on the rear end and said, "Time to go, Ang. Busy day ahead for me."

Then she headed for the bathroom to brush her teeth. She liked Anjou, but there was definitely an expiration date on this relationship, as there had been on the past few. It was hard to find the right people to love, or even to like, and harder to keep them, in the age of flying paparazzi flitters and spyeyes. Chloe's little gift from Twoclicks worked great in a zone about one hundred meters in radius, but her friends and lovers had no such privacy tool, so they had to be careful when they weren't with Chloe.

Anjou was stunning, with those Algerian good looks, those long legs, those cheekbones, those eyes, that pout. Sure, she was much too young for the likes of Chloe Cary, and Chloe knew it as she put the toothbrush back into its holder. Hell, things moved so fast these days that their twelve-year difference in age meant they might as well have grown up on different planets. Anjou, sweet little Anjou, thought it was perfectly normal to have aliens dropping in at the soundstage to watch Chloe, or standing by when Anjou was posing for that *Top Shot* cover. For her, the aliens (S'hudonni and otherwise, as the tourists from the other six planets were starting to show up) were, she always said, no stranger than people from Ohio. Chloe, an Ohioan at heart, found that amusing, though for her it seemed like the S'hudonni had arrived yesterday, changing her life—for the better, mostly.

There'd been changes all over the place in the year and a half since those ships had first been dancing around over her and Peter's heads while they looked up at the dark sky on that Florida beach.

Peter, poor dead Peter—they'd never heard otherwise—had loved her, bless his heart, and if the sad truth was that she hadn't loved him back, well, that wasn't something you could admit to anyone, was it? Plus, he was a sweet guy.

She wondered what he'd think of what was happening on Earth these days. Would he have any qualms about the new S'hudonni cloud that Two-clicks waxed on about, which was ever so much better than the other clouds that it was good they'd all been shut down? As Hanratty explained to her, the servers—if that's what they were—were in orbit and were untouchably safe and secure. And Earth's boring old sat phone systems had never worked all that well anyway, so it was good those satellites had been disabled (and probably vaporized, though Twoclicks didn't say that's how it had gone down) and replaced with generous gifts from S'hudon. Those wonderful ships that could do so much. And all of this in less than two years! Think how wonderful it would be in the years to come!

And maybe it would be, she thought. What were the options, after all?

Putting some whitener on her teeth, staring at the mirror, Chloe thought about those options. More changes were coming, she was sure, and she had to be ready for those, ready to stay on top of things. Right then and there, she decided that the timer had, in fact, buzzed. Game over. She didn't want to bring Anjou along to tonight's twice-monthly friendly dinner at the consulate with Twoclicks and the revolting Hanratty. Instead, in a few minutes here, she'd have to break the news to her. It's me, it's not you. All of that.

Later, at dinner at the consulate, as the servant class worked to clear away the sea bass and fennel salad and some very nice Chilean wine (Twoclicks's taste had improved markedly, with a little help from Chloe), Twoclicks, working on his sorbet, had an announcement.

"We have an Importance coming here to your country and your world, dear friend Chloe. And you must be the one to escort this Importance. You," he said, smiling, as he pointed one of those delicate fingers right at her.

"An Importance " was coming? What did that mean?

Chloe looked at Hanratty, who, as always, had an explanation ready. "He means to tell you that his son is coming to Earth and will be here soon." He clicked and whistled his name—Hanratty was very good at that. "In English, we call him Treble. A grand tour is being arranged, Chloe, and we would like you to escort the young princeling."

"A grand tour?"

"Yes, a global tour, to all those places where Two has an economic interest. The American Midwest, the British Isles and Ireland, France, Italy, Greece, South Africa, Chile, Argentina, Brazil, and then on to Asia."

"You will be along, as well, Hanratty?" God, she hoped the answer was no. She'd learned that Hanratty had his uses, but learning to get along with the guy didn't mean she wanted to travel with him.

"No," he said. "And no Twoclicks, either. There are significant matters of state that we need to take care of here."

Chloe looked at Twoclicks, who was busy spooning sorbet into his mouth.

Big slurps off the spoon. A satisfied smile. He said, "Thiss iss very tasty, dear friend Chloe."

And Chloe smiled and slid her goblet of sorbet over to Twoclicks. This goofy creature with strawberry sorbet dripping down to what passed for a chin was the world's leader, in fact if not in name. So, in a day or two, he'd be attending to matters of state. With Hanratty at his side.

"Oh, and dear friend Chloe, iss more!" Twoclicks said as he lifted the spoon to his mouth and slurped again. "Kait Holman, sister of our dearest friend Peter Holman, is on same ship as my sson Treble! Coming home for her!"

"Kait is back!" Chloe exclaimed. This was wonderful news, unless it wasn't and Twoclicks was about to add that something horrible had happened to Kait.

"No, no!" Twoclicks said, reading her mind again. "Iss perfect! Perfect health! Perfect happiness! Perfect homecoming! But must be quiet, yess?"

Quiet, yes, thought Chloe. The world didn't know the details on Kait's death and life and copy and all the rest, and Twoclicks didn't *want* the world to know, either. Fair enough. "I will want to meet her," Chloe said. "I know her and her wife, Sarah. They're wonderful people. Sarah will be incredibly happy to have Kait back."

"Of course!" said Twoclicks. "All happening ssoon, sso soon!"

She smiled. Kait's return, really, was wonderful news. It might take a little media massaging, keeping Kait's return out of the spotlight, or out of the news entirely, really. But Chloe was an expert on that, and with the studio's help they'd get it done.

Twoclicks had more to say. "But the perfect Treble! Will be great expossure, dear friend Chloe! Whole world will be watching you with my sson."

The ratings had been slipping again, so the whole world watching was a fine idea. But the perfect Treble? Chloe had looked again over to Hanratty, who just smiled and said, "Twoclicks thinks highly of the princeling. The two of them get along famously."

Chloe thought about things. This gig would shore up the ratings for the looming third season of *The Family Madderz*, and her love life would be fine, now that the clingy Anjou was out of the picture. It would be good, great even, for Chloe's face and name to show up all over the place, certainly. And with the help of her little suppressor device from Twoclicks, she'd be able to keep her public face public and her private life private, especially when she was home. Her publicist would be very, very pleased, and so would the studio and all the rest of the hangers-on. They'd make sure she had a full complement of stylists and publicists and PAs and all the rest with her, too. She'd be taken care of.

Plus, the truth was you couldn't really say no to the Scion of S'hudon, the Sultan Who Might Swat You, the Jovial Genius, the Man Behind the Curtain for Earth's Future. So her answer was, "Yes, sure. I'd be delighted"

And that earned her a hug from Twoclicks and an attempt at the same from Hanratty, which she neatly avoided with a pat on the shoulder and a sweet smile.

A thought occurred. An ingratiating one, to be sure, but . . .

"You know," she said, "I could show Treble around the studio and bring him onto the soundstage when he gets here. Would he like that?"

"Yess!" said Twoclicks, with even a bit more than the usual exuberance. "Perhapss on Friday?"

Friday was tomorrow. Could she make it happen that quickly? "Sure," she said.

"Iss wonderful Morning!"

Perfect, thought Chloe, and sighed and smiled. Tomorrow the studio, and a day or a week or whenever later, the rest of the world. Such was life when Twoclicks was your dear, dear friend.

9

IT'S ALIVE!

At six the next morning, myBetty woke up Chloe with a cheery version of "It's My Party," by Robin Patel. The song, a remake of a hit from the 1960s, had been Chloe's favorite when she was twelve and playing soccer for Strongsville United, starting her competitive swimming career, and continuing her straight-A grade trajectory that would, in due time, get her into Stanford.

The way she'd planned her future, back then, was to lead the women's national soccer team to the World Cup title, swim her way to a gold medal in the backstroke in the Olympics, and meanwhile get her degree from Stanford, just like Mom had.

And damned it if didn't almost work out that way, too. Until Hollywood called, when she auditioned in Palo Alto and got the *Sharpshooter* TV show gig, playing Annie Oakley. She lost her best friend—the one who'd dragged her along to the audition—but in return she gained fame, fortune, failure, and revival, with Peter Holman and Twoclicks and all the rest. It was a strange, strange world, for sure.

She looked at the clock and said, "It's six a.m., myBetty. What the hell?"

Robin Patel stopped singing, right in the middle of the chorus, so myBetty could say, "Priority from Twoclicks, Chloe."

Oh, hell. What could it be that couldn't wait till a decent hour of the morning? Still, it was Twoclicks, so . . .

"Put it through, please," she said to her helpmate. A second later she heard Twoclicks say, "Big newss, dearest friend Chloe! The biggesst newss! Ever!"

Choe sat up.

"The Importance has arrived! Ssmall ship in Ssalton Ssea has our Treble! We will visit you today at sstudio!"

Well, Chloe thought, that was just fine, and it meant Kait was home now, too. Lovely news. Good. And now maybe she could get back to sleep for a couple of hours. In her lonely bed, mind you, having said farewell to Anjou.

"And guesss what?" Twoclicks was saying. "The Importance brings great newss! Great, great, great newss!"

"Great news?" Chloe asked, when there was long pause at Twoclicks's end, no doubt for dramatic effect.

"Our dearest friend Peter Holman. Your true love and dearest friend Peter! Iss alive! Peter iss alive! He is on S'hudon and alive! Alive!"

Alive! Peter was alive!

Well, that should help those sagging ratings.

After that, there was no time for any napping. Someone broke the news within a few minutes—someone named Twoclicks, no doubt—and Chloe was so busy spending the morning dealing with the repercussions that any sleep was out of the question.

Peter Holman was alive! Someone had rolled the stone away from the cave mouth of his death and he'd arisen! Alive!

myBetty reported that the Trebnet led with the happy news on all fronts when anyone logged on, with Chloe Cary mentioned suspiciously often. The news on Kait's return was so hushed as to not exist. Not a peep, said my-Betty.

It was no surprise when, inside of ten minutes, the paparazzi had gathered at the end of her gated drive and the drones were flying around outside the hundred-meter perimeter that they'd all learned to love. Zooms and soundscoops and other new gee-whiz devices had made seeing her and hearing her possible, though they all knew she was in control of when that would happen. If they trod too close, well, Chloe had quite a collection of downed drones and spyeyes and flitters sitting in a big open container out in the yard. Message received.

But Peter Holman was alive! So they had to risk losing a drone or two to get the news, and risk it they did, until, by seven a.m., Chloe called for the limo and darted into it, from front door to car door in five or ten seconds. And off they went to the studio, where she could safely spend the day and hope that an earthquake or a volcano or a war or a plane crash or something else would take over the news lead.

Alas, by nine a.m. there was still nothing bigger in the news, so when Twoclicks and Hanratty and the Importance arrived in their limo at the front gate of the studio, it took a phalanx of police to clear a path and get them inside and into the relative calm of the studio grounds.

When the limo reached the main office building, Chloe was out front, waiting for them. A big hug from Twoclicks, a nod toward Hanratty, and then a quick introduction by Twoclicks followed, as Chloe met young Treble, a very excited princeling.

He was a cute kid, thought Chloe. Leaner and shorter than most of the S'hudonni she'd seen before, with slick, black skin and legs a little longer for his frame than they were for the adults. Same fragile look to the arms, but his grip was firm and strong when he reached out to shake Chloe's hand and said, in perfect English, "It's very exciting to meet you, Miss Chloe. Uncle Peter asked me to wish you the best and give you a hug. May I?"

"You've met Peter?" she asked, shocked. Chloe realized she hadn't quite put two and two together. Treble hadn't just brought the news of Peter's survival; he'd maybe been part of it.

"Of course!" Treble said. "We had adventures together! He loves you so much!"

Well, great, thought Chloe. More of that *love* thing. But Chloe was nothing if not adaptable, thinking on her feet and all that. So when Treble opened his arms for a hug, she opened hers, too, and leaned right over to give him a nice squeeze.

When that ended, Treble laughed, a kind of whistly giggle, and said, "That was from Peter! He said to hug you and say he misses you and wishes he could hug you himself. And he asked me to give you this, too." He handed Chloe a thin metallic sheet that had been folded into its own envelope.

"Here," he said, reaching over to point toward a small indentation. "If you press this spot, it opens. It's a letter from Peter!" He paused and grinned at Chloe and then added, "And he said you should read it in private."

There were chuckles and a heavy-handed wink from Twoclicks at that news. Great, thought Chloe. This was just what she needed. She knew it had to be some sappy and effusive love note.

Whatever. She'd have to find out later. "Thanks, Treble," she said.

She slid the letter into her purse before reaching down to take Treble by the hand and head toward the lot where the carts were, chatting away with him as they walked, pointing out what was done in each building and listening to Treble as he raved on that "Uncle Peter is the best! We are wonderful friends!"

Behind them, the most powerful being on planet Earth waddled along, gawking at all the sights, with Hanratty, glum and foreboding, right next to him.

As they clambered in, Treble looked around, and they were, for the moment, alone enough for him to say, quietly, "Kaitlyn says hello and she hopes to see you soon. Father Twoclicks tells me you've heard the news about her and reminded me to remind you that all this has to be quiet for now. OK?"

"OK," she said, as she got behind the wheel to do the driving, and gave him a quick smile. He smiled back and whispered, "She was so brave! She'll be in her home later if you want to see her."

Wonderful, Chloe thought, thinking mainly about how great it would be for Sarah, who she still considered a pal these days, though she didn't see her often. Drinks and hugs on the QT? That sounded marvelous.

And on they went, with Chloe at the helm of the big eight-seater cart and acting as tour guide. They drove down several streets that were exterior sets, which she talked about: a block-long New York City, a long block of the Old West, a street in Paris and another in London. They reached the soundstage for *The Family Madderz* and got out of the cart to walk inside the cavernous building.

Just inside the door, Chloe was amazed to see Joan Kadinsky , the studio head, standing there with an assistant to greet them. Kadinsky got an uncomfortable hug from Treble and a nice handshake from Twoclicks as Hanratty and Chloe stood off to the side. Then Kadinsky walked them over to the set, where the cast and crew, gathered underneath a WELCOME sign, gave them a burst of applause and a few minutes of polite introductions before splitting up to get to work, filming a scene that Chloe wasn't in.

Clark Perry, the showrunner, came over to say hello, and he too got what Chloe was already thinking of as the Treble hug: bend down, hug, and grin. He then introduced them to the executive producer, the director and writers, the script supervisor, and others.

This went on for hours. It was quite a day, and Chloe was pleased that it went well. She was also pleased with Treble, who was cute and seemed guileless. There was nothing threatening about him, as there could be with Twoclicks. No matter how funny or informal Twoclicks acted, his ultimate power was always in the background.

Surely it was the same, really, with Treble. All he had to do, after all, was tell his father that some Earthie had threatened him and that would be that. Chloe knew this, but Treble was so polite and curious that within an hour of meeting him, she quit worrying about it. With Twoclicks, she never forgot.

Treble even seemed to have gone to some trouble to learn about Earth's curious behaviors, from the hugs to the shaking of hands in one culture to the polite bows of another. Maybe he learned these from Peter, back on S'hudon?

She held Treble's hand as they walked back to the limo after a a few hours well spent. Chloe realized that Treble couldn't really have any awareness of the essential purpose of a studio, or soundstages, or even the entire movie and television and sweep industries. To him, she suspected, the streets of New York were real, as was the Old West, with those swinging doors into the saloon, and Paris, with its scaled-down Eiffel Tower and Arc de Triomphe. All false fronts. But perhaps he'd learn what it all meant after the fact, watching television or a few sweeps. In fact, it would be fun to get together to watch a show or two that had been made at the studio, and she could point out how it was done. It would give them something to talk about.

Chloe was relieved to find that she really liked the kid, so maybe the global tour thing wouldn't be so difficult after all. In any event, she'd know by next week. Today was Friday. They were leaving next Wednesday, traveling on Twoclicks's Earthie private jet. Just the two of them, and a dozen others on board to keep them safe and keep them famous. Chloe would be outfitted with the latest generation of sweep equipment, so thin and light you could hardly tell she was wearing it. The contact lenses were the only question, really. But if they bothered her, she had the backup glasses, which looked great, changing tint to meet the demands of the available light and, just like the contacts, video recording everything. myBetty would be in charge of that and had told Chloe she'd already downloaded the software for it.

So things looked all right for the moment, and Chloe was feeling pretty good as she sent them on their way. Then she decided to walk back to her trailer and think it through. Sure, she knew enough to be wary about the S'hudonni in general and Twoclicks in particular. And sure, it could all go south in a heartbeat. But she was in it so deep now, there was no climbing out. She decided to be optimistic that the tour would work out fine, that everything would be fine with Treble, that Twoclicks would live up to his promises. That it would all be fine. Strange, but she never did get to hear about Treble's adventures with Peter and Kait on S'hudon. That had to be fascinating material.

Speaking of which . . . On the limo drive home later, she had myBetty give Sarah a call on the private smarty line and, lo and behold, there were plenty of tears and laughter and virtual hugs. Kait was back and looked great and had stories to tell—so many that it took the full forty-five minutes of drive time to just tell some of them before they had to hang up. It was warm and wonderful to see how Kait and Sarah were in constant contact with each other, always a hand on a knee or an arm over a shoulder. It wasn't quite so warm or wonderful to hear Kait talk about Peter and how much he missed Chloe and all that. Absence made the heart grow fonder, of course, but Chloe decided she didn't have to worry about it. She wouldn't see him for months or years, no doubt, so let the poor guy have his distant love, right?

Later, back in Malibu, she got a real fire going in the fireplace, using the wood she'd split herself, a couple of weeks ago, from logs she bought at the green store, fallen wood from storms and that last quake in in San Jose. Very California.

Splitting the logs in the fenced-in side yard felt great. Hands on, that was Chloe, and she stayed in shape, and not just because the current role in *The Family Madderz* called for her physical heroics. She'd always been in shape, from the time of her youth in Ohio, where she climbed the trees and, later, played on the soccer and swim teams in high school, and then both again at Stanford. In shape. Always.

Working to stay that way was another reason to like the suppressor that Twoclicks had given her. Whether she was splitting logs or, an hour after that, getting in a good jog, if she wore the ball cap and sunglasses, dressed herself in baggy sweatpants and a T-shirt, she could sneak out the back way, get the car service to drive her to the park and wait, and then carry the suppressor with her as she jogged, getting in a few quick kilometers with no one watching. It was heaven.

Now, back from that jog and the Abe Lincoln log-splitting session, she took a hot shower and was in her favorite comfy chair, admiring her fire-making skills as she finally opened the letter from Peter, who was still the love of her life, as far as the celeb journos knew. It was just another gig for her, really, playing the part of Penelope, here in her California coastal version of Ithaca, waiting for Odysseus. It wasn't true, but it did make for a nice little story. Hell, he might well show up at the ten-year mark. Wouldn't that be something?

She laughed. She read.

Dear Chloe,

I'm alive! And better yet, Kait is alive and well and I know you've already talked with her or will soon. What an adventure I had with her! I've started writing it up in what I hope will be a true and honest account of my time here. I'm calling it "Notes from Holmanville."

My little pal Treble promises me that he will hand deliver this to you the first time he gets to meet you. He's a great kid and I'm sure you and he will be friends. He's been enormously important to me.

I've been writing up a storm here, since there have been long lulls in my routine, times when I don't have much to do and without any of my tech or my books or anything else since everything was lost in that explosion on Twoclicks' ship.

It's hard to stay busy, but it only took me a few days to realize that everyone on Earth, starting with you, probably wanted to know what it's like here and since one thing I do have is this way to tell my story, that's what I'm going to do.

So, here's the story so far. My college professors will be delighted to find out that I'm finally writing.

P.S. I miss you terribly, Chloe. I know I have no hold on you; no reason, really, to have any expectations for any possible future for us. Hell, for starters I don't even have any idea if I'll ever return to Earth. But of all my memories of my years on Earth, those weeks I spent with you are foremost.

Now. To the story.

PART THREE

NOTES FROM HOLMANVILLE

Entire worlds followed the fascinating travels of the inept upright biped from Earth and his adventures with his guide, Prince Treble of S'hudon, as we walked the path of the Old Ones, our adventures documented by the tiny flittercams that I thought were insects. There are large parts of that adventure that I'd like to leave on some cutting room floor.

—Peter Holman, *Notes from Holmanville*
(S'hudon City and New York:
Trebnet Press, 2035)

10

HELLO, EARTH

Hello, Earth.

The last time you saw or heard from me I was wearing my sweep equipment and was transmitting to more than a billion of you as I left my quarters on that S'hudonni ship and headed up to Twoclicks' quarters for a formal state dinner with the governor-general and his aides.

A couple of weeks before that I'd left Earth behind. At Twoclicks' insistence I'd made a ceremonial swim of it, wading into the warm Gulf of Mexico from my home in Florida and doing a steady breaststroke through mostly calm waters to reach his ship, which had been parked in sight of my home, about two klicks or so offshore, since the day of the Arrival, when all those ships landed in shallow waters all over Earth, two dozen of them, bringing both promise and chaos to Earth.

I was one of the lucky ones when that happened, picked out of the crowd of eight billion to be S'hudon's documentarist on Earth. I suppose the emergence of sweep technology had something to do with that, since I got into that early on.

I'd been a pretty good second division basketball player in Europe, hoping to make it to the top leagues, and then when an injury ended that dream, I took up sweeping as a way to stay in the game. I was doing well enough at my interviews with sports heroes and media celebs to call some attention to myself, I suppose. And then that success led me to my friendship with Chloe Cary, a real star, and that helped make me a bit of a celebrity myself.

At any rate, Twoclicks and his aides asked me to document their visit through my sweeps, and that's what I was doing when that trouble broke out between the two S'hudonni princes who'd come to open trade with Earth. You know how that went, the trouble it caused, the lives that were lost, the uncertainty about what our alien friends really had in mind, and which prince was right and which was wrong.

We almost died in the middle of all that, me and Twoclicks and his aides. We had to survive a bombing attempt and a crash landing of our plane and more. Then, when things calmed down and the princes agreed to sit down and talk with each other back on their own world, I was offered the chance to go along, as well. I knew the risks, but I saw the opportunity, too; and so, after a frightening and very long and very lonely trip, here I am, on

S'hudon itself, to tell you about what this world is like, what the S'hudonni and their friends from other worlds in their empire are like.

I've been given complete freedom to tell the truth as best I can, and that is what I'll do, starting now, right here, in this first message. If I'm lucky, I'll be able to update these essays regularly and send them along with S'hudonni ships headed Earth's way. We'll see how that goes. If I'm unlucky, this will be my only communication with Earth. Let's hope it doesn't come to that.

THE NOTHING

When I first was rescued from the blowout of Twoclicks' ship—all of us sucked out into the nothing from that wide hole that opened in the side of the ship—I thought myself very lucky, indeed. I know you saw what happened as we abruptly exited the ship, spinning helplessly out into the void, but the lifeboats had already been launched and were outside the hole waiting for us to come floating by. I'd grabbed the hands of two of those little daffodils and was hanging onto them when we were sucked up like dirt from a rug, landing in a kind of protective jelly that filled the inside of the lifeboat.

I was lucky to be alive and I knew it. But as the gel evaporated I realized just how desperate my situation was. The daffodils hummed back and forth to each other in their own language, and each of them tried to whistle and click to me in what must have been S'hudonni; but it meant nothing to me. I was hoping one of them was the crew chief, since he or they or she or whatever it was spoke English. But no such luck.

The lifeboat seemed to be tumbling. I was in a small tall-backed chair, and held in place by loose restraints. I could feel myself pushing against the restraints one way and then, seconds later, in another way. It was dizzying and nauseating and as the daffodils hummed at each other, I vomited, a loose glob of vomit that then broke apart and widened and widened again. I tried to sit back in my seat, couldn't do it, and gave up, floating against my restraints.

There was a hard bump from behind me, and the lifeboat started clicking, a loud, demanding clicking that started loud and got louder, with the clicks coming faster and faster. The daffodils looked at each other, hummed, then hummed to each other some more, and then, as another thump banged against the hull, this time in front and the clicks were blurry and violent and very, very loud, the two daffodils walked quickly over to the single control panel, stood in front of it and turned to clasp each other, and then, amidst all the chaos a bubble erupted from the control panel, encapsulated the daffodils, but not before one of them punched a spot of that control panel and I felt the headrest of the chair come up around me, and felt the restraints tighten, and then there was a sharp pain in my right arm and then a bubble somehow surrounded me that was filling with gel and I wondered *what the hell* as abruptly it all went dark.

In what seemed like the next moment I was lying on my back, hooked up to devices that whirred and whistled and clicked, and I felt good. Really good.

I tried to sit up. Couldn't do it, so I tried again and nearly made it. Then I put my hands on the side of the bed I was lying on and pushed as hard as I could to sit up.

I was in a small room. There was gravity. There were no daffodils and no anything or anyone else. The device tabs that had been on my arms fell off as I slowly, weakly, sat up.

A door slid open and in walked a face from home, an Earthie. Heather Newsome. You knew her as an aide to Twoclicks during his time on Earth. Always in the background. Quietly professional, occasionally whispering in Twoclicks' ear.

But I knew her as the woman I'd fallen in love with and then, once I knew the reality of her, fallen right back out. And now here she was, smiling at me. That face. That smile.

"Heather," I said, though it came out as a weak mew from my dry throat. I felt great, yes, but I was weak as a kitten.

"Close enough," she said, and followed that with "Hello, Peter. We're so glad you're alive." And then she leaned over and kissed me on my forehead and supported my head and shoulders as she lay me back down and off I went, back to Nod.

HOLMANVILLE

I'd been in stasis for almost a year, Earth time, and a good three months or more, home world time. I'd been encased in that gel, frozen in time and space, as my lifeboat had gone spinning off into the nothing, its locator beacon smashed by the debris from Twoclicks' ship so it couldn't be found and eventually the search was abandoned. Space is big, the lifeboat and me within it were small and inconsequential.

I was found when a daffodil salvager showed up to find anything useful from the wreck and, lo and behold, there I was with my two daffodil compatriots, getting in the way of the salvager's approach.

They found us, and left me in the stasis cot, and brought me to S'hudon, the home world, where they figured someone would know what to do with me.

That someone was Heather2, of what I now know is a one of several Heathers in this world and the others in the system, including Earth. Shifting shape and shifting politics and shifting societies, that's what Heather does. Or what Heathers do. Are they all of one mind? I think so, so I stuck with calling this one Heather.

I spent three ten-days in isolation, getting poked and prodded and probed. Then two more ten-days in isolation letting all the nanos get their work done on me. Then another ten-day in isolation doing absolutely nothing, as far as I could tell.

But then, eventually, I was released to the wild. Or to Heather, who came to get me and sign me out and then take me by a kind of open-topped sled that hovered silently six inches over the paved roads that led us, ultimately, to my quarters.

Where I now sit, three days into my new life in the village, writing this down in longhand. I'm in my rocking chair on the front porch of my little frame bungalow on Elm Street, just up the block from Center Street, in my town of Holmanville, on the south edge of the largest island of the many in the archipelago that houses the population of the world of S'hudon. I even have a picket fence for my small front yard.

Yes, the S'hudonni built a whole empty village for me. Heather said they wanted me to feel at home after all I'd been through, as if the time spent in stasis had made any impact on me. It hadn't. I went under and, months later, I swam up to consciousness on S'hudon. And then went through the too-many ten-days of boredom and isolation, which about drove me nuts. I had a lot of questions and no one who was willing—or even able—to answer them. Where was my sister Kait? What you on Earth knew about my departure on that S'hudonni ship with Twoclicks was that I was headed off to the home world to document its wonders and, while I was at it, the negotiations between Twoclicks and Whistle over which one would control which parts of Earth. Important stuff, right?

But what *really* mattered to me was rescuing my sister. What you knew on Earth was that she'd been murdered as part of a plot to assassinate Twoclicks and Heather and me while we were traveling in Ireland. What you didn't know was that the Kait who died there on that hillside in County Clare in the West of Ireland was a facsimile, a copy, of the original true Kait, who'd been kidnapped by Whistle and brought to S'hudon as a hostage, a tool to make sure Whistle got what he wanted from the negotiations with his brother Twoclicks. I knew she'd been taken when I accepted the invitation to leave Earth and come to S'hudon. I was here to find her, get her released, and bring her home to her wife and the calm life she'd led on Earth.

So where the hell was Kait? That was question number one, but there were plenty more that needed answering, too. What was going on back on Earth? Had Twoclicks survived? And what the hell was the multiple Heathers all about? And were there still peace talks to cover? And Chloe Cary. I'd been in a contrived relationship with the beautiful and talented Chloe, a love affair conjured up by her agent and mine to bolster our two careers, and then it had started to become more real for me, though not, perhaps, for her. It was too much to expect her to be pining away for me; Chloe was too strong and vital for any swooning, that was for sure. But was she alive and well and still thinking about me, at least? There was no way to know.

And most importantly, there was this: Where was Kait? And where was

Kait? And where was Kait? It had only been a couple of weeks to me since I'd watched that copy of her die horribly back on Earth. But it had been six months or more to her, and more than a year year back on Earth, if I was getting my time-dilation anything close to right.

I had to know, and the more I got over the shock and awe of my near death and ultimate rescue, the more these things mattered to me. But it didn't look like I'd get any answers anytime soon. My Heather, the one here, had to wait for updates from the Heather back on Earth. Those updates came by ship.

It was during my time in isolation that the update arrived that told my Heather here about the terrible accident where lives had been lost, including mine. But Twoclicks and the Heather from Earth had been rescued and had returned to Earth, mourning my loss. That Heather had taken on another form—an Earthie form, but one that suited her role in the consulate—and then sent along the update for the Heather here on S'hudon, who gave me the news just a few days into my isolation. She'd also found out that Kait was being held in Whistle's compound, just a few hours by sled from where I sat listening to the news.

I wanted to leave that very moment to go get her, but nothing is easy. There was the long quarantine first, and then there were politics. Kait was alive, and said to be well, so that was good to know, but it might be a lot of ten-days before I'd even get a chance to visit her, much less winkle her out of there.

So, many ten-days later, as they count time here, I sat in Holmanville, my very own little village which the industrious little daffodils had constructed just for me, from plans they'd received long before I'd ever left Earth. Twoclicks and Heather had set those plans in place a long time ago, and only now was I becoming aware of them.

It was crazy, to be so far from home and sitting in a rocker on a porch, but here I was in Happy Holmanville. Keep Our Village Clean. The Village with a Future. We Welcome Business. We Love Visitors. Home of the Sweetest Peaches. Where the Sun Never Shines. State Champs 2032. Holmanville, in the district of Dissonance and in the state of Chaos on the world of S'hudon.

THE VILLAGE LIFE

Let me take you on a little tour. It's easy enough to do; the village is small and though I've only been here a few days, I already know it well. I'll ease my way out of this comfortable rocking chair and here we go.

We'll start at the bottom of Center Street and walk the six blocks uphill to the bluff that's at the edge of town. From the bluff we'll take in the magnificent view of the Great South Bight and then walk down the switchback path to the beach, bouldered, but with several small sandy coves and a number of steamy hot springs. There, by the water, is a lovely spot, about one hundred meters long, with rough, granular sand, large boulders at each end, and three hot springs. I call it Holman's Cove.

There are more of those hot springs offshore in the shallow water. So, while it's cool and damp here in Holmanville, the thermal springs in Holman's Cove keep the water warm. We'll take a dip in there later, maybe, to enjoy the warmth. It will be foggy, but I think you'll see how that adds to the charm.

If we're lucky, we may be joined by a few S'hudonni as we swim. The warm water appeals to them, too. Their village is about a kilometer from mine and directly on the tideless shore. I'm guessing a few hundred of them live there in small, round one-story homes that have a short, wide door on the beach side and another at the waterline on the opposite side. The homes seem strangely low-tech. Heck, no-tech. So I wonder if these are vacation getaways or something.

Their village has an unpronounceable name that requires the usual tongue-twisting mix of clicks and whistles, so unless I get better at the language, I'm just calling it The Village.

I'll need to be careful as I walk. The sidewalks in Holmanville are made of uneven paving stones, created to simulate the paving stones on the sidewalk near the Florida beach house where I grew up. There, the stones were laid directly on top of the sand and it was easy for the stones to slip out of alignment and rise or fall with the rush of water from the summer storms. Here, it's a good, firm clay soil, but the creators of Holmanville have spared no details when it comes to giving me the feel of home, and so the paving stones here are as uneven as those back home. It's easy to take a tumble in Holmanville.

As I walk along, a light rain is falling. I like the feel of the rain against my face. Alien rain. Amazing, really, that it's so much like home. Water is water, Heather tells me, and I believe her about that.

To our right is the small park that holds the town gazebo where, Heather says, in the summer the jazz fest takes place in front of a large, appreciative audience. This is Heather being funny. There will be no large crowds here, ever. And there is no summer here. In fact, there are no seasons at all. No days, either. The large, red sun, they call if the father, sits about one-third of the way up from the horizon and never wavers from there. No night, no day, no seasons. Just the same climate, the same clouds and mist, the same dark, hazy, reddish light even on those rare days when the clouds thin out.

Now, back to our uneven sidewalk as we head up Center Street. Over there is Nicky D's Pizza Palace. You can see Nick—or something very much like Nick—in there making pies. He's just an image, holographic I suppose, forever tossing a spinning pie into the air. But the pizza they bake is real, and you can get used to it.

And next to Nicky D's is the Brazen Head, the oldest and most authentic and absolutely best—and only—Irish pub in the entirety of S'hudon. Let's go in. It's empty, as it always is. But the Brazen Head looks and feels just like the real thing back in Dublin and serves a passable shepherd's pie that you heat yourself in a bread-box-sized device that sits on the counter. Place it in the small cabinet and then draw yourself a passable pint of porter as the pie heats. The handcraft porter is the real thing, I think, with the bubbles sinking in the beer while you wait patiently for your shepherd's pie.

That pint of porter—it tastes just like Guinness as far as I'm concerned—is proof, as it were, that Heather tells the truth when she says that S'hudon has begun shipping the first batches of Earthie alcohol, very pricey stuff indeed, all handcrafted small batches of this and that, from grains grown on small farms tended by hand with no pesticides and no machines.

Heather tells me the first products are heading out from here to the other worlds where S'hudon trades, and so far so good. I think of it as selling pet rocks, or tulips, but Heather says the spyeyes that hover around the entire production of these ales and whiskeys and vodka, oh my, show off the careful workmanship by the hardworking Earthies, and the consumers on the other worlds love that.

So, she tells me, all these things here for me have come from those first few ships to arrive with Earthie alcohol. This explains how that French roast coffee at the Calico Cat in my village of Holmanville can taste so authentic. It is. The same with the porter and the meat and potatoes for the shepherd's pie and all the rest.

Lucky me! It's all good! Except, of course, that this village is my enclosure. My zoo. My artificial home. And I'm not doing a damn thing except living here. And writing this, a little bit of it every day.

Heather tells me things will change soon. Sure. And she tells me every time she stops by that my sister Kait is safe and sound in the care of Whistle's people. Sure. Heather tells me a lot of things, and some of them are even true. After she left the village this last time, I sat down with a pint in my faux Irish pub and mulled it all over. The porter tasted fine. As did the next, and then the chaser of good Irish whiskey, the Dew of Kenmare.

FRIENDSHIP

It's five ten-days later and time to catch up. Once I settled in, every five-day or so Heather would take me to a formal or informal gathering of the S'hudonni elite, where I was shown off as a kind of Pocahontas—you know, the "Civilized Savage" from Earth.

That's how these people, the beings I've met here, think of us, my friends. The wild and woolly savages of Earth, not quite capable of rational thought, but willing to kill each other rather regularly and capable of interesting primitive art—which is how they classify our handcrafted beers and wines and ouzo and whiskey (from the Irish) and whisky (from the Scots) and saki and aquavit and baijiu and all the rest that's showing up now regularly in ships from Earth. It's our art, and it's a must-have, Heather tells me, on Melody and Harmony and Downtone and Sibilance and even on Adagio, where only the wealthy few can afford such luxuries as the Dew of Kenmare.

Is this true? Well, all I can tell you is what Heather tells me as she visits, often bringing me new clothes and food and drink and more from Earth. I'm glad to have these things, don't get me wrong. I'm glad to have the T-shirts and the blue jeans and the running shoes and the Murphy's and the Dew of Kenmare and the Niagara ice wine and all the rest. But I'd be a lot happier if I had a chance to see Kait and get her out of that captivity, and it sure would be nice to be reunited with myBob, my helpmate who went spinning off into the ethereal nowhere when Twoclicks' ship had that blowout that nearly killed me.

Heather swears the replacement hardware has been shipped and it will arrive this five-day or next or the one after that. It won't be connected to any clouds here on S'hudon, so only what's locked into the hard drive will be available to me. OK, OK, I tell her. As long as it's myBob and he recognizes me and I recognize him, that will do fine for starters. We'll talk about baseball or something. myBob will, at least, be a voice from home, I tell her. And Heather, usually in her S'hudonni form but now and again in the form I knew so well back home, smiles warmly and says yes, yes, soon, soon. And then I wait. Soon enough there's another show-and-tell, where I smile and nod my Earthie head and pretend to be intelligent.

LOVE AND DISAPPOINTMENT

I knew her as Heather Newsome when she first came to Earth in that human form. She seemed intelligent, educated, beautiful, passionate. I wanted her and wanted her to want me. Perhaps I still do.

She came to Earth, a sort of vanguard, or a spy, and sought out my brother Tom for seduction, and through him, me for the same thing. She and Twoclicks had a plan that I couldn't see then and can hardly see now, but I can look back at it for what it was. They needed me, and, sure enough, they got me. At the time it seemed like love, a kind of commitment to something I hadn't known before, something so overwhelming I was willing to create a rift with my brother that even today hasn't healed. She came, she conquered, and then, when I realized how purposeful it had all been and came to my senses, she welcomed me as a confidante and now, here, in Holmanville, I've accepted her in that role. And, on several occasions, her other roles as well. I am lonely here, that is my only way to explain it. And in a faux village with a faux pub and a faux rocking chair on a faux porch, why not have a faux lover? Don't we all create ourselves? Can't we all become someone new when we need to? A loss in life? A gain? Changes? Growth? Youth? Old age? All of these and many more are the various people we are as we go through life. It's all good.

That's what Heather tells me as we're making love. I'm prone to agree, and I see her point about changes and growth and all that. But I do have to wonder what Chloe, the real Chloe back on Earth, would think of Heather's offer to present as Chloe, to be a perfect facsimile of Chloe, that voice and intelligence and beauty and strength and wit and all those things I liked so much—perhaps even loved—about Chloe? Would Chloe, the real Chloe, be horrified by that or would Chloe, the real Chloe, see it as acting, excellent acting, her art form perfectly done?

Hard to say, isn't it? After, in that delicious and warm after, when we're in my bed together, her right arm over my chest, her nibbling on my earlobe her saying, "That was lovely, Peter. You. Me. It's all good." And then, usually, she rises from the bed, and just to avoid confusion I look away so I don't have to watch but only listen as there are uncomfortable crackling and tearing noises that last for a minute or so before she says, as Heather in S'hudonni form, taller and thinner than most of them, more shark-like than porpoisy, that my next appointment, my next show-and-tell will be in four hours and I need to be ready to leave in three hours and be ready to talk about life on Earth.

Heather is always in that shark form when she picks me up in a small, roofless two-seater sled for these, and I always bundle up for the ride, which is windy, cool, and always with smatterings of rain. Because that's S'hudon, more often than not.

Usually the back of the sled is filled with metal crates when she arrives. These are filled with goodies for me that have arrived recently from Earth. We carry these things into my cottage, the clothing, the food, the craft beer or wine or whiskey or books or toilet paper. I unpack them and store them, and then off we go to wherever she's showing me off. The empty crates are always gone by the time I get back to the cottage.

At first, I thought I was really doing something useful, showing these creatures that Earthies can be worth talking to. Always in the back of my mind was Kait. Did it help her if I was popular among the S'hudonni elite and their off-world friends? Did it give our side of the talks a little leverage? I was confident I could help our cause.

I was wrong. I turned out to not be very good as a show-and-tell. Sure, I looked and sounded all right as a narrow example of an Earthie. A tall, white male in my thirties, I wasn't very representative of Earth's great diversity, yes; but Heather would translate as I talked about that, about our genders and our cultures and how proud we all were on Earth to be part of the great palette of human possibilities.

I didn't mention how often we failed at that pride, of course. Things are better again now on Earth, I hope. When I left there was turmoil and anger and worry; but it was directed outward, toward the common enemy of a culture that wanted us under its webbed thumb. Maybe that was the silver lining of the arrival of S'hudon. After the ebb and flow of leaders—in my dear old U.S.A. and, I bet, in your country, too—who moved us forward and those who moved us back, those who included and those who excluded, those we admired and those we feared, S'hudon brought us into a common fold. We were all part of a colonial empire, one that might play nice with us or might not.

So I wanted to talk about that. About Earth and what it was like there; the rain in Dublin, the sunshine in Florida, the Alps and the Andes and the high Himalayas and the melting Arctic and the Ring of Fire and the Gobi and the Sahara and the Taj Mahal. All of that, or all of it I knew well enough to talk about. That was Earth to me.

But not, as it turned out, to them, the S'hudonni elite or the ambassadors or trade representatives from the other six planets. The ambassador from Downtone was nearly my height, and our conversation—with Heather translating—started of just fine and then went all to hell. His feathers were ruffled, literally, when I couldn't talk about opening up diplomacy with the billions of ducks (that's what they looked like to me) who knew about Earth and wanted to know more. Mainly, he was interested in all our handcrafted alcohol. How are the grains grown? What are grapes like? Which are the best for which kinds of wine in which area of Earth? What is the history of beer? Is beer an ale? Where is ale grown? What are hops?

These and many, many more questions came at me with a pleasant patience as his eminence, a tall, blue duck dressed in a red tunic and gray pants, whistled and clicked through a mouth that looked strange on that feathered face, speaking in S'hudonni to Heather, who spoke to me in English. Several others wandered over: a daffodil from Harmony, those dewlaps enlarging in surprise at my ignorance of just about everything; a leg or arm rose up out of the water to our left and then opened into a funnel, some official from Melody was listening, and then twice that horn reshaped to a kind of bright purple mouth through which whistles and clicks emerged to ask questions; three of the quadrupeds from Adagio trotted over, dog-sized with elephantine trunks that ended in a three-fingered hand that included a thumb.

They rattled me, all of them. How large was Earth? What percent of arable land? How large the population? Atmosphere? Geology? Ocean depth? Ocean acidity? Intelligence on land? Intelligence in the oceans? How stable the global government? No global government? Ha! That brought a great flaring of dewlaps and trunks raised high and laughter from the water and vigorous head shakes up and down from the duck that had started it all. Global productivity, global gross product, climate, transportation systems, intelligence, strength, atmosphere, on and on.

And I had almost no answers. In fact, what I didn't know for sure I was afraid to guess at. This was me, Peter Holman, ex-jock with a bachelor's degree in English Lit, a celeb sweeper who got caught up in all this to document peace talks that hadn't yet begun and to somehow be a hero and rescue my sister. And now I was supposed to represent the nine billion Earthies. Me? I was a tiny sliver of that reality, and, I confess, pretty damn stupid without myBob whispering in my ear. He'd have had all the answers, but he wasn't here. I missed him. A lot.

I was a major disappointment to everyone there, and I knew it. This wasn't what I'd had in mind, or they, or Heather and Twoclicks.

HELP WANTED

On the sled on the way back to Holmanville after that last wretched experience I asked Heather for help, some kind of S'hudonni version of a helpmate, something that had all the knowledge of my home world and knew about this one, too. Something that could whisper in my ear the facts I needed.

She said she had something in mind, but a five-day went by and I hadn't seen it yet. That was typical, I was discovering: lots of promises on S'hudon but not a lot of follow-through. Sure, I'd have myBob any day now, but he never arrived. That had to be purposeful.

That five-day later I was sitting on the bluff overlooking the Great Bight and asking myself the usual questions. What was wrong with me that I found pleasure and peace in making love with Heather, when I knew she was artificial, a contrivance that was being nice to me? And if, after we made love, as we lay there on the bed, that contrivance promised me again that sister Kait was fine—comfortable, safe, and healthy—why then couldn't I go see her, at least? Every time, Heather's answer was a deflection, hemming and hawing and turning her face to smile and kiss me or reaching to touch me, and never, ever really answering directly.

Same with the peace talks. Remember those? That's the other reason I came here, to document those as S'hudon decided Earth's fate. I was going to meet Twoclicks' and Whistle's mother, right? And she was *the* Mother, right? She would sit in judgment, right? When were those talks going to start? Never? So, why had they brought me here if I was just going to sit and vegetate?

Oh, hell. I was on an alien planet, under a huge red sun they called the father, in a damp and cool climate that never changed, with plant life that was just the same and dramatically different at the same time, and with animals on land and in the sea and in the air that were hard to imagine. The blimpies, for instance. That's what I called those gray things the size of a bus back home, which floated serenely along fifty meters up over the bogs that surrounded Holmanville. They were amazing. It was all amazing. No humans except Kait and I had ever seen these things, so I should shut up and take notes. Heather said my moment would come. I'd be busy and important. Patience, patience.

That five-day later, after I'd begged again for Heather for help to give me some answers, I sat on the edge of the bluff that fronted the Great Bight.

Open sea lay in front of me, a declining bluff on both sides. I sat, legs over the edge, at the highest point. The view was good.

There'd been heavy fog when I first got to this spot. Now, less than an hour later, the fog was offshore and I could see the bouldered beach below, pockmarked by steaming hot springs. There was one huge boulder that looked for all the world (my world, not this one) like an elephant at rest, seeming to stare up at me from the far edge of that beach. There were two blimpies out over the water, and the only sounds came from the shore break water hitting the rocks below and the steady low background whine and drone from the insects that seemed to follow me around but never bite or land.

It was what I chose to call midday and I was thinking I might stand up and head back to my little cottage with its picket fence and its charming porch with a white rocker on it, and eat some lunch and have a pint of porter. Or maybe, I thought, I would stay here and feel sorry for myself as the damp fog rolled back in, as it surely would. Neither idea seemed particularly profound or useful, but what the hell; lunch would at least take my mind off my boredom for a few minutes.

I started to bring my legs in and put my hands down so I could stand. The soil here at the edge of the bluff was mostly soft, almost bouncy, and covered in a thin moss, but there were bare patches of flat stone and pebbles.

There was the rattle of those pebbles scattering behind me. I finished standing and turned at the same time. It was Heather in her S'hudonni form, gray, upright on short legs. She was smiling, and next to her was a shorter, younger S'hudonni. He held up four fingers, two spread wide on each side, and said, "Live long and prosper, Peter Holman." And then he brought the hand down and reached out with it to shake my hand. "I am Treble, the princeling son of Twoclicks and his brother Whistle, as you call them."

I laughed, and it was my first laugh since I'd left Earth. The greeting was silly, sure, but the kid had done his cultural homework.

"I'm very pleased to meet you, Treble," I said as I shook his hand. "Thank you for that excellent greeting, and for coming out here just to meet me."

"Oh, it's better than that, Peter," Heather said. "You talked about needing a tutor and translator, and someone who knows Earth, as well. Well, here he is. Treble is very bright, and I'm sure he'll be able to teach you our language, our customs, our history, and all the rest. Plus, he's very knowledgeable about Earth! You two will be great friends, I'm sure of it."

"I am sure, too!" Treble said with enthusiasm. "I know everything about Earth! I hope to visit there soon! We shall be great friends!"

"Well, OK," I said to them both. "When do you want to start?"

"Right now!" Treble said. "Please!"

Heather laughed, said, "I'll leave you two to it, then," and walked away, back to that floater and then, I was sure, back to Twoclicks' compound. It was funny to think, as I watched her waddle away, that we'd been in my bed a couple of days ago.

Treble plopped down on the mossy soil next to me, patted the ground, and said, "Sit! Sit, please! There is so much to talk about!"

As I sat he rattled on: "Warm seas, blue skies, billions of natives making things. Earth is wonderful! I want to go there so much!"

He pulled me down by the hand to join him there on the edge of the bluff, looking out over the Great Bight. He looked up at me and I down to him as he grinned and said, "I will tell you stories about S'hudon and then you will tell me stories about Earth and we will ask and answer questions and we will be friends. How does that sound?"

He was a little bubbly, I thought, but at least he was aiming to end my boredom, which was all to the good. So, "Great," I said. "Let's start with stories. Tell me one of yours." And he did.

"A long time ago, when I was very young," he said, and I laughed at that, since he looked so young to me that it was hard to imagine his being much younger. He smiled at my laughter and started again. "I was swimming and playing and eating lunch off this very spot with my two fathers, the ones you call Twoclicks and Whistle, though really they are . . . ," and he whistled and clicked two separate, surprisingly long names in S'hudonni. Perhaps I heard some double-clicks in the one name, and I was sure there was extra whistling for the second.

"The eating was playful and fun, and there was a strange light as the great star shone through the mist to warm us, and spending time with both of my fathers was wonderful. Even though they did not get along.

"Then there was a shift in the weather," he continued, and I stopped him there.

"The weather changes? It seems to me it's always the same."

He nodded. "Almost always, Peter, but sometimes the dark side with its great frozen seas sends cold air to our archipelago, and sometimes the bright side with its hot oceans sends warm air to us, too. When those two meet at this archipelago, the storms are terrible. Lightning, winds, great waves, great destruction.

"But in those days, we were complacent. We came to this world generations ago and found it habitable and accommodating and filled with gifts that had been left behind. There were no native forms of intelligence on land or in the sea except for the . . . ," and he clicked a name and pointed out to sea, where the same pair of blimpies I'd seen before were coming over to take a look at the two of us. "Those," he said, in English.

"I call them blimpies," I said, "after the lighter-than-air flying machines on Earth."

"Blimps!" he said, clapping his hands in delight. "I know about them! And dirigibles and zeppelins and more!"

"But here? The blimpies are intelligent?"

"Oh, yes. Agreements were made after First Landing. The air is theirs alone, and the fens and bogs where they feed must be left alone."

I thought of the whales and dolphins back home, and what Earthies had done to them, as Treble went on, talking about the great storm that came when he was swimming with his two fathers.

He pointed. "We were just offshore, right out there," he said. "My fathers were showing me how to catch the quick ones by herding them first and diving into the herd. It was great fun! Then we came to the surface to breathe and the father , you'd call it the sun, shined down on us. We thought it was wonderful!"

He shook his head. "But it was not wonderful. It was the start of the great fury, the clouds and mists blown away by the approaching storm. By the time we next came to the surface, all had changed, the storm was on us, sheets of rain, high winds and huge waves and terrible currents that pushed us toward the rocky shore. If we were pushed to that shore, we would be trapped and crushed on the rocks and we knew it.

"My fathers, even then, were competitors. Both sought the Mother's favor, both sought control of Downtone, the third of the six planets that we came to barter with, using the gifts we found in the bowels of the abandoned city."

There was an abandoned city? That was news to me.

He went on: "They were very different, my father Twoclicks and my father Whistle. They shared nothing except me. Both had given their essential milt to the Mother's eggs and both had been there when I burst forth. Together they'd then raised me through the stages of life. And that day they saved me in that storm. They worked together perfectly. There was no way to avoid coming ashore, the currents and the wind and the waves were too strong. But the river Esk is that way," and he pointed, "and where it empties into the Bight the shore is flat and wide, and the estuary protected by the boulders and the bluffs on each side. So we went there, Father Twoclicks pushing me along the shore toward the mouth of the Esk, while Father Whistle pushed to keep us both out to sea long enough to make that mouth."

"And you did," I said.

"And we did," he said. "They saved my life, my two fathers. It was very exciting! And I learned so much from that, about everything."

I looked at him. "That's quite a story," I said.

I believed him, and that said something. I wasn't sure I'd ever completely believed anything that Twoclicks—sorry, Treble's father Twoclicks— told me.

Treble looked me expectantly and said, "Your turn! Tell me a story about Earth! How many fathers do you have?"

"Just one, Treble," I said. "And he died a while ago."

"But you have stories?"

I did. I'd been giving it some thought as I listened to him. Should I tell him about how my father died driving off a bridge in a blinding thunderstorm? Should I tell him about the time when I was a high school senior and I saw him through a window in the back office of his clinic, fucking the receptionist I had a bad crush on? Should I tell him about how my father told me to my face that I was a disappointment and had wasted my education by playing professional basketball?

No. All those were true, but this was not the time for the truth. Instead, I told him this, which was, at best, just slightly true, and had the merits of involving a storm, a child, and a heroic father.

"Where I grew up was a small island connected to the mainland by a bridge, and to our west was the warm water of the Gulf of Mexico. People came, many thousands of them, to play in our warm water and under our bright, yellow sun.

"But that warm water meant that sometimes we faced storms born of that heat. Once, when I was a tiny baby, the water was so warm that a huge storm developed late in the season, one so famous that people on Earth still remember it: Hurricane Robert."

"I will see your home someday, Peter. I promise," Treble said, smiling up at me from where he sat, on the edge of that bluff looking out over the Bight. "I want to see your bright sun."

"I hope I get to show you around, Treble," I said, smiling back at him. "You'd like it there. But the storms!" I added. "You don't want to be there for one of those, trust me. Winds that knock down buildings, surges of water that drown coastlines, rain so strong that you can't see what's happening a meter from you when you try and walk or drive through it."

Treble shook his head in wonder. I laughed, said, "Some years they don't come, Treble, and the weather is wonderful, if a little too hot. We'll make sure you don't have to be there during a storm."

"No!" he said. "It would be wonderful! To be in such a storm, out in the water, being part of that. It would be exciting! Like here! Like home, only warm!"

"And windy and frightening and dangerous, Treble," I said. "A lot of Earthies died in that storm. Nearly five hundred just in my city. The water washed right over several of our smaller islands, washing people and buildings away. It was terrible."

"Ah," he said. "I forgot that Earthies can't swim."

"We can swim, but not well enough for that," I said. "So we have to hide from the storm and run away from it. And some people, too many of them, stayed for Hurricane Robert and paid a terrible price for staying."

"Didn't people help them?"

"Yes, some very brave people stayed so they could help others who were trapped. My father was one of those brave people. He was a doctor, and he tried to save as many people as he could."

"He was a swimmer?"

I laughed. "No, not really. But he stayed at his hospital to care for those who suffered from the storm. The hospital was built to last through any storm, and it did. After it had passed, they opened up the doors and stepped outside. My father said he stood there in amazement for a few seconds. The storm surge had turned the hospital into its own tiny island, just inches above the flood. There was water everywhere, with things sticking up out of it: top halves of cars, power lines strewn across everything, upended street signs, roofs off of houses, about a million palm trees floating or stuck in the muck."

"Terrible!"

"Yes, it was terrible. My father said it was so quiet that it was eerie. He could hear the splash of water against an upturned car or the hiss of the breeze going by.

"Then he heard some yelling, a child's voice, calling for help. There was a small arm coming out the back window of a car that was up to its windows in water in the flooded parking lot. That small arm was waving, and he heard a child's voice calling: 'Help us! Help us!'"

"So he did!" said Treble. "How brave!"

"The water wasn't deep," I said, "but Father said there was a lot of debris floating around, and it was so mucky you couldn't see into the water at all, so he had to shuffle along to walk toward the stranded car. And there were power lines down, and if the power came back on while he was near one of those and in the water, that would have been very dangerous. But he was a doctor, and thought he had to do what he did."

"Others went with him?"

"No, everyone had assignments, including him. But he figured he would help that child first, and then come back to work in the hospital's emergency room.

"When he got there, the window with the child's arm out of it was broken, with jagged edges from the glass coming up out of the door. He looked in and it was a mess, the water almost up to the window level and a bleeding child, a boy, his arm bleeding badly, looking up at him. In the driver's seat, a man, moaning, sat behind the wheel."

"And your medicine is so simple," Treble said. "No medcots, no nanos, just simple medicine, yes?"

"Yes," I said. "We think of it as advanced, but compared to yours, well, we're not."

"So sad!"

"Yes," I said again, waving away the insects that buzzed around us as we sat there on the bluff, talking, "it *is* sad. But my father did what he could. The boy was on the brink of going into shock and all Father could think about was his own children and how much he loved them. He had to do something, so he took off his shirt, tore it apart in the back, and used a large section of that and the stem of a palm frond to make a tourniquet. He got that on the boy's arm, made it tight, and then he checked on the driver.

"Blunt trauma, my father figured. All he wanted to do was stabilize him until they could get him into the ER. But when he felt for his pulse, it was gone. He'd lost him in the time it had taken to put the tourniquet on the boy's arm. He couldn't believe it; all that work to get to them, the boy waving that bloody arm at him, the tourniquet, all of that, all of it, and now this poor man was dead."

Treble seemed rapt in his attention, and even the insects seemed to have paused in their buzzing. Everyone liked my little story, I was thinking, as I wrapped it up.

"Father said he was so angry about how unfair that seemed that he shouted, and then his training took over and he thought maybe the guy's heart had gone into ventricular fibrillation and that a thump on the chest would be worth a try. If Father could get the heart started again, the guy might pull through. There wasn't much chance of that working, but then there was no chance at all that he'd survive if Father didn't try.

"So he pulled his legs out to get a good angle on the guy's chest and then hit him, hard, right on the chest, right on the heart. Nothing. So he hit him again, about as hard as he could, and put his ear down to listen to his chest and there was nothing. So he tried again, and then again, and then, on the fifth try, he put his ear down to his chest and there it was, a heartbeat. He was alive. It wasn't the strongest heartbeat Father had ever heard, he said, but it was there.

"He saved two lives!" Treble said. "What a great story. Your father is a hero!"

"Yes," I said. "And he saved more than those two that day. The hospital was filled with patients, and the whole staff saved lives, a lot of them."

"Even with your simple medicine! That's wonderful!" said Treble.

"Yes," I agreed, "it was."

"Great story, Peter!" Treble said. "I knew it would be!"

And that was the start of my friendship with Treble, the princeling son of two fathers and the Mother. I saw him the very next day. And the day after that. He was often at my side, helping out, translating, offering advice, explaining things about abandoned cities and about how his fathers' father had died. He'd been genial but powerless, a figurehead, really. It was the Mother who ruled, he said. Soon enough, I saw that in action.

THE MOTHER

I was on the Mother's royal barge, drifting along the South Canal while I held a small, beating heart in my hands and considered the merits of eating it.

The bendie's heart was still fluttering when Treble handed it to me. I told him that I hoped it would taste like chicken, and Treble got the joke but said, "Not now, Uncle Peter."

So I did what Treble had told me to do, holding the heart up in the palm of my right hand and slowly turning full circle so everyone could see it was still beating. The entire pod of S'hudonni royals, fifty or more of them, was watching. Even the Mother, up on her ornate wooden throne, had her eye on me. For the first time all afternoon, she was smiling.

I saw that smile and had to wonder if the joke was on me. Was this all set up so the Earthie would do something stupid and silly, or was it an important step toward acceptance, meant to test my willingness to embrace this world's culture? That's what Treble had said it was.

I didn't know, but I trusted Treble, who was about the only S'hudonni that I *did* trust. A good kid. And if Treble said it had to be done, then I had to do it.

All that time I'd spent in isolation and inoculation when I'd first arrived, drinking down the nanos the daffodils had designed for me, meant I was protected from anything deadly that I ingested, so eating the live heart wouldn't kill me, differing biologies be damned.

But a few seconds ago that heart had been doing its work, pumping away inside the body of one of the bendies, those cute, small mammalian things that populated the riverbanks and seemed to have so much fun in the shallow water. This heart had been having that fun five minutes ago and now here it was, fluttering in my hands while the various royals and hangers-on watched me.

Sitting to the Mother's right was Heather, in S'hudonni form of course. She was smiling, and winked at me as I caught her eye. To the Mother's left was an empty seat. Whistle would sit there whenever he arrived.

Everyone else was there because the Mother had invited them. Also, I was sure, because no one wanted to miss a major fracas, should it come to that. Heather was there in her S'hudonni form to speak for the missing Twoclicks, who was back on Earth. Treble had told me that Heather and Whistle didn't get along. No one, it seemed, got along with Whistle.

On the spacious barge were fifty or more of the S'hudonni: royal cousins and their various mates and children, a few well-connected merchants, and the servants with their towels and spray hoses. It was quite a gathering; many of the S'hudonni were fractious with each other, disagreeing about everything, and especially about Earth and its future, which was why we were here, the start of the talks at last.

But not right at the moment. Right now, here on this barge, all eyes were on the Earthie who had the beating heart of a bendie in his hands and had promised to eat it. I brought my hands down and looked at the heart, about half the size of an apple, a four-chambered heart that beat in rapid pulses, several a second. It was more a dark green than red, but otherwise it looked disturbingly like the heart of any mammal on Earth. Somehow this made the whole idea of eating it even more disturbing than if it had looked more like a piece of shivering alien something.

I looked at Treble, who looked back at me and smiled but said, quietly and firmly, "You really need to do this, Uncle Peter. Please."

All right, then. I didn't want to let the princeling down, did I? I brought the heart up to my face, sniffed it—the smell was vaguely metallic—then put it slowly into my mouth and took a bite. There was a rush of blood, warm and tasting of pine and iron, that filled my mouth and threatened to spill out. Instead, I swallowed the blood.

It was hard to tear off a piece of it with my teeth, but I bit harder and got through the muscle and the beating finally stopped as a piece came free. Small favors. I chewed some more. It was rubbery, even more metallic in taste, and I couldn't get my teeth to break it down very much, so after a few more chews I gave up and swallowed it. Then another bite, bigger this time, and I swallowed that, too. Then another. Then another three bites and it was done.

I finished swallowing, then raised both arms separately, fingers open and palms visible as Treble had instructed me, and showed the S'hudonni what I'd done. There was a burst of chittering and whistles, some awkward applause, and then a group whistle of appreciation, all together, rising higher and then higher again and then done.

Treble was happy and reached out to hand me a small towel and say, "Well done, Uncle Peter."

Everyone else seemed happy, as well. They chittered and whistled away with each other some more, and then one by one they came over to me to talk. Each of them reached out stiffly to take my right hand in theirs and then shake, carefully and formally, before talking. A handshake was obviously something they'd learned just for this occasion.

This was my first public outing since Heather had sent Treble to be my tutor a few ten-days before. Now, Heather had decided, Treble had me ready for public display in front of the Mother. I hoped that I'd lived up to their expectations.

So I breathed a small sigh of relief. Maybe the sessions with Treble had been worth it? Maybe this time around I'd be more of a hit and less of a disappointment? One could hope. I wanted to be in the Mother's good graces, certainly, so I could renew my prodding of the powers that be to allow me to visit with my sister Kait and maybe try for more than that.

Why couldn't she stay with me in the little faux village they'd built for me, for instance? There was plenty of room, god knows, since I was the only live resident. And it made no sense for Kait or me to escape the place even if we'd wanted to. It was a tiny faux village in a small island on a planet unthinkably distant from Earth.

But politics was politics, and so I was taking it step by step. I'd even picked up a few ingratiating phrases in S'hudonni. With any luck I'd get a chance to show off my language skills. Anything to curry some favor.

It had taken me those several ten-days under Treble's tutelage to acquire the few phrases I had. Treble was great when it came to teaching me the language. He was both patient and persistent. But I had never been a good student in any subject other than English, and even here, in this incredible setting, I hadn't made a lot of progress. I had, at least, learned to whistle hello and click a thank-you here and there.

For the rest of it, Treble translated for me as I answered a steady stream of questions, two or three from each S'hudonni before he or she (or it, I was still shaky on their odd multiple genders and how often they could switch) stepped aside and let the next one in line go through the same procedure. I did my best to be friendly and conversational as Treble stood by my side and listened to one after another ask me politely if I was enjoying my stay on S'hudon, and I heard Treble's click and whistle translations for "Yes, very nice" often enough that I tried to duplicate it, and Treble laughed and said it was very good and I should use it, so I went with that for a while. A declining sort of bird trill and a double-click of the tongue against the roof of the mouth and suddenly I was the hit of the party, at least for a few minutes.

"It speaks S'hudon!" one of them—a minor royal from a small district on the second island—whistled loudly enough for everyone to hear, and that brought a cacophony of whistles and clicks in response. Treble told me what the minor royal had said and added that the response was appreciative laughter. And then Treble gave me a hug around the waist, his small arms not able to reach all the way around.

"They find you as charming as I do, Uncle Peter," he said. "The Mother is pleased, I'm sure."

I looked up to the far end of the barge, where the Mother sat in regal comfort. She was looking at me and nodded.

Treble was watching this. "Bow a little bit, Uncle Peter," he said. "The Mother would like that." And so I did, and when I came back up from the bow, the Mother had her right hand up, too, acknowledging me.

"Whew," said Treble, taking me by the hand and leading me away to the far side of the barge. "I was worried, Uncle Peter, since the Mother doesn't usually like aliens. But it seems that she likes you. That is so good!"

Later, when things had quieted down, I stood alone at the edge of the barge as it traveled along a canal, the shore no more than a few meters away on the starboard side.

Treble, dutiful child, had left me to go sit at the feet of the Mother. He looked happy, clicking away to her, and her to him. When he saw me looking his way he waved and then cheerily said good-bye to the Mother, stood up, and headed back toward me, grinning.

When he reached me he came with a formal request from the Mother herself. I was to visit with her for a "small conversation," he said.

So I walked across the length of the barge to the raised platform where the three thrones sat, the Mother in the highest and in the middle, the smaller thrones for the two princes on the sides. Both of those were empty at the moment. Heather had left to go for a swim, and Whistle hadn't made an appearance.

We walked to stand in front of the Mother. She was smiling, and she clicked and whistled to me as she slightly nodded her head.

"You should nod in return, Uncle Peter, and thank her for the day," whispered Treble.

I did that, saying I enjoyed almost everything, and Treble whistled back to her. She tilted her head back and clicked and whistled loud enough for everyone around us to hear. Then she paused and clicked some more.

"She is laughing," said Treble. "She finds you very funny. She wants to know if eating the heart of the bendie was the thing that you did not enjoy."

I smiled and returned the laugh. I kind of liked the Mother. Could S'hudon's great queen have a sense of humor? "Yes," I said, "let's just say that that was not my favorite meal on S'hudon."

Treble whistled that to her and clicked back.

"She asks what was your favorite meal, Uncle Peter," said Treble.

I had an answer for that. "Tell her that meal I had with you and Heather a ten-day ago was wonderful. All fresh-caught swimmers from the sea. The creature called . . ." and I tried to whistle it, doing that from memory, hoping I got it right but knowing it would be amusing if I didn't. "The long fish. It was especially good. Firm flesh, with a taste not unlike a sea creature we have on Earth."

Treble laughed even as the Mother did the same. Then she whistled a long question to him. "You said the long *book*, Uncle Peter, instead of *fish*, but she knows what you meant. And she asks if you are happy here. Is there anything she can offer you?"

Well, that open door was too good to be true. Maybe it would be a diplomatic disaster to ask, but I felt I had to try. "Treble," I said, "tell her I want to see my sister. She's being held by Whistle. I know she's all right, but I want to see her. I want her to see me. Can the Mother arrange a meeting for the two of us?"

Treble looked at me and gave me a strange smile and a nod, then turned to whistle and click to the Mother, who listened very gravely to the question and was whistling back to Treble when, out of nowhere it seemed, it all went to hell, with some hooting noises that I'd never heard the S'hudonni make before, and when I turned to look to see what was happening, there were S'hudonni walking onto the barge as a group, most of them wearing a kind of uniform, dark brown coats over black pants. Many of them were carrying weapons, lightweight rifles with thick, round barrels that looked porcelain rather than metal. They looked very Earthie, in fact, so I had to wonder if that was one of Earth's contributions to S'hudon: weapons.

There were ten of them on the dock, two fives as they would say. I had nothing to record it with, but I wanted to remember it in all its details, and so I focused intently on what was happening, trying to build some memories I could conjure up later in the day when I got home and could write about it. I had an idea that this was going to be an important next few minutes.

Where had these S'hudonni come from? I didn't know. And then there was another stir among the attending royals as they all looked toward the shore of the canal, and there I saw a squadron of four floating blimpies coming in low over the barge. They held a palanquin, open sided, festooned with banners, and with two S'hudonni in the front, dressed in dark gray uniforms, holding tight on reins that went up to harnesses wrapped around the blimpies. In the middle of the palanquin was a kind of throne, whereupon sat an imperious looking S'hudonni, holding a staff.

It looked ridiculous. The S'hudonni didn't usually go in for gaudy shows; their power was more subtle than that. But not this one. He wanted everyone to know he'd arrived.

"That's Whistle," Treble said to me calmly, showing no emotion. "He always makes a show of his arrival, but this . . ." He shook his head ever so slightly. "This will not please the Mother. Those harnesses are barbed so the blimpies fear for their lives. If they are punctured . . ."

I'd admired the blimpies I'd seen around my faux village. They seemed serenely calm as they foraged, and almost friendly in the way they came close to look me over.

"It is forbidden to use the blimpies for such purposes, Uncle Peter," said Treble. "They are very intelligent; sometimes we can talk with them, in a way, a kind of emotional sharing. We honor them in our culture. Whistle debases them."

The blimpies eased the palanquin down until it bottomed out on the barge, and then some handlers helped Whistle off the palanquin and onto the barge, and the blimpies rose and drifted away a few dozen meters, still carrying the palanquin.

Whistle was immediately surrounded by his entourage. Now they walked toward me and Treble. Whistle was shorter than any adult S'hudonni I'd seen. They are generally short anyway, and stocky. But Whistle was the shortest of the ones who stood there, and the thinnest. He wore a kind of bandolier belt that wrapped around his right shoulder and traveled down below to what passed for a waist, where it wrapped around again as a belt.

His bandolier didn't hold any weapons, but his thugs had short blades hanging down, and some kind of wrapped wire looped and tied to the belt, and ten of them or so held those Earth-style weapons with the porcelain barrels. As I looked, a half dozen of those without the weapons dived right off the dock into the water and disappeared from view. It was easy to forget that underwater was where they truly belonged and only at that moment, watching them dive in, did it occur to me that until I had a good mask, some fins to wear, and a breathing device, I'd never see the S'hudonni in their real element.

Whistle reached me, smiled, and said, in perfect English, "Peter Holman, it is my great pleasure to meet you."

I know I shouldn't have been surprised. There were only two Earthies on S'hudon, and one of them—my sister Kait—was captive at Whistle's own compound, so that made me pretty damn obvious.

"Yes," I said, walking toward Whistle. "I'm Peter Holman. And you, I take it, are . . ." I hesitated. What was appropriate? This was another opportunity for a major diplomatic error. Aim high, I thought. "Prince Whistle."

Treble nudged me, whispered "*Prince Whistle* is correct, and he likes that. But bow your head, too, Uncle Peter." And so I did that.

Whistle smiled at my clumsy protocol, but seemed forgiving. He turned to his right and addressed the throne in whistles and clicks. Treble translated.

"Mother, you asked us to attend, and now we are here. I regret that we missed so much of the pleasant day."

The Mother was not smiling as she clicked back. "You bring weapons to the royal barge, my son?"

"Not done. Never done," whispered Treble to me.

Whistle turned back to look at me and Treble, and then spoke to the Mother even as he looked at us. "We were told there were dangerous visitors on the barge, Mother. We wanted to be prepared." Then he added, drily, "We know you are aware of how violent the Earthies can be."

Treble squeezed my hand, whispered, "Say nothing, Uncle Peter."

So I said nothing, but I did stare at Whistle, trying keep my face impassive. Then the Mother, thank god, finally spoke, leaning forward on her simple, wooden throne to say, "You should not have brought these thugs with you, Whistle. And you should never, ever have allowed them to be armed in my presence."

Treble translated that for me, but, for a change, I didn't really need it. Though the Mother was, to me, an alien, glistening porpoisy creature, I felt like I could read her body language; a general tensing up, the eyes narrowing, a slight lean forward. Whistle had overstepped. And dangerously so.

And then Whistle doubled down. He walked up to the three thrones and stepped up on the low platform, turned around, and sat down on the throne on the Mother's right—the throne of the heir. Twoclicks' throne.

"I cannot believe what I am seeing, Uncle Peter," whispered Treble. "That is not possible. Whistle seeks to replace Twoclicks at the right hand of the Mother. That is unbelievable."

So, a kind of coup d'état was taking place right before my eyes. Incredible.

Treble reached up to take my hand. Squeezed it. Whispered, "Remain silent, Uncle Peter. Say nothing."

And so I said nothing as Whistle turned left to look up at his mother. "It is regrettable that I felt I had to, Mother. But the situation on Earth grows dire. Your son Twoclicks, the one who should be sitting here now, next to you, has lost control. Violence tears at the fabric of the short lives of these Earthies, and now I hear of the death of two of our own people from the house of S'hu. Young lives, gone, none of them having Traveled, so their lives are truly lost.

"And these lives are gone through the actions of the Earthies! They are angry, these Earthies, and violent. They want to destroy everything they don't know, everything they cannot understand. And this despite all we have done for them. All that we offer."

"Not true," Treble added, after telling me what had been said. "One of them, at least, had Traveled and is safe."

"It is my understanding that in those parts of the planet where Twoclicks serves as governor-general, the Earthies are more accepting. Do you dispute that?" the Mother wanted to know.

"They have been lied to!" Whistle said. Then he pointed his hand at me and added, "This Earthie lied to them at the urging of Twoclicks! And he will lie more from here—our home world!—if he is given the chance. He will send out propaganda about Twoclicks, glowing reports that convince the Earthies that all is fine, all will be fine, with Twoclicks as their leader. Bah!"

Treble translated that for me and I saw the Mother look at me and, maybe, there was a hint of a smile. Then she turned to Whistle. "He has sent no messages since his fortunate arrival here, Whistle. You know that. And if he does, it will be handwritten messages, ink on Earthie paper, carried by hand to a few on Earth. A slow process. And a nearly private one. Not very good as propaganda."

So that explained my lack of technology, I realized. The Mother herself was making sure I had no myBob and no tech at all. I wondered just what she thought of me, really.

"But before!" Whistle said. "It was unfair! This one," pointing at me again, "and even now his partner, the female Earthie, she reaches billions! If he is allowed to write to her, yes, ink on Earthie paper, she will then tell all of Earth!"

The Mother looked at me. Treble nudged me. "She wants you to speak, Uncle Peter. Talk about your friend Chloe."

I looked at the Mother. She nodded her head. All right, then. In terms

I thought might work for her, with Treble translating as I went along, I explained.

"The prince refers to the Earthie named Chloe Cary, Mother, and she is, indeed, my friend. This much is true. We spent time together on Earth before I left to come here, to see this world and report on it to Earth.

"But I have sent her nothing yet, not even ink on paper."

Whistle, annoyed, blew air out his airhole and clicked furiously for a few seconds. No need to translate that. But the Mother looked at him and held the gaze. A polite whistle. "She says *Silence, my son* to Whistle," said Treble.

That was an effective reminder of who was in charge. Whistle shut up and I went on as Treble whistled the translation. "It was Chloe and I who first reported the arrival of your ships in our night skies, and I was using a new technology, a way to send all the Earthie senses from one person to many, to millions or billions, even. So perhaps it made sense for Twoclicks and Heather to approach me with an offer. I would travel with them and be free to document their diplomacy, their travels, all of it. Through my sweep system, as we call it."

I shrugged. "I did that. I traveled with them and recorded everything, and then there was violence. It seemed like the start of a war between Twoclicks and your other son," and the Mother smiled at my oblique reference to Whistle. "I recorded that, too. And then, when they agreed to meet and work out their differences here on S'hudon, I came along to document that, too. And so I am here."

"And so you are," said the Mother. "Sometime soon we must get you fitted with new recording equipment, mustn't we?"

Whistle erupted with a long string of violent clicks, rising from his seat. Treble translated for me as Whistle said, "He is an Earthie, Mother. They are not to be trusted! I know many of them."

"We know," said the Mother. Then added, "Sit, son. And over here," she waved, "on my left."

Whistle was outraged. "I will not!" and sat back down firmly onto Twoclicks' throne. There was an immediate rustle from a dozen S'hudonni standing behind and to the sides of the throne, a sort of imperial guard, I was guessing. But they took only one step when the Mother raised her hand to stop them.

I shook my head, but Treble whispered to me, "Do not worry, Uncle Peter. Just family squabbles. Look, see over there?" And he pointed to spot some fifty meters away on the far side of the canal.

I looked and didn't see anything and admitted that to Treble.

"Oh, Uncle Peter, you have much to learn. See the dorsal?" And I looked where he was pointing and, sure enough, there it was, coming our way and fast. "That is Heather. She will set things right."

I watched as that dorsal fin approached, and then saw behind it four, five, eight, or more other fins coming up behind it, all of these in a hurry.

The dorsals were coming up to the back of the barge, so Whistle and the Mother on those thrones couldn't see the fins, but a lot of excited whistling and clicking on the part of the gathered royals on the barge who could see them made it obvious something was going on. So Whistle and the Mother stood and turned to look.

It was Heather, in her S'hudonni form. I watched as she climbed up the ladder at the side of the barge. She was trembling in anger, a reaction I hadn't seen before in any S'hudonni. And she was bruised and beaten, green welts along her right side and several large bruises the size of dinner plates along her front and both sides.

She stumbled as she reached the top step of the ladder and then stepped over to put first one foot, and then the other, on the barge. She walked forward. Behind her, others came aboard, a half dozen of them, two of them firmly in the grasp of the other four.

Heather approached the Mother. She didn't look at Whistle, who sat impassively on Twoclicks' smaller throne. "I am sorry I wasn't here to greet Whistle," she clicked to the Mother, as Treble translated for me. "I was busy enjoying some playful exercise with these two," and she pointed back at the two who were being held. "The exercise, as you can see, was rough. But I would like to think I gave as much as I received."

She turned to her left to address Whistle directly. "Good to see you, Prince Whistle. What do you think? Did I give as good as I got from these two?"

Whistle remained impassive.

"It was very entertaining," Heather said directly to Whistle. "They rammed me, they tried to slash with the short blades that are no longer in their possession . . ." Two of the S'hudonni who held the captives raised blades to show them to the crown.

"It was great fun," Heather said. "I fended them off, and then my friends arrived to grab them and bring them along as I returned to the barge." She turned back to look at the Mother. "And to you, the Mother of all."

Heather smiled, slumped down a bit, and added, "I would like to sit down. It's been a tiring experience." A dozen or more S'hudonni around the throne took steps forward to ensure that Heather could sit where she was meant to, as Twoclicks' surrogate.

Whistle rose. The day was not going as well as he'd hoped, I was sure. He walked between Heather and the Mother and took a seat on her left.

"What happens next?" I whispered to Treble.

"This is very serious, Uncle Peter. Whistle is in big trouble. He could lose everything—his rank, his colonies, all of it."

"And why do this with the talks about to finally begin?"

Treble shrugged. "Anger? Envy? Fear of losing everything in those talks?"

Yes, that sounded right to me. It was interesting to know the S'hudonni had some of the same motivations as Earthies. It was all about power, and, like Treble said, the anger and the envy that drove one to seek or defend that power.

The two who had been caught accosting Heather were escorted from the barge along with the other thugs who'd come with Whistle, and then everything seemed strangely all right for a few minutes, Heather chatting with the Mother and her smiling and agreeing with Heather about what was being said. Whistle sat, aloof, alone, on the Mother's left.

The throng around the throne slowly dissipated and I even walked away, Treble at my side, thinking maybe it was time to leave the barge and bring this strange day to a close. But then there were some whistles and clicks that I'd missed, and suddenly all three—Heather, the Mother, and Whistle— were rising and walking to the ornate wooden gangplank that connected the barge to the wharf. Before they reached it, the Mother looked over at us and whistled something. Treble, for the moment, didn't translate but just whistled back.

As the three of them reached the wharf, they had a retinue of twenty or more S'hudonni walking with them. Some of them, it seemed to me, were in custody. I heard a hard *thump* behind me and looked to see the palanquin on the ground not far from where I stood with Treble. The blimpies floated above it, still harnessed. Without thinking much about it I walked over and found the clasps that held their harnesses to the palanquin. I opened those clasps, all eight of them, and the harnesses fell free. I looked up to see the blimpies, released now, eyeing me as they drifted away.

I looked back to the group of S'hudonni and they all had walked to a line of wagon-shaped sleds. The first wagon in line was impressively ceremonial in design, enclosed with carved wood figures along the top and sides and doors that opened wide, with windows that had curtains. The two royals and the surrogate stepped into that wagon and the others filled the ones behind and off they went. Treble and I stood there watching. We had not been invited along.

Then, as they turned to go, Treble said to me, "The Mother said that she agrees to consider your plan to visit your sister."

"Consider?" I asked

"It's as much as she is able to say right now, I think, Uncle Peter, but it is a very good signal, yes? And I'm sure that she liked your release of the blimpies, but Whistle surely didn't."

I shrugged. I hadn't given that any thought, really. They looked trapped and I let them go, that was all.

"Oh," Treble, said, "the Mother said I should warn you that storms are coming and you should be prepared."

"What does that mean?" I asked.

"That storms are coming, Uncle Peter," said Treble, as if speaking to a child, or a pet. Like me.

Ah, yes. "Sure," I said. "Please convey my thanks, Treble."

Later, I found out that Whistle was to be detained indefinitely in the Mother's compound. That was fine, but indefinitely was indefinite. Somehow I had to persuade Twoclicks and the Mother to let me go find Kait, let me bring her to my place, let me make her safe. Somehow.

A KNOCK AT THE DOOR

After that meeting with the Mother and her son Whistle, I feared for my life. I thought for sure that Whistle would arrange to have me killed in my sleep, or killed while walking down Center Street in Holmanville, or drowned while taking a soak in my favorite hot spring. So I spent a very nervous five-day being wary, locking doors, staying away from those lonely walks along the Great Bight that I'd so enjoyed.

But nothing happened until, at the end of that five-day, there was a knock at the door, and when I answered it—very carefully—Treble walked in to tell me our rescue trip had been approved. Off the books, with no support, with no technology, with nothing but ourselves and a floater sled, so no one but us could be blamed if it all went wrong. In fact, Treble said with a laugh, "It's officially unofficial, Uncle Peter! You're going to kidnap me and force me to take you to Whistle's compound, where you'll force me to rescue your sister. It will be great fun!"

I got it, and it sounded fine to me. It would get me moving in the right direction, so off we went that same day.

TRAVELS WITH TREBLE

Waiting for death a five-day later, but serene in my drugged state, I was being carried facedown over the edge of a two-hundred–meter cliff above the rocky shore of the Great Bight. We were apparently going out to sea, me and the blimpie that had a firm grip on me.

All I could think about was how disappointed my sister Kait would be. I'd sent her a handwritten letter as we left the cottage a five-day before, bringing her up to speed on all that happened, from her copy's death to the purpose of her own kidnapping and the promise that I'd be there in a ten-day to bring her back to my little cottage and something closer to real life. Now it wasn't going to happen. Treble swore the letter would get there, but I hadn't been so confident. Now, perhaps, it didn't matter.

Instead, I was being carried away over the bogs and the woods and the meadows and the coastline of Curved Island and now about to go over the Great Bight, the water below alive with mares' tails as the offshore wind ripped the tops off the waves. We were just high enough that if the blimpie holding me decided to let go, I was a dead man. Which I was maybe anyway. The various options didn't look good, which I found amusing.

The blimpie was struggling, rising and dropping a few meters erratically and making sudden jolting moves left and right. No surprise, given my weight and the gale we were sailing along in, the wind pushing us along the coast, sometimes far out over the Bight, sometimes over the bouldered shore.

I was held by a half dozen of those long tentacles I'd seen trailing along underneath the blimpies as they'd cruised over the bogs, grabbing small creatures and plants and bringing them up to that wide mouth and tossing them in. It had been fascinating to watch but it was frightening as hell to literally get carried away by the experience.

I'd been tethered to the sled that held our gear, thinking it was heavy enough to keep me grounded in the fierce winds, but then a gust hit us that sent the sled and me both up into the air, the tether snapping so the sled went one way and I the other.

The blimpie had grabbed me midair after the sled and I parted ways, me going up and the sled crashing down the shoreline below. There were small hooks at the end of the tentacles, and they'd grabbed onto my clothes and dug into my skin to haul me up, up and away. I'd struggled at first, but then another tentacle, and then a few more, had come down to barb me and now I felt very relaxed, indeed, now that we were out of the gust and into spatters of rain and a steadier gale.

I'd be lunch, I'd supposed at first, but now I'd rethought that as the blimpie carried me along instead of eating me. Maybe I was on my way to some nesting site where I'd be fed to youngsters? Maybe I was on my way to a blimpie cookout, where a whole flock of these things would dine on the rare Earthie?

You'd think I'd be terrified to have that thought. Instead, I was at peace. Some sedatives must have come out of those barbs, I realized, and that sounded just fine. I was calm, watching the scenery go by as the tentacles turned me so my head was forward and facedown, seeing the bluffs and rocky beaches and then the wide-open water of the Great Bight.

So, I thought, this is how it ends. My grand plan to be the hero and rescue my sister Kait was about to end up with me dying of my own stupid hubris on this alien world, leaving Kait alone and terrified in Whistle's compound. She'd never again see our brother Tom, or her wife Sarah, or anyone or anything else on Earth. She'd rot there in captivity.

It was tragic, and all of it my own damn fault. We'd been doing fine, young Treble and I, hiking the dark paved path of the Old Ones on our way to Whistle's compound to find Kait and escort her to safety. It had been perfect walking weather, as it usually is on S'hudon, cool with a mist and an occasional rain shower rolling in from the Great Bight to our left. The gray weather, the constant red-wine twilight, the dark green and purple hues of the ferns and mosses that were everywhere, the constant light buzz of the insects that hovered around us, the blimpies cruising slowly overhead with those large downward-looking eyes searching for food—these were the sort of things that made S'hudon what it was, constant and dark and full of wonders.

The path was ancient, Treble had explained to me, though it looked new. It had been paved a thousand years before with a kind of living macadam that grew when and where it needed to in order to repair itself. It even redirected itself when that was called for, which happened often enough, I guessed, as the bluffs wore away from the encroaching sea.

Was it alive? Was it intelligent? Treble laughed when I asked that, and said, "Of course, Uncle Peter! Everything the Old Ones left behind is alive and intelligent. Haven't you noticed that?"

"Sure," I said, but that was a lie; I hadn't noticed anything of the sort. His saying that, though, changed how I saw this pavement we walked along. I hoped it liked me.

The path brooked no intrusions from the grasses and bushes that were along it on either side, so the footing was sure as we walked this way and that, the path a winding one. We tugged the floater sled along behind us on its long leash. It was packed with our camping gear and food. We were roughing it.

We saw no one else as the kilometers slowly slipped away. There was a major roadway a few kilometers farther inland, and that road was a straight shot from S'hudon, the capital that was not far from my little faux village of Holmanville, to East Song, the only other city in the entire archipelago. Surely that was how everyone traveled, in bigger, larger floaters that zipped along in a hurry, carrying people and freight to and fro, the imported beings and their imported products from six other worlds to S'hudon, the hub of the empire.

Whistle's compound lay not far from East Song, so it wasn't more than a three-hour trip between cities if you sledded it. But Treble and I were traveling the slow and scenic way because we must. I had no tech, and Treble had disengaged his external links so he couldn't be traced or use his tech either, because that's what the Mother had demanded.

Yes, sure, we'd been given permission to attempt this rescue of Kait, but no, certainly not, we couldn't have any help in getting it done. Heather and the Mother couldn't appear to have anything to do with it, and no detectable tech could be used. So we were on our own and stealthy, me and the little S'hudonni princeling. Or so we hoped.

The path was a good four or five meters wide and ran along the shore of the Great Bight as we headed toward Kait. It wound its way alongside small coves and atop headlands and through occasional stands of forest, weaving and curving with the terrain as it went. Occasionally the bluff lowered and for a while the path would wander along the outside edge of the boulder-strewn beaches with their coarse, dark sand before again rising to fifty or even one hundred meters above the shore, often sweeping for a while into one of those headlands, which we would round before getting back to the more direct path toward the compound.

It felt great, having the chance, at last, to do something, to take some action, get moving, go forward, I was happy to be out in the real wilds of Curved Island in the archipelago, walking along, the two of us, toward the chance to rescue my sister Kait.

At first, I'd been overwhelmed by the scenery. I'd seen none of this from the little faux village they'd built to house me. But here! The dark wide leaves of the plants folded and unfolded, moving in the breeze to outwit the neighboring plants in the struggle for energy from the dim, red father, that emerged now and again from the clouds and the mist. Treble kept naming things for me, first whistling and clicking in S'hudonni and then following that with an English translation. I was free to rename things as I chose, and he found that hilarious. I was, to Treble, almost always funny and cute. Back on Earth, the kids' term for what he thought of me as would have been *adorable*.

I didn't feel adorable, but I did feel adventurous, out in the wild at last. There were bogs everywhere, watery and shallow, covered by an algae-looking plant that seemed to sense I was walking by, the tiny individual plants rushing together to form a single table-sized, dark green, flat surface that then opened to let large bubbles fly free from within.

Near the far end of one of the larger bogs, we'd stopped so I could watch the first time this happened. A large pod of plants suddenly coalesced as we walked by and out came bubbles the size of basketballs, blown by the onshore breeze right toward us. They popped dramatically, and as a thousand tiny sharp particles scattered to the breeze, some of them washed right over us.

There was the rotten smell of decay and death after they burst. Then, when I saw more bubbles drifting toward us, I panicked and tried to run out of the cloud of them before they burst, scrambling madly down the path and brushing myself as I went.

"Uncle Peter! Uncle Peter!" Treble shouted at me in English as he did his best to keep up. "Stop! Stop! They're harmless!"

I stopped.

He trilled a laugh. "Well, *almost* harmless," he said, "but sticky! After a while they begin to dig into the skin. You have to wash them off in water to get rid of them before they implant and you have a thousand itchy seeds growing under your skin!"

He came over to take my hand. "Come on, Uncle Peter, we'll wash off." And he led me off the path, over to a small bluff where we found a way down and out onto the grainy dark sand of the beach, and then out into the water. We were stripping as we walked.

That was easy for Treble, who stepped out of his footwear, dropped his kilt, shrugged off his tunic, and waddled into the water. Me? I had laces to loosen and a belt to unbuckle and buttons to undo, so it took a little longer. Both of us carried our clothing into the sea with us.

The water was clear and cold and salty, just like the water back home in Florida during a rare winter cold snap. I guessed it was about ten or twelve

Celsius, which was bracing, indeed. But after diving in and then standing in the shallows and then ducking my head under the waves that came in, I adjusted. I stayed in for a few minutes, rubbing my face and hands and hair, anywhere those tiny seed pods might have stuck to me.

Then I rinsed out my shoes and clothes and waded back ashore. Treble was already there, waiting for me.

"Good job, Uncle Peter!" he said with his usual enthusiasm. "Those seeds can't live in salt water, so we're fine!"

He could have told me that before I'd done all the scrubbing, I thought. But that was all right; the dip had been refreshing. We'd left the sled behind, up on the path, so I stood there, naked, and slowly turned to let the sea breeze blow me dry. The day was dark and chilly and damp, but dry me it did, and not long after that the two of us, the princeling Treble and your faithful correspondent, walked back up the beach, barefoot, put our wet clothes back on, and sat on boulders to brush the sand off our feet and to put on our shoes (and damp socks, for me), then we squished our way back to the path.

We hurried past more bubbles and on up a slight rise that led into a small stand of treelike plants that stood three or four times my height as I walked through them. In ten minutes we reached the far side of the tiny woods and the path dipped underneath us, back into marshland.

There were plenty of blimpies keeping an eye on us, for whatever their reasons. Mostly, they stayed forty or fifty meters up, but occasionally one would drop down lower to feed, getting within a meter of the bogs, where tentacles emerged from the bottom of the blimpie to reach down into the bog bushes and small trees to literally grab a bite, one of the small squirming animals that peeked out from the shadowed higher branches of the banyan-like trees, or the large purple fruit—the size of volleyballs—that hung down from those same branches.

The blimpies had two huge eyes right on the front of a flat snout, and below that a wide mouth that opened for the food brought to it from one tentacle or another, and below that the single lower eye. Back when I'd first seen them along the bluff near my village, I'd thought they were mechanical, some sort of floating communication device, maybe, and that's why I'd given them that name. But now I knew better, having seen them in action and heard about them from Treble. They were intelligent living things that had been here from long before the arrival of the S'hudonni, back when the Old Ones had been here. They were solitary or in small flocks or herds, moving in a leisurely fashion, drifting with the breeze or using a kind of oar that emerged from the bottom to steer or even propel them into the wind. They were beautiful in their languid mystery, floating in the mist and light rain, and I was the first Earthie to see them, unless Kait had seen them first, and wouldn't that be a wonderful thing to argue about with my sister? To argue that would mean we'd rescued her.

Anyway, I decided to stick with the Earthie name I'd given them, at least for now, and that led me to a spate of naming as I walked along. The strange, dark sandy soil with the dark green streaks running through it? Sea sand. The animals that lived in caves at the base of the bluffs and ran out into the waves to catch a meal and then carry it back across the sea sand to their caves? They were quick. The size of beavers, maybe. A kind of mossy fur on them, that same deep purple color I saw in other things. Call them otters, or purple otters, or purple people-otters. I'd pick one of those later.

And that had led me into silliness for a while: a jub-jub bird and a squirrel-looking thing that hopped like a frog: a bandersnatch. And a small, very ugly reptilian thing that lay on the path and refused to move, then squirted me on my pants-leg as I walked by. Urine, or some kind of weapon? There was no smell, but in a few minutes the blue of the denim pants began to fade to white. There was a small stream cascading over the bluff. I washed off the pant leg in the water and wrung out the leg and put the pants back on. Acid test, I decided to call the thing.

I had a goal; I was intent on reaching Kait. So I tried not to ogle at the headland's view of the combers rolling in from the cold sea to beat against the sheer face of the bluffs below as the cold sea spray rose from the rocks. We went on, Treble and I, taking turns in the harness that tugged the mag sled along behind us, its bottom a few centimeters above the pavement.

This went on for hour after hour in that steady, never-ending twilight. We made good time and I was actually starting to think about what we would do to rescue Kait once we got to Whistle's compound. He wouldn't be there; he was under a kind of house arrest at the Mother's. But surely his staff would try and stop us. We had no weapons, so it would be up to Treble to get her released into our charge.

I was talking that over with Treble when the weather changed. We were walking along the top of still another headland, and had rounded the corner to head back toward the main shoreline, when I saw the father, huge and red, slowly emerging through the usual low, gray clouds, the wind picking up out of the south, and thunderheads, the first storm clouds I'd seen on S'hudon, building up above us in all directions.

"Big changes coming," said Treble, standing the middle of the paved trail and looking up.

I wanted to keep going. I'd waited a whole lot of ten-days for this chance to find Kait and bring her back to my little village. But I trusted Treble. If he said we needed shelter, then we needed shelter.

I'd grown really fond of Treble. He, or him, or her, was a terrific, personable young princeling or princess or royal. He'd been explaining to me as we walked along that he wouldn't have to decide on which of the three states-of-being he wanted as his primary for another year, when he reached productivity. At the moment, he was male, and what we would call a young teen. In a few ten-days, he was thinking he might give the princess side a try. Later, he said he would give the royal state a try, too. Would he be the Mother some day? Only if he felt like it, he said.

Treble was friendly, bright, energetic, and honest, none of which were traits I'd associated with the adult S'hudonni I knew, including both of Treble's fathers. They were royals, and I now knew what that meant. They were interested in power and leadership, and no longer interested in reproduction. They'd been there and done that, and Treble was the result.

I looked at Treble. "Big changes coming?" I asked, thinking maybe trouble was headed our way.

But no, not that kind of trouble. He meant in the weather. "A storm?" I asked. "Like the one you were in with your fathers?" It was always misty, cool, cloudy, and dark on S'hudon, so I was thinking a storm would be interesting, even fun, if it didn't slow us down too much.

Treble nodded. "Same thing. Terrible storm. We'll need to stay safe somewhere, and soon."

"Can't we just keep moving on through it, Treble?" I asked him as the path wandered along the top of a bluff, the open water to our left. Waiting is something I'd done too much of during my time on S'hudon, and now here I was, doing something at last, getting close to Kait so I could bring her to safety, my prince being better than hers by a long shot. "I'd like to just bundle up in rain gear when it starts to pour," I said, "and then we could push on through, right? It'll be fun."

"I don't think so, Uncle Peter," Treble said. "These storms can be terrible, and this is coming right at us. It's going to get very ugly."

"I'll be all right," I said.

"I don't think so," he said firmly. "But if you insist, then I'll stay with you right through it, Uncle Peter."

And so he did, the two of us pushing into the rain and the wind that grew and grew in strength until we could barely make our way into it. At one point we'd been struggling along as the path edged along the top of a steep bluff that looked out to an angry sea in the Great Bight. The gusts nearly blew us both out to sea. We were happy, a few minutes later, to curve inland a bit and get into a small woods.

What passed for trees on S'hudon were five- or ten-meter-tall plants with multiple fibrous trunks that wound around each other until at the top they spread out with large, wide, deep purple leaves. Gourd-shaped seedpods hung down from the multiple trunks, and if you bumped them, I'd discovered, they exploded with seeds.

These trees swayed in the gale, but also dampened it so we could keep moving. Then, when we emerged on the far side into another low-lying bog that bumped up nearly to the cliff edge, the wind increased steeply again. I put my head down and trudged on, tugging the sled along behind me, with Treble in front.

I heard a shout from Treble and looked up to see a deep-black funnel cloud emerging from a low desk of clouds just ahead of us. "Back! Back!" Treble was yelling as he turned toward me.

But it was too late. The funnel danced across the bog toward us, and then met us. I reached for Treble, who'd lost his footing and was sliding by me, but I couldn't get to him, and then I watched in horror as he rose and then rose again and then went spinning out over the cliff edge toward the distant riot of the open sea.

I was next, lifted by the vortex even as I hung on to the sled's harness. After a few seconds the strap broke and I was carried toward the water myself, flailing toward certain death, when I felt the first tentacle wrap around my right arm and when I looked that way I could see another reaching for my chest, finding it and wrapping around it. Another went around my waist and yet others grabbed my legs and my left arm, all of this in the middle of that ferocious wind.

And so the blimpie had me, tightly wrapped, a kind of carryout meal for the family, I supposed.

Once the sedation took hold, I lay there with time to wonder, as the blimpie shook and trembled in the wind. How was Treble? I wondered. There was a chance, I thought, that if he'd landed in the water he might be all right.

And then I thought of Kait and wondered how she would manage without me. I'd spent my life trying to help Kait deal with a world full of problems and challenges, and I'd promised her often that I'd always be there to help. Bad friends and worse drugs had almost done Kait in several times as she'd gone through the dark cycle of being lost, then found, then lost again. Through it all, I'd been there for her. But not this time.

The blimpie trembled again and headed down toward a cliff edge of the bluff with its beach below, huge rock outcrops on coarse sand. The squall line and the funnel cloud were well past us now as we passed over that bluff edge, and the rain that hit us was blinding and pushed us down and out toward the sea. But now there was lightning as a huge bolt with its massive thunderclap nearly hit us. Then another crashing bolt and then another still as we neared the water and then, just when I thought perhaps I felt us begin to bank toward the sandy beach and safety there came a blinding light and I felt the tentacles lose their grip on me and I was falling, falling, falling and feeling very sorry for myself and feeling very sorry for Treble and for Kait, who'd believed my promises that now weren't going to come true, and feeling very sorry and regretful, most of all, for not having listened to Treble, who'd warned me about the dangers of these storms.

THE WAVE

I was dreaming about my Florida childhood. I was playing on the beach with my sister and brother, our mother watching over us from the protection of her beach umbrella, stuck into the firm sand that ran for more than a klick in each direction from the spot directly in front of our home on our little barrier island.

We were snorkeling, the three Holman kids, in water two meters deep and crystal clear. We were searching for sand dollars and crabs, both of them easy enough to find in these shallows, bright with morning sunshine. I watched as Kait found a sand dollar, alive and covered in its brown fur, as we called it. Its tiny legs that ran all around the outer edge of the sand dollar were flailing furiously. Carefully, Kait put it back. Sensitive Kait, our eco-warrior and soccer player and our actor in all the school plays.

I was following Tom, the young scientist. He'd be catching crabs and bringing them in to the kitchen table to dissect them. I gave my fins a quick flip to catch up with him but, funny, instead he seemed farther away. He was swimming easily, effortlessly, headed out to the deeper water of the Gulf. I knew I had to get out there and catch him, grab a fin, turn him around and bring him to safety.

But he was swimming faster and faster and I couldn't catch him and I panicked, looking around for Kait but she, too, was gone now; and so I surfaced and looked around and it was a rocky coast and a cold rain and not Florida. Not Florida at all.

The water was angry but shallow. I stood. The rain pelted down but the wind had calmed. I looked around and thought I was very, very lucky to be alive. I remembered flying off into the nothing, tied to that sled before it let go and went its own way and I went mine, tightly wound in the grasps of that blimpie's tentacles.

The sled. I looked around and all I could see was a wide, wide strand of sand and rock-strewn beach, a bluff in the distance, hundreds of meters away. There was a jumble of flotsam on the beach, left behind by the retreating water. Was any of that from the sled? There was no way to know except to see if I could walk over there.

I started wading to shore. I was shaky, but everything seemed to be working and I steadied after a minute or two. In a hundred meters I reached the beach, soaking wet but still clothed, still wearing my walking boots.

The beach seemed to be at some sort of extreme low tide. The puddled sand and various rock outcrops extended out for hundreds of meters before reaching the water. I trudged across the sand toward the distant bluff. It was cold and getting colder as I walked. The bluff was farther away than I'd thought but there was nothing to do about that except keep moving. At least I started to warm with the exercise.

Ten minutes later I didn't seem to be any closer to the bluff, but the wind that had been in my face as I'd started this long walk was now shifting, coming around all the way to behind me, which was good, pushing me gently toward that bouldered shoreline and the bluff. The wind seemed a little warmer and I was feeling better as I walked, so I started to organize my thinking: First, I needed to reach that shore and hope that among all that debris on the beach was some material from the sled. Second, I needed to figure out a way to contact Treble. I was hoping he was fine and had fallen into the water and stayed there to get through the storm. Third, I needed to figure out where I was and what I could do to recover from the storm and get back to rescuing Kait.

A good plan, right? First, second, third, and done, right?

The day was brightening again, the clouds thinning out, the air fresh and warm at my back. I stopped for a second to rest, closed my eyes and turned to my left to feel the strange but welcome heat from that red father up there.

I lowered my face and opened my eyes to look around. Everything was going to be all right, I decided. Everything would be fine.

I looked around. Out to sea there was some wave action, maybe the tide coming back in? No problem, I turned and started the final few hundred meters to the bluff, splashing through the puddled sand, looking for anything from the sled, taking my time.

I was looking around for anything, a piece of clothing, a tie-down, a broken harness, anything. There, over by the largest boulder, very near the upper part of the beach. An upended cart? The sled? Maybe. I headed that way, taking a sharp right turn to get there. As I turned I looked out to the distant sea, which wasn't so distant now. Not a tide coming, unless this was the right geology for some kind of tidal bore. No, this was bigger than that. A wave, at least my height but maybe twice that, coming right at me, and coming fast. I froze for a second, processing that, and then turned to run toward that boulder where that might be my sled. I didn't want to get caught by any kind of wave, tidal or tsunami or tidal bore or seiche— whatever the hell it was on this strange planet with its red star and awful storms, I didn't want to get caught in it. I figured I had a minute, maybe two, to get to the sled and tug it higher up the beach.

I splashed through some puddles and ran as fast as I could to that boulder. Got there and saw my sled, on its side, most of it in one piece but most of the equipment and supplies long gone. It was stuck into the sand, not deep, really, but certainly deep enough to slow me down. I turned and looked and there was that wave, yes, at least twice my height, coming hard. A minute away? At best. Probably less.

Damn. I tugged at the sled. Nothing. I leaned into it to shove and loosen the sand's grip on it. That helped. More shoving and it came loose with a quick sucking sound. Now, to get it higher up the beach.

I had to turn and face the oncoming wave to get a grip on the sled, and when I did that I saw I had run out of time. The wave was twenty meters away and coming fast. I could see it was three times my height or more. I needed to get to high ground, and fast. I turned and ran, going up the beach toward the bluff and safety.

The sand was looser here, the running harder. It was all I could do to struggle through it, and then I heard the wave behind me, and then I swear

I could feel it behind me and then it had me, lifting me, tossing me face-first into the sand, pushing and shoving me around as it carried me all the way to the base of the bluff. Mostly I was lost and tumbling under water, but there was a moment when my head came clear and I could see the driftwood and the rocks at the base of the bluff and I reached and grabbed at the driftwood and hung on for dear life.

The water withdrew and I'd survived. I watched it withdraw and I could see, out there in the backwash, the sled, floating, turning and spinning in the currents and eddies, and then, as the wave ebbed and left me high and dry, the sled came to rest in the shallows.

But I couldn't go get it, I was stuck, my right arm wedged between two boulders, and my left knee, that one in such bad shape they'd considered amputation a few years ago, was screaming at me and felt like it was bending in the wrong direction.

My left arm was wrapped around a piece of driftwood, and despite the pain from the knee I was able to brace myself, move around a bit, and free the left arm. It was bruised and scraped but otherwise all right.

But the right arm was so deeply wedged between the boulders that I couldn't move it. The wave action must have pushed those boulders slightly apart and my arm happened to find its way between them as they came back together.

I leaned there, trapped, as what had been a dull ache from that arm became something more painful and then something truly agonizing, coming at me in waves, contending with the pain from the battered left knee. I thought the S'hudonni nanos were protective, would heal me and dull the pain. But apparently not. I threw my head back and screamed. I yelled for help, I begged for help. I looked to the sky and wept with the pain.

Two of the blimpies came into view. I was, perhaps, entertaining in my agony, or they thought I might make for a good meal to be shared between them. One came close and a tentacle came down to touch my trapped arm. It was a horrifying moment. I had no idea what the blimpie had in mind. And then I felt pinpricks from that tentacle and the pain finally ebbed and then disappeared as I drifted off into a troubled sleep.

SCYLLA AND CHARYBDIS

When I awoke the insects were buzzing around me again, five or ten of them swooping in to check me out and then swooping back out when they realized I was not something they were interested in biting or laying eggs in or sucking blood from.

I tried to move that arm but it was hopeless, I was firmly stuck, and it occurred to me that I could die here. I would die here, in fact, if someone didn't come help me. The water was coming in again, more slowly now, so maybe there was some kind of sloshing effect going on. I was keeping an eye on that, though I didn't think it would reach as far as the boulders where I was trapped. A lot of time had passed, hours, since that wave had placed me here, and wedged my right arm between the boulders. It was hard to tell how long it had been under S'hudon's red, still star. Strangely, the clouds had cleared again and the father sun was out. I'd been on this planet for three months, and where I lived I'd never seen more than hour or two of clear sky in total. And now, along this coastline, I'd seen clear days twice, with that massive storm in between.

It had clouded over and rained on me twice, the first time before I'd realized how hopeless things were—I'd been thinking someone would come by to help me soon—and so I'd welcomed the rain and looked up at the rain to hold my mouth open and get some raindrops. But I hadn't thought to capture any of it, and when the shower ended it wasn't long before my thirst returned and I had no water. I had it everywhere, of course, but not a drop to drink.

There were indentations on the top of the one boulder I could reach with my left hand, so I brushed one of those clear of pebbles and debris so I had a shallow depression in the rock that might hold some rainwater. Then I used my finger to open up a few paths in the mossy surface that might, if I was lucky, give the raindrops a tiny streambed to follow to lead to the cupped area I'd cleaned out.

Spending ten or fifteen minutes doing that exhausted me, but took my mind a bit off the deep ache from my arm. After resting for a minute or two I tried once again to pull that arm free and the pain was immediate and terrible. Something was broken in there, for sure, maybe crushed. I felt faint with the pain and started to collapse against the boulder and that raised the pain to a level I didn't know it could go, with incredible shooting pains, like someone was cutting through my arm just above the elbow with a very dull blade.

I looked up and there were those blimpies again, a pair of them, a hundred meters up, apparently waiting for me to die so they could come down with those tentacles and make a nice meal out of me. So I stood up to prove I still lived, and if I stood straight and held that arm and elbow in just the right way I could get the pain to ease. It wasn't gone, it wasn't even tolerable, really. But it was the best I could do.

I started shouting again, yelling, "Help! I need help!" over and over again until my voice gave out. At some point, I hoped, some S'hudonni would hear me, but I knew the odds weren't good. Apparently, only the blimpies found me interesting. The smaller of the two drifted down toward me again, that barbed tentacle came down to touch my arm. Pinpricks again.

I waved away some insects. I croaked out another "Help me, please," but it wasn't very loud. I didn't have the voice for that. With that big red father shining down and a suspiciously warm breeze blowing again I was hot, and thirsty, and in pain. I felt a drop of rain, then more. I looked up and saw one dark cloud scudding by, a rain shower falling from it. Please let it rain, please let my tiny reservoir fill so I could quench my thirst. Please let some S'hudonni hear me and save me. Please. Please.

The rain reached me, and for ten minutes or so I was cool and wet, my head up and my tongue out to catch a few drops. When the shower ended my little plan had worked and there was a pool of rainwater on the top of the boulder. I sipped from it. The boulders had trapped me but now were giving me water.

This was a perfect example of the S'hudonni paradox: promise always held peril in equal measure, as it had right from the beginning of this little adventure.

Again I dozed, and then a few minutes later, or an hour, or ten hours later—who could tell?—I was licking the bowl dry on the boulder, that little reservoir of rainwater gone so only some moisture remained, when I heard some splashing from the sea. Painfully, I turned to look. It was Marina, beautiful Marina, emerging from the waves to walk on the beach toward me, holding a gray pitcher of water in one hand and a sturdy piece of driftwood in the other. "Peter!" she yelled to me, and held up the pitcher for me to see.

My coterie of insects buzzed off and zoomed toward her. She smiled at them and then came within a few meters of me, insects trailing. "Peter, what a mess you're in," she said.

I knew I was hallucinating, I'd fallen in love with Marina a trillion kilometers ago, back on Earth, back in my basketball days, when I'd been the off guard for the Dublin Rovers. I'd met her in the Prado in Madrid, seen her again in the Picasso Museum in Barcelona, and then later she'd come to visit me in Dublin. I'd fallen hard for her. It was one of those things where you know in the first few minutes that this is the one, this is forever. She was beautiful, intelligent, strong. I couldn't believe a woman like that could care for me at all, much less love me.

And then she'd left Dublin to go home to Madrid for a visit and I'd never heard from her again. No response to my messages and calls. I went to her apartment in Madrid on a crazy off-day expedition from Dublin and she didn't live there and never had. She could not be found. She'd been too good to be true and I knew it and, finally, a long time later, I got over it.

And now here she was. On S'hudon, leaning over me with the pitcher in her hand to splash some cold water on my face and to let me drink my fill. She leaned down to kiss my chapped lips and said, "I've missed you, Peter," and then added, "but, really, I think it's time."

"Time for what?" I asked her. Death, I assumed she'd say. Time to give up. Relax. Accept it.

She set the driftwood next to me and said, "Really, Peter. It's time." She reached out to touch my cheek and then turned and walked away. I wept. I knew I was dying. I slumped down against the boulder, and howled with the pain that tore through me with that effort.

Later, how much later I didn't know or care, I'd finally given up. No help was coming.

I closed my eyes and slumped down further. Let it end. And then I felt a jab in my shoulder and I awakened to see a tentacle there and two shadows over me. Fucking blimpies again, one of them right above me now. There were marks, scratches, and long swipe marks on the boulder, like the blimpies had tried to move it, hoping for easier access to lunch, I supposed. They'd given up and so, I thought, should I as the blimpies drifted away.

An hour went by, and then another and still another. I wept. I knew I was dying. The pain was back, I slumped down against the boulder, and howled with the fiery sharp edges that seemed to tear through me.

Time passed. How long had it been? I'd lost track completely. Hours? Days? It seemed hot to me, the sand on my feet as hot as the beach I'd grown up on in a slowly drowning Florida, rising water eating away at the shoreline year by year, and the heat and humidity rising and rising again. I wondered if I'd ever go back there, and then answered that to myself. Not bloody likely.

It rained again, filled up my little pool on the top of the boulder. It's time, it's time. I swatted at the insects. Missed them all, of course.

I drank. I stood. The clouds and mist were back. And then I finally understood what Marina had told me. It was time for me.

It was going to be terribly painful. The boulders lay on sand. If I lowered myself as much as I could and ignored the searing pain that came with that, I could use that piece of driftwood that Marina had left me and I could dig out the sand behind the boulder to my left. I tried it, gasping with pain but able to get the end of the branch into the sand beneath the boulder. I poked and scraped, a cupful of sand or so at a time, pushing it back and out of the way, digging out that loose sand from beneath the boulder, small handfuls of it at a time, but making progress.

This went on for long time. Too long. I stopped and drank the last of the water from the top of the boulder. A thick fog was rolling in from the sea. I stood, I braced myself with my back against one boulder and my feet against the one I hoped to move. The pain from that trapped right arm was dreadful and demanding. It wanted me to quit. But Marina said it was time, so I pushed with my feet. Nothing. Pushed again, nothing. I stopped, returning to digging out the sand. Returned to pushing with my feet. Did that again. And again. Excruciating pain. And then, at last, some movement. Just a hint of the boulder moving, but I screamed in excitement, "Yes! Yes! God damn it, yes! Move, you son of a bitch! Move!" And it did again, a centimeter, then two. I tried pulling out my trapped right arm and it moved, too! Not free yet, but it had moved. I returned to pushing and then, at last, the boulder seemed to sigh and admit defeat, and rolled a good five centimeters. My arm was free. I saw blood oozing from it, a lot of it, too damn much of it. I collapsed onto the sand and sat there, in terrible pain, watching as the blood oozed, and I knew that after all that pain and all that effort, I would die here on this beach. I yelled, "Help me. Please!" and then screamed that again and then I lay back and closed my eyes and waited for the pain to end.

And then felt a hand on my cheek, and hands on my arm and felt water being poured, a tiny bit at a time, into my mouth. I opened my eyes to see who my savior was. Treble, I bet.

But it was Kait, my sister to the rescue. Sweet Kait. "It's OK, Peter, I'm here," she said. "You'll be fine. I'm here."

I thought I was hallucinating again—or, more likely, I was dead. And I was all right with that, really, but did that mean Kait was dead, too? I'd failed to help her, then. My One Good Thing and I'd failed at that.

Well, too bad. I closed my eyes and drifted off.

PART FOUR
KAIT WITH SMILES

On Sibilance, Brave Kait is their idol. The wide-eyed wonder on an alien world, struggling for freedom while finding friendship, is still popular in constant reruns. They hope to see her some day in person. I used to doubt this would ever happen.

—Peter Holman, *Notes from Holmanville*
(S'hudon City and New York:
Trebnet Press, 2035)

11

THE WIND WHISPERS

Kaitlyn Mary Theresa Holman is out of breath but still stumbling forward, trying to move as fast as she can through the boggy ground that's covered in dark purple bushes with wide leaves edged by small, sharp thorns. There are puddles all over the place. One of those puddles left her waist-deep in cold water when she tried to splash through it, so she's trying to avoid them all now. The perpetual red twilight and the light rain and mist of S'hudon doesn't help her do that. It's the murkiest damn place she's ever been.

In front of her, the S'hudonni guard she calls Smiles is waddling along briskly on those short S'hudonni legs that provoke so much humor back on Earth but that seem to be working just fine here on the home planet. Smiles moves smoothly through the brambles and puddles, leading the way, even though she's slowed by a backpack that she's apparently had ready for this moment for a while. She grabbed it in seconds when the moment came to leave.

Smile is Kait's one friend on this whole world. Smiles befriended Kait over the many, many ten-days of captivity, and now Smiles is the one who is leading Kait to freedom and her brother Peter and, someday, back home to Earth and wonderful Sarah, the love of her life.

Behind them there are whistles and clicks from some kind of loudspeaker. Kait stops for a second to take a quick glance back toward the compound and sees several S'hudonni coming through the narrow gate in the stone wall. Oh, hell. Kait and Smiles had planned to get over the crest of the hill in front of them and down the other side to the Old Ones' path before anyone in the compound knew they were gone. Looks like that hasn't worked out.

"Hurry!" says Smiles in her excellent English. "I don't think they've seen us yet."

"Right behind you," Kait whistles back to her. Kait's S'hudonni is getting better all the time.

They are surrounded by insects, large double-winged things that look like dragonflies back home, and smaller, quicker, darting things that are always in front of her but never land and, like the dragonflies, don't seem interested in biting. They're annoying, but they are the least of her worries right now. What Kait and Smiles are trying to reach is a paved trail and a vehicle that will take them to freedom, but getting to the trail isn't easy. There's a kilometer or more of this thick ground cover with its hidden puddles; you don't see them until you're in them, especially when you're busy trying to dodge around and through the bushes and any number of things that look like ferns.

She wishes she had more time to look at all the plants. There are some small tree things with a deep purple fruit hanging down to touch the ground, and when Kait tried to brush one of those out of the way it exploded with pulpy fruit and a thousand sticky purple seeds. And there are algae mats the size of tables on top of the puddles. When those mats sense you nearby, they send out large bubbles that can pop and spray you with sticky little dots that Smiles says you have to wash them off, but there's no time for that now, so the dots are staying.

It all makes for hard going. Smiles walks through it easily, but Kait stumbles every five or six steps, dodging puddles and bubbles and hanging fruit, and once falling flat on her face into the ferns. These ferns on this strange and dark world look just like the spear ferns back home in Florida where she grew up—lots of long, narrow leaves with rows of spores on the underside of the leaves, ready to reproduce. They don't need much sunlight. Good thing, since it's always a cloudy twilight here. The sun doesn't rise or set. There are no days, no nights, just the perpetual twilight of the huge red sun that Smiles says they call the father. Kait has only rarely glimpsed the father through the cloud cover and rain and mist on her daily walks around the grounds of the compound where they held her.

Today, oddly, it's dry and there are hints of the father in the sky. There's a strange warm breeze blowing and Kait is sweating in that warmth and from her own exertion. She's exhausted and exhilarated both. Six months she's been here, mostly confined to the two rooms that Whistle has set up for her. One room is a kitchen and toilet and living room, all in one. The other is an exact duplicate of the bedroom in the family home where she grew up, in Florida. Nice idea, Kait supposes, but she hated that room and went through hell to be rid of it and all that it meant—and now, look, it's back.

It looks exactly as Kait remembers it from a very terrible night during her sophomore year of high school: the soccer posters, the trophies, the flat screen that doesn't work, the desk with her schoolbooks on it, the tile floor and the wood-paneled walls and the closet and the bed.

The bed. After the Terrible Thing happened, she never slept in that bed again. For months afterward she slept on the floor, using blankets and sheets from the linen closet. She didn't want her mother to know, so she would mess up the sheets and blankets every morning so it would look like she'd slept there. She'd wash the sheets like usual, make the bed every morning like usual, all of that. But for those long months she didn't lie on that bed again. Not once. That bed.

She'd played Ado Annie in the school play, and her father, Mr. Famous

Pediatrician, Mr. Respected Citizen, Mr. Too Busy for Her all the time, actually showed up at the play. He sat next to Mom and, at the end, during the ovations, he stood right there with her and clapped and clapped and clapped. It was her first try at acting, and she'd been pretty good. And then. After.

It didn't help, of course. It was all too much, the Terrible Thing. It had grown in her mind, expanding, dark, so dark, taking her over, on her mind all the time.

So, finally, she left. Went toward school in the car, with Peter driving, dropping her off at Catholic before heading off to all-boys Jesuit High for him. Neither one of them saying anything really, some classic Hendrix on the sound system talking about watchtowers and then the wind whispering about Mary as they backed out the driveway, went down Gulf Drive to the ferry, and then across to the mainland and onto the Bayway and then left turn into the drive to Catholic. Pulling up to the front, opening the door as if it was all OK, she stepped out, slammed the door shut, waved to Peter, and then, as he left, she started walking, away from school, away from home, away from the Monster who'd done this to her, away from her mother and her brothers, away from life as she'd known it. Away, away.

That *away* lasted for years, with her talking only to Peter, the brother who couldn't understand but always listened, always cared, even as she fought those demons and lost, time after time.

Then, finally, she found some peace and love with Sarah, wonderful Sarah, who could and did understand, and cared, and loved her. And then, one bright Pasadena morning, a car door opened as she jogged by, rough hands grabbed her, threw a hood over her head. Then came a long drive, followed by darkness, until she woke up here, in the strangest of all places, and with this strangest of all friends.

But the room! My god. So here, even here, she pulled the sheets and covers and the two pillows off the bed, spread them all out on the floor, and slept fitfully. That helped keep the memories away, away, away from all the horrible comforts of home.

All of that just added to the terror and fear of being captive here. Prince Whistle came to visit her on five different occasions over those six months. What an awful creature. A bully, for sure. And Kait knew bullies when she saw them. She was his guest, he told her, and she could leave any time. And he didn't know why Peter, who was not that far away, didn't come to see her. He could, if he wanted to.

Which was a lie. Kait knew it. If Peter could be here, he'd be here.

But he isn't, and Whistle is, and she's running away from him as best she can, trudging through the muck, trying to keep up with Smiles, who keeps turning back to urge her forward: "Almost there, dear friend Kait! Almost there!"

They hear a loud, high-pitched whistle behind them. It goes on for five seconds or so and then becomes a series of urgent clicks, going from two or three per second to ten or twenty, rapid fire, urgent.

Kait looks over at Smiles, who looks back and says, in her near-perfect English, "They're looking for us. Please, dear friend Kait, we have to hurry."

Kait looks up and there are two—no, now it's three—of the blimpies coming sedately toward them. To watch? To help? To attack? She has no way to know and can't watch anymore anyway. Hurry, hurry Kait does, struggling to keep up. All that time in the compound has left her out of shape. The walks in the courtyard just don't cut it. Her legs ache; she's struggling for breath. She just wants to sit down, smack in a puddle if she must. She starts to do just that, when the clicking ends, the whistle returns. Smiles comes back and takes her hand. Wonderful Smiles. Her only friend. Kait keeps moving.

They hurry, and then, finally, they crest the hill and start down the other side. Ahead of them, no more than two hundred meters away, is the path that was built by the Old Ones, and above the path are those three blimpies, huge open eyes, dark pupils wide in the dim light, watching Kait and Smiles reach the path. It's several meters wide and straight as an arrow, heading off along the seacoast, toward Peter's little town and, beyond that, great S'hudon City itself.

They push through the brambles and the puddles and they don't look back until they get to the path and step up a good ten centimeters to get on it. Kait thinks it feels like asphalt, maybe with a little bounce to it. It seems ordinary. They look to the left, and the path is empty. They look back, and there are those four S'hudonni, pushing their way through the brambles as they crest the hill and head down, but now the blimpies are between the S'hudonni and Kait and Smiles. They've come down to just a meter above the path and are touching each other, side by side, three gentle giants blocking everything. The attackers slow, and that buys precious moments for Kait and Smiles to run away from their pursuers, down the path.

In fifty meters, Kait looks back and three of the pursuers have managed to get around the blimpies, the other one is tangled in blimpie tentacles and is flailing away as that blimpie rises. Kait can't stop and see what happens, but as she turns back to run again she hears the S'hudonni whistle loudly and there is a crunching noise behind her. That pursuer hit the path hard. But the other three are still coming.

They need her alive, Kait knows. But Smiles? She's helped Kait escape, and they don't need her alive at all. Better, in fact, if she's not. And they're a few minutes away.

It's hopeless, she thinks, but whistles to Smiles anyway, "We have to run!"

But Smiles is just standing there, looking down the Old Ones' path. "Listen!" she says, in English.

Kait doesn't hear anything. But then, "There! There!" cries Smiles, and points toward something emerging from the mist. A few hundred meters away and coming toward them in a hurry. Some kind of wagon or sled or cart, the size of a small truck back home, but with no wheels, no sides on it. It floats over the pavement. Magnetic levitation? Could be.

As the seconds tick by, Kait turns to watch the S'hudonni getting closer, the blimpies off to the side of the path now, watching, as Kait turns back to see the wagon getting closer, too—so close that she can see there are two rows, front to back, six seats deep, with just two seats in the front occupied. A pair of S'hudonni are sitting upright, their dorsals poking through open slots in the seatbacks. One of them looks older, perhaps wiser, with a look of quiet command. The other, younger and energetic, is clicking and whistling like mad—"We are here! We are here!"—as the wagon pulls up, silently, and comes to a stop.

"Mother!" Smiles whistles to the older one, as Kait hears a *pad pad pad* behind her and turns to see the three remaining S'hudonni waddling up the path, wearing uniforms, dark purple shirts and black pants held up by suspenders, with devices attached to them. She can see the fourth slowly rising from back down the path where it landed. It stands and starts hobbling up the path toward them.

Two of the S'hudonni are carrying what looks a lot like leashes and collars. A third carries what Kait guesses is a weapon—small, held in one tiny hand, with a single narrow stick that juts out the front so, she guesses, the user can aim it. It's the first weapon she's seen here, and she doesn't want to find out how it works. The fourth one, only fifty meters back by now and walking steadily, is dressed differently, in a kind of jacket, wearing long pants and wide footwear and a hat, a ridiculous assemblage of cloth and ferns with a single eye in the middle of it, staring forward. Is that hat alive? Maybe. It seems to look at her, and then slowly blinks. It's creepy as hell.

It—he? she? they?—finally gets close enough to speak. It clicks at her angrily as the eye blinks twice, and then it says, in English, "Kaitlyn Holman, you should return to your quarters."

Kait stares at that single eye as it blinks again and clicks and whistles the same message in S'hudon. Kait clicks and whistles back, saying, "I don't think so." She's pretty good with the language now.

There is a burst of sound from behind her, and she turns to see the older of the two S'hudonni on the sled raising one arm to point at Kait as she says to Single-Eye, with an emphatic high-pitched whistle, "You must leave! This Earthie is coming with us! I am her protector!"

Next to Kait, Smiles whistles softly, "That is our mother, dear friend Kait. And no one dares disagree with her."

There is another angry burst of clicks and whistles from the Mother, and Kait looks back to see her pointing at the S'hudonni who carries the thing that looks like a weapon as she is saying, "Put that thing away or I will tell your fathers!" And when Kait looks back, the S'hudonni is busy packing the weapon away into the small bag held by a belt that goes around his shoulders.

"Better," says the Mother.

"Isn't she wonderful?" says Smiles to Kait, in a whistle full of admiration, though it's so low in volume that Kait can barely hear it.

"She sure is," Kait whispers in English. "But I wonder if—"

But there is no time for wonder. The Mother is waving her hands and whistling firmly and Kait and Smiles are helped aboard the floating sled by the very ones who had been chasing them. And then the sled is spinning on its axis to face the other way, and the Mother, doing the driving, is pushing a handle forward, and off they go, heading away from Whistle's compound, away from their silenced pursuers, and on toward . . . somewhere. Kait wishes she knew where. Toward her brother Peter, she hopes, who must be waiting for her, anxious, worried sick. Peter, the strong one, the big brother. Always. Off to the side, just ten meters up, the blimpies accompany them.

12

THE STORM

There is a name for everything: the sun, the air, the clouds, the plants, the things like trees, the buzzing and the flying and the soaring things from tiny to huge, the crawling things, the leaping things, the things like grass and the things like mud and the water and the bog and the rivers and, when they reached it at the end of that first day outside, the sea. These things and a thousand more have names, whistles and clicks that rise or fall and come fast or slow or repeating or not. And Kait is learning them. One by one, she is learning.

Smiles enjoyed pointing all these things out to Kait as they rode along at a leisurely pace on the Mother's sled. The path went for kilometers along a canal, and then along a river, and then, at last, they reached the sea. The weather was as the weather always was, cool and foggy and an occasional light rain. The red sun they called the father was not often visible, but Smiles said she could feel a change in the air, something different.

The blimpies had kept company with them for a long while, and then they slowly drifted—foraging, said Smiles. She thought they'd be back; they seemed to like Kait for some reason.

No one else had followed them, so perhaps Whistle hadn't sought vengeance after all. But they were on their way now, so on they went, not bothered by the buzzing insects that swarmed around them but never seemed to bite.

When they reached the sea, they had to leave the path and the sled behind, so they tied it off at a shed that was there for that purpose and walked down steps cut into the rock to reach the sea. The cove there was protected water, the bluffs rose steeply all the way up to the path that ran along the coast. The tiny village that Smiles came from sat huddled up against the base of the bluff. There were a couple of dozen homes, each of them built halfway into the water, with a small door at the back that opened to the beach and, in the front, a hole that allowed the villagers to dive right into the shallow water from inside their homes.

Smiles introduced Kait to the villagers, most of whom were related to Smiles in one way or another. The wide range of what Kait would call fathers and aunts and uncles and cousins and brothers and sisters was mind-boggling. Watching over all these introductions with a benevolent smile was the village elder, the leader, the mayor, the arbitrator, the calm voice of reason: the Mother. The one who'd rescued them.

None of the villagers had ever personally met any creature from any of the planets in the S'hudonni Empire. In fact, village life seemed completely divorced from the empire and its reach to Earth and Downtone and Harmony and Melody and the rest. Life here was simple.

Kait was fascinated by what she found. The living seemed communal, with the Mother's opinion the one that mattered. Smiles explained that there were many Mothers; each village had one. But all of S'hudon was ruled by the one Mother Over All. She was the parent of both Twoclicks and Whistle and even of their child, Treble.

Kait saw no farming going on, not even small gardens, so it was the sea that provided the food, and responsibility for gathering that food seemed equally shared.

Kait and Smiles went for a swim, then rested there, and slept, and ate. The raw fish had been cut for her, and the seaweed—if that's what it was—was prepared as a bed for the diced fish, which had a light sauce poured over it. It was delicious and filling, but Kait had to wonder just how her body had been changed during her quarantine after her arrival. There had been lots of nanos to drink and inject, so that must be how she could safely eat alien food on an alien world. The food she'd been eating in her captivity had been Earthie in style. She assumed it had been imported for her and that Peter was probably eating the same sort of food, wherever he was, but maybe that wasn't the case.

She felt safe here. No one seemed worried about anyone coming after them—or concerned about anything much at all, really, except the weather. The Mother warned them a storm was coming and that they should stay safely in the village for a day or two while it blew over. And so Smiles and Kait made plans to do that, with Smiles putting together a kind of bed for Kait in the same hut where she would be. The S'hudonni seemed to sleep lightly and not often, preferring frequent short naps to long stretches of sleep, but Kait didn't know whether this was related to their aquatic lifestyle or their locked star that sat forever on the horizon, never rising or falling, a permanent evening.

The bed looked comfortable, but Kait wanted to take one more look at this remarkable place before sleeping, so she wandered outside, alone, to stand on the narrow strip of shingled beach and try to capture in her own memory what it looked like here, what it smelled like, and how the air and the mist tasted and felt on her arms and her face as she walked along. The buzzing insects were there, as always, sharing her walk with her.

As she strolled along, the sky brightened, still dark hues of green and purple and reds, but brighter than usual. Then, in a strangely clearing sky, the father emerged in all its rouge glory.

It seemed wonderful. Kait stood atop a boulder on that beach and stretched out her arms to embrace the rare appearance. The wind had been from the shore and pushing the water out to sea, flattening the waves. The beach had widened and there were stranded fish squirming in the sand and small pools of water left behind.

Now the wind was starting to shift, a big change, nearly a one-eighty. And the breeze was something warmer and easier to embrace than the usual cold chill. She took off the jacket she was wearing and laid it down on the boulder, then she sat down on it, put her hands down behind her, and leaned back so she could close her eyes and feel the heat of the father on her face. That, and the warm wind, reminded her for a few precious moments of her youth in Florida, on warm beaches with a hot, bright yellow sun.

Somewhere out there in the Gulf, Peter and Tommy were snorkeling, looking for sand dollars or crabs, out past the first sandbar, where the water was a little deeper. Mom was behind her, sitting in the shade of that big umbrella and reading a book while she kept an eye on her children. Father, the pediatrician, was off at his important work, like always.

Kait's mask was next to her, and her snorkel and her fins. She stood up, kicked over the halfhearted sand castle she'd been building, grabbed the fins and mask and snorkel, and headed toward the water, shouting at her brothers, "Hey, wait up!" Then she was splashing into the shallow water, then wading deeper, then slipping on the fins and spitting into the mask and swishing around the spit on the glass so it wouldn't fog up, and diving in, putting the snorkel mouthpiece between her teeth and giving one good blow out to clear it, and then off she went, catching up with Tom and Peter. The three of them swam together between the two sandbars, checking out the crabs and sand dollars and pockets of seaweed with the minnows darting around. Warm and wet and thoroughly wonderful, those shallow waters.

It had been a wonderful childhood, no question, until Father ruined it, ruined everything. The bedroom they'd built for her in Whistle's compound had brought all that back to her.

There was a lot of whistling going on. She came out of her daydream and saw Smiles coming up toward her, waving, whistling some kind of warning, pointing at the sky. Kait turned to look, and there, out to sea, was a squall line, dark and green, with waterspouts, a line of them, dropping down into the water. Behind it there was a wave, a big one, coming their way. The word came to her: *seiche*. That was why the water had receded; it had been pushed away by the wind. And then, when the wind shifted, back the water came, a kind of tsunami. It would wash all the way up this small beach, and partway up the bluff, probably.

It was headed their way, and coming fast. Kait scrambled down off the boulder and ran toward Smiles. When she got to her, Kait turned around once more to look at the squall line and the waterspouts and that wave, and it all was coming, too fast.

She looked around. All the S'hudonni were gone, into their homes and into the water pools. They could stay down for hours; they'd be fine under the water, swimming back and rebuilding when it all passed by.

But Smiles had stayed with Kait, who couldn't hold her breath for more than a couple of minutes at best. Kait had to climb. Smiles went with her, trying to get to the bluff and get up it before the squall line and then the wave hit them.

Together, the two of them ran toward the steps that went up the bluff fifty meters or more, and then they were on them and climbing. The wave caught them about three flights up, and as it turned out, that was just high enough.

Kait and Smiles had to wait a full day before the storm was finally done with them. They couldn't get back to the village even after the water receded; the wind and rain were too much for Kait. They found a cave near the top of the bluff, though maybe cave was too grand a term for the indentation in the soft clay. It went into the bluff for four or five meters and it angled slightly to the right, so it got Kait out of the wind and the rain, at least.

After the height of the storm had passed by, Smiles left the cave and walked down to the storm-tossed beach, huge waves still crashing in right up to the bluff, to see how the Mother and the other villagers were doing. Then she swam out to get Kait a meal.

After a while, she brought back the news that the villagers were fine, having weathered the storm underwater for the most part, and that they would be rebuilding as soon as the wind let up. And she held in her small hands two eel-like creatures. She told Kait that they were delicacies, and Kait was hungry enough to not question that idea, though they were repulsive to look at, covered in a kind of mucus with a greenish tint to it. They had large oval eyes that dripped the same mucus, and nasal slits that did the same. They looked long, thin, and awful. But they tasted fine, and she felt better for having eaten one of them, chewy and slimy though it was.

A few hours later the storm was finally done with them and they walked down to the village together, thinking they'd help where they could, but the villagers had it all well in hand. They had even shoved Smiles's backpack into a safety hole, and when they pulled it out it seemed fine. So now Kait and Smiles had a backpack full of food and water, and rain gear for Kait, and it was time to say good-bye to the villagers and, especially, to the Mother. Then they were on their way, walking up the switchback path to the top of the bluff, where they found the paved path. Kait marveled at seeing it dry and clear. How was that done? She whistled that question to Smiles, who whistled back that no one knew, that the Old Ones had left behind many things that everyone used without really knowing how they worked.

And so the conversation about the Old Ones took up the next couple of hours as Smiles and Kait walked the path, knowing that if they kept on it long enough they'd reach Peter's village. At first there was a lot of talk about the Old Ones, who'd left behind so much technology that S'hudon had learned to use: the screamships and freighters, the Travel beds, the power units that ran everything from the sleds that ran over the paths to the great ships that traveled the stars.

When they ran low on conversation, Kait had time to think about all that had happened to her to get her to this point in life, and what the future might hold. Funny how her life back in Pasadena with Sarah seemed an impossibly long time ago. This—escaping from Whistle's compound and walking along with her S'hudonni friend on an ancient path, heading toward safety with Peter on this alien planet—this was reality now, and it seemed strangely normal. Of course it was always evening; of course the strange insects buzzing about, the clouds, the light rain, the exploding plants, and the floating blimpies.

The blimpies! She looked up as she had that thought. She looked, and there, inland as they walked the path, were three of the blimpies—escorts, she supposed. She waved at them and Smiles laughed and clicked and whistled at them, but there was no response.

It was full of wonder, all of this, and she knew it. But she missed the hell out of the life she'd had. She'd struggled mightily to wade through a lot of deep trouble and construct a good life with Sarah—sturdy, reliable, loving, caring Sarah. She wanted that life back. And what she was doing here was taking steps—literally!—to make that happen.

She laughed at herself and her little joke, and Smiles cast a look her way to see what was up, but Kait waved it off and grinned at her. They were doing fine, walking along with their blimpie escort, all of them heading toward Peter and the safe comfort of his home.

Somehow the path stayed dry even as it wound through flooded bogs and then through wet, decimated stands of trees. The trees here along the Old Ones' path had several narrow trunks each, which wound around one another and became a merged unit, ten or twelve meters tall, with huge, wide, dark leaves that spread open at the top to get what energy they could from that dim, red sun. Seedpods hung from small branches off the multiple trunks. If you bumped the tree's base, the pods burst, with small, black seeds pouring out.

The first stand of these trees they came to had been flattened by the storm, especially on its outer ring, which had faced that ferocious wind. Farther in, the crush of fallen trees finally eased, and a few stronger trees had survived upright. Farther still and the survival rate looked much better, with most of the older and stronger trees still standing.

Somehow, the paved path was clear of debris all the way through the woods, as if the fallen trees had been careful to avoid blocking the path.

And on the boglands, the path seemed to rise as necessary to stay slightly atop the shallow water they crossed. Within a day or two, she supposed, much of the water might drain away, but for now it would be impossible going if not for the path.

Smiles was a lot better at swimming than walking, so she kept parting ways with Kait, heading off on her own when the path wound close to the sea and then swimming forward to reconnect with Kait two or three kilometers down the road.

This gave Kait plenty of time alone—there was no one else on the path the entire time they walked it—to recall what she missed the most about Earth and home. Sunshine and blue skies, for one. Hot weather, for another. Busy streets, human chatter as you walked along. Restaurants! Baseball games! Museums! She would give about anything right then to take the tram up the hill to the Getty Museum and just walk around, inside and out, to marvel at the art and the scenery. To be home. Earth. California. Los Angeles. Pasadena. Sarah.

It was good to think of these things. To hope she'd have them again. And then she came out of the woods and the path angled toward the water and there, walking toward her, was Smiles, waving.

If it weren't for Smiles and her friendship, the months in that compound would have driven Kait into madness. It was Smiles who'd made it survivable. And now, after their Great Escape, here she was, walking along on an alien world, with a friend who was about as different as a friend could be, and on her way to see her brother, and together, the two of them, they would, eventually, go home. She'd get there. She'd be with Sarah again, in their little house on their little street in Pasadena. Life would be good again. She promised herself that. Heck, Smiles could come visit; she and Sarah would get along great.

And then she swatted at the inevitable insects that had followed them all the way from Whistle's compound and were back again within a couple of hours of the storm ending, buzzing around her but never landing, never biting. She was too different for them, she guessed, and she laughed at that thought. Too different; that was her.

This went on, but by the third time Kait reconnected with Smiles, Kait was getting tired and asked Smiles about their taking a break for a while to eat and rest. So, at the next stand of flattened forest, they got into the middle of the woods, in a place where at least half the trees were still standing, and settled down on the path to rest.

Smiles's backpack was surprisingly capacious, and she happily dug into it to find something special for Kait: some Earth-style bread that it didn't seem possible for her to have found in that village, and some salted fish, which Kait thought was a much improved meal over the mucus-covered eels. And then they talked, the two of them, in a kind of Shunglish that they'd stumbled into, a combination of English and S'hudonni that didn't convey much information but they both found hilarious. It was a good, pleasant hour, and then Smiles let Kait have another hour for a nap and they were off, an odd pair to be best friends, but that's what it was, friendship, thought Kait, as she walked alone, mostly, while Smiles did her swimming.

It was three such stops later that Smiles heard something. They had met on a spot where the low boglands edged right up to the beach for a kilometer or more. Smiles was sitting on the Old Ones' path, waiting for Kait, who emerged from a distant wood and followed the path as it slowly angled toward the beach and then started climbing up the next hill, which made for another bluff overlooking the beach.

Smiles, as she often did, walked along for a while, climbing the hill with Kait. If there was a path, she'd take it down the bluff after walking awhile. The path wound along the cliff edge, offering impressive views of the rocky beach below and the Great Bight, open water seeming to stretch away into the distance forever, though ultimately, Kait now knew, that sea grew warm and then terribly hot on the sunstruck, unlivable side of the planet. Go far enough in the other direction and there was nothing but the frozen wasteland of a perpetual ice cap that covered about one-third of the planet.

The weather was cloudy and cool, misty but with no real rain, and a light breeze coming in from the water to rise up over the bluff and ease its way past Kait and Smiles. Pleasant for walking, really.

But the blimpies stopped them. All three of the blimpies had moved toward them without Kait and Smiles really noticing, and now the blimpies floated in front of them, no more than ten meters up, facing them, those huge eyes, the tentacles hanging down.

Smiles held up her hand to ask Kait, "Did you hear that?"

"Hear what? From the blimpies? Why are they stopped like that?" asked Kait.

"It certainly sounded like a cry for help. In English."

It took Kait a second to process that, and then she stopped in her tracks. "*In English?*" There were only two Earthies on the whole planet. Peter!

The blimpies now were moving, straight toward the edge of the bluff that ran along the shore, then out over the beach, as Kait ran to the edge of the bluff herself, with Smiles right behind her. They looked down to the base of the small cliff and the beach beyond and could see it covered in detritus from the storm. There was a small travel sled upended, empty, wedged into some boulders at the base of the low cliff on the far side. The waves must have washed right up to the bluff.

And there, nearly at the footpath that led from the beach up to where they stood, was someone, yelling and waving. Peter. Peter!

"We're coming!" she screamed into the wind, and started running, scrambling, tumbling in her hurry to get down the path, which had two switchbacks to navigate. Smiles did her best but lagged behind.

It wasn't more than a minute before Kait reached the bottom and could see Peter there. He was sitting next to two large boulders on the beach, leaning back against one of them, his right arm soaked in blood. She ran to him, kneeled next to him, and took a little of her fresh water and splashed it on his face, put a few drops into his mouth.

His eyes opened. "It's OK, Peter. I'm here," she said. "You'll be fine. I'm here."

"Kait," he said, mumbling. "Thank god."

PART FIVE

TOGETHERNESS

I thought I'd lost my only friend on S'hudon, poor little
Treble. But I'd found my sister. Or, more properly, she'd
found me. It was a very emotional moment, and we later
heard that on Harmony the whole world was watching,
and those who could afford it were drinking the Dew of
Kenmare in my honor.

—Peter Holman, *Notes from Holmanville*
(S'hudon City and New York:
Trebnet Press, 2035)

13

COMMAND PERFORMANCE

Kait and her S'hudonni friend, Smiles, brought me out of the cold and wet and into a shallow cave in the bluff. I told them about Treble, and Smiles went to search for him, but found nothing. Without any electronics to help, it was, I knew, an impossible task to do more.

While Smiles was gone, Kait told me her whole, long story and I've added it into this narrative, including material I heard from her later, too.

While she talked, she propped up my knee and bandaged my right arm enough to stop the bleeding, and then rigged up a sling for me before sitting me up against the back wall, so that I could see out the cave mouth opening to the coarse sand and boulders on the beach and the gray sea and gray sky beyond.

When Smiles returned she dug into her backpack for some Earthie meds that she'd brought along for Kait. She dosed me up with naproxen and a lot of freshwater and some self-heat Earthie food. That helped. The arm's bleeding had stopped, so they cleaned and wrapped those scrapes. All in all, I'd survived, and after a couple of hours of this I thought maybe I could walk out with them, getting back on the Old Ones' path and heading toward my little fake village of Holmanville and the safety it held for us all.

But that didn't help Treble, and that was really the first thing on my mind once I'd recovered enough to think straight. Yes, I was overjoyed to be rescued by Kait and her S'hudonni pal, and yes, it was wonderful to be alive. I'd thought I was a goner, I told them, and Kait laughed as she explained to Smiles what that meant.

But Treble was my friend, and my guide, and my mentor despite his apparent youth. Plus, he was the son of Twoclicks and Whistle and so the heir to the throne. So I stood up—pretty damn shaky, to be honest—and started hobbling toward the cave mouth. At the moment, the knee hurt the most. I'd twisted something in there badly, and the knee hadn't been any good since I tore it up playing basketball a few years before, trying to penetrate the trees and dish the ball out to the shooting forward. Still, damn it, I was going to get out there and look for the princeling.

Smiles clicked and whistled at Kait when I did that, and Kait came over to me, put her hand on my shoulder, and said, "Don't be stupid, Peter. We know how important he is. But you're not capable of doing any searching right now. Just sit back down."

That seemed sort of like a command from my sister, probably the first one she'd issued me since we were kids on the beach together and she'd tell me to behave myself when I came near her sandcastle.

I sat back down and listened as Smiles and Kait did a lot of whistling and clicking back and forth, with a few words in English tossed into the mix: *sled*, and *quicker*, and *tent* were what I heard popping up in that animated conversation.

"You're pretty damn fluent, Kaitie," I said to her when they paused.

She just smiled at me and said, "Here's what we're going to do, Peter. We found a small sled stuck into the sand and rocks. Smiles has pulled it out and walked it up to the top of the cliff edge. She says it's empty, but it works fine on the path, so you and I will get you onto that and head toward your village and some help.

"Smiles, though, will move much faster in the water than we all will on land, so she's leaving in a few minutes to swim along the coast toward that same place. She's left us the camping gear, including a nice little tent that will do fine for us. We'll all meet up on the path, near Holmanville. If she gets there first—and that's likely—she'll get help and they'll come on the path toward us. The sooner we can get you into a suitable medcot the better."

"That's fine," I said. "But what about Treble?"

"Smiles will leave a message for him here, then while she's in the water she'll keep an eye and an ear out for any sign of Treble. We'll do the same as we take the path."

"Treble is what matters," I said, and was about to offer some thoughts on how we could walk the beaches instead of the path, but Kait wasn't paying any attention to me. She'd already turned away to have another quick conversation with Smiles, who nodded her head yes in a very deliberate Earthie bit of communication, aimed at me, I'm sure.

Then she came over, put her hand on my shoulder, and said, in English, "I will get help, Peter. You stay with your sister, all right?"

"Sure," I said. "I'm feeling better all the time." Which wasn't quite true, but I managed to get to my feet again to show off my mobility. The arm hurt like hell, but there was plenty of naproxen, and moving toward safety and some medical attention seemed better than sticking it out here in this cold, damp cave.

"You'll feel better as soon as we can get you back to Twoclicks' staff," Smiles said. "I'm sure they have a medcot with Earthie settings on it for you."

I nodded my agreement. There was no use pretending I'd be any use at all in a search. Hell, I'd just slow things down. So I watched as Smiles reached into a small pouch she was wearing around her waist, pulled out a small device, and spoke to it. Then she left the cave and headed off down the beach, where she stuck the device into sand next to the boulder where I'd been trapped. She turned once to wave to us, then she waded into the water for a few moments, dived forward and was instantly gone from sight, heading out to get help, or find Treble, or both.

We watched her go, and then I held Kait's hand as we left the cave and walked along the sand toward the switchback path that wound its way up the bluff, and there, at the top, to the path of the Old Ones. It took some time and three different stops for me to rest, but eventually we got there, and after we loaded up the battered sled, I sat down on it as Kait walked ahead of me, towing it. It was the very one that almost killed me, of course, so there was a certain irony to using it now to save my sorry ass. And off we went, walking back to Holmanville, a place I never thought I'd miss but right then was anxious to reach. Home, sweet home.

Time passed all too slowly as I rode behind my sister. I had plenty of time to think about things, though there was a deep ache in my right arm and a sharp, breathtaking stab of pain when I tried to adjust the sling. I felt feverish and weak. But I was glad to be alive, and able to talk with my sister. I just wished that we'd already found our way to that promised medcot where I could sleep as the thing healed me.

But the whole point of the exercise had been to not have an electronic footprint, and Kait said that was true for them, too. The device that Smiles had left on the beach didn't broadcast or receive, so it was safe enough. If Treble was alive and came to that beach, he'd run across it, listen, and know what was up.

That all sounded pretty damn unlikely to me, but what the hell did I know? Nothing, really. So I sat there, and occasionally got off to stretch my legs and try to walk along, using my good arm to wave off the inevitable buzzing insects that hovered around all the time, rain or shine, though "shine" wasn't anything we were going to see again anytime soon. The weather had returned to its stable, misty, dark gray, light rain self. It was warm enough, fourteen or fifteen Celsius, which was great for walking as long you could ignore the wet. I was getting good at that after a few months on the planet. The weather always reminded me of Ireland.

14

SOMETHING HONEST

I sat on the cushioned floor of the tent, my back against one wall, my legs out in front of me. There was no way the left knee was going to bend enough for me to sit any other way on that floor, and we had no chairs; even the backpack wasn't big enough to serve as one. I didn't care. We were out of the wind and rain, there was hot food and cold water, and I wouldn't have to step out into the nasty weather except to relieve myself. I promised myself to hang on and only do that once.

I was surprised at how easy it had been to set up camp after the light mist that we'd been traveling through had hardened into a good rain and threatened to turn into a downpour.

Kait said it was time to get out of the weather and into the tent. I was dreading trying to use my right arm in any useful way to hurriedly set up the camp, but Kait told me not to worry, she had it all under control. She pulled a small black box about the size of an old hardcover book out of her backpack and pressed a black dot on the top of the box and stepped back to watch the tent unfold. It unfolded by itself again and again, larger with each unfolding, turning itself into a dry, comfortable tent with a padded floor and a space big enough for two to sit or lie in and tall enough for Kait, at least, to stand.

The unfolding took about a minute and then Kait pulled back the flap and we both crawled in, grateful to be dry. Let it rain!

We took a few minutes to get out of our rain gear and hang it up to dry, and another few for Kait to pull out the heat-and-eat Earthie meals and pull the heat tabs on them, and then we were quite comfortable, thanks.

We ate, Kait talking about the raw fish and slimy eels she'd eaten with Smiles. "Better than you'd think," she said with a smile. "But mucus is mucus, you know?"

I laughed my first laugh in a long time, and that led us both into some silly cackling that lasted a minute or two, the safety of our current situation relieving the tension we'd both felt building for months, maybe years. I was here. Kait was here. We were safe.

When we calmed down from the giggles, I told her this reminded me of the time we'd camped in the backyard back on our little island, the three of us: Kait, me, and our brother Tom.

She laughed. "It was pretty damn crowded, wasn't it? The three of us crammed into that tent that Mom bought for the family camping trip that never happened. Remember how complicated it was to set that tent up? Took the three of us an hour, I bet. Tom was the one who finally figured it out."

"Yep," I said. "Not like this Taj Mahal we're in here."

"And flashlights!" she said, and I laughed again. We'd forgotten the flashlights when we set it up, so the three of us ran inside the house to get a couple and Mom was baking cookies for us and one thing led to another, so we wound up back in the tent a half hour later with plenty of chocolate chip cookies and still no flashlights. It became a family joke that lasted for years: *Flashlights!*

"Good memories, Kaitie," I said, "eating those cookies and some popcorn and crawling out at three in the morning to look up at the stars."

"And finally getting a flashlight," Kait added, smiling.

We paused. I was thinking of Tom and Kait and me and how we'd got along so well as kids, before it all fell apart.

I said, quietly, carefully, afraid to bring this up, really, "I'm so sorry about Tom, and Whistle, and what they did to you, Kaitie. It was horrible."

"Tom?" she asked. "What did he have to do with all this?"

So she hadn't seen the letter I'd sent; she didn't know about her own part in the violence on Earth. She didn't know that she'd died—or some version of her had died—and that Tom and Whistle had made that happen.

"You didn't get the last letter I sent, Kaitie?"

"I never got any letters from you, Petey. If it came, I never saw it. It all happened so fast! I left everything sitting on my desk in my hateful little bedroom in that compound." She shook her head. "I'm sorry."

I took a deep breath. This was not going to be an easy thing to talk about, but it had to be done. "All right, Kaitie," I said. "I sent you a letter because the Mother gave me permission to contact you that way and guaranteed that Whistle or his people wouldn't read it first."

"*The* Mother?" she asked. "The one in charge of everything?"

I nodded. "Yep. I'll tell you that story later. But first, in the letter I told you some things you need to know, things about what happened to you back on Earth, and why. And I have to warn you that it's tough stuff."

"But nothing happened, Peter," she said. "I was in a car, and then out cold, and then I woke up . . ." She stared at me. She saw the expression on my face. "Oh, god, Peter. What did they do to me? Oh my god!"

That had really set her off, and I couldn't blame her. But I didn't think anything like what she feared had happened, though I couldn't swear to it.

I raised my hands to calm her down. "You need to hear this, Kait, OK? Please?"

She glared at me, a kind of anger in those eyes that I'd never seen before. But I had to tell her. "Just fucking tell me," she said, in a calm, strong voice.

So I told her, in as calm a way as I could, about her death, about Tom's part in it, about that terrible, terrible day back on Earth, when Whistle tried to seize control, using her as a weapon to make that happen.

"Kaitie, the S'hudonni have a device that can send people instantly from one place to another."

"I know," she said. "Smiles told me they call them Travel beds, and they're just one of the hundreds of things they found here when they first landed, stuff that the Old Ones left behind. Most of it a thousand years old or more but still working. Even those screamships that tore up Earth so bad. They're hand-me-downs from whoever the hell those Old Ones were."

I nodded, said, "Hell, Kaitie, unzip that flap and go outside and look up and what do you see?"

"Our shepherds," she said. "Those blimpies, keeping an eye on us."

"How do they fly?" I asked. "And how does this path stay dry and perfectly paved? And how do those screamships really work? And on and on. The S'hudonni don't know. And those daffodils from Harmony, smart as they are, I don't think they really know either. Treble is the smartest S'hudonni I've met, and he just brushed off my questions about those things. And if he doesn't know . . ."

"Maybe they don't want *us* to know?" Kaitie said. And she had a point. Maybe that was it. Or maybe not.

I went on. "The sending unit copies the person exactly and then sends that copy to the receiving unit, which can be thousands of kilometers away. The original person is still there, back on the Travel bed. So after he kidnapped you and drugged you, Kaitie, Whistle put you on a Travel bed and copied you. Then he sent you, the real you, off somewhere, maybe to one of his ships. They took that drugged-up copy of you and loaded it up as a bomb and put that drugged-up copy in Ireland, where I was on that diplomatic tour with Twoclicks and Heather. The idea, I'm sure, was for the bomb to kill you, and Twoclicks, and Heather, and me. Twoclicks and Heather have copies, so killing them didn't really end them. But me? No copies for me, that would have been it, and that was Whistle's point, I'm sure.

"And it almost worked, Kaitie. Twoclicks was safe but it did nearly kill me and Heather. I survived because Heather got me into a medcot that patched me up.

"Kait," I said, squeezing her hand, "I thought you were dead in that explosion. I didn't really know about the Travel beds then, and I'd only seen it work once and that was for Heather, and hell, she's one of them, not one of us.

"So I thought you were gone, and I've never hated anyone so much as I hated our Tom and his pal Whistle just then."

She was still staring at me, her face impassive. She could have been listening to somebody talking about a baseball score or a movie they'd seen or a politician they didn't like.

"Tom was part of it, Kaitie. Later, he came to see me and denied he knew anything about their using you, but I think he did. I've never been violent, Kaitie, but if I could have wrapped my hands around his neck that night after the explosion, I would have. And choked and choked until he was dead. I would have.

"But then Heather explained to me that the original you—You! The one sitting right here with me in this tent!—was probably still alive, held by Whistle and his people. We found out a little later that Heather was right, that they'd put you on a ship and brought you here to the home world as a hostage. And so that's why I'm come here, Kait, to find you and bring you home. The real you, back to Earth and Sarah and safety.

"On my last day on Earth I told Sarah about you. She knows the real you, the original you, is alive. She told me to say that she loves you and she's waiting for you and praying for you to come home."

Kait was still holding my hand. She said, "Oh, Petey," and gripped it tighter.

"You saved my life today, Kait," I said.

"Oh, Petey," she said again. "This is all pretty hard to believe. I mean, I'm me, right?"

"You're you," I said, and squeezed her hand one more time. "You are so you, Kaitie."

We slept fitfully for hours after that, listening to the raindrops bounce off the tent material—something else made by the Old Ones, I guessed, or maybe those crafty daffodils on Harmony. Then we got up after the rain had eased, ate some warm food, packed ourselves up, and got back on the path, not talking much about the great revelations of the night before.

On we went, quiet for a good hour, me sitting on the sled and occasionally trying to walk along some with Kait. Woods, shoreline, bogs and repeat.

Finally, I asked, "How'd you find me, Kaitie? Did Smiles have some great tech that pinpointed where I was somehow?"

Kait smiled—and that was awfully good to see—and said, "I thought it was just dumb luck, Petey, that we happened by, and that Smiles has great hearing. But, you know, there were blimpies tagging along with us, and they came a lot closer to us when we were up on that bluff above your beach there. Maybe they were trying to tell us something? Could be."

"Yeah," I said. Could be. And then I looked to our left, inland, and there were three of them over there, over the bog, browsing to feed as they followed along with us, those tentacles reaching down to grab plants or small animals and bring them up to the mouth. Seemed pretty clear to me that the blimpies were very much keeping an eye on us, helping where they could. I wished to hell I had Treble with me to explain the hows and whys of that help, that interest in us. And that made me hope to hell that Treble was all right, that he'd survived the storm and found his way home and was waiting for us now. I really liked that kid.

"Really," Kaitie said, "it's Smiles that's the one responsible for any life-saving that went on, Petey."

"That you were there at all is because you broke free, Kaitie," I said. "And thank god for that. How'd you two get to be such friends? And where did you pick up these language skills? I'm impressed."

"There's a story there, Petey," she said.

"I bet," I said, and chuckled. "And this is a good time to tell it."

She smiled again, said, "True enough," and then, as we walked, she talked about her time in captivity.

The story started off with joy and satisfaction, I could tell. Kait had never thought of herself as a risk taker, even in those darkest days when she was strung out on horse and oppy and meth and every other damn thing that came long. That wasn't taking risks, she explained; that was running away from risk. Did I understand that?

I did. Family trait, in fact, I thought at that moment.

But now, here, she'd attempted—and succeeded—at the Great Escape! The way she said it sounded to me like it deserved being capitalized. She'd done it. Without hesitating, without worry over it and wondering if she'd be killed or caught and punished; she'd summoned up the courage and held hands with her S'hudonni pal Smiles, and now here she was, with me, nearly home, nearly safe.

Now she could put things behind her, she said. The cold mornings when she'd wake up in her strange and awful bedroom—exactly like the one she'd grown up in on the beach all those years ago—from the usual troubled sleep with the usual bad dreams.

Day after day after day, for ten or fifteen ten-days—it was hard to keep track—she would come awake as the room powered up and the lights rose and some heat drifted in from the walls. She'd get up. She'd be cold. She'd be wondering if this was one of the mornings when Whistle would pay her a visit and blame all her problems on me and on Twoclicks. She'd hope like hell it wasn't; he scared the hell out of her.

But then she'd get things moving. She was always cold in the morning—if you could call it morning in a place where the red father never sets or rises. Always, she could see her breath in the cold and humid air. Breathe in. Breathe out.

She would kick off the covers, she told me, then stand to put her feet on the cold floor, then roll her neck to get the cricks out, and then walk over to the tiny bathroom, with its sink and toilet. She'd pee first. The toilet seat was cold, but at least it was from Earth, and at least there was a toilet and at least it worked. And at least there was the luxury of toilet paper.

Then she would rise from that seat, take one step over and be at the sink, where she'd turn the single tap and cold water would emerge. She'd cup her hands and drink some, grateful to have it. Then she'd splash some water on her face, use the toothbrush and Colgate toothpaste—Toothpaste! From Earth!—for that whiter smile as she faced her day of, basically, doing nothing.

At least the water seemed safe. Smiles told her on the very first day they met that water is water, just like home. Sure, she thought, after you've been injected with enough nanos to handle the parasites. Ha! That had been a pretty horrible ten-day, the whole decontamination thing they'd put her through after she woke up in the compound. Flushing everything out that was old; injections or pills or suppositories for everything new.

I told her they'd put me through the same thing: a full ten-day of decontamination and nano injections. It was no damn fun at all, but at least I felt safer in this cold, dark, damp alien place.

There was the three-drawer dresser, a facsimile made here on S'hudon, she was sure, since it was made of some kind of fiberboard, though it looked exactly like the one made of pine that she'd grown up with. On the top of that dresser lay her soccer trophies and sand dollars from the beach and the poster on the wall of the smiling faces of Temple of Justice, the boy band she'd loved so much when she was ten.

Smiles always made room on that dresser to place Kait's clothes for the day ahead. They didn't fit her very well, but to have Earthie clothes at all seemed remarkable. Blue jeans that she'd roll up the cuffs on and tighten at the waist with the leather belt that was provided. A long-sleeved plaid flannel shirt that hung on her loosely, but she'd tighten it at the bottom by knotting it, and that worked OK. So did the shower that had hot water once a day, and the hot food that appeared in the desk drawer opposite her bed. It was usually rice or pasta, with some kind of diced meat. Best not to know exactly, she supposed. And there was that cold water to drink, and once a day a large mug of hot coffee delivered by Smiles.

That was how Kait and Smiles became friends, talking about hot coffee on Earth and Kait saying how amazing it was that Smiles could conjure up a passable cup of black, one sugar, every morning.

It turned out that Smiles had learned English just for this job, and studied Earth culture and medicine and nutrition so she could take care of the Earthie who was coming to the compound. Smiles had been given two ten-days to learn these things and handled that with ease.

Kait, once she was past the shock of her arrival and into the phase where boredom replaced fear, told Smiles she wanted to learn the whistles and clicks of S'hudon. It seemed like a smart thing to do, and it turned out the language wasn't too hard once you get the hang of it, at least for Kait.

They would talk in each other's language for hours each day, about life on S'hudon, the cities, the towns, the people, the wider world of S'hudon and how her people came to populate it, and about life on the other worlds in the Six. Those worlds with their beings and their cultures, and how Kait should act when first she had the chance to meet the daffodils of Harmony or the ducks of Downtone or any of the others in S'hudon City or East Song. Now, with Earth making it the Seven, they would all want to meet her.

It was strange how, after several ten-days of these lessons, Kait came to think of Smiles as a friend, someone she could talk to about life on Earth and how that had been for her—the good and, too often, the bad.

I told her how much I envied her that friendship. I'd had something like that with Treble, I told her. I really liked the princeling and it was hard to believe he was gone.

Kait came over to lean down over the sled where I sat and give me a hug and I hugged her right back. Then she stood up and started walking again, holding onto the sled's leash, while I sat on the sled and rested my knee and worried that I could feel the blood flowing again from my right arm. Onward. One more day, I figured, or maybe two, and we'd be back.

15

WHISTLE STOP

Whistle, second son of the Mother of All Mothers, brother of Twoclicks, father of Treble, Administrator of Trade for three worlds in the Mercantile Empire, Governor-General of Canadian North America, South Asia, China, Korea, Urals, and Sahel Africa, is visibly upset. Dressed in formal attire for the ritual he intends to perform, he has a tunic festooned with medals and he wears his bandolier. It holds no detectable energy weapons but has a wonderfully sharp blade half the length of his arm.

Sitting on his throne on his grounded palanquin in the middle of the spacious courtyard of his commodious compound, he waits for the royal blimpies, tamed and trustworthy, to float in above him, drift down to attach themselves to the upper rigging of the palanquin, and take him to the Old Ones' Path and the Earthie and the traitor who are part of the cabal that has cheated him of his rightful place on Earth, that newest colony and the one where Twoclicks, his brother, has caused such problems that only Whistle can fix.

The blimpies are late, and the blimpies, his blimpies, are never late. He will teach them a lesson later, he thinks, but only after today's obligations are met. After his release from the five-day detention at the Mother's palace there was a great rush on ground transport to this compound, where he demanded the Earthie, Kaitlyn. His guards had to explain that Kaitlyn and her tutor, Smiles, had fled to the path of the Old Ones, where a village Mother had come to protect them. They waited out that storm there, and now, his guards are certain, they are on the path of the Old Ones, walking toward the village that Twoclicks built for his pet Earthie, Peter Holman.

So he sits on his palanquin throne, waiting for his blimpies, planning how he will do what he wants to do with Kaitlyn Holman and the traitorous Smiles. It will require some negotiating with the local Mother, and the price will be high. But he will have his way with them, of that he is certain.

There is a deep, soft sigh from above and Whistle looks up. Four blimpies are coming in toward him, easing down into the courtyard, hovering over the palanquin, their tentacles with those fingers at the end reaching down to the top frame of the palanquin. It is not his usual team of blimpies; these don't wear the barbed harnesses that allow Whistle the control he likes. He is too angry to care. These will do. They will carry him, all but undetectably since he'll carry no technology, to wherever on the Old Ones' Path the despicable human Kaitlyn and the traitor Smiles are walking. He will end this whole charade then. His blade, of excellent steel from the planet Harmony, where the energetic daffodils make wonderful weapons of all sorts, will certainly get the job done.

All four blimpies are sighing, with those deep soulful exhalations that mark a blimpie's descent, as they reach down to grasp the palanquin and then rise, taking Whistle where he needs to go.

Kait brought me awake with gentle prods and more naproxen to dull the deep ache in my arm and knee that became shooting, searing pain when I stood and tried to walk. But walk I must, so in a few minutes we were back in motion, me hobbling along or sitting by turn, Kait walking and pulling the sled, with me or without me on it. We headed down the switchbacks of the slope.

We were, I was sure, nearly to Holmanville. I remembered these steep hills from the walk out, when it had all been so much easier for me than now, on the walk back.

Three final hills. Switchback paths up and down, a few hundred meters of flat, dry turf at the top. Which was where we were now. The climb up to the top had worn us both out. I'd had to get off and walk the steeper parts where Kait couldn't tug me up on the sled. We'd done it, in spitting and cold rain that made it all the more miserable, but we'd gotten to the top and, there, had opened the tent and taken a break.

The downhill side turned out to be easier for Kait but just as difficult for me as the uphill side. My torn-up knee, the one that had ended my basketball career, was more painful going down than going up. The only silver lining was that the pain from the knee temporarily blocked the pain from the arm. Ugh.

To add to the misery, the rain kept on, hard enough at times to be stinging. Soon I had to take another break and sit for a spell, with Kait doing all the hard work, handling the simple hand brake on the sled as down we went, with my leg propped up on the sled's rail.

We had rain gear, of course, thin-ply, rain-repellent ponchos, one for her and one that was meant for Smiles but worked, mostly, for me. That square piece of material was too short to have done me much good if I was walking, but for something to hold over my head as I sat there on the sled it worked fine. I wasn't dry, but I wasn't soaked, and so, eventually, we reached the flat swamp below and began following the path across that fen, and then we started uphill again. We were making progress.

But then conditions got even worse. Walking steeply uphill and away from the coast seemed to mean more wind and colder temperatures. As we struggled along, the wind picked up and the temperature dropped and dropped again, all in the space of thirty minutes or so. The wind was coming from the north, the cold, perpetually frozen, sunless side of S'hudon, and even after traveling across two thousand kilometers of open water, it still carried a bite.

We trudged upward, me walking when I could, sitting when I must; Kait doing all the hardest work—busy saving us both, I kept thinking, as I did my best.

The cold rain turned to sleet, the first I'd seen on S'hudon, as we climbed higher, and that slushy mess started to accumulate on the sled and on my little square handheld roof as I sat on the sled. I was cold, and getting colder fast. I decided to try and walk for a while again and eased my way off the slowly moving sled and stood there. The left knee ached. The path stayed wet but the sleet melted on contact and the water ran off rapidly to the sides, so the footing was good.

The wind went up a notch again. I'd walked this path in the other direction just a few days ago, and there'd been nothing but deep purple clouds and a light rain. That had been downright pleasant to walk in, by comparison.

It certainly wasn't pleasant now. We had to get over the spine that was still a steep half kilometer or so ahead of us, and then down the other side, where the path ran downhill at an angle that led to the Great Bight. I could hope that it would get warmer as we went downhill, and if I remembered it all correctly, it wasn't more than five or six kilometers or so after that and we'd be back in Holmanville.

I couldn't handle the walking. My knee was screaming at me with sharp daggers, and I could feel the wounds in the right arm oozing through the bandages. I was warmer for the effort of walking, but the pain was too high a price to pay, so it was freeze on the sled or limp along slowly on foot.

I climbed back on the sled, slowly and painfully, shivering in the wind as the sleet disappeared, and in the space of ten minutes, no more, the clouds thinned and that red father up there started to poke through. That made the struggle up the last switchback a little easier until, thank god, we reached the top of that hill and collapsed, the both of us, behind a huge boulder that blocked the wind and faced that thin, cruel bit of red father and warmed us a bit and we felt better.

The blimpies that had been over us all along this journey—one and sometimes two of them ahead or behind or beside us, up a few hundred meters, watching us, through wind and rain and even that horrible sleet—made a deep, rumbling sigh. Then they turned to face back where we'd been and started drifting in that direction.

I was too tired to move, but Kait stood, brushed off her pants, and then walked back to the edge of the steep incline we'd just come up. "Petey," she said. "I see trouble coming our way."

Crap. I managed to stand, and I hobbled over to be next to her and took a look. There, on the far side of the valley we'd crossed a couple of hours ago, was a little flock of blimpies—or a pod or a school or a squadron, you tell me. Four of them. And together they seemed harnessed to a kind of flat deck, or maybe they were just holding on to it with their tentacles. The deck was festooned with banners, and in the middle of it, a large chair, a throne. Oh, hell, I'd seen that before. A palanquin, and in the middle of it, on his throne, was a S'hudonni. I knew who that had to be.

"Hell," I said. "Kaitie, that's Whistle. That's how he showed up that time I told you about, on the royal barge. Him and his tamed blimpies making a real show of landing on the barge and playing king."

"Oh, no," she said, and I added, "Yes, oh, no," myself.

Our own blimpies were now right above us. The one near me lowered its tentacles, put one around me, then another, then another. I could feel pinpricks and then a calm acceptance. I knew that feeling from my rescue in the storm. My knee pain and arm pain were still there, but somehow I didn't care. Was this the same blimpie? I couldn't tell, but I thought maybe it was.

I turned to look at Kait and she was wrapped, too. She looked calm, un-afraid, brave Kaitie. "I'm hearing them, Peter. Yours, mine, the ones over there with Whistle. I can hear them talking, a kind of humming. The blimp-ies? They're not so tame as Whistle thinks."

"So this is OK, do you think?" I said. "You know they saved me before, during that storm."

"Maybe the one that has you now is the one who saved you, Petey."

"I don't know," I said, and then it lifted me up, put me into a kind of sitting position, tentacles beneath me and behind me and across my lap.

We moved out over the crest of the hill and headed toward the palanquin that held Whistle. I managed to look back, and there was Kait, held by her blimpie and rising now and coming toward us.

I turned back. We were ten minutes away, at least, from our little midair meetup—me, Kait, and Whistle. What did the blimpies have planned for us? I was in no shape for any kind of physical confrontation, to be sure, but loaded up with sedatives from the barbs at the end of those tentacles, I felt up to having a little verbal joust with Whistle. Heck, that sounded like fun. Anything, in fact, sounded like fun.

I sat there, serene, held in the grip of those tentacles. I had plenty of time to study the tentacle that crossed my lap as a kind of seat belt. It was about as thick around as the business end of a baseball bat. It was dark gray with almost a bluish tint to it, and with hundreds of tiny suckers that opened or closed depending on the need. It was those suckers on the four different tentacles that held me so firmly in place. At the end of the tentacle was a four-fingered kind of hand, one of the fingers slightly set apart—maybe to serve as thumb for gripping purposes? I was guessing, of course.

I didn't see any barbs, so I wondered where they were. As I wondered, a good dozen of them emerged from the top of the tentacle that crossed my lap. *Well, all right, then*, I thought. *So they read minds, do they, the blimpies?* That would explain a lot.

Peaceful and wistful at the moment, I leaned over to look down. We were maybe two hundred meters up over the boglands, the hard pavement of the path to our left and the steep hills right in front and back behind us. It was all very scenic. They should bring Earthies here for fun rides, I thought. It was so incredibly peaceful. I could clearly hear the blimpies humming.

And then I felt a jab in my buttocks and in a few seconds all the pleasantries came to an end. I was suddenly alert, and tense, as we approached Whistle, the obscene creature who'd threatened me any number of times, had kidnapped my sister and brought her here, a zillion kilometers from her home and wife, so he could threaten and torment her and use her as a pawn in some power play he was making. It was awful. He was awful.

And he was smiling. As I got close enough to see that round face and those cruel eyes, I could tell he was as heavily drugged as I'd been. As I, in fact, still was, some small part of my brain was telling me. It's the drugs! It's the drugs!

So I tried to corral my emotions and stay calm. It wasn't easy. "Prince Whistle," I yelled to him, "how odd to meet you here."

"Peter Holman!" he said back. "Nice to see you! Beautiful weather we're having!"

Right. It had, in fact, stopped raining. I was surprised that Whistle could tell. He was doped to the gills—which, I thought, maybe he actually had.

"I have been looking for you, Peter Holman! And for your delightful sister, Kaitlyn Holman. Is that her?" He pointed toward the blimpie coming up beside me now, with Kaitie sitting in the tentacled seat. "Ho! Kaitlyn," he said. "I've been looking for you!"

"I bet," Kaitie said. Then she turned to me and said, "We are to keep him busy for a few moments, Peter."

I smiled. Easy enough. I turned back to face Whistle. "Prince Whistle, I see you've been released from detention. How nice that must be for you."

He laughed so hard that he shook, and then said, "All a big misunderstanding, Peter Holman. The Mother loves me! She would never harm me. I have too many friends!"

"I bet," Kait said to me again, quietly.

Whistle went on. "I will make corrections for you both, Peter and Kaitlyn Holman. Then no more problems!"

The humming was louder, a throb underneath it now, too.

Whistle stood up from his throne, reached into the bandolier that was wrapped over his torso, and pulled out a blade, something like a short sword you'd see in an old Roman-era movie. I remembered it as the same kind of blade that was used to dismember that little bender back at the dustup on the barge, gutting it and then pulling out the heart, which was handed to me.

Whistle held the blade up high and then stepped down from his throne and walked unsteadily toward us on his palanquin. He was whistling and clicking like mad, something furious. "He really hates you, Peter, and blames you for everything," Kait said. "He tried to kill you on Earth twice, he says, and didn't get it done. So now he's going to finish this."

"Sure he is, Kaitie," I said, as I wondered how I was going to get out of this midair tentacled seat to try and stop the carnage. Not that I could. That sober part of me, down deep, saw the situation with some clarity. It wasn't pretty. Even if I could manage to get out of my tentacle-chair position and onto the palanquin, I was in no shape to get into a fight. I'd get hacked to pieces.

But whatever chemicals were coursing through me at the moment had me thinking otherwise. I could handle him! I'd twist that sword out of his hand and stab him with it, that's all. Easy-peasy!

But I didn't have to. Kait, my sister Kait, the one who'd run and run from trouble all her life and finally found peace back home, but had then been yanked to this strange world and its strange inhabitations, had taken action. I watched her blimpie move forward and dump her right onto the palanquin, upright and ready to go, with some tentacles still holding her. There she was, ready to take on Whistle.

"Kait!" I yelled, but she didn't look. Instead, she stepped toward Whistle, who clicked like crazy at her, and her right back at him, and now the background rumbling and vibrations from the blimpies was louder and louder. I was vibrating with it over in my weird chair, and I could see the palanquin vibrating with it, too, and swaying and yawing. Whistle was trying to stand upright but only barely succeeding, as Kait, steady Kait, walked over to him, one tentacle from her blimpie still wrapped around her waist as she ducked underneath a wild swing of that blade and stepped toward Whistle to shove him, hard, so that he staggered to the edge, pointed the blade at the base of the palanquin and shoved it down to steady himself, turned to glare and make a noise I could barely hear over the thunderous vibrations from the blimpies as he steadied himself, started to pull that sword out from the palanquin floor and then, in a heartbeat, that all didn't seem to matter. The noise and thunder from the blimpies reached a deep crescendo and, all at once, the tentacles holding the palanquin all let go and down it went, fluttering like a piece of paper with Whistle, going end over end, plunging past it and down and down again and into the bog, a thousand meters down.

16

THE MOTHER

The blimpie had held on firmly to Kait and then reeled her in and back into a seat so that she and I both could be carried back to the top of the hill where we'd started all this. It only took a few minutes and then there we were, both of us standing there, looking at each other, whatever drugs those blimpies had injected us with wearing off as we stood there.

I sat on the sled. "Kaitie, did that really happen?" The effect of whatever had been injected into me had ebbed in seconds, so I was back to pain, a lot of it. I couldn't see how I could possibly make it the rest of the way to Holmanville, even with Kait's help.

She walked over to the edge and looked down toward the bogs below. She pointed, "Do you want to see where it landed?"

I didn't, that would require standing and walking. "No thanks," I said. "Is he dead?"

"It's a long way off, but I can't see any movement. I can't tell what's Whistle and what's the palanquin, though. They wound up piled up together down there."

"Great. Kait—" I said. And she cut me off, walking toward me.

"I know. We'll stop here for a while now, Petey, and I'll give you the last of the naproxen. And then I guess we'll go down the other side and make our way to Holmanville. Only two more of the hills to climb."

It wasn't possible, but I didn't have the heart to tell her just then. I just sat there as Kait gently moved me a bit and then poked around in the sled and got out the magic tent. She hit the button and as we watched it slowly unfold we heard a noise. Higher pitched, a kind of distant screaming. Blimpies, back and angry?

No, I'd heard this sound before, back on Earth, and had been terrified by it. A screamship, the weapons that had pacified Earth in one terrible day. I'd watched people die by the hundreds from a "necessary police action" by one of these ships. I'd watched my best friend try to run away from the deadly light that came down from the ships and then watched, helpless, as she was turned to dust. This was Whistle's personal guard getting even. Too late to stop the blimpies, but not too late to do away with the Earthies who had caused all these problems. Soon, I knew, there would be a bright beam of light, so intense you couldn't stand it, and anything that was in its way would be vaporized, bits scattered in the wind. That'd be me, that'd be Kait.

I was too tired to care. Instead, as the scream overwhelmed me, I fell back onto the sled, waiting for the final moment when that light would pull me and Kait apart and scatter the bright, glittery bits of us into the wind and rain of S'hudon.

Kait came over to me and threw her arms about me in a hug. So this was it. Hell, I thought we'd made it and now this. At least it would be quick. I wondered if anyone on Earth would miss me. Would Chloe Cary weep when she heard the news? Would my brother Tom?

And then the chaos and lights and screaming ended, over, done—just like that. The screamship hovered right over our heads, a huge thing, slowly coming lower and lower. A hatch irised open. Several S'hudonni were there, looking down at us, a platform dropping down with them on it.

"Uncle Peter!" yelled Treble, alive and well. Smiles stood next to him, waving at us. Twoclicks and the Mother stood behind them. "So glad we found you!"

Two ten-days later, I stood on the pavement at the S'hudonni landing field, where a dozen huge freighters floated just inches off the tarmac. More remnant technologies from the Old Ones, I was sure. Whistle had been given a state funeral. It was very sad that he'd fallen to his death and the Mother said some very nice things about him at that service. Then his body was given back to the ocean; a squadron of blimpies, ten of them, ceremoniously took the body out over the Great Bight and released it. Kait and I were whispering back and forth during that ceremony about how we were certain that the blimpies were as glad to see Whistle rejoin Mother Ocean as we were.

Whistle was dead, but we assumed there was another version of Whistle on Earth that needed to be handled, one way or another, and Twoclicks was on Earth, too, and needed to hear from an impeccable source the real story of what had happened, so the Mother had told Treble to pack his bags, he was heading to Earth to be with his fathers. Treble had work to do there, for sure. Kait was headed home, too, to Sarah and a normal life. Smiles, her tutor and friend, was staying behind. The Mother had declared her a Hero of S'hudon, which meant whatever it meant.

And so we stood there, the four of us, having hugged all around after I gave Treble all the things I wanted him to take back to Earth: the handwritten notes, the expressions of love, the promises to see them soon, and even, in my case, a manuscript I'd spent a lot of time on. It was the opening chapters of this magnum opus: *Notes from Holmanville*. I hoped it wasn't awful. I asked him to give it Chloe Cary, who'd know what to do with it.

The princeling led the way up the ramp to the ship, and then stopped, turned around, and waved, along with my sister. Then they boarded.

"Treble has important things to do, Peter," Heather told me. She'd been standing there the whole time, quiet, letting Kait and me deal with things. She was in her S'hudonni form: a shark, upright, dangerous. "And he'll be back before you know it."

"Sure," I said, with a certain dry sarcasm. "Before I know it." Which turned out to be about half right.

PART SIX

THE TREBLE TOUR

I often wondered if there was some Great Plan that Two-clicks or Heather had in mind, some particular reason they'd chosen me. Was it all just for profit and power, or was there something bigger in the works, some great confrontation or some great opportunity or some great threat?

The very short answer to that is yes.

—Peter Holman, *Notes from Holmanville*
(S'hudon City and New York:
Trebnet Press, 2035)

17

THE ST. LOUIS BLUES

On the first day of the Treble tour, as Chloe thought of it, they started out early in L.A. with a formal opening of the tour, replete with appearances by Twoclicks and other S'hudonni and a carefully orchestrated walk out to the plane, a brand-new Earthie Boeing 797 kitted out just for the tour, with enough rooms for her publicists and stylists and Nanci, her new personal assistant, to each have their own space, while Chloe had a suite for herself, as did Treble. Smack in the middle of the plane was the shared space, lounge seats and ottomans dotted all around—and plenty of attention from the flight attendants, of course. This was the right way to fly.

Their first stop was the Midwest, where they admired the Gateway Arch in St. Louis, sampled the wares at a couple of microbreweries, and walked along with a large gaggle of media through the celebrated Saint Louis Zoo.

Treble was awestruck by what he saw at the zoo. It was one thing to know that such creatures existed, he told her, but another thing entirely to see them alive. The giraffes, the penguins, the big cats, the monkeys and apes, the elephants and rhinos, the raptors. He saw them all, and happily took a ride on the small train that ran all the way round the zoo. He sat next to Chloe and chattered in English about everything he was seeing. Which was, in a word, "Wonderful!"

"So much better to see it all this way," he said to Chloe. "I will have to do this on the other planets when I visit them, too."

"Absolutely," she said, and patted his hand. The other planets. Right. And he probably would. She'd have thought of that as crazy, until the day the S'hudonni arrived and Chloe Cary and Peter were elevated from minor celebrities to global importance. A lot had changed since then. More than a year and a half of wrenching reorganization and new ways of thinking about Earth and its place in the cosmos. Humbling, it was.

"It'll be even better when you get to see some of these animals in the wild in Africa," she said to the princeling. "You'll be amazed."

They'd be in Kruger National Park within a week. First, though, off to France for the wines, then Ireland and Scotland for the whiskey or whisky, take your pick, then down to South Africa for more wines, and onward from there to India and China and South America and back home. A celebrity whirlwind!

But first the whirlwind of the tiny train that ran around the zoo, with real steam coming out of a fake smokestack and a polite bell that rang at crossings where the zoogoers and paparazzi lined the track to take pictures and yell to Chloe, mostly, that she was wonderful and beautiful and could really kick ass.

Chloe just smiled and waved and thought, hell yes, she could kick ass. A solid two years of hard training and conditioning went into being an action hero on *The Family Madderz*. It wasn't easy. She was glad they noticed.

"I am excited by all this!" Treble said to her, turning to take it all in.

"Me, too," said Chloe, with something of a forced smile. The fans were nice, but a fan to cool off with would have been even nicer. It was hot as Hades, even in September. Thirty-five Celsius, myBetty had warned her, back when they sat in air-conditioned comfort in the chauffer-driven limo. "*Be prepared, Chloe*," myBetty had said, and Chloe had laughed it off. She wasn't laughing anymore, and myBetty, she thought, was probably gloating.

Treble leaned out to feel that hot St. Louis sun on his face. Sure, it was broiling, but Treble just smiled and nodded and waved at the photogs and the fans, who had fought hard for tickets to the zoo on this very day to see two—count 'em, two—celebrities: Chloe Cary and the princeling! Twoclicks's own son, Treble! Right here in St. Louis, seeing their zoo and sampling their beer! The King of Beers, that's St. Louis! Just like the old days.

When they finished the train ride, instead of heading straight to the airport, there'd been one change to the itinerary. A small brewery that had been handcrafting beer just for S'hudon had been attacked by insurgents a few days before and there'd been some damage and some casualties. Treble wanted to go see the place for himself.

It was still an active crime scene, so the police chief and the mayor said no at first. But Treble insisted, and one quick call to Twoclicks by myBetty on the Trebnet changed the mayor's mind, and he, in turn, changed the police chief's.

They saw one burned-out vehicle that had belonged to the insurgents. It was being towed away but Treble wanted to see it, and the major had learned his lesson when it came to Treble, so the towing waited while Chloe and Treble got up close. The vehicle, an old van, was a blackened, melted mess, but there were no bodies in it, so Treble moved on to see the scorch marks on the outside walls of the brewery building and on the pavement in front, from an explosion that was meant to kill people but had only scorched things. Inside, all but one of the vats was ruined, but already repair and replacements were under way. In a week or two they'd be back online and their St. Louis Toasted Ale would be headed across the Mississippi to S'hudon's distribution center over in Illinois, and from there off to the other worlds. Profit!

For now, there was still some forensics work going on, but not a lot else. The good guys had won a resounding victory, the mayor told Treble and Chloe, and the police chief said that this particular group of insurgents had been working their way through the lightly policed rural parts of three states and that the St. Louis attack had been their first attempt to do something in a city. It had failed, and the thought was that the group had been hit so hard it had probably disbanded. Eleven of them had died in the attempt to blow up the brewery.

They were more of these crazies all over the Midwest, the chief said, but this sent a message they'd get. So, one down and a dozen more to go. Bring 'em on. St. Louis was ready and here, today, was patting itself on the back.

Treble was quiet after they got back into the limo for the drive to the airport. They were headed out for the next stop, Paris and the South of France, and from there to the West of Ireland, where Chloe had never been but where they made Twoclicks's favorite whiskey, the Dew of Kenmare. The day after that they'd be in Scotland, so they'd have a chance to compare what the Scots did with whisky to how the Irish handled it.

On the long flight, Chloe had plenty of time to think back on that brewery and the battle. She'd been reading up on these militias, worried they might go after her and Treble. They were crazy, no doubt, but you almost had to admire their attitude. Whoever was left of that gang was probably somewhere in Illinois right now, laying low for a few days, licking their wounds, and then getting back to what they did best: burning crops, destroying some more small-town livelihoods, killing people to make a statement. She wondered what they had in mind next.

18

THE HARVEST

Tom Holman looked out the second-story window of the old farmhouse, toward Nikki and the new recruits, the Thompson twins, Billie and Billy. All three of them stood ready with their drip torches. The twins, runaways who'd been hitchhiking on a two-lane pavement near Carbondale to get away from some small-town trouble in Red Bud, Illinois, were just the kind of troublemakers Tom had been looking for. Not a political bone in either one of those husky, farm-bred bodies, but at eighteen they were already hard drinkers who loved a good fight. Billie, the girl, was fifteen minutes older than her brother and bossed the hell out of him. Billy, the boy, was big and strong and stupid, which worked fine for Tom's purposes.

The twins had been with them now for a week, and had enjoyed the hell out of setting one small brewery ablaze in Metropolis, Illinois—"Hometown of Superman!" is what the battered road sign outside of town had said—and then burning down a wheat field in Tiline, Indiana. There'd been lots of whoops and hollering in both cases. Now they were ready to see if they could burn all this acreage. That would really get the twins excited.

Tom had Chloe Cary on his mind. The bitch. She'd started on a world tour now with the kid, Treble, the son of Twoclicks. If you saw a newspaper or a television or went on the new fucking Trebnet version of the internet, you couldn't miss them. Cute kid, and together with Cary they made about as cute a couple as you could imagine, spreading all that Twoclicks good cheer around the globe. The wonderful world of an Earth that was part of S'hudon's empire.

Bad enough, all that, but now it turned out that Tom's own brother, Peter, was alive and well and living on S'hudon, the fucking traitor. Somehow he'd lived through the explosion and destruction of Twoclicks's ship and had been rescued by those cute daffodils.

Tom admitted to the momentary relief he felt when he saw the news on a flat screen at a bar that he and Nikki had walked into in Elmer, Indiana. Sweet sister Kait had been killed stupidly by Whistle, back when this all started, and it about broke Tom's heart. He felt in some measure responsible for that. Had he known about it, he might have been able to stop it. To have Peter killed, too, just a week or two later, and to know he was complicit in that even though he hadn't known it was planned, flattened him.

And then, later, when he pulled himself together, he found that it energized him. All of it, all of the death and destruction, was because of the

S'hudonni in general and Twoclicks in particular. All that fake goodwill, all those promises. At least Whistle, for all his violence, was honest about it. Tom knew where he stood with Whistle, and it was right here, taking action. Now that he knew Peter was alive, back on S'hudon and safely out of the picture, Tom could breathe a little easier, carry a little less guilt, and still go out and get the job done.

But really, the news was all bad. More propaganda, more acceptance, more normalizing of the occupation by these greedy alien bastards. And no one cared, especially in towns like Elmer, Indiana, where the corn crop was making a mighty fine handmade white corn whiskey. White lightning for those daffodils.

He and Nikki left that bar shaking their heads at the tragedy of it all. Now he stood at the edge of the field and wondered if the sweet corn here in Seelyville, Indiana, had in fact been knee high by the Fourth of July. It was sure ready for harvest now, in September. The fields stretched off in all directions, as far as Tom could see. Another few days and the S'hudonni spyeyes would be swarming around, watching it all live and sending it on to the other worlds of the empire, as the happy, industrious Earthies walked through the fields to handpick the ears of corn and toss them into horse-drawn wagons.

The corn looked good, too, Tom had to admit, given the lack of artificial fertilizers or herbicides or pesticides. All natural, this corn, and soon enough it would have been ready to start its path into becoming the kind of corn whiskey or handcrafted bourbon the S'hudonni demanded. Hoosier Bourbon and Hoosier Lightning, distilled over in Terre Haute, sold for a hefty price to the S'hudonni, who then put it on board one of those ships leaving from the new American Bottoms launch port near St. Louis and headed out to one or all of The Six.

Downtone, most likely, would have been the first stop, where whiskeys of all kinds were favored by those odd upright duck-like things that lived in teeming billions there. And then S'hudon, the home world, where the elite could skim off the best of the best. And then to wherever was next, selling at a higher price each time as the supply dwindled, all the way down to Adagio, the poorest of The Six , where the royal families of those weird quadruped houyhnhnm things with the one long arm would have been the only ones able to afford the luxury.

Would have been, thought Tom, and smiled, because none of that was going to happen now, at least not for these fields. It hadn't rained in weeks here, and the corn was dry, which was perfect. The fields were abandoned, which meant the family that lived here had gotten word that trouble was coming their way and they'd fled. Smart. With the S'hudonni suppressor keeping the spyeyes away and with Tom and Nikki and the Thompson twins avoiding any tech signatures, they should have all the time they wanted to do it right this time, with lots of smoke.

Tom waved away the flies that swarmed around them here—part of farm life, he thought, but annoying as hell. Then he watched out the window as Nikki talked with the twins, the three of them each carrying a drip torch. It was ten a.m. now, and by noon they'd have this whole area in flames. There was a nice breeze out of the west. With any luck, it would burn east for a good while, all that smoke sending a message that the S'hudonni couldn't stop with all their technology.

Nikki was hearing someone or something. Tom looked, and there was dust rising in the distance. Someone was coming, but the fucking silo was right in the way and he couldn't see who or how many.

Nikki ran to see past the silo and put up her hand to shade her eyes and looked back down the long dirt road that led from old US 40 into this farmstead.

She ran back, looked up at Tom, and waved, yelling, "Visitors!" which meant some of the locals were going to come and try to stop them after all.

Shit. Tom didn't want to see any more death. Nikki, though, was crazy, and those fucking twins . . . god knows what they might do.

Nikki was running toward him. She stopped at the foot of the barn, looked up at Tom. "It's the National Guard!" she yelled. "Old Humvees and the whole thing. What do you think?"

"How many?" he yelled down to her.

"Six or seven vehicles, so maybe a couple of dozen people? But they'll be armed, and some of them can probably aim, you know."

Damn, Tom thought. He and his old Irregulars had learned their lesson about that the hard way, back in St. Louis. The police and the guards there had been well armed and could aim like all hell. He hadn't had the time to use his S'hudonni tech in St. Louis and maybe that was a good thing. The same thing happened to some Irregulars in Georgia, who'd run into some trouble outside of Atlanta and they had used their S'hudonni tech to wipe out most of a town that harbored a bunch of quisling microbrewers. Tom had heard from a furious Whistle that now some Earthies knew that S'hudon tech was involved in the insurrection. That was a no-no, damn it, last resort only if they wanted more help from Whistle.

So they'd have to be a little careful here. Even crazy Nikki. He'd remind her of that. They had a job to do, and if they wanted that all to work out the way they had in mind, they needed to stay in one piece, pick up some more talent along the way, and make their way east and north, heading toward Niagara Falls and those specialty wines that the cuttlefish of Melody were so enamored of. All those vineyards along the shores of Lake Erie and Lake Ontario would be great to burn. And then the big blow, knocking down that free energy tower that Twoclicks, Mr. Benevolent of the S'hudonni, was building out in Lake Ontario. Free power for all! Right. If you believed there wouldn't be a price to pay for that, Tom Holman had a bridge he'd like to sell you.

Better, he thought, to just cut and run.

"Let's get the hell out of here," he yelled down to Nikki. "Tell the twins to shut it down and get to the truck!"

"You're the boss!" she yelled back up at him, but she shook her head as she did that.

She'd rather stand and fight, thought Tom, as he rattled his way through the room he was in, over to the staircase and down it, then out the front door of the farmhouse.

No one was there. What the hell? They should be right in front of him, dousing the torches and heading toward the truck, which was out back.

"Nikki!" he yelled. "What the hell?"

Then he smelled the smoke. Shit. They didn't have time for this.

He ran, sprinting around the barn and seeing the three of them, the twins and Nikki, walking fast through the corn, torches on full, trying to get the fire going.

He yelled at them, "Cut that shit out! Stop! We have to go!"

Damn it, they weren't seeing the bigger picture.

But Nikki saw him. She waved, and yelled at the twins, and then ran back toward Tom while twisting the valve shut on the torch. "Let's go! Let's go!" she was yelling as she ran, but the twins were having too much fun.

Tom heard the roar of the engines as the National Guard rounded that last turn and came into the main yard, great clouds of dust rising.

Nikki came running, laboring with the drip torch heavy with kerosene. Out in the cornfield, the twins were hooting, having a great time, and it looked like the field might catch.

"The back way!" Nikki yelled at him, and sprinted for the barn. Around the back side of that, and then around the farmhouse and they'd get to the car. There was a two-rut road that ran up from there into a wooded knoll.

That might work. The bigger picture, the bigger picture. The fucking Niagara Tower. That was it. Run now and see another day.

Tom ran, got to Nikki, yelled, "Ditch it!" and saw her heave the drip torch into the last row of corn before the barn.

They made it, got around the corner, and then heard a woman's voice over a loudspeaker. The sound carried pretty good over the corn.

"This is Colonel Joy Adrian, First Squadron, One Hundred Fifty-Second Cavalry, Indiana National Guard. Put down your weapons."

Tom and Nikki made it past the house, and there was the car, an old pre-tech Oldsmobile they'd stolen two towns back. They ran for it.

Behind them, from the corn, they heard the twins shouting, "Fuck you!" and then a rapid run of gunshots. They'd unstrapped their assault rifles and were shooting at the guards.

Then came a heavier sound, then another. Fifty-caliber machine guns, Tom guessed, mounted on top of a couple of those vehicles. Jesus Christ. The twins weren't yelling anymore.

Tom and Nikki got into the Olds, cranked it up, and headed for the ruts that aimed toward the woods. Behind them, more machine gun fire, but not aimed at them—yet.

Up the ruts, raising their own dust, but the Guard didn't seem inclined to follow, at least not yet. So on they drove, just the two of them.

The fucking twins. Tom felt sorry for them, but that had been a stupid, stupid way to die. Shit. Now it was just Tom and Nikki again, the two of them fighting the good fight by themselves.

He swatted at the flies buzzing around in the Olds and thought, one more time, of how he could have cut off the head of this snake back on that beach in Florida. Taking out Peter and Chloe and dead Kait's mourning wife would have done it. A whole different world now maybe, if he'd hit the trigger like he was supposed to.

But it wasn't. It was this world, damn it, so he'd just have to hope for another chance to right the wrongs. Peter was out of reach forever, it seemed. But Chloe Cary was reachable, and what a target that would be, taking her out and the kid prince at the same time. A worthy goal to work toward.

Maybe, if he could reach Whistle's people again and get some S'hudonni toys, he could meet that goal, do something about Cary and the kid. Maybe. Worth a try, anyway.

19

WHISKEY OR WHISKY

As far as Chloe knew, the S'hudonni liked warm and shallow water. That's where their ships landed, and they put many of their consulates in cities that sat near warm, shallow estuaries.

But now, after the summer heat of St. Louis and the warmth of the South of France and then Paris, at Twoclicks's insistence, they were heading to Ireland and then to Scotland. Both places, she'd been warned, would be cold, drizzly, and gray in September—or in any month, for that matter.

So she was surprised when little Treble seemed happy. "Just like home!" he said, when he and Chloe stepped off the plane and into the rain at Kerry Airport in the West of Ireland, walking down the rolling stairs and across the tarmac. Chloe held his hand, as always, as they maneuvered clumsily down the steps; the S'hudonni were not great at climbing or descending, though they got the job done.

Chloe had argued a little with Twoclicks in a long face-to-face call on their smarties during the flight from Paris to this tiny airport in gray, wet County Kerry, Ireland. She'd lost the argument, but, damn it, felt pretty good that she'd had the nerve to disagree with him to his face. Yay, Chloe.

On the call, Twoclicks had insisted that the two of them visit a pub he'd been to with Heather and Peter nearly two years before, Hussey's, in Ballina. But it was two hundred kilometers north—too far to drive, and even by helicopter it would take an hour or more.

Treble and Chloe wanted to stick with the plan, meet the taoiseach—Ireland's prime minister—and the mayors and other officials at the airport, pay a quick visit to a pub in Killarney that was right on the way, and then get to Kenmare and tour the distillery where the famous Dew of Kenmare was made.

Problem was, Chloe was wearing that sweep gear and recording everything all the time. myBetty was saving it all, editing it into frequent highlights, and sending it out to a global audience of several hundred million sweep receivers. This meant their visit to Ireland was no surprise, and since Ireland was where all the trouble had started for Twoclicks, Heather, Peter, and poor Kait two years before, security would be tight. No one wanted a repetition of that horrible day when Whistle and his gangs had attacked Twoclicks, Heather, and Peter and nearly killed all three of them.

But Twoclicks had *really* liked that pub, and those Earthies who'd been there. And he was paying for all this and expected to reap the benefits. So they compromised and did exactly what Twoclicks wanted, with the taoiseach coming in from Dublin by helicopter to meet them at the airport and then offering the copter for the day to get them all to Ballina and Hussey's pub, and then from there back down to Kenmare, in the south.

But first they had to meet the local officials, starting with Niamh O'Shea herself, the taoiseach, who was standing in the light rain under a welcome tent just thirty meters from the plane. The plan was to greet O'Shea and the others with a hearty handshake and a Treble hug before signing a few autographs, saying a few words to the media, and then getting on the helicopter that was waiting for them on a pad to the left of the tent.

But it's hard to greet and go in Ireland. This was County Kerry's first look at a S'hudonni, and a cute one at that, so . . . There were dignitaries to meet and shake hands with, and another two thousand people or more behind the tent and in the rain, holding their umbrellas, hoping to at least catch a glimpse of the television star and her cute little alien friend. There was a stage, and the tent was open on two sides so the people could see. When, mercifully, the rain stopped and the sun suddenly shined upon the proceedings, Treble came onto the stage to a great round of applause and seemed in no hurry to leave.

"Hello, everyone!" said Treble, holding up both of those thin arms as if to embrace the crowd as he leaned forward to speak into the microphone that had been lowered for him. "We are so glad to be here in Ireland! My father, Twoclicks, has told me such wonderful things about you and your country!"

The crowd roared, and Treble waved and started talking about Ireland and the Irish and why he loved it all so, so much. Where had he learned all these things about ceilidhs and Carrauntoohil, and Dingle and Donegal and Brian Boru and the Easter Rising and shanachies and so forth and so on? Ten minutes he regaled them with this outpouring, then he put his palms toward them to quiet them down and said a simple "Go raibh maith agat," which means "May you have goodness."

Oh, my, Chloe thought, this kid really does his homework. Treble was a hit! Chloe heard myBetty whispering in her ear as he left the stage, "Twoclicks is watching, and is very pleased."

"Good," said Chloe. "I'll try not to say much, then, and let our young star carry the load."

"A heads-up, Chloe," said myBetty. "I'm going live for the feed now, at Twoclicks's insistence."

Chloe rolled her eyes. Sure, go live. But she had nothing prepared, so if they asked her to speak . . .

And of course they did, a minute later, after Treble left with a wave and all that applause. Chloe's turn now. So, with a deep breath, a small sigh, and then a smile in that welcome sunshine, she stepped up to the microphones and cameras and swarm of tiny drones and started speaking, leaning on help from myBetty as she talked about how very, very much she enjoyed learning about Ireland's history and its people and the scenery they were going to see today—and, of course, the whiskey!

That got a great round of applause, so she stopped and smiled for a few seconds and then added that they hoped to sample several fine boutique whiskeys at several fine distilleries and pubs and were especially looking forward to the handcrafted whiskey they would see in Kenmare. The owner of that distillery was next to her on the stage, and Chloe and Treble made a show of publicly shaking his hand and promising to visit with him later in the day. Treble gave him a hug, which seemed to please them both.

Chloe hadn't hit it out of the park like Treble had, and she knew it, but she'd gotten it done and smiled her biggest smile and hugged little Treble and that seemed to make it all right. The taoiseach herself seemed as pleased with Chloe as she'd been with Treble. It was all very pleasant as the sun brightened the day, and then together with the taoiseach and her assistant, they all walked over to the helicopter and headed for Hussey's.

Flying low over rolling hills and green pastures with grazing cattle, they watched out the window as Ireland passed beneath them, vales and mountains and boglands, by turn. The day was turning gorgeous, the air smooth, the helicopter a fast one, and it wasn't much more than forty-five minutes before the pilot said they'd reached the place. He would set it down on the front lawn of Ballina House, the old manor house turned into a five-star hotel. From there, a limo would take them into town and the pub.

It all worked fine, but the mood in the pub wasn't as celebratory as the mood down in County Kerry. Here, close to two years before, the pub had been going full swing, with Twoclicks holding forth and Heather and Peter off in a corner watching him on that terrible day when the screamships struck, wiping out some of Earth's best weaponry inside of fifteen minutes. It had been a painful lesson and it all began right here, even as a band played a session—jigs and reels, and fiddlers fiddling away, and the bodhrán pacing the lot. And then all hell all over the world as warring S'hudonni brothers had brought fear and terror into the village.

Twoclicks and Heather and Peter had tried to leave it all behind them on that day, but angry Irish insurgents had come close to killing all three of them, and they'd used Kait—or that copy of her, anyway—as the weapon to get that done. So the pub was filled, but understandably somber, as Taoiseach O'Shea came in with her guests, Chloe Cary of television fame and Treble, the princeling son of Twoclicks.

Really, the locals would just as soon not be singled out for this event. Did Chloe and Treble really have to remind the whole world of what had happened here, with the S'hudonni screamship in the sky and the great lights flashing down? They'd seen that, some of them, and they had told others, even though there'd been a media blackout of it that had held for weeks before the news trickled out. Those days were done, surely.

But here they were, at Twoclicks's insistence.

"Twoclicks had me set up a live link to all four of their screens, Chloe," said myBetty, when they all walked into the pub.

"And?"

"And he plans to speak to them. Starting in five seconds."

The screens hadn't been on, and now, suddenly, they were. And it was Twoclicks, sitting in a chair in the consulate in L.A., who looked at them through the TV sets and said, "Dia dhuit, my Irish friends!"

"That means hello," whispered myBetty to Chloe and she to Treble.

"I know," said Treble. Chloe just smiled and thanked myBetty.

The level of tension in the room went down a notch or two.

"We are sorry we cannot be there with our sson and his friend, and with all of you, in my favorite pub on Earth!" And Twoclicks raised a bottle of the Dew of Kenmare for them all to see—always the salesman, that Two-clicks. He poured some into a tumbler, raised it in front of the camera, and toasted the room. "Sláinte!" There were a hundred *Sláintes* right back at him, and then Twoclicks waved and the screens went dark and the show was over.

Then Taoiseach O'Shea stood on a chair to say to everyone that the Irish were proud to have their famous visitors and proud to have them see a classic pub like Hussey's and to share a pint or a whiskey.

It was Treble's turn next, and Chloe had to help him stand up on a chair—and then higher, on a table, so he could be seen. She was nervous. myBetty had been whispering in her ear that Twoclicks had warned her to look for trouble, someone in the back of the crowd, perhaps, or someone crowded in at the bar. Someone who didn't look right. She should watch, and if she saw someone, whisper it to myBetty so that Twoclicks would hear it. Help was there, ready, if needed.

But she saw nothing. Not everyone was overjoyed to have Treble going on as he had before down in Kerry, about Ireland's history and all that rot again. They'd heard all that too many times to count, and this wasn't a tour-ist town like down in Kerry. But no one looked like trouble to Chloe's eyes, and then it was her turn to speak, and even while standing on the table next to Treble and saying a few words about being glad to be there, she didn't see anything threatening.

Instead, it turned very nicely from glum to happy, and now the whole world knew about Hussey's pub in Ballina, where you could come stand on the very table where Chloe Cary and Treble from S'hudon had stood! And you could have a pint of porter, just as Chloe did next. But you couldn't have any Dew of Kenmare, since that was solely for export to The Six. There was one bottle left in the bar, and Chloe and the taoiseach and Treble had a few sips each and then passed it around until it was gone, and that was that for the Dew of Kenmare.

Another few minutes of signing autographs and shaking hands and being pleased to meet you and then they headed for the limo that would take them to Ballina House and the helicopter ride to Kenmare, where the holy dew itself was made.

It had all gone very well, indeed, at Hussey's, and Chloe was relieved about that. Until they reached the limo and there, tucked under the windscreen wipers, was a small piece of paper with a handwritten note on it. Chloe reached it first, and pulled it out from under the wiper blade. In a large scrawl, written with a Sharpie, probably, it said, "D'fhéadfadh muid a bheith."

Chloe looked around. No one was there except for the throng back behind them that had followed them outside to send them off. She waved to them, smiled, and then opened her door and held it for O'Shea and Treble, who smiled back at her and clambered in. O'Shea's bodyguards got in on the other side.

Chloe climbed in, sat, and then handed the note to O'Shea, who took a look and asked her, "Who handed this to you?" And then showed it to her guards.

"It was on the windscreen," Chloe said. "I found it there, just now."

The two guards were already out the door, scanning the crowd. The taoiseach looked at them and they both shook their heads slightly. "Get in," she said to them, and as they did she said to the driver, "Get us to that copter, please, quick as you can without causing a panic." Then she shook her head and looked at Chloe and Treble. "It says, 'We could have.'"

Chloe didn't need to report that; myBetty was recording for the sweep and video and the raw footage went directly to Hanratty and Twoclicks, so they could comment when they wanted to.

"This meanss someone iss bragging?" Twoclicks asked Chloe, through the smarty link. The limo was rounding the corner from the small parking lot and out onto the main road that led to the manor house, where the helicopter sat on the pad, guards around it, waiting for them.

"Yes," said Chloe. "And it's a warning, certainly." She looked at O'Shea, who nodded grimly.

It was a tense ten minutes, Chloe expecting trouble at any moment, seeing things in the fields they went by, noticing shapes in the woods that seemed to be moving. She'd never felt quite so awake, quite so aware, in her life. The only moments that compared at all to this one had come during her athletic career in high school, and later at Stanford, when there were times she'd been so focused, so intent on what was happening, that time had slowed. The goal she'd scored against Cal, off a perfect cross from Naomi Harper, the ball taking forever to come off Naomi's foot and soar through the air and Chloe moving past and through the defenders and then leaping, rising to reach the ball with her head and steer it toward the upper ninety, the top-near corner of the net, out of the reach of the goalkeeper and into the back of the net. A marvelous, marvelous moment, seconds that seemed to take minutes. Fully aware. Fully immersed in the moment.

Those moments were hard to find, and here she was in one of them right now, seeing things with a clarity that seemed pellucid, everything with the edges sharp, every part of a second distinctly clear.

There, at the edge of the woods, as they reached the long drive into the helipad, someone stood there, watching. Tall, thin, a black leather jacket, a knit cap. She said, "There," to O'Shea and the guards, and pointed.

The guards wore thin headsets and spoke into their mics to let the others at the helipad know, and then they stopped the limo for seconds while one guard jumped out and ran, hard, toward that spot. Then the limo sped up, heading to the helipad.

"How exciting this is!" said Treble. And Chloe smiled at him. She felt fearless, unharmable, as they rounded one final curve, and there was the helicopter, blades turning. They pulled in and the guards opened the doors and they ran for the helicopter and climbed in, leaving the guards behind as the copter rose, and off they went toward Kenmare.

Later, the guard still with them listened through his earpiece and relayed the message to O'Shea. "False alarm, ma'am. The man there was a local, walking his dog, watching us go by. There was no threat."

Chloe felt strangely let down by the news, and when she looked at Treble, he smiled and shrugged, a purely Earthie form of nonverbal communication, for sure. Pretty funny, really, to be disappointed that they hadn't been in danger. She wondered how they'd do, the two of them, if and when some real threat appeared.

An hour later, in Kenmare, they were met by the usual coterie of local bigwigs, and then Treble happily surprised the group by stripping and diving right in when they drove by the harbor. He frolicked a bit with some bewildered seals, then came back out and dried off in the armored van they were in. Then it was off to visit the distillery and sample the wares with Chloe. She was unimpressed with what she'd tasted, but the decision wasn't hers to make, so she smiled and agreed with Treble when he said it was excellent.

By three in the afternoon, the taoiseach dropped them off at Kerry airport, and she headed back to Dublin while they took off for the Hebrides.

They landed at Edinburgh's Rowling Airport, walking down some roll-up steps and into the rain. There, under a capacious tent warmed by heaters, they met Scotland's prime minister, Ailsa Robertson, and chatted with her for a few minutes in front of the assembled multitudes. Scotland was new to independence and the economy was struggling, so a visit from a representative of the S'hudonni Empire—especially one with a direct line to

Twoclicks—was a welcome event. The prime minister raised her glass and offered a toast, "Slainte Mhor!" and they all enjoyed the good feelings with a long sip of single malt. After that, the prime minister spent most of her time talking about the whisky industry and its close attention to craftsmanship and small batches.

Chloe smiled and nodded throughout. Of course the Scots did small batches and handcrafted everything, from the oak barrels to the hand-reaped barley for the single malt. And of course they'd be happy to have the entire process and all of the many small-batch distilleries watched over constantly by S'hudon's spyeyes, buzzing around and sending live video to all the planets of The Six. Single malt made under those spyeyes brought fifty times as much income as that which wasn't watched so carefully.

After saying good-bye to the prime minister and reboarding the plane for the short flight to Skye and then the helicopter to Lewis, Chloe heard a *ding* from myBetty and asked her what was up.

"Twoclicks checking in again," she said. And Chloe took the call on her smarty, smiling back at Twoclicks's smiling face on the screen as he greeted her with his usual sibilance.

"We watched," he said, using that royal *we* he used so often. She couldn't see anyone else in the room behind him. "Sscotland iss often wet, yes?"

"Yes," Chloe said, "that's what they tell me, and especially in the Hebrides," which she knew now that myBetty had whispered it in her ear.

"And my Importance enjoyss, yes?"

Chloe assumed that Twoclicks was in constant communication with Treble, probably a live feed, in fact, through a contact lens or something like that. So this was an odd question, but it did give her a chance to let Twoclicks know how impressed she was with the princeling.

"Yes," she said, "he seems very happy. And he's done his homework. He knows about us, our habits, where we live, what we eat, our languages, our cultural differences. He's amazing, Twoclicks." She didn't mention how ready for some danger he had seemed to be when they were leaving Hussey's pub and there was that threatening note on the windscreen.

"Iss good to hear you ssay that, dear friend Chloe. We have great planss for Treble. You know?"

Did she know? Well, she did now. "I'll take good care of him, Twoclicks, promise," she said.

Twoclicks grinned, said, "Of course!" and clicked off.

Chloe sat back in her seat. The plane was already trundling along toward the main runway and the flight attendant was buckling himself in, so Chloe looked over to Treble to make sure he was buckled in, too, and then she did her own.

"I liked Ailsa Robertson," Treble said to her, and pronounced the name correctly: *ail* and then *suh*. It was curious how perfect his English was, considering Twoclicks's imperfections with the language. Hanratty was the one who often had to translate Twoclicks's fractured English into something understandable.

They were landing almost as soon as they'd taken off, and then they had to hit the brakes and reverse thrusters hard to squeeze the big jet onto the runway at Portree, on Skye. But they made it with room to spare and then went through the same tented welcoming from the locals from Skye. Again, Treble did most of the talking. Then a walk over to the helicopter and off they went, headed to Lewis.

Chloe pulled out her smarty and started writing longhand a letter to Peter, describing how the day had gone. She'd started writing these when they first left L.A. It gave her something useful to do on the plane, and she knew she was writing for posterity. She'd finish it up tonight at the hotel in Lewis, telling him the usual Tales of Treble that she wrote a little about every night. Then she'd hit Send and it would go to Twoclicks at the consulate, and from there it would be printed onto paper and put into a pouch and onto a freighter that was on its way to S'hudon and already loaded with Earthie artifacts, including, she was sure, a lot of whiskey—or whisky, take your pick.

In the letter, she told him how interesting and charming young Treble was and how he'd handled himself so well in France, where the French president didn't know what to make of him. Treble was the first S'hudonni to visit France, and there was quite the ceremony over that. And then, of course, the private talks about the way the French made wine and how there might have to be some changes in that. Lots of sniffing over that, but then Treble had discussed pricing and profits and the French had come around. Well, perhaps some of the wineries might choose to follow this new system. Oui, thought Chloe. They might.

They'd started in Bordeaux and then helicoptered even farther south, to Limoux, with its ancient sparkling wines. Chloe and Treble had both liked those. Then they'd flown up to Paris and taken the rest of the day for themselves, just the two of them on an adventure. Chloe swept it as they walked incognito—the blond woman with a ponytail, dressed in blue jeans and a worn, old Stanford Swim hoodie, and the unfortunate child in the motorized wheelchair that trundled along next to her—along the Rue des Jardins and onto the Champs-Élysées and then along the Seine, before stopping for pastry and a coffee at Café Panis, with its great views of Notre-Dame, site of that famous fire and now perfect in its rehabilitated state. It had been long enough since the rebuild that the new stones were beginning to weather to match the old ones. It would take another half century for that process to be complete, but the French were taking the long view, so that was all right.

myBetty had held all that sweep material just long enough for them to finish the excursion and then had sent it out to the hundreds of millions who had receivers. Those receivers got it first, savoring the smell of Paris as they walked past patisseries and the taste of their croissants and the dark, rich café coffee. And then, an hour after it was done, the simple high-res audio and video version went out to billions more.

Billions. Chloe could only shake her head over that. And then she turned her attention to the scenery, as their helicopter approached the airstrip on Lewis. She pointed to the mountains, and Treble smiled and nodded. There would be the usual greeting party, they both knew, and then they'd been promised a scenic drive and a more private tasting of several single malts made on Lewis.

Then they'd take a Land Rover to Amhuinnsuidhe Castle—a name that looked more unpronounceable than it was. Chloe would count on myBetty whispering the pronunciation in her ear when it mattered. They had tonight and most of tomorrow at the castle, with privacy promised, so the plan was for some swimming for Treble and hiking for Chloe. That sounded like fun, and Chloe might try a swim herself. You only live once. And then it would be off to Cape Town, and then to Argentina, and then to whatever was next after that.

Meanwhile, *The Family Madderz* was in planning for the next season and Chloe wasn't there for the meetings. It wasn't a problem; a lot of the cast and crew were doing their own thing during the time off, and not one of them was getting anything like the publicity for the show that Chloe was. Still, she missed the energy and focus of working on the show.

She looked out the window as they were hovering over the airstrip. She could see the local dignitaries huddled in a group down there, all of them with their umbrellas open.

Chloe stopped writing and hit Save on the smarty. Time for more fun with Treble, so she tucked the smarty away. But it was fun, she had to admit, writing an old-school letter, even if it was on a smarty tablet. She really didn't do much writing by hand, but the skill had come back to her nicely. Thank you, Ms. Martinez from fourth grade! If Ms. Martinez hadn't insisted on her students acquiring the skill, Chloe Cary, TV star and big-time celebrity, wouldn't have been able to write her letter to Peter.

Later, when she had her chance to finish the letter and hit Send, she wrote about what she was doing here on her travels with Treble and about how often, during the long plane flights, Treble would talk about Uncle Peter and the great adventure they'd had trying to rescue Kait—and how Kait had wound up rescuing Peter! Wonderful Kait! Treble had shared the details of that adventure, from getting swept away in the storm to meeting up with Smiles, Kait's S'hudonni friend, who'd helped her get away from Whistle.

And then Whistle's death! Treble had seen it happen, not live but through the spyeyes that were capturing every moment of all the excitement that Peter and Kait were going through on S'hudon. Eventually, Treble said, those recorded videos and sweeps would make it to Earth and everyone would see what had happened.

But first, things had to settle down on Earth and the version of Whistle on Earth would have be dealt with, one way or another, and then all the truth would come out! Peter. Kait. Whistle. All of it!

It was a long letter for someone who hadn't written in longhand in many years. She finished it by talking about all the mess with Tom, the self-styled revolutionary leader, burning fields and teaching lessons to those people willing to try to make a living selling boutique alcohol to the S'hudonni. They were trying to stay safe and alive and to make a living, those people. But Tom Holman, on his high horse and still filled with anger, was determined to show them that they shouldn't.

She was in a bedroom suite hours later when she finished the letter. Should she have been so negative about Tom? What a mess that was, but she felt she had to tell Peter about it. His brother, Tom, still a deadly menace. She left it unsaid, but in her mind there was only one way that menace could possibly come to an end. And she hit Send, and off the letter went.

20

LOVE AND VIOLENCE

Tom Holman was thinking that, hell, he could love that woman, as he watched, through the binocs, Nikki work her way down toward the prefab building that housed the winery near the vineyard in Harborcreek, Pennsylvania. It had some nice design touches on the facade, clearly meant to appeal to wine tourists. Tom and Nikki were sure that was where the grapes were crushed and pressed and then tossed into the vats for fermentation. After that, the usual clarification and into the small barrels for aging. All of this watched over by the S'hudonni spyeyes to make sure it was handcrafted by real Earthies.

The south shores of Lake Erie and Lake Ontario were good for growing grapes and had been for a long time. Most of the Lake Erie grapes became grape jelly, and Tom was thinking they should buy a couple of cases of that while they were here, just to make the point about what was OK and what could get you killed.

He watched Nikki as she crept around the side of the building, bringing out one, two, three small bricks of CXX84, the latest and greatest plastic explosives, attaching each of them to the side of the building and then pushing in the igniter. Easy as pie.

Then she disappeared from his view for a good thirty seconds, doing the same on the other side. When she reappeared she looked toward where he lay, atop the little knoll to the south. She waved in his direction and then moved away in a low crouch, off into the vineyard itself. All set.

The plan was to be humane about it. Tom was going to start peppering the front of the building with shots from his position on the knoll. When they came out of the building, he'd fire over their heads or into the dirt, and then when he figured they'd figured out where the shots were coming from, he'd stand, take another shot or two, and turn and run back over the crest of the knoll, down to where the no-tech old Ford F-150 pickup they'd liberated back in Ohio was ready for him. He'd even backed it in, so he'd be heading in the right direction on the narrow dirt road as soon as he turned the key.

They would follow him, probably pretty slow and cautious, and that's when Nikki would hit the button and the S'hudonni devices would go off and take the building down. That would confuse the hell out of them and they'd run back toward the building—or split up, with some heading back that way while the rest went after Tom. It didn't matter which thing they chose, because by then Tom would have reached the old F-150, cranked it up, and sped off on the side road. In a kilometer or so, there was an intersection, where he'd take a left and head on down to the Lake Erie shore. On the way, he'd pick up Nikki and off they'd go, message sent.

It was a good plan, and it would have worked, too, if the fucking old "classic" F-150 had started on the first try, or the second, or the third.

Tom sat in there for a good thirty seconds, turning the key and getting nothing but some clicking. Dead fucking battery.

He turned in the driver's seat to look back up to the top of the knoll, and two guys, one of them wearing a business suit and the other wearing overalls, crested the top and saw him. One of them raised a pistol and took a shot, and then another, but Tom wasn't worried about that. The guy was way too far off.

There was a huge explosion behind the two, so Nikki's charges had taken down the winery and she was off and running to get to the rendezvous point.

Now the guy in the suit was really pissed. He started loading up his rifle, some kind of bolt-action thing, pushing a bullet into the breech, pushing the bolt forward and snapping it down, and then taking aim, all while Tom watched, transfixed. A huge cloud of smoke was rising behind the knoll.

The guy fired, and a fraction of a second later the bullet hit the ground not ten meters away. Holy Christ.

The guy started the process over, even as the pistol shooter kept pulling the trigger, and even as one of those slugs slapped into the ground not far away, pinging off some rock.

The old F-150 was a manual, of course, so it finally occurred to Tom that he could push-start it by rolling down the hill that was right in front of him. Should have thought of that earlier, damn it, but it would work now, wouldn't it?

He opened the driver side door, stepped out, and started pushing, getting the truck over a little mound of dirt that had held the left front tire in place.

It started rolling and he hopped back in, turned the key to On, and jammed the stick into second gear while keeping the clutch all the way down.

The back window exploded. Christ, that was close. He popped the clutch and the engine, bless its heart, caught, and off he went, one more bullet from the rifle hitting the truck bed somewhere behind him. And then he was flooring it, shifting into third, bouncing along, farther away with every second, until he reached some trees and clattered through a stream, shallow in the late summer drought, and disappeared from the gunmen's sight.

Ten minutes later he picked up Nikki, and an hour later they dropped off the F-150 and liberated an old Volkswagen Beetle with a huge sunflower painted on the hood and stayed on some back roads until, at last, they felt like they'd cleared the danger.

Nikki was so excited by the action that she was bouncing on the seat right after she scrambled into the truck. "Boss! Boss! Did you see it? It was fucking fantastic! A huge ball of flame and then smoke and even a fucking shock wave. God, it was good! It was great!"

Then she noticed the shattered back window and said, "Holy fuck! You had some excitement! What the hell happened?"

He told her and she grinned and leaned over to hug him in her excitement, and kissed him on the cheek. "That was so fucking great! It was great!"

"Yeah," Tom said. "It was great."

And maybe it was. Maybe, now that they'd made a getaway, it had been pretty fucking great. Nikki's excitement was infectious.

She was amazing. Courageous, nerves of steel, plenty of smarts to go along with the bravery. A little reckless maybe.

He laughed. No *maybe* about it; she was reckless as hell. He turned to look at her. "You're something, Nikki. You're really something."

All right, so he'd fantasized about her every now and then, but he'd never followed up on that. There was too much at stake to mess it up with some schoolboy infatuation. He caught her looking at him every now and again, and he was thinking maybe she felt the same way but had come to the same conclusion. Keep it professional. But this. This was different. Just the two of them. Hot as hell.

Later, long after the sun had set and it had gotten cooler, in an old farmhouse not too far from West Seneca, New York, Tom and Nikki lay on an old mattress in the bedroom of the abandoned house.

The sex had been passionate and angry and loving and gentle and rough by turns. And wonderful. Tom was on his side, one arm stretched out so that his hand was on Nikki's hip. He shivered a bit in the cool night air that came in through the broken-out windows. She was on her side, looking at him.

"I thought you were never gonna get around to that, Boss," she said, smiling, and then reached over to trace a finger across his left cheek, his lips, and then to touch his nose.

"Didn't know if you were willing," he said. "And I didn't think it was a great idea, anyway."

"I was willing. Jesus Christ, I sure let you know. All those touches on the hand? Every time I gave you a pat on the shoulder? That was me telling you, Boss."

He shook his head. "I'm pretty much an idiot on that kind of stuff, Nikki. I thought you'd figured that out."

"I did," she said, and then leaned over to kiss him. "But this means we gotta be careful, right? We can't let this screw things up. I'm thinking this may or may not ever happen again and we should take advantage of the moment while it's here." And then she smiled, and added, "What do you think?"

Tom Holman had been a professor, a researcher, an invited speaker at seminars and conferences, a notable scholar in his particular corner of the biology world. He'd been important, and careful with his words, and careful with his deeds, and in full control of his passions, such as they were. And look where that had gotten him.

Now, here, she wanted him again, and some inner ape-mind of his liked that a lot. She was in control, not him, and it was her world, not his, and that sounded fine, so he leaned into her for another kiss and then, for the next little while, the passion took away the chill for both of them remarkably well.

Afterward, sated, he gave some thought to what was next, and then next after that. He'd been watching, when he could, the tour that the S'hudonni kid was making with Chloe Cary. Everyone was watching it, and everyone loved that fucking alien kid who was Twoclicks's son. Cute as a little bug's ear and all that.

And Chloe, of course, was a bigger star than ever. She was beautiful, he had to admit. Just like fucking Peter to wind up with her. There he was, a zillion kilometers away on the alien home world, and Chloe Cary did nothing but talk about him all the time. The celeb zines were still full of that crap, had them both on the covers every damn issue. Well, they'd sure be on the covers again in a few days, when the group in South Africa had at it. Tom hoped so. And then he leaned over and gave Nikki another kiss, rolled to his right, and put his feet down. Time to get back to business.

21

CAPE TOWN

The trouble started at a beach near Fish Hoek on their second day in South Africa, near Cape Town, with Treble excited about seeing the penguins in the wild.

"We saw these at the zoo in St. Louis!" Treble said, excited to see the cute little Cape penguins waddle along a sandy path to the beach. He saw no resemblance between himself and the penguins that ran along the path ahead of them. In fact, he mimicked their walk, more or less perfectly. Chloe laughed at that, her first laugh of the day.

Chloe really liked Treble, but they'd been at this for a while now, and traveling with him was wearing. She was enjoying all the hoopla and appreciative of the ratings, but really she just wanted to go home and get back to work on *The Family Madderz*. Instead, here she was, half a world away, on a bouldered beach near Cape Town, young Treble holding her hand as Anodiwa Pinaar, the hottest item in the stable of Cape Visions, the fifth-largest media entity on Earth and a sister studio to Chloe's, since both of them were owned by Totalcom, showed them around.

Just a couple of hours before, Pinaar had stood with them on the bluffs overlooking False Bay and showed them where to look for whales. There were none in sight, to Treble's great disappointment.

But they'd seen plenty of other things in Cape Town. They'd taken the new zoom lift to the top of Table Mountain, encased in that glass bubble that rose up the side of the mountain. At the top they'd had lunch at the Table, the restaurant that seemed to be suspended out over the nothingness, with the city to the left, the enormous bay in front, and the shoreline curving away into the distance to the right. You could maybe see Cape Point down there, the end of Africa.

Then, after lunch, they'd driven to the TruNature park entrance and walked into the interpretive center, where they'd helped Treble put on the modified sweep receiver, sliding the altered helmet onto his conical head and helping attach the earbuds, the taste buds, the smell tips, and all the rest. It wouldn't be the same experience for him as it was for humans— his hearing extended into both higher and lower ranges, for starters—but it would give him a good idea of what humans received, and that was the point. myBetty turned out to be indispensable for the attachment process. She was linked in with the Trebnet servers at Twoclicks's consulate in Los Angeles, and those servers had the answers to myBetty's questions. In fifteen minutes, Treble was hooked into one of the wandering caracal cats for the better part of an hour as it roamed the scrub brush and fynbos looking for a meal of dassie or guinea fowl or mongoose.

Treble was immersed when the cat found, killed, and ate a young dassie, tearing and chewing, tendons and muscles and bones all cracking and the blood flowing as the cat fed on the warm meat. When it was over, Treble said, in his best colloquial American English, "Wow, that was awesome!"

Chloe had her second good laugh of the day, and Pinaar had really cackled. He was a tough kid, was Treble. Cute as he could be, yes, but one tough kid.

Then they'd come down off the mountain and driven for a couple of hours to reach Cape Agulhas, the southern tip of Africa. There they'd stood next to the stone marker with the line down the middle. On it was printed "Indian Ocean" in English and "Indiese Oseaan" in Afrikaans, with the arrow pointing left, and "Atlantic Ocean" and "Atlantiese Oseaan," with the arrow pointing right. You could look out from there and see where the lighter blue of the Indian Ocean met the darker Atlantic.

They did a little business, too, of course, visiting the Stellenbosch wine country to the west of Cape Town. Treble tasted the wines from three of the vineyards that had bid to be providers of boutique wines to S'hudon and The Six. He gave a thumbs-up to each one, showing off his knowledge of Earthie wine idioms and making some new friends for S'hudon.

All of this was amazing to watch, even to Chloe's jaded eyes. The young alien, walking around with his small hand in hers, oohing and aahing over all these Earthie wonders, tasting Earthie wines, eating Earthie food. And he seemed completely genuine in his delight over what he was seeing and doing. Everyone he met, no surprise, seemed to feel the same way about him. He was smart, cute, friendly, and approachable. Good thing, because he was also exhausting.

For Chloe, a large part of the exhaustion was worry. Billions had been watching, day by day, as Chloe showed Earth off to Treble—or at least those vast swaths of Earth under Twoclicks's nominal control. Earlier in the tour, the billions had been watching when Treble had gone for a swim in the warm water of the Gulf of the Napoule, off Cannes. No one was quite sure how long he could stay underwater, but when thirty minutes had gone by, Chloe had quietly had myBetty send an emergency query to Twoclicks, back in Los Angeles. He'd replied, "It iss not to worry, dear friend Chloe. The Importance iss fine!"

And he had been. Later, she'd worried when he disappeared into the distance after diving off the pier at Kenmare, in Ireland, and had gone swimming out to Rossmore Island. That had been a nervous ninety minutes, waiting for that small dorsal to reappear. And then Treble climbed up the ladder and onto the pier and said, "Wonderful!"

And here in South Africa, the world audience had watched with delight as charming young Treble dived off the rocks at the end of Africa and took delight in the chance to swim in two oceans almost at once, swimming through the demarcation line between the Indian and the Atlantic, unworried about the great white sharks and orcas said to be there, and hoping to see and play with the whales. No luck with the whales, but no harm from the sharks, much to the relief of the watching two billion or more.

As Treble was out for that worrisome swim, Chloe had been thinking again, as she had in Cannes and in Ireland and even in St. Louis, that Twoclicks needed to get going on that custom-built sweep system for Treble that he'd promised but hadn't yet delivered. Imagine the sweep audience for an alien as lovable as Treble!

"myBetty," she said to her helpmate, "remind Twoclicks, please, about the necessity of getting a sweep system built for Treble, so he can send and not just receive."

"Done," said myBetty a few seconds later. "I'll report his response."

"And remind him, too, please, about my worries about our security," Chloe said.

She wasn't sure why Twoclicks had been so hesitant to beef up the security details that came along with Treble and Chloe on their adventurous diplomacies, but hesitant he had been. Often—too often, she thought—there didn't seem to be any guards detailed at all. Chloe assumed they were out of sight; but if that was the case, how quickly would they be able to react if something happened?

"Done," said myBetty, and then, seconds later, followed up. "The sweep equipment is ready and will be waiting for us in Buenos Aires, Twoclicks says. No response on additional security. I'm pretty sure he doesn't think you need that." To which Chloe could only sigh and shake her head.

It was here, on Boulders Beach, toward the end of the day where it all came down. Anodiwa had said she had a great surprise for them and took them to Boulders Bay, in Simon's Town, some twenty kilometers south of Cape Town. They snuck away from the usual gaggle of paparazzi by using Anodiwa's little runabout, a boxy Nistoy electric with tinted glass that they got into down in Anodiwa's capacious garage. They drove through the back alleyway, away from the house, and headed down to the bay.

Away from the media, Anodiwa felt free to pull over in the empty parking lot at Boulders Beach and told Chloe to look in the trunk. She did, and lo and behold, there lay Anodiwa's surprise: a wet suit, a full face mask, and a snorkel that Anodiwa helped Chloe get into so she could join Treble on the swim and get it all live on her sweep system.

Once she got into the gear, Chloe led the way as they wandered down between the house-size boulders and onto the grainy sand. She wasn't worried about the swimming; she'd done well enough on the swim team at Stanford and she still did a morning ocean swim often enough in Malibu—down the wooden steps to the beach, out and into the cold Pacific, and then straight out for a few hundred meters and left or right from there, depend-ing on the whim of the day, and then back for a good half hour. Refreshing.

This was sure no Malibu, though. There were penguins all around, eye-ing them suspiciously but unafraid. They were noisy as hell when a crowd of them got together. She hadn't quite realized that before, seeing only a few of them on a path at one time. Here, together, they raised a great ca-cophony, calling to one another with loud squawks. Chloe could barely hear herself think.

Treble, Anodiwa, and Chloe worked their way through the penguins and then, as they got close to the water, Treble let go of Chloe's hand and ran—his own version of a penguin waddle—right into the water. Chloe, close be-hind, had to stop and slip on the fins and the mask, and then she was in the water herself.

It was marvelous. The water wasn't any colder than in Malibu, and it had a lot less wave action, so she had no trouble snorkeling. She could see about twenty meters underwater, not great but not too bad, either. Even in that range there were penguins next to her and around her and beneath her as she snorkeled out to deeper water. She paused once to float and look around. A number of boulders were big enough to rise out of the water, and one had a large flat area just above the waterline, wet and sparkling in the sun, crowded with penguins.

It was a playground! She laughed, right through the snorkel and mask, as she watched the penguins leap out of the water to land, standing upright, on the flat surface of the rock. Then they waddled around for a few paces, seemed to take stock of one another, and dived right back in. It was comical to watch.

Treble surfaced just a meter away from Chloe, a huge smile on that bul-bous face. He was having fun, a lot of it. "Race you to that rock!" he said, and dove back in.

"myBetty, you getting all this?" Chloe asked her helpmate.

"Absolutely, Chloe. Looks like fun," myBetty said.

"OK, then. Here I go," Chloe said. She ducked down into the water, went down a meter or two, and started porpoising her fins to maximize her speed. She couldn't possibly beat Treble, who was already halfway there, but she'd give it her best shot. The penguins bumped her several times, which was somewhere between funny and frightening. But she worked her way through the crowded water to the flat rock and clambered up. Minutes later, sitting side by side on the rock, surrounded by pushy penguins, Chloe and Treble grinned at each other. Then they turned to wave to Anodiwa, who was watching through a binocular cam that was getting good video of the whole thing.

Together with myBetty's video through Chloe's mask, and the sweep that caught the tang of the salt air and the warmth of the sun on a cool, South African day, and the feel of the wet rock beneath her, this made for a great segment. The playful young alien from S'hudon, the star of *The Family Madderz,* whose boyfriend was now on S'hudon itself, and the glamorous Anodiwa Pinaar, their host, all having a great time.

The water, the cute little penguins, the stunning scenery—their numbers were going through the roof! All the world was paying close attention to charming little Treble and the woman he called, in English, Aunt Chloe.

Better yet, as soon as myBetty turned on the sweep feed from Aunt Chloe, the paparazzi were on their way, in cars and on motorcycles and with drones of all kinds unpacked and ready to go: flitterbys and spyeyes and gnats and even, in the case of two very smart paps, water-capable drones. Toss them into the surf and send them on their way, speeding along on the surface or diving down below it.

The paps had locals on the payroll to identify the beach, and locals on hand to do the driving, and locals on hand to work their way through the Cape Town traffic, and so in ten minutes they were starting to arrive, and so were the drones. Great stuff!

So they were all there watching, and Chloe was sweeping, and Anodiwa was live with her binoc cam, when a Zodiac rounded the headlands to the south and came toward Chloe and Treble. There were three men aboard, one at the helm, another with a mask around his neck and carrying a speargun, another with a rifle. The outboard in the rear was pushing them along in a hurry, moving them from one thousand meters away to nine hundred and then to eight hundred in one damn hurry.

"Chloe, get the two of you off that rock!" myBetty commanded, seeing the feeds from the others—the paparazzi and Anodiwa and even one, incredibly, from the prow cam on the Zodiac. The bad guys were keeping their own cam going while they tried to assassinate the princeling and the Hollywood star!

Chloe was confused by myBetty's command but started looking around. Treble didn't hear the warning through the din from the penguins and was unworried. In fact, neither of them heard it when the distant pop of a rifle sounded, and then a second one. But when that second shot hit the boulder they sat on and the whole rock seemed to vibrate as it rang like a bell, Chloe reacted, grabbing Treble's hand and pushing them both off the rock platform and into the water. Good thing, since a third shot rang the bell again as it slammed into the rock right where Treble had been sitting moments before.

Chloe's decision was choosing where to go. Into deeper water? Treble could stay down for hours, apparently, if he needed to, but not Chloe. She couldn't protect him there, but he'd be able to swim away from any danger. Into shore? She could protect him there, and they would have help from Anodiwa. Yes, that.

But Treble didn't wait for Chloe to decide, so no, not that at all. He stayed above the water just long enough to tell her, "Get to shore!" and then he dived, disappearing from view. Chloe, her decision-making over, struck out for the beach, which turned out to be the longest minute of her life as she ripped off her mask but left the fins on and swam like a demon for the sandy shore, where Anodiwa Pinaar stood there waving, foolishly perhaps, and yelling at her to "Swim! Swim!"

Which she did, and very well. Chloe had finished third in the Pac-12 hundred-meter freestyle as a Stanford sophomore. She'd quit competitive swimming the next year, when fame and fortune struck her in the form of a what-the-hell-why-not audition that turned into her first starring role as young Annie Oakley in the *Sharpshooter* series. But the body remembers, and the muscle memory kicks in when you need it to, and Chloe Cary most certainly had her personal best time as she plowed right through the low swells and the moderate shore break and reached the beach in one damn hurry.

Chloe stood and hurriedly waded the last five or ten meters to the beach and then turned to look out toward the Zodiac as it slowed and the diver front-flipped over the side, holding on to what looked like a speargun. He was going after Treble, which in a long-short moment of utter clarity Chloe realized was utter stupidity, unless that wasn't a speargun but some kind of S'hudonni weapon—and oh, my god, it might be.

But she couldn't worry about that at the moment; a bullet whizzed by her and hit a large branch of driftwood behind her, spraying wood chips. Close.

"In my bag," said Anodiwa calmly. She was ready, with a pistol in her right hand and the left hand steadying it as she let off a round. Hopeless, but worth the shot.

Chloe reached into Anodiwa's bag and there was another pistol, a SIG Sauer, which she knew how to use. Now to put that target practice she'd done for *The Family Madderz* to good use. She grabbed the weapon, thumbed off the safety, cocked it, and aimed out toward the Zodiac, now bouncing along over the outer edge of the low surf line that Chloe had just been swimming through. They were more than one hundred meters out, but no use waiting for a better shot. She squeezed the trigger once, and then again, just as she saw the muzzle flash from the rifle and heard a deep grunt from Anodiwa, standing next to her.

Chloe glanced over and Anodiwa was standing there, still, looking at her right arm. "Jesus," Anodiwa was saying, but Chloe could see she'd only been winged, an open cut along the forearm.

Anodiwa glanced at Chloe, and damned if that wasn't a smile as she raised that arm, flexed her wrist, moved the fingers, was satisfied, and raised the gun again to take aim.

Another shot from the Zodiac, and this one hit the bag at Chloe's feet. The guy out there was a good shot, but the bouncing of the Zodiac over the waves wasn't helping him a bit.

Chloe turned to see the Zodiac making a left turn to give the shooter a clear shot toward the beach, as the boat settled into a trough. But this also gave Chloe and Anodiwa both a clear view of the shooter, now closer than one hundred meters away, and they both fired at the same time.

The shooter crumpled, fell onto the gunwale of the Zodiac, and then, when the driver hit the gas to get them out of range, fell over the side.

Chloe and Anodiwa fired again, both aiming for the driver. They missed, but the windscreen in front of him shattered as someone's bullet hit it. They fired again, but he was bouncing along on the waves now and it was hardly worth taking the shot. But, hell, they both kept firing anyway, and then one of them got lucky. The driver threw up his arms in the distance, then fell back into the Zodiac. Got him.

Chloe looked at Anodiwa, who was looking at her. There was a kind of joy in this, a oneness with the moment, with the danger, with the killing. Anodiwa smiled. Chloe smiled back. There was a lot, everything in fact, said in those smiles.

"Good shooting," Anodiwa said, and it was. It was, for both of them. "But now, you look for the swimmer while I wrap this up," she added. She reached into the bag for a first aid kit and sat down to bandage the bloody open wound on her forearm.

The swimmer. Right. He was the other attacker.

Chloe looked out to the water. No swimmer in sight, and now, behind them, she could hear people running toward them. She turned to look and it was the paparazzi. Hell.

She knelt down and helped Anodiwa bind the wound, turning to look a few times out toward the water. She didn't need that swimmer to come out of the surf while she had her back to him.

But he didn't come, and she finished the bandage and stood and turned to look as the paparazzi rushed right by and down to the water, where Treble, the prince and heir to the throne, emerged from the water, swimming in and then standing to walk when it shallowed out. He held a line that went back into the water, and he pulled on it as he walked.

He was grinning, was Treble, and waddling happily toward Chloe, whistling and clicking and then saying, in English, "So much fun! So much fun! Here, Chloe, help me!"

Chloe did, walking over to pull on the line, and then, with the help of a few of the paparazzi, brought in the swimmer who'd attacked Treble. He was still alive, if half drowned and wrapped in the line, the only attacker to survive the day. The paparazzi and Chloe's sweep feed and all the drones and flitters and spyeyes and everything else went live with the moment as Treble and Chloe and Anodiwa hugged and then sat in the sand. Wailing sirens announced the arrival of the cavalry in the form of the Fish Hoek police and EMTs. The audience numbers for this event, counting live and replayed worldwide, reached four billion on Earth and many billions more throughout The Six.

To be honest, making love with Anodiwa a good five hours later, back at her place, after the interviewing and the police work and the two state departments and the calls back to Twoclicks and all the rest, seemed as natural and perfect as if they'd known each other for years. They hardly even talked about it, exhausted, bandaged, Treble in his own room, they in Anodiwa's. There was a cautious first kiss and then on it went from there, slow and languid and careful, given Anodiwa's wound. But beautiful, in its own way. At least that's how Chloe saw it.

Afterward, Anodiwa slept while Chloe lay on her back and stared at the ceiling. Where had Anodiwa's weapons and her ability to use them come from? Who was she working for? Twoclicks? The South African Special Forces Brigade? The latter, probably, Chloe thought, and then she rolled over on her side to put her arm over sleeping Anodiwa and snuggle in. Safe.

They were still sleeping and spooning, the two of them, when myBetty dinged her with another call from Twoclicks, who'd been calling all afternoon to shower praise on her and Anodiwa and, mostly, on Treble, telling her the tour had to go on, billions were expecting it.

And now, lying here in Anodiwa's bed, answering the ding from myBetty, she heard otherwise. A new message from Twoclicks. The tour was over and Chloe and Treble were heading back to L.A. Anodiwa would be staying in Cape Town, where her promo team was taking full advantage of her new global profile. She had things to do.

A few hours later, Chloe sat in great comfort in a nice lounger in her suite in the big 797, and Treble, "the Importance," was elsewhere on the plane, relaxing in a suite of his own. On her third glass of a very nice Fish Hoek Kaapse Riesling that soon enough would be finding its way to Harmony and Melody, Chloe wondered if Twoclicks had set the whole thing up. Would he risk his son's life, not to mention Chloe's life, for all that global attention? After all, Treble hadn't really been in danger, had he? Would Twoclicks do that? Chloe—a real hero now, not just a Hollywood version of one—realized that, yes, of course he would. And then she finished the very nice Riesling.

PART SEVEN

THE NIAGARA GORGE

Violence is rare for the Harmonics, and so it was with a mixture of disgust and guilty pleasure that they all watched the action that took place in the Niagara River Gorge and sent the ratings through the roof. Earthies are so passionate! Actual death! Fabulous!

—Peter Holman, *Notes from Holmanville*
(S'hudon City and New York:
Trebnet Press, 2035)

22

PEACHES

Tom Holman sat in a wrought iron chair on the back deck of Shadrach's Steakhouse in Pekin, New York, thinking about how easy it was for most Americans to fool themselves. Next to him, and in general agreement, was Nikki Freeman, drinking a beer. An hour ago, in a small hotel on Niagara Falls Boulevard, they had broken their rule about no more sex between the two of them. They didn't say it to each other at the time or afterward, but they both knew that they might not make it through this afternoon and evening's excitement, so the lovemaking had been earnest and passionate. Now, on the back deck of Shadrach's, they were calmer.

They'd just watched the news on an old flat screen behind the restaurant bar. They were drinking Budweisers—no microbrew crap for them—as they saw the news reporter showing snippets of the heroic actions of Chloe Cary and Prince Treble and Anodiwa Pinaar from the week before, capturing one attacker and killing two more in an incident in Cape Town, South Africa, watched live by nearly four billion people worldwide.

And Chloe Cary and Prince Treble were coming here! Today! To Niagara Falls! To celebrate the completion of the Niagara Tower and throw the switch to start the power flowing—free electricity!—to the entire Northeast of the United States and all of Ontario!

The news reporter was breathless with excitement. Tom and Nikki felt differently. They looked at each other, then quietly clinked their glasses. Now it was up to them.

Tom liked it here, sitting and sipping and looking out over the edge of the Niagara Escarpment to the scenery below. You could pretend everything was fine. To the north, Lake Ontario glistened on a cloudless and warm late summer day. It was midafternoon on a Wednesday and tourist season was over, so business was slow and they had the deck to themselves. The staff seemed uninterested in stopping Tom from smoking, so he'd lit up an unfiltered Camel—hard to get them these days, but worth the effort and expense—and now he looked out to that splendid view.

Below them, the escarpment tumbled down into the back edge of the fertile bottomlands with their peach orchards and vineyards stretching out to the east and west, busy with workers bringing in the harvest, all those neat rows of S'hudon's profit, reaching all the way north to the distant lakeshore. Below, just north of where the escarpment met the bottomlands, Ridge Road ran arrow-straight east and west, the self-drives moving along smartly, in nicely ordered, careful patterns, just as safe as safe could be. A beautiful day, a beautiful view, everything nice and tidy. Prosperous. Nearly two years into the occupation now and everything was fine. Life was good in some places, as long as you were on board with the new way of doing things.

The Niagara Tower was the greatest symbol of that. The Earthie friends—emphasis on *friends*—would prosper. But get on the wrong side of a changing world and you were fucked. That was the deal, like it or not. There were a lot of promises that had been made: the new S'hudon Trebnet cloud that was free and fast and capacious; the new roads and bridges and tunnels that were being built to move freight around; the promised new transcontinental hypertubes to move the people coast to coast in three hours, with spurs off to everywhere; the med-doc automata to keep the happy workers healthy and fit. The endless fields of grain. The vineyards and the orchards. The endless and mindless entertainment, like that fucking *The Family Madderz* show, with Chloe Cary kicking ass both literal and figurative, what with Hollywood awash in big money from Out There.

All of this was the bright and shiny future for Earth as S'hudon's nature park, filled with billions of happy peasants tilling the soil and reaping the crops. For booze. For the handcrafted Earthie alcohol in all its permutations that was all the rage of The Six, those settled planets in S'hudon's empire.

It seemed like an idea concocted from a drunken frat party at some school in the Midwest. Stanford and Caltech can have their science nerds, man. We'll make beer and schnapps! Hey! This will make millions!

Dr. Tom put his binoculars—classic old Zeiss 20x60s that had belonged to his father, a wonderful guy, a pediatrician and serious birder—to his eyes and searched the near shore of the lake. There it was, the image stabilizing as he settled on it. The Niagara Tower, buzzing with drones and barges and helicopters on this Big Day of the dedication, when the symbolic switch would be thrown by superstar Chloe Cary, the hottest ticket in Hollywood, the girl who'd shot to even greater heights of global fame by plugging the bad guys in Cape Town. And the girlfriend of Peter Holman, traveler to the home world—and, oh, by the way, Dr. Tom Holman's older brother. Fucking Peter. Humanity's greatest sellout. Ever.

"Take a look," he said to Nikki, and handed her the binocs. She looked toward the tower, a latticework construction that, like all the S'hudonni buildings and ships, looked like a Tinker Toy, all flimsy scaffolding with round connections where the beams met. No wonder the new Tinker Toy sets were so popular again.

"I don't know, Boss. That tower is a son of a bitch, tough as all hell. You sure you can knock it down?"

"Yep," he said, and blew out a cloud of smoke. "I talked to Whistle's people this morning. They say it'll work if I get the damn things attached to the pylons. I think, despite it all, we got to trust him one more time, Nikki."

All of the barley, the rye, the flower of the hops, the wheat, the corn, the grapes, the potatoes, and all the rest. Grown by hand, furrows dug behind a horse-drawn plow, trees and vines tended by careful hands, no pesticides, no fertilizer, just humble Earthies working the soil and then carefully picking the grapes and stomping around in a vat to macerate them, or picking the corn or the hops and barley and then small-batch brewing the perfect beer, or distilling the perfect vodka, the perfect rum, the perfect gin, the perfect ouzo, the perfect mescal. The latest rage, in fact, centered on those very workers in the peach orchard below, carefully climbing ladders to pick peach by peach to meet the demands on Melody, where Earthie peach schnapps was what one's conjoined family had to have. All for one and one for all. Distilled peaches. Those cuttlefish creatures scuttling around drunk. Christ almighty.

All of this was so very hand intensive, with hardworking native artisans creating liquid art by the millions of barrels, vats, tuns, bottles, and kegs. All of it very carefully supervised by spyeyes at every step, to ensure authenticity. You can't trust those Earthies, you know; they're lazy, and they'll cheat. But their libations? Yummy. And there wasn't enough to satisfy the demand on Downtone, on Harmony, on Melody and all The Six. And you will be the seventh, Earthies, honest, once the markets meld. Nearly two years into the process and the world was changing fast. Planets-worth of markets will do that to you.

He took a drag on his Camel, flicked it out over the railing, and watched it arc down the escarpment, down toward the vineyards. He was sure there was a spyeye seeing that, and some algorithm sussing out what he'd just done. In a minute or two some helpful Vichy having a drink in the restaurant bar would set down his glass of handcrafted Niagara wine and come outside to admonish Dr. Tom Holman. Fuck that.

"Let's go," he said to Nikki, and they both rose, turned their backs on the splendid scenery, and walked around the building to the parking lot. They got into the little rented Nistoy. They didn't want to call attention to themselves. Not yet, anyway.

They waited for the buckles to belt them in, and then Nikki spoke to the car, told it to go manual. Then she looked at Tom and said, "Hit the button on that suppressor thing so we're not tracked."

Tom smiled, hit the button, and then Nikki got them going, on their way to the Niagara Gorge and the town of Lewiston.

23

NIAGARA FALLS

It was six days after the Cape Town excitement and the long flight to LAX, then home to Malibu, then a few hours of rest, and then back to work on the show for a couple of days when the usual priority call came through for Chloe, right in the middle of a table read. That myBetty let the call through meant it was Twoclicks, and everyone at the table just smiled politely when Chloe took the call; no one stepped out of the room. They all knew which side their bread was buttered on.

There was a very private party for that night at the consulate. Could she come? "Sspecial, special people, dearest friend Chloe!" Twoclicks said. "Just arrived! Can you attend? I need you!"

Could she? Would she? As if there were any question. She would. And she did, later that night, using her suppressor to dodge the paparazzi technology as she took the back way out from her house and the back way in to the consulate.

It was, in fact, quite a gathering. Chloe Cary on Twoclicks's arm, wining and dining her way through the evening with a small group of Earthies and the first daffodils and ducks she'd ever seen live.

The Earthies in attendance were all influencers, she was sure, though she only recognized a few. myBetty said their bios were blocked for her, so Chloe never did find out all their names. They were heavy hitters in tech and energy, mainly, it looked like.

These were people not easily impressed, but they were agog to be in the presence of Twoclicks and his alien pals: daffodils from Harmony, just like the ones they'd all seen through Peter's eyes back when his ship had blown apart; and three of the tall feathered ducks from Downtone, the ones who were all female, laying eggs that were fertile.

These alien emissaries had all just arrived for their first visit to Earth, the source of so much entertainment and profit for them all. They were ecstatic to meet Chloe Cary—a lot more excited than the Earthies, to be honest— and at first she couldn't figure that out. There was no reason for them to care about a (let's admit it) slightly aging actor whose show they'd never seen on their own world or, she suspected, on Earth. But one after another they'd come up to her to express their delight. Hanratty did the translating for her as they talked about her courage and her primitive daring and her deep friendship with the princeling.

Ah, *that* was it, then. They had seen some kind of replay of the Cape

Town attack. That had to be it. Still, it was quite a reaction to a few minutes of excitement back there with the penguins in Cape Town.

She wanted to ask Twoclicks about how they knew so much about her, but he was too busy being expansively generous as a host, showing her off with exclamations of "Thiss iss our wonderful dear friend Chloe Cary!" and "Issn't sshe the most wonderful dear friend?" and on and on.

Then he explained what he needed from her. A little promo work with the new Niagara Tower. "Free power for millions, dear friend Chloe!" he said to her, in front of the gathered dignitaries. "Wonderful for you to dedicate, yess?"

She wasn't in a position to say no. Her debt to Twoclicks was a big one. Since Cape Town, she was followed now by billions, and swept up by ninety million. She was everything, in fact, that Peter had once hoped to be. Ironic, that.

So the next day, in the antiseptic room in the consulate—the one with the huge plateglass window along one wall so everyone, from Twoclicks to those Earthie movers and shakers to the duck and the daffodils, could watch as she stripped down—she held the hand of the small daffodil technician, who helped her lie on her back against the cold, hard surface of the bed. She heard a slight buzzing and then nothing—no dreams, no nothing—until she woke up in Niagara Falls.

One minute she was stripping in L.A., climbing onto that Travel bed, closing her eyes and relaxing, and then, *zap*. Seconds or minutes later, Chloe slowly came to consciousness, still lying on her back on what felt like the same hard glass of the Travel bed in the consulate.

She sat up, put her leg over the side, and then stood. It wasn't the same bed at all. She was in a different room, not the sterile and close white walls of the consulate Travel room but a spacious room with a single large picture window. She walked over to it and there, sixty floors below her, as promised, was Niagara Falls, impressive in the long light of morning.

She felt pretty good. Twoclicks had told her that the process was so painful that she'd scream in torment but that she wouldn't remember it, and sure enough, she felt fine, but her throat was very sore.

No dizziness, so Twoclicks had been wrong about that.

So now she'd Traveled, as Twoclicks and Hanratty called it. Capitalized. Scanned and copied and pulled apart, then squirted from Twoclicks's consulate residence in L.A. to this room in S'hudon's Ontario consulate overlooking the Falls, and reassembled here. Would the wonders never cease? She glanced at the clock on the bed table, which read a couple of minutes after noon. So with the three-hour difference from California, the whole process had taken about a minute, from lying down on the glass bed in the consulate to waking up here on the Canadian side of the Falls.

She walked through the bedroom door and into a dining room. Two-clicks or Hanratty or their minions had taken care of everything. A large table, mahogany, sat in the middle of the room, and everything she would need was laid out there—except for Treble, of course. He'd flown on Two-clicks's private 797 to Washington, DC, yesterday, to meet with the US president in her office—Chloe was not invited—and that same jet should be getting him here to Niagara Falls in an hour or so. She'd swing by and pick him up.

Her clothes, her myBetty and her smarty, her toiletries, and the sweep system she'd be wearing for the dedication were all there for her. She picked up the new myBetty bowl amp and put it into her ear. There was some buzzing, a few clicks, and then myBetty said, "Hello, Chloe. Nice to see you made it in one piece." myBetty had expressed her doubts about the whole quantum travel thing. Now, though, she faced the facts. Chloe had Traveled, and it was time to move on.

"Hi, myBetty. I'm glad to be here," said Chloe, offering a bit of an olive branch to her helpmate.

There was a moment's hesitation from myBetty. Then she said, "I've just heard from Twoclicks. He's happy to hear you've arrived and wishes he could be here with you, but he has two shows tonight at the StandUp Club."

"Right," said Chloe. That was so Twoclicks. It was often hard to tell whether Twoclicks was a brilliant and cunning actor just putting on a show for the gullible Earthies or a genuinely oblivious *Aw shucks* sort of being. As if to prove his good-humored love for the locals, while Chloe had been traveling around the world with little Treble, Twoclicks had started performing at the StandUp Club, and now he considered himself a comedic star. A movie was in the works.

He didn't seem to realize that the StandUp Club sold out through fear. If you were invited to see Twoclicks perform, you attended. To be a friend of Twoclicks was to have the inside track on all the tech and all that power. But to be on the wrong side of the same said Twoclicks was to risk annihilation. He'd only shown that side a few times, but everyone involved got the message. Recently there'd been that unrest in Fort McMurray, Alberta, and the trouble in the Inner Mongolia Autonomous Region and in Russia's Kuznetsk Basin. People in those areas dared to wonder whether giving up Earth's own energy supply was really that great an idea. They'd been squashed, although almost no one knew about it. S'hudon controlled the Trebnet, after all. Only the few insiders—count Chloe Cary among those few—really got to hear what was going on.

So S'hudon's wondrous towers were set to rise everywhere, broadcasting free energy for a happy Earth. Coal? Oil? Solar? Hydro? Tides? Bio? Not needed anymore. The towers were rising, and inside of a year, free power would be there for the asking. The first one of those, in fact, was why Chloe was in town.

Chloe finished dressing and then talked with myBetty about the plan as Twoclicks had outlined it: First, drive across the Rainbow Bridge to the US side, then down Niagara Falls Boulevard to the airport to pick up Treble. Then retrace that path and do a quick drive-through with fans in the city of Niagara Falls. Then a meet-and-greet up the road in Lewiston, a touristy village that was right on their way. Then back on the road, up to the village of Youngstown—right at the mouth of the Niagara River, where it emptied into Lake Ontario—where they would meet Anodiwa Pinaar, who'd helped save the day in Cape Town. There, with Anodiwa—dear Anodiwa, Chloe thought—the three of them would do all the meet-and-greet stuff all over again, including some interviews with the celeb journos and drinks on a barge that would take them all out to the new Niagara Tower for its grand launch, where Chloe was making a major speech about the prosperous future under Twoclicks's gentle guidance.

All of this was easy enough. So easy, in fact, that it was hard to understand why she'd had to be squirted out to here by that device; the studio's corporate jet would have done just fine. She could have red-eyed it and only missed one day's shooting.

Now, here, the final thing to do was to put on the sweep unit. It was still in the box, but when she pulled it out, the battery icon said it was fully charged and ready to go. So, OK, she put it on, another brand-new next-gen version. It was a flimsy thing, really, considering all that it could do, a single strand of wire that split twice to end with four contacts, which clicked over the imbeds when she put them into place, working the wire through her hair. The latest and greatest for sweeping everything she saw, heard, touched, tasted, and smelled. New stabilizers for the images, new sound clarifiers that she could control by thought, new touch and taste amplifiers controlled through myBetty.

Speaking of which . . . "Are you tied in with the sweep system, myBetty?" she asked her helpmate.

"Yes, Chloe, and I finished the diagnostics. We're good. I'll record it all as the default. You tell me when you want to go live. We're connected at all times through the Trebnet."

"Good," said Chloe. "Record away, dear. I'll let you know when to go live. Just for the speech, I think."

"Got it."

Chloe walked over to the bedroom window, which faced north. She looked out, away from the Falls, downstream, to where the Niagara River emptied into Lake Ontario. And there it was, the focus of today's activity, clearly visible from here: the Niagara Tower, Twoclicks called it.

OK. Go get Treble, meet the dignitaries, hang out with Anodiwa and the princeling, drink a little local wine, give her little speech, and, an hour after that, maybe an evening with Anodiwa before tomorrow's flight with Treble back to L.A. Easy enough.

And for a while, it was. An hour later she'd met the limo and they'd made the twenty-minute drive out to the airport. There, they'd been escorted by the local National Guard onto the tarmac where Twoclicks's 797 was parked. As they'd driven up, Treble had come hopping down the steps by himself, waving at everyone, a large smile on that face, and then hopped into the limo to sit across from Chloe, after giving her an exuberant hug and calling her Aunt Chloe once again. She kind of liked that, she had to admit.

As they drove back toward the city, Chloe got to hear all about his visit with the president and the flights from L.A. to DC, and then today from DC to Niagara Falls. It was dizzying, but good fun, to listen to him in his excitement.

"The president was great!" he said, and when Chloe asked what they had talked about, he said, "Top secret!" and laughed.

His plane had come in right over the Falls before touching down, and Treble was impressed. "Beautiful!" he said. "Can I swim there and go over the Falls, Aunt Chloe?"

"Please don't, for my sake, Treble," she said. The princeling was certainly crazy enough to try it. "I bet we could sneak you in down at the bottom, though. They have boats there that get up close, and you could just go over the side for a swim. How does that sound?"

"Perfect!" he said. "But first, I am hungry for Earthie food. Let's eat!"

Treble had discovered hamburgers while they were in the Midwest, and he hadn't let go of the interest yet. Chloe was certain there was a good place for hamburgers in Niagara Falls, and they had an hour before the scheduled drive through the city. She asked myBetty for some help on that and myBetty had a recommendation: the famous Sammy's Sammies, which had all sorts of sandwiches but specialized in the Samasita burger, which had a little Mexican heat added in.

But Treble had another idea. "Chicken wings!" he said. "Did you know they invented those in Buffalo, and we could be there in twenty minutes? Let's go!"

So go they did, changing course to go back and across one bridge and then another, both of them spans over the same circuitous Niagara River. From there on into downtown Buffalo, and after a little winding around, they were at the Anchor Bar, "Home of the Original Buffalo Wing." Treble had ten, mild, and then ten more, hot, all the while admiring and commenting on the autographed pictures on the walls of celebrities from John Lennon to Elvis Presley to many more. Chloe was not surprised to hear about them all from Treble, between bites of the second round of wings. By the third round, she was taking part. Mild, mind you. They both happily made a real mess of it, the wings and the dip were all over the napkins that Treble and Chloe wore around their necks. Then they signed autographs—messy with sauce—for a while, and then, with a little help from the owner, snuck out the back and darted into the limo. They were both laughing. What fun!

And it was good they had that fun, since the rest of the day took a darker turn, which happened like this.

Chloe was thinking, during the limo ride, *Cute little princeling. Cute as a button. Cute as he could be.* All of that, sure, but he'd be the Mother one day, he'd explained to her over a whisky in the Hebrides. He'd be the ruler over this whole empire.

"I'll be a good Mother," he'd promised her. "Once I choose my path, and take Motherhood, I'll be first in line. Fathers Twoclicks and Whistle have been preparing me for years! I am the Importance, next in line. I will be a great ruler."

Ah, the Importance. So that was really a term. Chloe had thought it was the usual Twoclicks-style enthusiasm when he'd used that term for Treble when he'd first said the princeling was coming. Well, hell, he was a great kid. Assuming he became a great Mother, and assuming he liked what he knew of Earth, that was a good thing, right? She hoped so.

And Chloe was thinking this, too, during the limo ride: Why had Twoclicks insisted on using the Travel device to get her from L.A. to here? To duplicate her? What the hell was that about?

She had an idea. "myBetty," she whispered to her helpmate, "can you send a message to the original Chloe Cary back in the L.A. consulate?"

"Certainly," myBetty said, apparently not finding anything odd about the request. And then, seconds later, followed up. "The number seemed to work, but there was no response from her myBetty—my first-ever call to myself, I should add."

"Did you leave a message?"

"I did. And here's something interesting, Chloe. I've been assigned a new number. The final two digits have been changed."

Interesting. Chloe had to admit she didn't understand how it all worked. Yet. She'd find out, though. She didn't like not knowing things.

Treble had left the Anchor Bar with a small box of leftover hot wings. "Delicious!" he said as he finished the last one, and by then they were driving by Niagara Falls on the US side.

They stopped the limo and got out to walk over to the railing and take a look. "Wonderful!" said the princeling. "I love it here!"

24

DOUBLE TROUBLE

The limo that was taking Chloe and Treble through the day's activities wasn't armored, and it had a human driver instead of an AI. Chloe realized later that she should have been worried about that, but the driver was nice, the limo was comfortable, and the driver would only have them for a couple of hours, including the planned stop in the village of Lewiston to do the usual visit with the mayor and other city officials. What could go wrong?

And, in fact, the afternoon started just fine. After the Anchor Bar and the quick stop at Niagara Falls, Treble wondered aloud what the Falls would look like with a full flow. "That will be something to see, won't it, Aunt Chloe?" he asked her.

What was that about? Without being asked, myBetty let her know: "About sixty to seventy-five percent of the water is diverted to power plants before it reaches the Falls, Chloe."

Treble heard myBetty, and added, "And when the new Niagara Tower is at full strength, there won't be a need for that diversion. Full flow over the Falls. Amazing!"

By then, they were on a parkway that took them along the Niagara Gorge. Chloe asked the driver to pull over at a scenic view sign, and she and Treble got out to walk to the edge of the gorge and look down the river. It was impressive, with a rushing ribbon of river down below, the mist from the Falls to their left, and to their right, just visible, the new Niagara Tower, where they'd end up in a couple of hours. It was all very stunning.

She must have said that aloud, since Treble responded with his usual enthusiasm. "It will be even more impressive with the full flow! Imagine!"

"It sure would, Treble," she said, but she wondered just where all the new water would go as it rushed downstream. She wouldn't want to be on one of those Maid of the Mist tourist boats when that additional water came thundering down.

The plan was to go right down the parkway to Lewiston and then, after that, to Youngstown and the big gala out on the tower. But it wasn't going to be that easy. They got back into the limo and hadn't gone more than a half mile when they made a turn to the right and found themselves facing a large crowd waving American flags and with a band playing Sousa music. The signs they were holding said "Welcome, Chloe Cary!" and "Love *The Family Madderz*" and "Treble Fan Club!" There were a lot of them, hundreds. It wasn't going to be quick getting through this crowd.

The whole point of this little excursion to Niagara Falls, though, was to build good relations between Twoclicks and the Earthies. He governed with a light hand, for sure, and he left things in place in most places most of the time. But Chloe had almost laughed at him in person a couple of times, when he seemed so needy. He wanted badly to be liked—witness the zaniness of his stand-up comedy routines in L.A.

So, without asking, she knew he'd want them to stop for a while. She didn't see anyone who looked dangerous, and Treble seemed happy to stop, so stop they did, to press the flesh, as the American pols say. As the limo stopped and the driver came around to open the door, Chloe told myBetty to go live on a sweep of this, and then she put on her sweep glasses. It was a bright, cloudless, late summer day, so they darkened immediately.

Chloe clambered out first, and then reached back in to take Treble's hand and help him out. The police hadn't been expecting them to stop, so there were barricades along the side of the road but not more than one officer every fifty meters. Chloe and Treble smiled and walked over to the waiting crowds and started shaking hands and signing autographs. Treble had mastered the art of a quick autograph during his time on tour with Chloe, and he put the technique to good use here. A quick scribble and a big smile and a hello was all it took.

Chloe was enjoying herself. It was always better to go unscripted with these things, she was thinking, since the pleasant surprise for the fans made it a lot more fun for her, too.

By this time, one of the police officers, a woman, had arrived, said hello, and then turned her attention to crowd control and security. Chloe watched as the officer reminded a few people to not fall over the barricades in their enthusiasm, and then noticed that she kept checking the crowd for trouble. Was she looking for someone with a weapon? Someone on a rooftop with a rifle? Someone looking angry and suspicious in any way? The officer wanted to head trouble off, wherever it came from.

At one point, the officer was standing next to Chloe, who took the opportunity to say, "We're sorry," and reached out to shake her hand. "We didn't mean to complicate your day."

"No problem," she said, and smiled at Chloe. "It's great to meet you. I'm Officer Chechele. Call me Karen. And I'm as big a fan as anyone here. But we do want to keep you safe, all right?"

"Absolutely, Karen, and thank you," said Chloe, and then Treble came over, too.

"I am so pleased to say hello and thank you," he said, reaching up to shake hands.

Chechele leaned over to take his hand. "Delighted to meet you," she said, and she smiled broadly at him before standing back up and surveying the crowd once again.

Ten minutes later, the impromptu event was over and Officer Chechele escorted Chloe and Treble back to their limo, where the driver, with a stern and worried look on his face, held the door open.

Chloe helped Treble in and then climbed into the limo herself. Next stop, the village of Lewiston, New York, famous for its rich history of hosting all sorts of dignitaries who'd visited the village, from Charles Dickens, James Fenimore Cooper, and Harriet Tubman to—here, today—Chloe Cary and the emissary from S'hudon, young Treble, son of Twoclicks, son of Whistle, and heir to the throne. Funny how much Americans loved royalty.

Lewiston sits on the shore of the Niagara River, just after the river emerges from the deep gorge that marks the path of the Falls as they've worked their eroded way south over the previous five thousand years. In another ten thousand years, the Falls will have worked their way to where the river begins at Lake Erie. Make that five thousand years, with the Falls returned to full flow.

Across the river from Lewiston is Canada, which meant freedom to pre-emancipation slaves in America. For many escaped slaves, the road to freedom, sometimes called the Underground Railroad, ended with a stealthy nighttime passage from Lewiston to Queenstown, Ontario, dodging the bounty hunters, who operated freely even in the North—but not in Canada. So when slaves who had risked their lives to escape in Alabama, Georgia, the Carolinas, Tennessee, or Kentucky traveled the dangerous path of the Underground Railroad and made that final passage across the swift river to the Canadian shore in the dead of night, they were slaves no more. Thousands risked the journey.

Chloe listened to the history lesson from Treble and was glad to hear it. They both were expected to say a few words, and then the town was unveiling a new statue, *Friendship*, constructed by a local artist who had used scrap metal to construct fantastic creatures of all sorts—including, apparently, a creature who symbolized the friendship between the citizens of Lewiston and the new friends from another planet who had brought such prosperity to the region.

Prosperity? Chloe wasn't so sure. Treble had wanted to see a real, live Native American reservation when they were here, and so the limo had driven a few kilometers out of their way to take them through the back roads of the nearby Tuscarora reservation. Things didn't look so prosperous there, with a nice home here and there but too many homes in poor shape and too many people, she guessed, in poor shape. The school they drove by had a basketball standard on the playground. The pole was leaning. The rim was halfway off. There was no net. Chloe wondered what Peter, the old pro basketball player, would have thought of that.

And then they were through the reservation, driving on a road that ran along the top of a steep escarpment. The views out over the old lake bottom below were great and she could see Lake Ontario in the distance, and there, where the river emptied into the lake, the tower they would be visiting later.

Finally, they angled down the hill to reach the bottomlands, and then, in minutes, they were in Lewiston, which looked prosperous, indeed. From the town square, complete with softball diamonds and signs reminding everyone that Peachfest was just two weeks away, Center Street ran downhill ten blocks to the Niagara River and a handsome yacht club building and a small marina.

There was an outdoor stage at one corner of the town square, where, according to the poster Chloe saw, the Peach Queen would be crowned. Today, though, the stage was hung with banners and American flags for the queen for a day, Chloe Cary, star of *The Family Madderz*, and her young pal, Treble, of the S'hudonni royal family.

The crowd was a happy one again. It looked like six or seven thousand people, Chloe guessed, as she and Treble walked hand in hand onto the stage, after the mayor had waxed rhapsodic about the benefits the S'hudonni had brought to Western New York, starting with the boutique wine and craft beer successes, products that now were being sold on distant planets under alien suns. Having heard a dozen of these speeches on her tour with Treble, Chloe smiled her way right through the mayor's glowing remarks and then got up from her front-row bench, helped Treble to rise from his, and the two of them walked onto the stage.

Chloe thanked the mayor and the other officials and talked about the history of Lewiston and its famous visitors and how proud she was to join the ranks of those luminaries. She finished by talking about the history of the Underground Railroad and its terminus in Lewiston and how the good people of the village had helped and welcomed people, runaway slaves, who were so very different but came in peace and sought only freedom.

And then she introduced Treble, who wowed the crowd in his perfect English as he talked about the wonders of Niagara Falls and the charm and prosperity of Lewiston and its fine people. He promised them that the ceremonial throwing of the switch to send power to all of the Northeast was only the next step in the economic friendship between two great societies, and that the profits and benefits to both worlds, to both societies, would be enormous.

It was all over inside of twenty minutes, though there was another half hour after that of signing autographs and talking with people. Eventually the crowd filtered away and Chloe and Treble were back in the limousine, with plenty of time to spare. Too much time, in fact. Even after they walked across the street to Hibbard's Ice Cream stand and sampled the product ("It's amazing!" said Treble), trailed by the paparazzi all the while, they still had time.

It was the limo driver who told them about the Niagara River Gorge path. If they made a right turn and drove up the hill to the parking lot, he could give them a short private tour of the paths that ran along the gorge, one at the bottom and next to the river, the other at the top and offering great views of the river and the bridges.

Of course they both said yes.

To get to the gorge paths, the limo driver took them through the town, down the River Road for a mile, and then circled back toward town and the narrow road to the gorge site. All of this, the driver said, was to make sure they were away from the fans, so the walk would be a private one for them.

Treble was excited. They reached the empty parking lot at the gorge entrance and he was the first out of the limo, not waiting for the driver to open the door or for Chloe to help him. Instead, he waddled quickly over to the edge of the parking lot and clicked and whistled in appreciation, and then he translated for Chloe as she walked up.

"It's beautiful! See the river? See the paths down there? See the people on the other side in Canada? Wave to them!" And he waved, and Chloe waved, and the people on the Canadian side of the gorge waved back.

"You're getting all this, right?" Chloe asked myBetty.

"Of course," she said. "But I thought I'd record it and show it afterward. Otherwise, in minutes you'll be awash in paparazzi and fans."

That made a lot of sense. A little privacy on her walk with Treble sounded fine. The last time they'd had that kind of privacy, sunbathing on a rock off the beach in Cape Town, hadn't worked out all that well, so a nice, safe follow-up here sounded fine. Plus, she needed the exercise.

The driver came up to them. "I'll let you go on your own, Ms. Cary. Probably the best way is to take the top path out for a couple of klicks, and then there's a path that leads down to the bottom path and you can walk that back. It will take you forty-five minutes or so. I'll wait here and keep an eye on things."

Chloe thanked him. It was odd that she didn't know his name, but he'd never offered it. And then she and Treble followed his advice and walked over to where the top path started. It was two-thirds of the way up the side of the gorge, with woods to the left and a steep drop to the right. The view of the river below was a good one.

They set out on their little hike, the path heading upstream and toward the Falls, the deep gorge tumbling over rapids down below, and the path following the contours of the gorge as it pretty much arrowed south.

Between myBetty and Treble, Chloe got all the details of the things they were seeing, the sedimentary rock walls that were laid down four hundred million years ago and then cut through by the receding Niagara River very recently, only twelve thousand years ago. They could see the fossils from an ancient seabed in the rock walls to their left.

myBetty told Chloe that the trees that covered the walls, despite how steep the gorge was, were mainly red oaks, white ash, and pignut hickory. The underbrush, Treble gushed, was asters and goldenrod.

It was a great walk, easy enough that Treble had no trouble on the path, unpaved but mostly smooth. The views were great, and the sun was shining on them even as the opposite side of the gorge was already in the shade.

In a few rough spots here and there, Chloe held hands with Treble, helping him over the rocks or, a few times, the upthrusts from roots of the large oaks that lined the path.

For the sake of the sweep that was being recorded, they talked about how much they were looking forward to tasting the Niagara wines, which they'd get to do at the reception in Youngstown. They'd heard great things about them, all the intensive hand labor that went into them, the pesticide- and herbicide-free vineyards, the microclimate that was perfect for them—northern sun and the relatively warm waters of Lake Ontario the two major factors in that. The wines were already selling well on three of the worlds, Treble said. He was excited to taste them.

That was all very interesting, sure, Chloe thought, but really, the trees were trees, the fossils were fossils. The view, she had to admit, was a good one. But her mind drifted again to how nice it would be to see Anodiwa Pinaar once more and to continue the explorations the two of them had so enjoyed after the Cape Town attack. A long night of lovemaking and conversation and wine with Anodiwa sounded marvelous.

But while that was on Chloe's mind, what she said for the sweep was how wonderful this whole experience was—hearing the roar of the river's rapids down below, seeing the views from up above, touching the fossil coral on the wall they walked next to. It was all wonderful and amazing. Really. Honest.

They reached the path that would take them down to the river's edge and it was suddenly a much trickier bit of exercise for Treble. The steepest portions of the path had been turned into steps, and though the steps were too wide for Treble to negotiate cleanly, he was able to slowly come down on them.

But then other parts of the path were slippery gravel on a dirt path, and that was especially tricky going. Chloe figured out that it worked best if she stayed just ahead of Treble and then reached back to hold his hand. This steadied him, and if he slipped he'd bump into Chloe and, she hoped, come to a stop before sending them both rolling down the path and into the rapids.

This system worked fine until very near the end of the downhill path. There, on the next-to-last step, Treble stumbled forward into Chloe, who at just that moment was starting to take her next step down, and the two of them tumbled forward, rolling once to reach the bottom and then sprawling after that, so that they were half in the water at the river's edge.

They were lucky; the eddies of rushing water at that part of the rapids meant there were a series of countercurrents at the shoreline, and they fell into one of those. It was sheltered by a fallen oak tree with plenty of branches to grab. So instead of being pulled into the roiling river, they found themselves sitting in a pool of calm water, which was cold but only bracing. When they came to a stop, they looked at each other and laughed, and then laughed some more. Neither was hurt, though Chloe had a good scrape on her right elbow.

"That was fun!" said Treble, and he splashed the water at Chloe. "Feels great!"

Chloe laughed and splashed the water right back at Treble. It was only funny because no one was hurt and they hadn't been washed down into the rapids. Treble might have survived that, but Chloe, even with her competitive swimming background, might not have. There were Class V rapids out there.

"myBetty, did you get all that for the sweep?" she asked her helpmate. But there was no response. A little water and a little tumble shouldn't have bothered myBetty at all.

"Treble, are you connected?" she asked.

"Of course!" he said, and he tilted his head a bit as he listened to his internal feed. Then he frowned. "But not. What has happened?"

"I don't know," said Chloe, "but I don't like it. Let's get moving, and let's keep an eye out for trouble, all right?"

"Yes!" said Treble, delighted that there might be trouble, which sounded to him like great fun. He rose, grabbed a handy branch, and pulled himself onto the muddy riverbank, as Chloe was doing the same thing. Together, hand in hand, they got back onto the path, and then they stood there for a moment, brushing off what dirt and branches and leaves and water they could.

The path here was flat, and easier. More people had walked on it, so the dirt and rocks were smoother and well worn. But there still were tree roots and branches and, twice, fallen tree trunks to deal with, which was easy enough for Chloe but a challenge for Treble. He was determined to stick it out, though, and Chloe didn't have to help too often.

They were, Chloe thought, about halfway back to the stairs that would lead straight up to the parking lot and the limo, when they took a break to look at a massive whirlpool out in the river. This gave Treble a chance to rest his legs while Chloe tried again to get myBetty to respond, with no luck. Treble tried to reach Twoclicks, too, but, again, no luck.

And then they both heard someone crashing through the woods that went up the slope to their right, and when they turned to look, there was a glimpse—no more—of someone in a light brown jacket, a ball cap and dark pants, scrambling to get behind a tree.

There was a frozen moment as Chloe and Treble processed what they'd seen, and then they turned to run, Treble stumbling and falling forward,

Chloe leaning over to help him. There was a sound, muffled, a light *crack*, and Chloe heard the *thunk* of a bullet striking the tree next to her. She threw herself atop Treble to protect him and heard another muffled shot being fired. The bullet struck the ground near her and skipped past the back of her head. She thought she heard it go by, a whizzing noise, the bullet tumbling.

She came to her hands and knees and pushed Treble toward the water. "In," she said. "Dive in. Get away from here."

Treble turned to look at her, excitement the only thing she could read on that round face of his. "You are so brave!" he said. "But we should work together, Aunt Chloe, like before!"

"No. Get to those docks in Lewiston!" she said to him, but he was already diving into the river, a perfect entry with no splash, and then, in an instant, he was gone.

There were footsteps behind her. Chloe froze, waited for the muffled sound of that pistol with that suppressor on it firing a bullet into her back. It didn't come. She stood, slowly, raising her arms, not looking back, not wanting to be killed for having seen the face of her attacker.

"Where's the kid?" a woman's voice asked. "He jump in the water?"

"He did, yes. He's unharmed. He'll be calling his father from out there and a screamship will be coming by soon, I'd think."

"Sure. A screamship," the woman said. Then she added, "Turn around, Miss Cary."

Chloe turned. The woman was in her twenties, probably. Black hair cut short, a pretty face, no makeup, dark skin, physically fit, holding some handcuffs. She wore a light, brown jacket and a dark ball cap. These were probably bad things to know.

The woman smiled. "You're thinking I'm going to kill you because you can ID me, right?"

"Are you?" Stall her, Chloe was thinking. Buy a little time for Treble to get linked and then get some help.

"No. We wanted to get hold of that porky kid, but he's long gone. So we'll take you, instead. Hell, that might even be better." She smiled. "Turn around; put your hands behind your back."

Chloe did as she was told, turning around and putting her hands behind her back. As the woman came up to put the handcuffs on, Chloe was thinking it was now or never. She didn't think the woman would actually kill her. No, she needed Chloe Cary as a bargaining chip. Killing her might come if that didn't work out, but for right now, she needed Chloe alive.

So when Chloe felt the woman grab her hands, she raised her right knee in a savate move she'd practiced a thousand times with her trainer for *The Family Madderz*, and then she followed that with a straight kick back with her right foot, hoping to hit the woman's knee and bring her down. She connected.

The woman cried out in pain, and Chloe wheeled around to see her falling and grabbing for her knee. That was enough of an opening for Chloe to put a few more of those savate lessons in Beverly Hills to good use and to kick out again, this time at the sternum, hoping to knock the wind out of her attacker and maybe, with any luck, crack a rib or two. The woman dropped the gun and fell to the ground, gasping. Chloe, not really thinking about it at all but just working on energy and all those hours of practice with the trainer, kicked again, a broad shot at the right hip this time, which sent the woman rolling away, her head banging into a fallen tree trunk. Chloe reached down for the gun, picked it up, and pointed it shakily at the woman.

The woman lay there, quiet. Maybe unconscious. Chloe turned to look out at the river. No Treble in sight. Had he heard her yell about the docks? She had to hope so, since there was no way to talk to him, or to myBetty, or to call for help.

She took one more look at the woman, pushing her with her foot and getting no reaction. Then Chloe decided it was time to get out of there and, gun in hand, she started running, thinking of those stairs at the end of the trail, which would lead up to the parking lot and safety.

The woman didn't follow her, probably *couldn't* follow her, and Chloe made it to the wooden staircase without anyone shooting at her or chasing her. Chloe was thinking she was going to make it now, so she didn't look back but just headed up the stairs, going as fast as she could. All that exercise and conditioning for the show was being put to good use as she negotiated the wide steps, up and up, a good eight flights of ten steps each, to make it to the top.

She got there, winded and near collapse but alive and well, and then she stopped at the top to catch her breath. This was all pretty damn exciting. Jesus, she felt great. She felt wonderful. This was better than acting, or competitive swimming, or soccer, or driving, or any damn thing. She was alive, vibrating with the adrenaline, humming along.

She'd get the driver to take them down to the docks, meet up with Treble, and boy, would they have things to talk about for years to come, she and the little prince.

Then there came a loud *crack* from an unmuzzled pistol, and a bullet went into the wooden handrail, inches from where she stood.

It was the driver. The unnamed driver. Running right at her, taking another shot, and then another, wild shooting but dangerous. He was trying to kill her.

Chloe held the gun in her hands, still with the suppressor on it. This moment, too, was the culmination of hours of readiness, hours at the range, shooting at round targets, never wanting to even shoot at the silhouette of a person. But here, now, she aimed for the torso, the largest target, as the guy approached. She seemed to have all the time in the world, even as he

stepped closer and fired again, and then stepped closer again, and then—
she felt very leisurely about this—Chloe pulled the trigger and the driver
staggered, still firing his weapon but his arm dropping as he did so, and
the bullet kicked up some pebbles off to Chloe's left and then headed off to
god knows where.

But he still stood there, looking a little puzzled, his brow furrowed, his
lips tightened. Chloe could see all this in great detail. He tried to raise that
right arm again and Chloe, still aiming at his torso, pulled the trigger again,
and then a third time, as he staggered, staggered again, and then finally fell
to his knees. Then he pitched forward, facedown in the loose gravel of the
parking lot. He was very still.

She dropped her arms but held on to the gun and walked, very calmly,
over to the driver. She realized she didn't even know his name. And wouldn't
know it, now.

Time was speeding up, getting back to normal. She knelt beside him,
rolled him over so she could see the wounds and perhaps try to stop the
bleeding. There were three separate wounds. One was up near the right
shoulder, that bloody spot growing larger as she watched, and then another
just below that, also with a bloody spot growing larger on his white shirt.
Then, as if she'd been correcting her aim, though she had no recollection
of doing that, the third wound was on his left, very near the heart, and the
blood was pulsing out of that wound.

She didn't think he had any chance at all. She put her hand on the heart
wound for a minute, thinking to slow the bleeding. His eyes opened briefly
and he looked at her, seemed to recognize her, and then the eyes lost track
of her, of everything, and she knew he was dead.

Chloe sat back on her legs, her knees still on the ground.

myBetty was working again. "Hello, Chloe, how can I help?" she asked.

"Call nine one one, myBetty, and get an ambulance here, and the cops.
This guy's down, but he has at least one friend, a woman, down by the river."

"I'm afraid we can't make that call, Chloe," said myBetty. "Twoclicks
wants to talk with you about why."

That conversation was a short one, but firm. And so Chloe, doing her
damnedest to stay under control, felt in the driver's pocket for the car re-
mote, stood up, walked to the limo, hit the unlock, and climbed into the
driver's seat. There, she took a deep breath, tried to calm down, and said to
her helpmate, "You drive, myBetty. Take me to the Lewiston docks." And
myBetty did.

25

NEW PLANS

Nikki showed up in bad shape, and with worse news. Things had gone south on the plan to grab the S'hudonni kid. Worse, Marco—their hired gun—had been killed, three bullets in the chest from Chloe Cary, the fucking TV star.

How was that possible? The plan was pretty simple. Marco dosed the limo driver, left him bound and gagged in an empty house on an empty street in Niagara Falls, then took his place. All he had to do was get the TV star and her pet S'hudonni to the hiking trail in the gorge and Nikki would take it from there.

And yet. Somehow Chloe fucking Cary turned out to be some kind of martial artist for real and the kid was a sneaky little bastard, and all of a sudden it was the worst-case scenario. They were both on the loose, and now they knew that people here were after them. Even the suppressor was lost.

This meant that Tom had to make contact with Whistle's people, which he was scheduled to do anyway, but the idea had been to report in that they had the S'hudonni kid, and instead he'd be reporting on how it had all gone wrong. He reached into his backpack and pulled out the S'hudonni communicator. He turned it on. It was easy to trace if you had the right equipment, and Tom knew that Twoclicks did, so that probably meant Chloe fucking Cary, who wasn't dead or captive but was, instead, alive and well, would hear from Twoclicks immediately about whatever call Tom got from Whistle.

Fuck. You spend months working hard and you think you're ready for the big play and then on the culminating day the whole thing fucking falls apart. Damn it.

His communicator dinged at him. He glanced at it. The screen showed "Unknown," and that meant Whistle's people. Well, get it over with. He hit the triangle, said, "Hello," and got the usual message to wait for a call.

A few seconds later he was listening to the right-hand man, a guy Tom knew only as Hanratty. Hanratty knew what had happened and was pissed off about it, sure. But Whistle always had a plan B, and so Tom listened, nodded, said, "Sure," and they ended the call. Some hired help was standing by. Get Nikki to their boat and they'd be back on track.

PART EIGHT

HOME AGAIN

The problem with pain is that it hurts so much.

—Peter Holman, *Notes from Holmanville*
(S'hudon City and New York:
Trebnet Press, 2035)

26

TREBLE TROUBLE

What the fuck?

Heather had promised me there wouldn't be any pain when I came awake, but here I was, waking up to my left knee screaming at me with the kind of stabbing agony I hadn't felt since I'd ruined it playing Euro hoops, driving the lane and getting tangled up with Barca's two big men and when I came crashing down onto the parquet my basketball career came to an end. Two surgeries, anterior and medial ligaments both ruined and needing vat-grown replacements, and there you go: career over and find something else to do with for the rest of your life. Like getting copied and squirted and reassembled on the other side of the galaxy. Heather had promised me that I wouldn't remember any of the pain of the Travel from S'hudon to Earth. But I did. I did.

Shit. I opened my eyes and a daffodil with a frown on its face—something Earthie she'd learned, no doubt, so she could fit in; pretty hilarious, that thought—stared back at me and asked, in good English, "How would you rate your pain on a scale from one to ten, one being least?"

"Fucking forty," I said, and tried to sit up, and that's where I felt something new, the stabbing searing pain of an open wound on my right arm. Christ Almighty.

I lay back on the Travel bed and took a long, slow breath, trying to gather myself. The pain was overwhelming. I couldn't think about anything else. Damn. I took a breath, tried to focus on something else, turning my head to the right to look at my arm. No wound, no sign of any damage at all. My wounds from where I'd pulled it free from that boulder at the beach were healed. No scars, no nothing but that agonizing pain.

"Phantom pain, I think," doctor daffodil said. "I've heard about that."

"Great," I said. "What can you do about it?" I was thinking that my grand plan for a heroic rescue of Treble, something I could do to make up for how I *hadn't* managed to rescue Kait, wasn't going to work out at all how I'd hoped. I could barely sit up, much less become the action hero that Heather had in mind.

The daffodil was musing, her dewlaps opening and closing in thought. "I suppose," she was saying, "that it isn't really phantom pain. You were told this kind of Travel hadn't been done before, yes?"

"Yes," I said. The Travel beds weren't meant for anything more than planetary Travel, or even, with some risk, planetary system Travel.

"It's very daring, very risky," Heather had told me, back in my bed in my cottage in my faux town of Holmanville, where she'd come to visit me and we'd drank, talked, and made love. These visits were more common, now that Kait had gone home to Earth and Treble with her. I was achingly lonely and depressed and trapped in this place. Heather was all I had, that's my only explanation.

Afterward, as we lay there, she reached over to touch my lips and run her finger over them, first the top and then the bottom, and then she said, "Twoclicks needs you on Earth, Peter."

I sat up. "Wonderful!" I said. "Send me on home!"

She sat up. "It's not that simple. He needs you right away. Treble is in trouble, lost and not in contact, and he needs you to find him."

"I don't get it," I said, putting my feet over the side of the bed and standing up.

"Twoclicks is beside himself with worry, Peter, and you're the best one for the job. He wants me to send you by Travel bed to Earth to make the rescue. And if it works, you—one version of you, at least—will be home with your sister and with Chloe Cary. That's a pretty nice upside."

"I thought that couldn't be done, sending someone all that way."

"It's difficult, and dangerous," she said. "We'll have to use all the available power on this island for the thirty seconds or so it will take to copy you and send you Earthward a few thousand times as packets, and then take the best parts of each of those packets to reconstruct the real you at the end."

There was really no way to say no thanks, I'd prefer to stay here in my Potemkin village and rot for the rest of my life, doing exactly nothing for no one. And, like she said, it was very daring. So only one version of me would sit, glum, in Holmanville. The other version, the new one, would be back on Earth, where I—he, it, them—would find and save Treble. Plus, I'd been wondering why Heather was stopping by so often in her Earthie form to spend time with me in my little cottage. Now I had the answer to that. Like everything else the S'hudonni did, there was a plan underneath the plan that was underneath the plan.

Plus, she said she'd keep visiting the me that stayed behind, if that's what I wanted. I said no thanks to that, but yes to the Travel bed, and so Heather gave me all my instructions and off I went within the hour. And now here I was, moments later, in serious pain but back on Earth.

"You had injuries in this knee before?" the daffodil asked me. "And in that arm, too, I suppose?"

"I suppose yes," I said.

"Good!" she said. "We can fix those with a medcot. Plenty of Earthie medcots here!"

"All right, then," I said. "Get me into one."

Her petals folded tightly into the side of her head and her color dropped from cheery yellow to a darker tone of purple. "Sorry. Sending you on this

Travel bed to a medcot in one of the consulates would kill you. Your reconstituted self is"—the daffodil hesitated, her petals sliding into a deeper, darker purple—"in a fragile state, I think."

Fragile state? "What does that mean?"

"Dissassembly is quite possible. An unwinding. Collapse. Liquidity!" She frowned again, though she seemed very pleased with her word choice.

Dead, in other words, I was thinking. I wondered about the me back on S'hudon. Was that me, the original, still all right, or had it puddled on the Travel bed there and dripped off onto the damp floor of the Travel room?

The pain was fucking awful. I took another deep breath. Jesus, awful awful awful.

The daffodil paused, hearing something in some internal comm unit. "I'm told by Prince Twoclicks himself that you have a critical mission, so there is no time to waste."

She turned around to rummage through a drawer, then turned back, and the dewlaps were yellower, and emerging. She held up a fat syringe, nothing you'd use on an Earthie, I thought. But she said, "This will stop the pain, I think," and jabbed me with it in the right arm, and then, without any hesitation, also in the left knee.

"There," she said. "In a few minutes you won't care so much about the pain. You'll be right as rain, good to go, all set, teeing off, stepping up to the plate, ready for action, ready and able!"

"Sure," I said, but stayed right where I was. And then came a nice warm glow, and the pain did subside. She was right. I knew there was pain there, terrible pain, in fact, but I didn't care. It didn't seem to matter all that much. The painkiller was something they must have conjured up from the blimpies.

I sat up, put my legs over the side, and stood. Shaky, but so much better. I took a step, and the left knee worked fine as long as I consciously thought about taking a step. I rotated the right arm. Same. Think about it and it worked fine.

"OK, then," I said. "Where am I, and how do I get to the Niagara Gorge?"

An hour later I felt fine, though I still had to remind my left knee to bend and my right arm to move. I was walking on a footpath at the top of the Niagara Gorge. Ahead of me, somewhere, was my little princeling pal Treble. It was my job to find him, save him. He had a locator embedded that should be blinking in and out, whether he was alive or dead, but wasn't. I wore a pair of S'hu-tech sunglasses that should be showing me right where he was, but weren't. At least their zoom lenses worked, and I could see the recording light in the top right, so everything I saw and said was being saved.

I was a local, that was the idea. The worlds, both Earth and S'hudon, couldn't know about Treble's troubles or my return to Earth to rescue him.

So I strolled along in a baseball cap, hiking boots, khaki shorts, and a long-sleeved gray T-shirt and looked hard for the princeling, telling my left leg what to do on every step, and every now and then reaching for a fallen branch or a rock wall with my right arm, telling it how to go about the task. Ahead of me, kilometers of Niagara Gorge. Behind me, Niagara Falls. Slowly I turned, step by step . . .

In my right front pocket was a wallet, with credit cards and cash and a fake ID. For the duration, I was Harold Gallatin. In my left front pocket there was a gun. "SIG Sauer," it said, up near the end of the barrel. "SP2022."

I'd never fired a gun in my life. In fact, I'd never held a gun in my hands in my life. So this didn't seem like all that great an idea. I had no idea how to use it, whether it was loaded or not. I could point and pull the trigger, but was that all that was needed? Did I have to cock it or something?

And what was even more worrisome was that someone thought I might need this. My daffodil faux doctor had given it to me, along with clothes and some instructions on where to start my long walk.

When Heather had backgrounded me on this whole adventure, she'd told me that I could expect to be in communication with Twoclicks while I searched, but I wasn't. No incoming, no outgoing. Nothing. Something, someone, had blocked all my electronics except for the glasses, so I was on my own, guessing where to look for Treble or, gods forbid, his body.

All I knew for sure was this: the whole mess was the work of my brother Tom. While I'd been on S'hudon, Tom had been playing at being a disruptive guerilla leader, burning crops and sowing terror. It was causing Twoclicks some trouble, eating away at the profits, and we couldn't have that.

I had about a half-hour walk to get to the start of the Gorge. I was avoiding leaving any digital signature, so no cars, no purchases, no messaging. Just me and my recording glasses and the small backpack I wore, with S'hudon medtech in it for Treble and some bottles of water for me.

So this was my first look at how things had changed in the two years of local time that I'd been gone. The city of Niagara Falls was in the midst of a building boom, it seemed to me, with hotels and condos rising to overlook the Falls. I knew the city had struggled for long decades after its industries closed down, but tourism was dependable, and some fancy casinos opening up had kept the place going through the bad years. But now, with the influx of jobs—construction and high-tech—brought by the building and operating of the Niagara Tower and all the new boutique wineries that required all that handcrafted labor, there was money to spend in Niagara Falls. And the Niagara Tower would be its own tourist draw, too, it seemed to me. Maybe Twoclicks had done a good thing here. Stranger things had happened.

The city isn't big, and in twenty minutes I was clear of it and walking along a shady two-lane parkway that carried me to the footpath that ran along the top of a deep gorge, with occasional paths running off from that, dropping down in a series of steps to the bottom of the gorge and the Niagara River itself, still carving its way through the rocks to run, full of rapids, below. They looked deadly, even for someone as aquatic as Treble.

That was part of the appeal of the Falls: the immense power and the danger. There was always the lure of the Falls for daredevils, men and women who chose to go over the Falls in barrels or unsinkable boats, sometimes surviving and more often not. Men and women walked across high wires stretched over the Falls, too, doubling down on the inherent danger of the place.

And that danger didn't end at the base of the Falls. Within a half kilometer of the Falls, the rapids began, and they went on down through the gorge until the river widened and calmed after it left the gorge at Lewiston and Queenston.

But that rush of water was what first drove the power here, all the way back to Nikola Tesla, who harnessed the Falls to bring light to the cities, back in 1895, with the world's first large-scale hydroelectric power plant. I saw why it made such great symbolic sense for Twoclicks to build the first of his towers in this area.

I took the first path down the steep switchbacks to the river, where the path ran right along the rushing water. Going downhill with a knee and an arm that needed a good talking-to was a challenge, but I got it done. There was a lot of pain, I knew, but my mind didn't care. I walked on.

The river was narrow here, and fast, the current tumbling over huge rocks out in the middle of the stream. There were constant backflow eddies along the shoreline. Step into one of those and I'd be drawn in and spun out into the main current in seconds. Something like that might have been all right for Treble, but it would likely be the end of me.

The edge of the river was also a patchwork of small rock beaches, muddy edges, fallen trees, bushes clinging to land but edging out into the water, roots from the tall oaks and maple trees at the edge that went out for meters in some cases, just above the waterline. I could see some younger version of myself loving it here, swimming in the eddies, fishing from the fallen tree trunks that were over the water, kayaking out into the main stream—all of that. But for me today, the troubled and broken adult, trying to look for Treble while also watching where I was going, while persuading my knee and arm to behave, was a challenge.

And I found nothing, walking along for a couple of hundred meters and then another couple of hundred. Nothing. The gorge, steep to my right as I walked north, rose almost straight up for hundreds of meters. The rushing water to my left hissed or roared, depending on the size of the rocks that caused the rapids.

I stepped out to the very edge of the water, grabbed a branch on a fallen tree that offered me footing, and walked out on that tree for a few meters to look downstream. The gorge cut deep here, but ahead it would widen and smooth out as the river neared Lake Ontario and its flat and fertile ancient lakebed. They grew grapes and peaches there, the lake and the escarpment the gorge cut through making for a microclimate that was perfect for vineyards and orchards and, inevitably, the handcrafted wines and peach schnapps that S'hudon would buy and then sell on those distant worlds.

To my left, I could see up ahead a huge standing wave. That had to be a Class V rapid. No thanks. But no sign in the water or along the shore of anything resembling a friendly young S'hudonni that I'd thought of as a great friend. I hoped to hell he was alive.

"Twoclicks?" I asked through my glasses. But there was still no response. Well, hell. I engaged the zoom lenses, looking toward a large rock in the middle of the river. Water was rushing by it and, now and then, washing right over it. The daffodil said the glasses took voice commands, so I said, "Zoom in," but nothing happened. I tried, "Please zoom in." Still nothing. Then I said, "Glasses, zoom in," and there it was; I was zooming in, the effect so dizzying I tried to grab an upright branch next to me. But that arm wasn't listening to me, and the left knee didn't understand why I wasn't paying attention to it, and the zoom had me so damn dizzy that I fell onto the path on my left side and then slid halfway into the water's edge.

Damn, the water was cold. And now my left knee was underwater, and whatever the wonder drug was that had kept the pain from bothering me was ebbing away as I lay there. Pain. Sharp pain, like needles driven into the knee. Damn, damn.

I put my arms down, explaining to the right arm why it needed to behave right now, and pushed against the dirt and rocks that held me. I inched back, and then back again and the knee was out of the water and, thank god, the pain ebbed away again. OK, lesson learned, stay out of the water.

It wasn't easy, but I used a fallen tree, a boulder, and a broken branch to good effect. The glasses were still on, so that was something. And I still had a job to do, finding Treble. So I stood there and looked once again out toward the boulders midstream and the muddy opposite shore.

It took me a second or two to realize I was seeing an insect, a beetle of some kind, crawling along in the mud. "Zoom out," I tried. And then, oh yes, "Glasses, zoom out slowly." That worked better. A few more ins and outs and I had it figured out and was standing there on a fallen tree, looking with crystal clarity up and down the shore I was standing on. Somehow the glasses stabilized the image, too, so I didn't have to hold them steady.

Nothing but leaves and branches and mud along the shore. The river was much wilder than I'd have guessed, but not right here along the shoreline. I used the glasses to record things as I walked along, knowing Twoclicks and maybe billions of others someday might like seeing what I was seeing as I went. Nothing. Then something, but just a bird, and then again, nothing.

And then, at the base of a distant boulder that lay a couple of meters out from the shore, a something, a movement in the still water at the base of the big rock.

I looked, zoomed in a little more, then a little more, and there, in the mud, was a small hand, attached to a small arm as I looked a bit to the right, and that attached to Treble. There he was!

But the way there wasn't simple. After a couple of hundred meters I had to leave the path and then faced a tough decision, indeed. I was going to have to wade out to Treble. He should have been able to see me by now, should be waving at me, but he wasn't. The way his body was twisted, I worried he might be dead.

And that water. Oh, god. I stepped with my right leg, no problem, and then the left, and in seconds there was that pain, knives being shoved into my knee, shoved in and then moved around. Incredible, staggering pain.

I wanted to hurry, but that led to slipping, and that led me to fall into the water twice, the countercurrent threatening to shove me out into the main flow, where death lay waiting for me, I was sure.

And the pain, my god. The wet right arm now was rippling with sharp, almost electric, spasms just like the left knee was. I struggled to clamber over boulders and past tree trunks and through shallow pools in several places where tiny rivulets from up the slopes of the gorge emptied into the river.

And then, finally, I was close. For the last twenty meters I could see him clearly in front of me, and that helped. I stumbled again, and yet again, searing pain from knee and arm, but I was somehow used to that now, until, finally, after one fallen tree and a little more wading through the knee-deep water to save a few minutes climbing over rocks, I was there.

And Treble was alive. When I knelt next to him and he looked at me and gave me a tired smile and said, "Uncle Peter!" I could hear a noise I'd never heard before from a S'hudonni: a whistle combined with choking noises. I think he was crying with relief. Or maybe that was me.

27

LIGHTING UP

Chloe waited for Treble at the Lewiston docks for almost two hours, sitting in the small park and keeping an eye on the river, talking to myBetty and Twoclicks—and once, as she came in with an update on the news, Hanratty. It did give Chloe plenty of time to clean up in the public toilets, which were cleaner and better maintained than she'd expected.

While she alternated between walking down to the river to look for any sign of Treble and sitting on the lone green bench in the park, she saw only a few locals. There was an older couple who emerged from the hotel that sat back a hundred meters or so against the river bluff, some high school–age girls who came to use the swing set amid a good deal of laughter, and one kayaker who pulled up, got his kayak off the top of his old 4Runner, and was into the water and paddling away downstream, all in five minutes.

But no Treble. Finally myBetty said, "Heather and Twoclicks are worried, Chloe, but they have a backup plan. You are to go to Youngstown Marina, meet with Anodiwa Pinaar, get out to the tower when the barge is ready to go, and then try to stall things if Treble doesn't show."

"Fine," she said. "But what if he can't be found?"

myBetty hesitated for a second, listened, and then said, "That's not possible. He'll meet you at the barge or, worst case, out at the tower. All right?"

Twoclicks was hard to fathom sometimes, but this was really crazy. He was the boss, though, and it was his son they were all worried about, so if this is what he wanted . . . well, OK. Chloe got back into the limo and myBetty drove them into town for a little clothes shopping in the stores that were still open, and from there down the River Road to Youngstown. She left the gun in the limo as they reached Youngstown and the security checks for the gala.

She arrived late, but not terribly so. The barge was still at the dock, and people were on it, drinking and chatting and enjoying both the good weather and the incredible sights of the river, the lake beyond, and that immense tower out there, which seemed to loom over them.

As she stepped out of the limo, Chloe was back in heels and a nice Nagawa dress that she'd found in a shop on Center Street. It wasn't the latest in fashion, to be sure, but it would get the job done, and if anyone asked, she could always talk about how she'd bought it right down the road in Lewiston, helping out the locals.

She stopped for a second to take in the whole scene. "Are you getting all this, myBetty?" she asked her helpmate.

"At Twoclicks's request, you're going live right now, Chloe," myBetty answered.

It was surreal. Had she been in a fight for her life just a couple of hours ago? Had that been some dream, some alternate reality that she and Treble had slid into? Everything here seemed perfectly normal and calm, limos pulling up and dropping off well-dressed people—and there, stepping out of a limo and looking around, was dear, sweet Anodiwa Pinaar.

Anodiwa wore a colorful long-sleeved gown, showing off the multicolored South African flag: the red, white, and blue for the old Boer republics; the black, yellow, and green from the African National Congress. Low cut in back, knee length, and a bright statement, a mix of haute and traditional. The blousy sleeves were white. She wore a Zulu isicholo hat, the band matching the dress's colors. It was stunning, and Anodiwa carried it all off with ease, with her mocha skin and that wonderful face and that smile as she saw Chloe and hurried over, arms open for a hug.

They did hug, and Chloe whispered in her ear, and then they both turned to face the photographers as they stood there, smiling, arm in arm.

What was on Chloe's mind was that she'd killed a man up close and personal today, she'd killed one or two back in Cape Town, and life had gotten very surreal. Here she was at a social event and sweeping it live to billions. This was a gala, a grand opening, as glamorous an event as you could want, but Chloe was still thinking about how she'd acted without any fear holding her back, lost in the moment, back there in the Niagara Gorge. She'd simply done what had to be done, and only now, long after the fact, could she take the time to realize she'd been exhilarated by the action, by the rightness of it, the truth of it. Here was this thing that must be done, and so she'd done it, just as she had back in Cape Town with Anodiwa.

The last two years of training for *The Family Madderz* had actually mattered! How about that? Her youth spent doing all those sports, all those moments of being lost in the act of shooting a soccer ball or swimming toward the touch at the end of the pool, had served her well—and how about that, too? She had a right to be proud of herself, doing something that wasn't acting, didn't have twelve takes to get right, didn't have any lines to memorize or marks to hit. Just action and danger—real danger. And here she was! Alive and well at the grandly named Youngstown Yacht Club, with its simple two-story building and its marina that held a dozen or so sailboats, and all of this along the Niagara River, wide now, where it emptied into Lake Ontario, half a kilometer, perhaps, over to the Canadian side.

Anodiwa walked with her into the yacht club's main building and the ladies' room at the back, saying, "Privacy, please," to her own helpmate even as Chloe whispered, "Record this, please," to myBetty, "but kill the live feed."

Anodiwa held Chole's hands, looking at her. "I rather thought maybe you'd want a moment to catch your breath," she said. "There's no green room here or anything like that, so this will have to do. And then we'll go to the barge and the show goes on, yes?"

Then she smiled that wonderful wide smile, reached out to touch Chloe's cheek, and added, "And then, afterward, dear one? The two of us?"

Chloe smiled, nodded, and then turned to look in the mirror, trying to figure out just who she was seeing in that image. Celebrity? Actor? Killer? Lover? My god, what a world this was now. Here she was, safe in the arms of Anodiwa, even as Treble, that sweet little odd princeling, was lost and gone. Insane, absolutely insane. Two realities at once. It was almost better not to think too much about it but simply to act.

Oh, but dear Anodiwa. Chloe turned back around, buried her face in Anodiwa's welcome neck, looked up and kissed her, and then held that kiss, and then backed away and burst into tears, all the suppressed fear and anger coming out in a brief flood.

Anodiwa hugged her hard, patted her on the back, and said, "Take your time, dear. Take your time."

Chloe calmed, took a deep breath, stood up straight, said, "Thank you, Diwa," to her friend, and then walked over to the sink to clear away any trace of the tears.

"I'm here for you, Chloe," Anodiwa said behind her. "And we'll talk when you're ready. They'll find little Treble, I'm sure, and everything will be fine. When we're done with this tonight, we'll stay at a private house I've found on the Canadian side. You'll like it. Very quiet. Then tomorrow we'll visit a couple of those wineries for Twoclicks's sake, and then we'll all go to the airport so Twoclicks's plane can whisk us out to L.A."

Chloe nodded. A plane. Sitting on a plane for hours and flying west, to California and normalcy. That sounded good; that sounded very good.

myBetty and Anodiwa's helpmate both went live again as the two women walked back out through the building and onto the ramp that led to the barge. There was a brief round of applause as they stepped up onto the barge, and Chloe and Anodiwa both waved to everyone, smiled, and then walked over to meet the locals: the mayors of several villages on both sides of the border, the prime minister, the governor, some famous football hero, the local big money, and the rest of the usual.

Chloe kept thinking about Treble and where the hell he was as she hugged and shook hands and signed pictures and the usual embossed handouts about the event. Had he been killed? Captured? Really, this was maybe the best acting she'd ever done, to appear calm and collected as she worried about the princeling while playing the role of the celebrity guest.

She made her excuses for Treble's not being there yet, saying he'd gone off on his own to a winery and would join them soon at the tower, and no one seemed to worry about it. The princeling would show when the princeling wanted to to show and that was that. Finally, a glass of local Niagara Cellars sauvignon blanc later, she and Anodiwa stood at the rail together as the barge pulled away and headed downstream in the wide Niagara River.

It would take them twenty minutes or more to reach the tower. Chloe looked out over the river, the current strong but the rapids long left behind, and took a sip of her wine. Anodiwa put her hand over Chloe's, there on the rail, as the barge turned, and now they were looking at big Lake Ontario—a freshwater sea, really, it was so large.

Straight across the lake was Toronto. The river and the lake formed a border that mattered less and less as S'hudon slowly changed things. States still mattered; nations still mattered. But Chloe wondered if such distinctions would still be there in five years, or ten. What plans did the mighty Twoclicks have for that? Was he thinking of those things while he was doing stand-up comedy in L.A.?

She sighed. It was a strange world, indeed. "Stay live, myBetty," she said, and then she leaned over and put her head on Anodiwa's shoulder. Anodiwa put her arm around Chloe's waist. They stood there, the two of them, for a long moment.

And then Chloe stepped back from the rail, looked around at the crowd, and saw there, at the far end of the barge, Tom Holman.

She was dead certain it was him, and she was dead certain he'd been responsible for the kidnapping attempt in the gorge.

The balls of that guy! There was no mistaking him, tall and thin and, no surprise, smoking a cigarette that he'd no doubt lit as soon as he was aboard.

Chloe didn't know what to make of this. Tom did, though. He saw her looking at him, flicked the cigarette out into the river—typical—and started walking toward her, working his way through the crowd, smiling at her the whole time.

"I'll be a minute, Anodiwa," she said. Then she added, "myBetty, kill the live feed but record it all as I talk with Tom Holman."

"Done," said myBetty, and then Chloe backed away from the railing and walked toward Tom with a smile on her face.

"Chloe," he said, when she got there. "It's wonderful to see you again." And he reached out to shake her hand.

She took the hand, shook it politely, and said, "Hello, Tom. I'm surprised to see you here."

"Yes," he said. "My friends and I had a little trouble on the way, but here I am. Wouldn't miss it."

He smiled at her. *The nerves on this guy,* she thought.

Then he said, "It's nice to see you looking so good. You must be staying in shape, despite how busy you are with *The Family Madderz* and the big tour with Treble and whatever else you have going with Twoclicks and friends."

The conversation was one more surreal impossibility in the strangest day of Chloe's life. Tom, she was sure, had been the one behind that murderous woman's kidnapping attempt deep in the Niagara River gorge, and the limo driver's attempt to shoot and kill her. What a bloody mess, the whole thing. And Treble still missing, out in the water somewhere, probably—hopefully—just lost and scared. She'd watched as little Treble had been swept underwater, and the last thing she'd seen was a hand raised out of the water as he went over the rocks, through the boil of the rapids' standing waves, and then disappeared downstream.

And now here Tom was, pulling a pack of cigarettes out of his pocket and casually pulling one free and lighting it, effortlessly—habitual, yes, but with no signs of nerves after what he'd been through.

Well, she could play that game, damn it. "I've received a letter or two recently from your brother, and he tells me he's written you, too, Tom. You should write him back." That was all a lie. Peter hadn't mentioned Tom at all. But it got the response she wanted.

Tom's smile was gone. "I haven't received any letters from him, but it's not like I have a regular mailbox or anything."

"Too bad, Tom. He wrote to me that you've never responded to any of them. I'll let him know that's why. You're not that angry with him, Tom, are you? He's your brother. Blood thicker than water and all that?"

Tom took one drag on the cigarette and then flicked it out into the river. That was at least a little signal of some emotions, some turmoil. "He's not the guy you seem to think he is, Chloe. He's not some great fucking hero."

"Sure he is, Tom. He's out there. He's seeing things the rest of us will never get to see, except when he shows us."

Tom shook his head. "You don't get it, Chloe. You can't see it. You're believing all the media bullshit and all the propaganda. You know fucking S'hudon controls all of it, right? Streaming, sweeping, broadcast—shit, all of it. Probably the fucking sales flyers you get in your mailbox."

He took a small breath, seemed to gather himself a bit. "We're defending ourselves here, Chloe. We're saving what's left, and then, once it's done, we'll rebuild."

She stared at him. "Tom," she said, and then again, "Tom."

But he wasn't listening, wasn't reachable. He saw treachery everywhere. All change was for the worse; all change was ruinous.

He caught himself, stopped talking. Chloe thought maybe he wished he hadn't said what he'd just said. "I'm looking forward to hearing what you have to say, Chloe. I'm sure your speech will be great. Interesting things happening here today, right?"

"Right," she said, and then she wondered what else Tom might have in mind.

He was still talking. "Are you leaving right away after your dedication?"

She nodded, lied a little bit. "Yes, flying right out. I have to be back in L.A. tomorrow for the show. On the set at five a.m."

"Ah, of course," he said. "You are amazing, Chloe, really. And I'm happy for you." And then he looked toward the tower as they slowly approached it and said, "I'm sorry, Chloe, I have to meet someone. Thank you for talking with me, though. I know it wasn't easy."

She smiled, at least a little. "It's OK, Tom. Take care of yourself. Write back to your brother."

"Sure," he said, and walked away. She lost him in the crowd at the far end of the barge, everyone drinking and talking.

Almost everyone. She realized that Anodiwa was at her side. She reached out to take her hand. "Your myBetty has been telling me through myWinnie what you two were talking about, Chloe. And then I heard from Twoclicks. He says you handled that perfectly."

"Confirm that," myBetty said to Chloe. "I didn't want to interrupt, but what you've done is exactly what Twoclicks needed, Chloe."

"All right," she said. "But what was it I did? I wanted to throw him over the side, you know. Or worse—a lot worse."

Anodiwa was listening to her helpmate, nodded her head, smiled, and then myBetty broke in with, "They've found Treble, Chloe!"

Chloe sagged a bit at the rail of the barge. Thank god. "He's OK?"

Anodiwa was listening to her myWinnie and nodding. Before myBetty could speak, she said, "He's alive, and seems all right."

"Chloe," myBetty said, "it was Peter that found him, and Peter is bringing him here now."

"Peter?" How wonderful, but how in the hell?

"He Traveled all the way from S'hudon to here to help, Chloe," said myBetty. "I didn't think they could do that. It's amazing technology."

Peter! And Treble! Chloe was suddenly ecstatic. From despair to joy in a heartbeat. "They're on their way here? Do we need to get this barge turned around to pick them up?"

"Coming by boat, and they'll meet us at the tower," said myBetty. Then she added, "Twoclicks wants to talk to you directly."

There was a click or two, and then, "Dear friend Chloe! I have newss! Your friend Peter has resscued my son! Pulled him from the water, rapidss, rapidss everywhere! Very dangerous, rockss and water and huge waves! Peter ssaved hiss life!"

Chloe felt like life had just taken a sharp turn toward getting better. But Peter? "You Traveled him all the way from S'hudon, Twoclicks? How is that done?" And she wanted to ask, *Why in the hell did you send him by the slow boat all the way out to S'hudon? And why all these letters and slow communication?*

But she didn't have to ask. "Very difficult to do, Chloe, and very rissky.

The Travel devicess are not meant for that, going through light pane. And longer the disstance more chance of erossion, losses of information. So thousandss of copies sent at great expense to have one complete on arrival. You know?"

All right. Now she knew. "And Peter made it through OK?"

"Almost perfect! To save our son! We are sso sso happy now!"

"I'm happy, too, Twoclicks. Thrilled!" she said. And then she wondered what the hell "almost perfect" meant.

There was another click, and Anodiwa touched her ear and nodded. She was now in on the conversation as Twoclicks said, "For both of you, a warning. All iss not over yet, dear friend Chloe and dear friend Anodiwa."

"How so?" Anodiwa asked.

"We are not sso sure we have stopped the planss that we feared. Tom Holman is blank to uss, and sso we think he must have a suppressor, or even two or three of them. And a weapon of ssome kind. We think he hass plans to use it. Ssomething big, dearest friends. But now! In few minutes will be four of you there! You can find out and stop it. Yess?"

No, Chloe wanted to say. She'd had enough action for one day in that fight just a couple of hours ago. She kept seeing the man bleeding out as she tried to stop the blood coming out of the holes she'd shot him full of. Awful. Terrible.

But she was here, and so was Anodiwa, and Peter and Treble were on the way. All right, then. "Sure," she said, and she looked around to see Anodiwa looking worried but determined. They nodded at each other, and then, without saying a word, they walked away separately, making sure they were keeping an eye on Tom Holman.

28

SHOWTIME

When the barge docked at the Niagara Tower, they all disembarked. Chloe had been half-expecting Treble to be there with long-lost Peter in some kind of disguise, but there were just two S'hudonni there to greet people as they came off the barge. Chloe and Anodiwa would be the last ones off.

Chloe, waiting, looked for Tom in the crowd, but she only glimpsed him once, and he wasn't looking her way. She didn't see him again until it all came down, about an hour later, as the sun set into the great lake, over in the west, toward tired old Hamilton, Ontario. That was when they each did what they thought they had to do.

For now, she and Anodiwa finally left the barge, walking up the ramp that ran from the barge to the lowest deck of the tower, two decks below where the event would take place.

Waiting at the top of the ramp were the two female S'hudonni. They were taller than the males she'd seen but carried themselves with every bit as much confidence. It was their empire, after all.

"Hello," the female said in perfect English. "The Prince Twoclicks welcomes you, dear Chloe Cary, and I bring a personal warm hello from the Mother herself, by whom I am employed. My name is . . . ," and she whistled and clicked, "which rendered in your English might be Careful. And here is my other, whose name might be rendered Cautious, and is in my employ." And then she gave a slight bow, which wasn't easy when you were built like the S'hudonni.

Careful and Cautious, thought Chloe. What great names. And polite as hell.

"Thank you, Careful," Chloe said. "And thank you, Cautious. It is my great pleasure to meet with you, and I am honored that the Mother is so gracious as to say hello. Please let her know of my warm wishes for her, and I hope to meet her someday."

Which was pretty good, thought Chloe, as she shook hands and bowed slightly to both Careful and Cautious before walking toward the elevator that would take her and Anodiwa up to the main hall. Treble had told Chloe about the Mother's importance, but why this hello from her?

There was a ding from myBetty. "Twoclicks apologizes, Chloe. He didn't know that Careful and Cautious carried greetings from the Mother. He said I should quote him, in English, saying 'Wow.' He's never seen any representative of any of the cultures on The Six receive a greeting like that from the Mother. It's quite an honor."

"Tell him thank you," she murmured to myBetty. So the Mother must know what was going on here on Earth, and in real time. How was that possible?

Then Anodiwa came up to take her hand and the two of them stepped into the elevator and rose to the occasion.

29

MISS CHRISSY

Jamie Sullivan's fishing boat was a classic, an old 1972 wooden Chris-Craft Sportsman. It went down the smooth water of the Niagara River like it was sliding on glass. Five minutes after Sullivan took us on, Treble and I were both standing at the wheel, the glass deflector in front of us blocking some of the wind, though the cool breeze of the water still got to us even as the warm late summer sun shined on down.

"Earth's sun is amazing, Uncle Peter," Treble said to me as he closed his eyes and looked toward that late afternoon sun. He seemed fully recovered from his hours of being trapped at the river's edge.

"It is," I agreed, and did just what he was doing for a few seconds. I felt like both of us had earned that little moment of enjoyment.

It started with the two of us walking downstream along the shoreline until it emerged from the gorge and the going got easier, which mattered a lot to poor Treble and to me, both. And by then my connectivity through the glasses was working and I'd reported in the good news to Twoclicks.

But our problems weren't over yet. Twoclicks insisted that we had to get Treble to the tower for the dedication. He was arranging some transportation, but it would take some time.

As the path we were on widened and the walking got easier, we approached the Lewiston docks and our transportation problem solved itself. There sat the beautiful old wooden *Miss Chrissy*, and the owner was gassing her up for a few hours of evening fishing on the river.

Jamie Sullivan, retired after forty years of teaching history and coaching soccer in the local school district, was the proud owner of the classic boat, and he was stunned to see the alien and a friend walking up to him on the path.

"Can I help you two?" he'd asked, and that was the start of a conversation that led to where we were now.

I turned to look forward and there, in the distance, was the Niagara Tower. It rose from a wide base through five stories of offices and meeting rooms and restaurants and lecture halls before it started to narrow dramatically to a single spire that topped out at five hundred meters, just a bit shorter than Toronto's CN Tower, the top half of it just visible through my glasses, all the way across on the far side of Lake Ontario on this clear, blue-sky day.

Sullivan, at the helm, was excited. He had recognized me right away. "This is something; this is really something," he kept saying to himself as he steered us toward the Youngstown docks, where he would drop me off. I needed to stay as incognito as I could, since as far as everyone on Earth except Jamie Sullivan, standing next to me, knew, I was still on S'hudon. No one here knew of the Travel technology that could quantum you from there to here in seconds, and Twoclicks wanted it to stay that way.

"You know, Mr. Holman . . ." Sullivan started to say to me, nearly shouting in the breeze and the engine noise.

"Peter," I shouted back at him. "It's just Peter,"

He smiled and said, "Hard to believe." And I smiled back at him. And then he went on.

"Peter. You won't believe this, but I saw you play basketball a couple of times. You were a heck of a player."

"Really? Were you in Dublin or something?"

"Yeah, something like that. The first time my daughter's college, Mercyhurst, played you guys in the first round of the Division II tournament, one of those parents' weekend things, and the game was part of the package. You guys beat up on us pretty good. You were hot from outside, six threes, I think. It was quite a show."

"I remember that game," I said, and smiled at him. "I had thirty-two points on the day, I think. One of the best games of my college career."

"And it had to be against Mercyhurst." He laughed. "You were fun to watch, anyway.

"And then the other time, I was one of the chaperones for a big group of high school kids in Ireland. The kids were driving us nuts, of course, so we took turns having our nights out. I went to see you play for the Dublin Rovers against Sunderland. Decent night, fifteen or eighteen points or something. It was fun.

"And then when you got involved with these guys," he nodded toward Treble, who looked over and smiled back, "that was pretty cool. Biggest moment ever, for all of us, and I felt like I knew you."

"That's great," I said.

"And now I *do* know you," he added. "You know, I was watching that day when you broadcast from the ship and it all went to hell. I'm glad you survived that. And you must have some great stories to tell about life on that planet."

"It's one interesting, interesting place," I said. "A big red sun that they call the father; lots of dark purples and greens everywhere, lots of rain, lots of weirdness—you know: the animals, the plants, all of that."

"And now you're back!"

"Not really," I said. "You'll have to stay very quiet about this, Jamie, like I told you. It's sort of spy stuff, OK? I'm just here for a little visit with my pal Treble here. Can you promise me that? I really need to confirm that."

"Or you'd have to kill me, right?" He laughed, and then he saw the serious look on my face and his eyes got wide. "OK, OK, I got it."

I was thinking that this was for his protection more than mine. What might my brother Tom's badasses do if they knew that Jamie Sullivan had helped us? Better, certainly, to keep it quiet.

Which is what we all did for the next few minutes, cruising along in that fabulous old classic Chris-Craft, admiring the view of the Niagara Tower and the shores to each side—Canada to our left and the United States to our right. It seemed like everything was back on track, but I regretted even having that thought as soon as I had it. We weren't done yet.

"Look," said Treble, and pointed toward the New York shore.

A boat was coming out from a small dock. It was large enough to hold half a dozen people, some of them standing, and it was headed downstream like it wanted to cut us off.

I was wearing the glasses, which had darkened for me in the bright sunlight on the river. I looked at that boat, said, "Glasses, zoom in," and they did the job.

"Wow," said Sullivan, followed by "Damn," from me.

The zoom has been perfect this time. I could see six people—five guys and a woman at the wheel. They were all armed, semiautomatic weapons strapped over their shoulders. One of them was looking right at us with binoculars, and as I watched, he turned to say something to the woman at the helm. She pushed the throttle forward and the boat rose higher on the plane and headed hard toward a spot ahead of us. Five minutes? Maybe less? We'd meet there.

"Anything you can do to get us past them, Jamie?" I asked our skipper.

He smiled. "I rebuilt this engine last year, Peter. We've been cruising so far, enjoying the day. Let's see what she can really do." And as he pushed the throttle forward, the *Miss Chrissy* showed her stuff, rising up higher on plane and going faster and then faster still. Maybe, I thought, we'd outpace them, force them to get behind us and try to chase us.

I kept an eye on them as we upped the speed, and the guy with binoculars was doing the same. He saw us rise up and go faster and he spoke to the woman at the wheel. She shook her head. That was all they had.

I heard Treble behind me, whistling loudly, and when I looked over he was waving his arms like a madman and whistling and hooting with excitement. He looked at me. "Wonderful, Uncle Peter! Absolutely wonderful! Such fun!"

Right. Fun. The kid was amazing.

I looked back at the other boat, and one of them on it had a rifle with a scope. He was aiming at us. "Down!" I yelled, and I grabbed Treble and pushed him down. The front windshield shattered, hit by a bullet from that scoped rifle. I had my pistol in my jacket pocket, but it wouldn't do any damn good at this range.

"I'll zigzag!" yelled Sullivan, who'd dropped down, too. He reached up to grab the bottom of the steering wheel and move it to the right and then to the left. It cost us speed but gained us some mercy from that rifle with the scope. I saw another puff of smoke but nothing hit.

I peeked over the gunwales and saw that we had passed them by, and now they were turning to come in behind us. The guy with the scope was unsteady as they crossed our wake and then turned. He lost his footing and had to let go of the rifle with one hand to grab the boat and hang on. That wouldn't last long, and he was probably accurate to a thousand meters or more with the rifle. But maybe not when he was shooting it from a moving boat. Let's hope that was so.

I turned to look ahead. The tower wasn't far off. The Youngstown docks were far to the right and out of the question.

"Get us to the tower!" I yelled to Sullivan, and he waved in agreement and mostly steadied the *Miss Chrissy*, just tweaking the steering wheel back and forth a bit to make us a tough target as onward we went, zigzagging toward the tower.

A shot from behind and a bullet buried itself in the wooden fishing locker that sat in the middle of the boat, wood chips flying. Sullivan inched us to the right and then to the left.

I looked back and they were falling behind, not that that mattered too much to the guy with the scope. I could see him aiming and saw a puff of smoke as he fired. I felt the bullet go by my right ear and then bury itself in the front control panel. Another shot or two and we were dead, I guessed. I was strangely calm about that.

Then, as I watched the guy aiming again, I saw him stagger, then fall to his left against the gunwales, and then collapse over the side. I stood up for a second, looked around, and saw a US Coast Guard boat at an angle to us, slipping by, full steam ahead toward the boat behind us.

Treble yanked on my arm. "Father Twoclicks called them in. They were at the tower, on standby for trouble. He told them the ones on the boat were insurgents trying to kill a prince of S'hudon."

"That would be exactly right," I said, smiling at him. So the cavalry had arrived. It must have been something for Twoclicks to watch live through my glasses.

Sullivan pulled back on the throttle as we approached the tower. The nearest spot to board it was to our left and no more than one hundred meters away. I turned to smile at Treble, but he wasn't smiling back. Instead, he was pointing up several decks of the tower, to where two people were fighting and everyone else—a couple of hundred people maybe, and even a couple of S'hudonni—was running, clambering down the stairwells to the bottom deck and the barge that was tied up there.

Then one of the people in the fight climbed atop the railing. I zoomed in and saw it was Tom Holman, my brother, the angry insurgent. Jesus Christ,

I thought, my own brother. The terrorist. Right there. So something awful, something major and awful, was happening.

I watched Tom turn and say something to someone, and then he turned back and jumped. It was a long way down. I was going to look there to see if he'd survived it, but the other person started climbing the rail, too.

It was Chloe. My god, Chloe. And as I watched, she stood up on the railing, holding on to an upright support, and then she dived—dived!—down to the water. I followed her and it was a good entry, so I was betting she was fine. Jesus, that was amazing to see.

"Jamie," I said, about to tell him to head there, get us there to help, but he was way ahead of me, pushing the throttle back up so the *Miss Chrissy* rose up on plane as we turned slightly left and headed toward the spot where the two had gone in. We'd be there in a minute, maybe less.

I started slipping out of my shoes and taking off my shirt and slacks. I was a good, strong swimmer. I'd grown up in big water on the Gulf of Mexico. I was unafraid, and hell, in high school I'd passed my Red Cross lifeguard test. Put me in, coach! I stood on the gunwale, turned to Treble, and said, "Stay here. Help Mr. Sullivan pull any survivors out of the water, all right?"

We were closer now, so close that Sullivan turned the *Miss Chrissy* so we wouldn't run over the people in the water. I looked over at Treble, my little pal, and he smiled and nodded his head yes. "Go!" he said. "You are so brave!"

And I went.

30

●

POWER SURGE

A few minutes ago, Chloe Cary had been sitting on a folding chair on the small, raised stage. To the side of the stage was an old-style electrical switch the size of a pup tent. After her speech, Chloe would walk over to put both hands on the switch, pause dramatically for a moment, and then pull it down to close the connection and send power to millions with the right receiving equipment all over the Northeast United States and the provinces of Ontario and Quebec in Canada.

The switch wasn't real, of course, but Chloe was used to props, god knows, and would have no trouble pretending to find the switch a challenge to bring down and make the connection.

The hosts for the event were the mayors of Youngstown on the US side and Niagara-on-the-Lake on the Canadian side. They both tried to be charming and funny, and didn't quite carry it off, as they introduced the people of lesser importance and had them stand for a polite round of applause. Then the two mayors stepped aside as the provincial governor spoke for Ontario, and then the governor of New York spoke, and she did a great job.

Then the new prime minister of Canada spoke, and her speech was gracious and admiring, specifically mentioning Twoclicks. That was interesting, thought Chloe, since Canada had been dealing primarily with Whistle about trade agreements and Chloe would have thought the prime minister would have focused on him. But no.

Then came the governors of Ohio and Pennsylvania and Vermont and Massachusetts, all of them delighted to be working with Twoclicks as major recipients of his new power system. Other states, Chloe guessed, were waiting to see if the new thing worked or not. The systems at the receiving end of the power broadcast were costly, both to the states and to the citizens.

Then, on the big screen behind the stage, the US president sent her best wishes, with another gracious acceptance of things as they now were. Chloe was next and had a fifteen-minute speech ready that would lead up to her walking over and tugging that thing down to get the system working.

She sat up a bit, thinking through what she would say. She didn't get nervous at these things anymore, especially not after the half dozen she'd done with Treble on that truncated world tour. But not being nervous didn't equate to not being ready, and Chloe had spent enough years in the entertainment industry to know that being ready mattered. She was ready.

Then she got a ding from myBetty and heard in her ear, "Chloe, there's an Urgent for you from Twoclicks. A request for a live conversation."

"Accept, myBetty," she said quietly, "but give me fifteen seconds." She rose from her chair, smiled at Anodiwa, who sat in the front row, and walked away toward the relative privacy of the catwalk that encircled the entire second deck of the tower. Metal ladders ran up from the waterline to the top of the five floors that served as the base of the tower. The ladders were connected to the catwalks on all four sides of the tower.

She had a speech to deliver soon, and Twoclicks surely knew that, so this must be some important bit of news. "All right," she said quietly to my-Betty, staring out at the lake, smooth as glass in the calm evening. It was nice on the catwalk, as long as you weren't afraid of heights. Heights didn't particularly bother Chloe, but she didn't want to clamber around to the outside of the ladder she was leaning on and go up any higher to prove the point. The view from here was fine, thanks.

There was a click, and then Twoclicks said, "Dearest friend Chloe." She had no way, right here, to see a visual display, but unless she was hearing it wrong, there was concern in that voice. "There iss ssomething terrible about to happen. You must leave there immediately."

"Leave?" What could be about to happen that S'hudonni technology couldn't stop? That was hard to imagine.

"Dearest friend Chloe, Tom Holman is there."

"I know, Twoclicks. I talked with him back on the barge an hour ago or more. I suppose Whistle got him credentialed for this. He seemed calm. Better, certainly, than the last time I saw him."

"We know, and that iss why we are worried. And checked into it. And he iss not better, dear friend Chloe. Iss worsse. And hass a device, ssomething from S'hudon, from Whistle. We are sso disssapointed in our brother Whistle. But this device is not detectable. Soon, we think, in minute or two, he will start processs, and the suppressor comes first. No more communication, so thiss iss only warning. If he uses this, many, many people will die. Everyone there on tower."

"A bomb?"

"Dear friend Chloe, not a bomb but worse. Things will disassemble. Fall apart. The legs of the tower will give way. All into the water."

"And you can't stop it?"

"We are trying. But this device iss from home planet. Prohibited. Not possible that it could be here. We were not prepared for it."

"And yet it's here. Damn. What can I do?"

"Dearest friend Chloe, iss ssimple. You must leave."

There was a pause and Hanratty came online. "Chloe, Treble and Peter are coming your way to help. They are in a boat and you could join them and all of you would escape. That really would be best, saving Treble and you and Peter. You might be able to see them now, if you look in the right direction, toward the south. We have warned Treble not to attempt to stop Tom Holman, but the princeling isn't listening. Chloe, please! It is very important that we save Treble, and I think that Tom has already set the device and it will go off soon. Perhaps only minutes remain. Please! Warn everyone to get back to the barge and away from the tower. Warn them! And then make sure Treble is safe, and protect yourself and Peter."

Sure, she thought, clicking off. Of course, save everyone, but especially save Treble. Well, hell, she'd do her best. She turned and was about to head back into the crowd to warn them when Anodiwa came through the doorway to stare at her.

"I've just heard from Twoclicks. I'll get everyone headed to the barge. I'll do my best. You do what you can, right? And then get to safety, right?"

"Right," she said. She watched Anodiwa go back and heard her shouting, telling everyone to move quickly, don't panic, get to the barge.

Chloe turned around and took two steps back to the catwalk railing to see if she could spot Treble and Peter. She looked out to the lake and saw a dozen or more small boats and one, a bigger one, white with red stripes on it—Coast Guard. It was moving fast toward one of the small boats, and that boat was turning and heading away.

She saw what looked like guns firing back and forth. Weird to see it from here and have it all look pretty mundane but to know that down there someone was being chased by the Coast Guard, bullets were flying, and people were likely to get hurt. She knew what that was like.

She heard scuffling on the ladder to her right and looked up to see feet coming down, and then, smiling at her from the ladder above, there was Tom Holman.

"Hi, Chloe. Fancy meeting you here."

"Tom," she said, "whatever you've done, these people are innocent. No one needs to die."

"Ah, so you've heard about the plan. From Twoclicks, I suppose. Well, fair enough. I've heard about it from Whistle," he said. Then he added, "You know, I'd like to stay and chat, but I'm sort of on a deadline."

"Oh, Tom."

He smiled. "Yeah, it's happening. Here and now, Chloe Cary, TV star and friend of the new leadership." He spat it out. "It's got to change, Chloe. We can't go on like this, licking the boots of those things, making money for them, changing our whole way of life for their profit. It's got to stop."

"Not this way, Tom, please. These people here, they don't have to die."

"If they're here, they do have to die, Chloe. That's how it works." And he started climbing down the ladder again.

Chloe grabbed at him, got him by the legs, pulled one of them free, tried to wrestle him back to the catwalk. Instead, he kicked and kicked again, and as Chloe fell back against the inside wall of the catwalk, he stood there on the railing and looked at her.

"This is how it has to go, Chloe. I'm sorry, really, for you and for your boyfriend and for that fucking S'hudonni kid. But this is how it has to go."

He turned to face out toward the great lake, turned to look back once at Chloe, smiled at her, turned back again, looked down, and jumped.

31

SWIMMINGLY

Chloe had never tried a dive from that kind of height, but it went well, and she hit the water within twenty or thirty meters of Tom and then sank deep and had to work hard to get back to the surface. When she did, there was Tom, staring at her as he treaded water.

"Oh, Christ," he said.

"Tom. Don't do this," said Chloe, spitting out some water and wiping her face with her hand to take a good look at him. "You don't want to kill those people, Tom. You don't."

"What the fuck do you know about it, Chloe fucking Cary, TV star and lackey to the ruling elite? I've killed a lot of people this summer. I'm sort of used to it."

Oh, my god, Chloe thought. He was nuts, murderously nuts. He would kill everyone, she was absolutely certain of it.

"You know," he said, "I *do* want to do it, Chloe fucking Cary. It kind of grows on you, you know? Righteous, that's what it is." And he held the device up for her to see. It was the size and shape of a deck of cards. Not much to it. But he was holding it in his hand, with his thumb on the narrow top of it, when he said, "If I press this, Chloe, right here? The whole thing comes down," he said.

Tom and Chloe both heard splashing from behind the big support stanchion that rose from the lake to meet the lowest of the five platforms. They looked, and Peter came into view, swimming hard, trying to see what was happening, who was where.

Peter looked terrible, Chloe thought, like his right arm was broken or something, so he was struggling in the water. He was even having trouble treading water. Back trouble, too? Legs?

"Tom!" he was yelling. "Don't do this!"

Tom, treading water, looked at him and laughed. He turned his head toward Chloe. "You seeing this?" he said to her. And then he laughed. "Fucking bad penny. Keeps showing up." He looked back at Peter. "Go to hell, Peter. I don't know how you got here or what you're doing, but this thing is going to go melt away to nothing in a minute or so, and with any luck you and your girlfriend will go with it. Got that?"

The river's current was pushing Tom away from her and from the stanchion, forcing Chloe to work hard to stay close to him and the girder. Then she heard myBetty speaking to her in her ear. Amazing that the dive and the water hadn't shorted myBetty out, but here she was, saying, "Twoclicks advises that until Tom attaches the device to the support stanchion, it's a bomb, but only as a triggering device and won't bring the tower down. Once it's attached, that explosion sets off the dissolution protocols and the whole thing starts to dissolve. Ten minutes later, there's nothing left of the structure."

OK, then, thought Chloe, keep that damn thing away from the support stanchion. She could do that, just let them all keep drifting slowly away, pushed out past the tower into the open lake.

She looked over at Peter. He was struggling to keep his head above water. He'd had a long, tiring swim, pushing hard to get here from that boat. Where was Treble? Better not to ask, she thought. Don't give Tom any ideas.

Chloe didn't think Tom realized how the current was pushing him away from the stanchion. Keep him talking, she thought, and buy time. They were all maybe ten meters apart now, Tom holding up the device, his thumb on some spot at the thin top of the thing.

"All right, Chloe, here's an offer. If you and Peter just swim away from here and leave me alone here to do this, I'll wait for five minutes before I attach this thing and press this son of a bitch down and there she goes. That'll be time for most everybody to get onto the barge and get clear."

Not likely, she thought, and then she heard Peter say, "Not likely, Tom." He was pushing hard with his arms to keep his head above water but then rising with some leg pumps to get up a little higher. "Come on, Tom. *Ten* minutes. Promise us that. Ten minutes."

Peter, too, was trying to buy time, she thought, and he was drifting toward her at the same time. He was gasping with pain, though. She wondered how long he'd be able to keep his head above water.

In pain or not, while he was begging his brother for time he was also reaching behind himself to get something. He drifted a little more and then he was next to her. He looked at her, smiled, and then seemed to struggle in the water, getting his hands down into the water to paddle some, the right hand splashing, the left hand staying down underwater.

She felt something. He was handing her something. A gun. She knew that gun, just by the feel of it, a SIG Sauer SP2022, nine millimeter. People laughed at that gun—it was light, not much recoil, a beginner's gun. A girl's gun. She owned one.

Would it work after being in the water for these long minutes? She didn't know, but she thought she was about to find out, unless Tom changed his mind.

Tom was smiling. "Look at you two. You two begging me? That's so sweet. The lovebirds begging me for just a little more time together, right, before this whole thing blows?"

"Tom," she said, "don't do this."

"Oh, you kids," he said, and then, hand up with the thumb on the trigger, he started backpedaling toward the stanchion.

"Tom! Please!" said Peter, and then he started to flail with his arms and sank beneath the water.

Tom watched his brother slipping beneath the waves but didn't say a word, still backing up. While he was looking at Peter, Chloe brought the gun up, aimed it toward him, and said, "Tom, stop. Don't do this."

He laughed. "A gun? One that's been in the water? I had no idea. But tough shit, little girl." He held up the trigger, said, "Fifteen seconds, kids," and pushed down hard with his thumb. There was an audible *beep*, and then he turned around to swim over to the stanchion. He was reaching toward it when Chloe fired.

The first bullet splashed the water next to him. Aiming was tough in these conditions, but now she knew the gun would fire. She steadied, shot again, and the bullet hit Tom in the back of the head. He stopped but didn't yet sink, and he was drifting toward the stanchion, his arm still out there. The trigger he had was magnetic, she was sure, and would cling to the stanchion with the slightest urging.

There was a gasp to her right and she knew it was Peter, rising, ready to help, but there was no need for that now. She fired again and hit Tom again in the back of the head. His arm dropped into the water. No connection, no dissolution. They'd saved the structure.

She turned to Peter. He came over to her. "Chloe," he said, and she was just starting to reach out to hug him when there was a bright, white, searing flash of light, a great *whoomph* of displaced air, a sharp shock wave that roiled the water and shattered and tore Chloe and Tom and Peter into small pieces of who they'd been.

From a distance, safe, standing next to his new friend Jamie Sullivan aboard the *Miss Chrissy*, the young princeling Treble watched. The explosion was dramatic, a great white flaring from the base of the tower and a shock wave that rocked even the *Miss Chrissy* at its distance, with a huge billowing of smoke, and water after that. But the tower itself was nearly immune to such trivialities, and while the five floors of office space and meeting rooms were battered and aflame, the tower stood there, firm, once the air began to clear.

Treble knew that Peter and Chloe could not have survived, and there was work to do as Sullivan took the *Miss Chrissy* into the site to pick up some of the unlucky guests who had jumped to escape. Treble helped for the next couple of hours, both in the water and out, as the *Miss Chrissy* made repeated trips between tower and shore. Other pleasure boats did the same, and most, but not all, of the guests were saved, two dozen of them by Treble himself, who went unerringly to the worst swimmers and kept them afloat as he brought them to one boat or another. Treble, the Princeling Hero!

32

TRAVELING

Inside the consulate of the Empire of S'hudon in Los Angeles, Chloe Cary heard a knock on the door, and before she could ask who it was, in walked Twoclicks, wearing a blue L.A. Dodgers baseball cap held atop his bullet-shaped head by a white elastic strap that went under what there was of a chin. His upper torso sported a Dodger-blue T-shirt that had his name in script across the back shoulders. Dodger-blue culottes completed the ensemble. He looked ridiculous, not that Chloe would mention that.

"Dearest Chloe!" he boomed at her, and came over to hold her hands. "Important engagement for me! Half-hour gig at Funny Man on Wilshire! My big break!

Good grief. I'm held incommunicado for hours and hours and then Twoclicks shows up to say he's getting ready for a stand-up gig. Incredible.

She wanted to tell him off, to let him know he couldn't treat people this way, that he couldn't treat *her* this way, after what she'd done for him—squiring around the Importance and fighting off the bad guys and all that on the abortive world tour.

But that would be stupid to say. He'd worked wonders for her; he really had. Twoclicks was the reason she had a career at all, to say nothing of one with a global audience. She shook herself, reminded herself of her Ohio roots and that Midwestern politeness, and said, "Break a leg, Twoclicks. Do I get to come watch?"

"Yes! Break legss! Thank you!" he said, which meant he knew the expression. "Will be great sshow! Baseball jokes! Very very funny! Who's on First?" And then he let go of her hands, stepped back, and said, "We have way for you to see the show! I have much new material for you to see!"

"I don't know . . ." Chloe said, wondering if Twoclicks would get the joke. But what did he mean—that this old Abbot and Costello routine was important for her? Maybe they were letting her out of this gilded cage? She'd been here all day. Three-room suite, and very nice and all that, but still, it amounted to kidnapping, damn it. They had myBetty blocked and she had no access to the clouds at all. She couldn't even place or receive any calls. Twoclicks was going to let her out of here now, she hoped.

But that turned out not to be why he was here. Instead, looking at her with a strained effort at a sad face, he said, "Dearest friend Chloe, I bear ssad newss and great newss both. Which first?"

"Tell me the sad news first, Twoclicks, please," she said.

"All right. Will do." And he stepped back toward her again and reached out to hold her hands again and said, "Dearest friend Chloe, you died a sshort time ago ssaving the livess of many people during attack on Niagara Tower."

He brought that strange face with its flat nostrils and no ears, and that fat, slick, porpoise-shaped body, close to her face and said, quietly, "S'hudon thanks you."

Chloe looked at him. Yes, she knew about the Niagara Tower gig, but that had happened without her, right? The glitch in the hardware, right? So, since Twoclicks fancied himself a comedian and had dressed for the part, maybe this was all an elaborate joke? "What the hell happened? And what do you mean I died? I'm very much alive, Twoclicks."

"That glass bed that you lay on sso early this morning, dearest friend Chloe? I explained to you that we would usse it to send you to a receiving unit at Niagara Fallss, yess? You Traveled, yess?"

"It didn't work, you said. I was unsuitable, you said."

"It worked perfectly, dearest friend Chloe. But we thought it besst to keep that from you, and to keep you here in great sssafety."

"I don't understand."

"The device copiess, dearest friend Chloe, and ssends the copy on the decoding bed. The original, the you that sstands here with me, remainss behind."

Chloe stared at Twoclicks. Was this really happening? Another fucking curveball from Twoclicks? "I knew that," she said. "You told me that this morning. But you said it didn't work. So now you're saying it *did* work, and a copy of me ended up at the Niagara Tower? Some other me?"

"Is imperfect processs, dearest friend Chloe, and not ussed often. But ssometimess is need. Even I have been copied! Imperfect, and in repose now, but could be brought awake. Ssafety in numberss!"

She nodded. Sure. Safety in numbers. What that really meant was that she'd died at Niagara Falls and stood here, alive and well, in Los Angeles. Sure, who'd have trouble with that idea?

Twoclicks took a deep, theatrical breath. He put a frown on that round face, reached up to tug on the bill of his Dodgers cap, and said, "There iss more, dearest friend Chloe. Iss worsse for you. No one can know of thiss. No one on Earth can know of thesse Travel devicess. They are few and need would be many, sso big ssecret! With you, necessary things musst be done, dearest friend Chloe. You undersstand?"

She smiled, took her right hand from his left and mimed zipping her mouth shut and swallowing the key. "Mum's the word, Twoclicks," she said.

"You do undersstand?" he asked again.

She looked him straight in the eye. Uh-oh. There was more to it than just staying quiet. Damn. Well, she'd face this shit head-on. What would be the worst thing? "Am to be killed?"

"Oh, no, dearest friend Chloe! You will be alive and doing important work for uss. Huge sstardom for you! Very famouss on many worldss! Famous Chloe Cary!"

Sure, she thought. Famous. But dead. "On many worlds? What important work?"

Twoclicks dodged the question and instead said, "Your new friend Anodiwa will be big sstar on Earth, Chloe. Huge sstar! Mournss your losss and then, with great reluctance, takes over your role. Great acclaim!"

Ah, so that was it. Somehow this all fit together. The South African wonder was the heir to Chloe's global fame. Had this been planned all along? Could she have been so stupid as to not see this? Anodiwa? Was all that love and lust with her just an act? Christ. Damn, damn, damn.

"But you, too, will be big, big sstar, dearest friend Chloe. Famouss on many worldss!"

Those many worlds again. What the hell? There was something she wasn't understanding about this, about how it all fit together. Not that it had to make sense. If Twoclicks willed it, so it was.

Chloe thought about laughing. Or crying. But it wasn't as if she had a choice in the matter.

"You will travel by screamship to S'hudon, dearest friend Chloe. No more copiess! You and me and the Importance. Great time to be had by all! You will be reunited with dearest friend Peter Holman! Wonderful! Famouss on many worlds! Treble will be home as great hero! The Importance! And I will be home for some time, too, before I see you off on great adventure! You and Treble and Peter go on to ssee the other worlds and they will ssee you! Live! In person! One night only! Chloe Cary from Earth!"

This was dismaying on several counts. Reunited with Peter? Why couldn't she be rid of that relationship? From the start it was a Hollywood fix-up to help two careers. Peter was a nice guy, sure, so it was easy enough for Chloe to act her way through it. But she had, to put it mildly, other interests when it came to love and comfort. Priya? Terri? Anjou? She could stand a few months with one or two of them, if she had to.

"Will there be anyone else along, Twoclicks? Can I bring a few people?" she asked. "I'll need a stylist, for sure, and a personal assistant. One or two others. Just the basics, not like the whole entourage we had on the Treble tour." That would make it all right. A few months with some friends, exploring the universe while faking it with Peter? That would be all right. That would be fine, in fact.

But Twoclicks had moved on with the details and wasn't answering the question.

"First we do sspecial funeral for dead you. Great mourning! So much sadness! Line of limos all the way out to to Malibu! Funeral will be global show for you! The Importance will sspeak of love and admires for you, his Aunt Chloe. Anodiwa will speak and weep for you! I will tell a few jokes!

And then your asshes into the Pacific, dear friend Chloe. Treble will say ssome final words about your wonder, and then pour them from Earthie urn. Sso sad!"

Sadness and tears. Fucking hell. And hey, she wondered, what about Peter? That was a copy of him that died, too. Why wasn't Twoclicks worried about that? Weren't people wondering about him? Dead, alive, dead?

"Never happened!" Twoclicks said, reading her mind. "Peter, broken, copied, dying, never happened! No one saw! Trebnet! Our perfect Trebnet! Change here, change there. All different!"

Shit. All different, she thought. Nothing is real; no truth exists except Twoclicks's.

"Correct! Never there at all, dearest friend Chloe! You alone were great hero who stopped Tom Holman. You alone stopped death and destruction! Amazing! Wonderful! But sad! Sso sad!"

Chloe wasn't surprised by all this. Routine stuff, really, even for Earthies. Deepfakes, they used to call it. Now it's just our truth, which is better than yours. Simple.

"After funeral comess very clever! Ssmuggle you out to ship on Ssalton Ssea. Very exciting! Dark of night! Your lasst excitement here, we ssuppose."

Crap, she thought. That sounded really lonely.

"Who will know the truth, Twoclicks? Can my parents be told? And Kait—surely Kait and Sarah can be told, yes?"

"Dearest friend Kaitlyn is one of uss now. The Importance ssays sso and you know Treble iss trusted. Completely. So, yess, Kaitlyn can know. Great hero and dearest friend Kaitlyn, yess! Of course!"

"And my parents?"

"Ssuch good people them! But no, dear Chloe. Mother and father, sso nice. But no."

Worse and worse, thought Chloe. But then she thought about her pal the young princeling, and her good friend the rescued Kait, and she realized she had some leverage over even the mighty Twoclicks. He needed her, right? *Let's make a deal.*

And so it came to pass that a deal *was* made, and Chloe watched live on her smarty as Twoclicks did stand-up for thirty minutes at the Funny Man on Wilshire, and she told him afterward that it was awfully good, though how does one explain to a comedian the difference between being laughed *at* and laughed *with*? If the being in question is the governor-general of all Earth, one ignores the distinction and praises said governor-general.

In return, before being smuggled aboard Twoclicks's sumptuous S'hudonni screamship, before her tearful good-bye to wonderful Kait and Sarah, before her own depressing five weeks aboard that ship—in great comfort, but that didn't help a bit—Chloe was able to spend time with her parents, telling them her sad but happy news as they signed their non-disclosure agreements and wept with relief and anguish both. They spent two days with her in the consulate, getting to know Treble and Twoclicks and saying good-bye to their daughter before she dressed as a stevedore to board the great ship that was taking Twoclicks and Treble home to S'hudon. Twoclicks promised Earth that he'd be back inside of a year, Einstein permitting. And Treble might be back, too, said the Importance, before the ramp closed, adding, "I love you, Earth!"

Chloe, though, would be back never. Probably. The thought was dismaying, though the five weeks of travel with Treble and Twoclicks was entertaining enough, with plenty of forced laughter while watching Twoclicks do stand-up, and plenty of time to run in the corridors for exercise, and plenty of time to start a memoir on pen and paper that would, somehow and somewhen, she knew, be read by billions, and plenty of time to hang out with Treble, who was, in fact, a great kid and prepped her for what was to come by regaling her on the wonders of blimpies and the joys of daffodils and dagios and ducks and melodists and all the rest of the wonders of The Six. They'd be touring all those planets, Treble and Chloe and Peter. They were already famous, the three of them, along with Kait and Smiles and some others. Those daffodils and ducks and dagios and the others had been watching their adventures for many months.

Fame! Galactic fame! Chloe smiled as Treble talked all about it. But Chloe was alone, and the prospect of many months of faking it with Peter didn't hold much appeal. And there wasn't anything at all that she could do about it.

But then there was.

Once they arrived on S'hudon, Chloe was put into a special two ten-days of quarantine in a little fake village they'd built for her, all false fronts, like any good set on the studio lot. She called it Carytown.

There they poked and prodded and nanoed her up. Her quarters were fine—amazingly good, actually, at making it feel like home. As did her visitors: Treble every few days, and Twoclicks now and again, and Heather, wonderful Heather, who wound up moving right in. Heather: the construct, the device, the diplomat who could, and did, make anything of herself and be anyone. Be Anodiwa.

And so it was that on the last of the second ten-days after arriving on S'hudon, Chloe Cary woke to the sound of Robin Patel singing "It's My Party," dredged up from myBetty's capacious internal memory as a song from home. myBetty didn't have access to S'hudon's planetwide Trebnet and had to hobble along with the two petabytes of memory she'd arrived with, including all five versions of "It's My Party."

Cry if you feel like it, for sure, Chloe thought, but then she rolled over on her back and no sooner got into that position than Anodiwa—or the nearest possible thing to Anodiwa—reached over to touch Chloe's nose and say, "Bzzz, time to get up, dear."

Chloe sighed, moaned a bit for effect, and grabbed Diwa's hand to give it a kiss. Then she let go of it and rolled left to get her legs over the side of the bed and sit there for a few moments to contemplate life as it was here in Carytown, in the district of Dissonance, in the state of Chaos, on the planet of S'hudon, where the only thing in the whole town that was really what it seemed was Chloe herself.

She stood, walked over to the dresser to look at the souvenirs from her youth and her career—the prop six-shooter, the Annie Oakley doll, the sports medals from high school and college, the posters from *The Family Madderz*, with Chloe in those dramatic action poses, the People's Choice runner-up statuette, and more—on top of the dresser and framed and hung behind it. All of this just exactly the way it was back home in Malibu.

"Are you all right, Chloe?" she heard from behind.

She turned to look at Anodiwa and smiled. "Fine," she said. "Just fine."

"We leave in an hour. I'll have to change for that, you know," said Anodiwa, the beautiful and smart and witty and talented and deadly and loving Anodiwa Pinaar, who was, at the moment, the love of Cary's pretend life, the costar of act one, scene three of *The Life of Chloe Cary*.

It was a good way to look at the world, Chloe thought. She was a damn fine actor, so grab it, inhabit the character, give it some agency, make it your own, work it!

Heather did a perfect Anodiwa. OK, a little wooden maybe, but very close to perfect. Working together, it seemed they were made for each other, here in *LoCC* (yes, she'd shortened the title already!). They were two great talents, Chloe and Anodiwa, the action heroes who'd fought the bad guys—twice!—and won. Brains and beauty and shared knowledge of the difficulties of a public life. They hadn't known each other long, but they already could finish each other's sentences. They *knew*.

And the fact that it wasn't *really* Anodiwa? No problem! Ian McKellen wasn't really Macbeth, either, in the Scottish play. It's called acting!

She, or it, or sometimes he, or they, wasn't the real Anodiwa, wasn't the real South African star of stage and screen and sweep and stream. That one, the real one back on Earth, had replaced dead Chloe, the copied one back on Earth, as the protégé of Twoclicks, governor-general of the whole damn planet, who was currently in a mud pot somewhere, waiting for Chloe and Treble and Anodiwa to show up, to meet Peter, and then, *Action!*

Back on Earth, the real Anodiwa Pinaar had graciously agreed to take over the lead role in *The Family Madderz* after the heroic death of copied Chloe as she and Peter Holman had given their lives to stop Tom Holman's act of terror at the Niagara Tower. In that show, Chloe would hate her.

But here? This role is even better. And here, the real Chloe hasn't died!

No, this Chloe, the real Chloe, the nondead one, the not-really-the-hero-of-the-Niagara-Tower-incident one, stood here and looked at the not-real Anodiwa Pinaar, who was looking back at her with a lustful gleam in those eyes, saying, "We do have time for a little more, Chlo."

You'd swear it was Anodiwa saying it; that South African accent was perfect. Thank god for Heather! It, she, them, him had been Heather in one form and a shark-like S'hudonni with a whistle and a click in another, and then despicable Hanratty in the L.A. consulate with Twoclicks in yet another, and god knows what other people or beings from anywhere she, they, it, or he had been. What a talent!

And now here she was as Anodiwa, beautiful, deadly, crack shot, SAA trained, sitting up in bed, smiling at her and saying, "Just for a few more minutes? It could be quick. I wouldn't mind."

Inhabit the character, Chloe! God, she smelled so good. So. What the hell. Why not? All of life is a lie, if you look close enough. It's all acting. It's all of us making it up as we go. Sure, we're changing all the time. Heather or Hanratty or Anodiwa, take your pick, was just doing it a lot faster, that's all. And Chloe climbed back into bed.

33

INHABIT

The hot spring was no more than four or five meters in circumference, with steam rising from the hot water that bubbled up from the pebbled bottom. It was empty. Overhead, a pair of blimpies circled slowly, looking down at the proceedings. I saw them about every day now and could recognize them both. They were keeping an eye on me. The usual insects were flying around, too.

Twoclicks was back on S'hudon and had invited me here to meet with him. He'd been back for a couple of ten-days, and I'd been expecting an invitation, or perhaps just a visit, with him waddling up to my little cottage to say hi and bring me up to date on matters political and Earthie. We had a lot to talk about, me and Twoclicks.

There'd been no visit, but yesterday there'd been a formal invitation, handwritten in a flowery script.

> *Dearest Friend Peter,*
>
> *Twoclicks of the House of S'hu and Governor-General of your Earth would like to meet with you on the morrow at your afternoon two o'clock at the hot spring at the beach you call Same Ole, near the rock you call The Elephant. We will bathe and reminisce and then discuss a matter of some importance.*
>
> *Yrs, etc,*
> *Twoclicks*

The invitation was exactly the sort of thing I'd expect from Twoclicks. It was delivered first thing in the morning by hand, a young S'hudonni female knocking on my door and handing it to me and waiting for my reply. Very Victorian.

I'd told the youngster to tell Twoclicks that I'd be there, and thank you, and now here I was, my afternoon two o'clock on the beach I called Same Ole and near the huge boulder I called The Elephant. I kneeled next to the hot spring, put my hand in the water. It was warm, even hot. A good thirty-eight or thirty-nine Celsius, I guessed. It was no wonder the S'hudonni elite spent so much time on this rocky coast.

I looked toward the water and saw a slight ripple in the calms offshore. Then a form emerged, slowly stood, waist deep, and walked toward me, the body emerging as the water shallowed. *Portly* always came to mind. Slick, porpoise skin, one hundred fifty or so centimeters tall. Thin legs that didn't seem able to hold up that thick body. Spindly arms and small hands with four fingers and a thumb. All that folded away into side pouches when he was swimming. Twoclicks, the first son of the royal family for all of this archipelago, which ran a business empire that stretched to six other planets. The strange S'hudonni. So few to control the lives of so many billions on seven worlds, counting Earth.

It must be their charm. Twoclicks came completely out of the water, laughed, and shouted, "Cold!" Then he ran forward a dozen tiny steps to jump from the side and into the hot spring with a splash and more laughter, as he went underwater and then popped up quickly. "Hot!" And he laughed some more.

Twoclicks, who had won the struggle with his brother for control of Earth's profits and its future, then said, "Join me, friend Peter!"

And I did, thinking all the while of how Twoclicks, who'd just invited me for a quick dip in the hot water, paraded a kind of charming buffoonery but could decide the fate of Earth's billions and act on a whim. But, hell, he professed to like me, albeit in a way not unlike how I, as a child, had once loved my dog Zorro, the bright and cheerful border collie. Twoclicks. Enigmatic. Odd. Dangerous. Alien.

He waited until I was immersed up to my shoulders, then looked at me sadly and said, "Friend Peter. I have ssome very bad newss for you."

Oh, no. What kind of news could be "very bad news for you"? It must be about Kait, or Tom, or Chloe, or Treble—someone who'd been there on Earth with Twoclicks.

"I am sso ssorry for you, but I must ssay there wass much death very recently on your Earth, dearest friend Peter. And all of thiss was caused by your brother, dear Tom Holman, who was one of many killed during an attack on our new enterprise, the Niagara Tower, built just for humans. Built to pleasse you! Free energy!"

I suddenly felt foolish, silly, sitting in a hot spring on an alien world while my brother had died violently back where it all mattered, back on Earth. I stood up, sat back on the edge of the spring, legs still in the water. That, too, felt wrong and stupid. I rose, naked and honest and human, to stand across from Twoclicks and ask, "How did it happen?"

"Your brother, dear Tom Holman, had a device, dearesst friend Peter. A weapon of S'hudon. It musst have come from Whistle. Terrible device. Deadly! And Tom Holman was using thiss device to bring down the Niagara Tower. Many would have died, great friends of ourss, supporterss. All those who were there, human and S'hudonni, had come to see your friend Chloe Cary and my sson, Treble. Dedication for free power! Your brother Tom meant to kill them all. He wass not a good human, friend Peter, but he was your brother. I am sso very ssorry for you."

I trembled, was suddenly chilled to the bone. Tom was dead. The brother I'd pitied and envied and battled against. The brother who'd nearly killed me two different times. But the brother I'd grown up with in our little beach town. The brother that my sister Kait and I had been swimming and snorkeling and kayaking with a hundred times.

The brother who'd fallen in love with a woman I'd then had an affair with—a woman of uncertain truths, certainly. A woman who was a device, a creation who could change shapes and manner and be anything she wanted to be for whatever reason she wanted. A woman I'd loved, who'd left him for me.

I had others, better people, to worry about. "Treble?" I asked. "And Chloe?" I wanted them both to be alive, to be fine. But from the way Twoclicks was looking at me, that wasn't the news I was going to get.

"Iss more, friend Peter," he said, rising from the hot springs to stand, waist deep, and stare sadly at me. He shook his head slightly in dismay. "Iss sad," he said. "Iss so very sad."

I could only stare back at him.

"Yes," said Twoclicks. "Your friend and mine, dearest Chloe Cary, was great hero. And you, too, friend Peter; and my son the Importance! The you that Traveled there became great hero, too! Saved hundredss of livess, you and Chloe and the Importance. Some died, but many more lived. I ssing your praisess." And he whistled something I hadn't heard before, a kind of trill that, even to my ears, sounded heroic.

"And Treble?" I'd been wondering—hoping—that the copy of me that had arrived in Niagara Falls had done his job and gotten Treble out of there. But if I'd died, perhaps Twoclicks was saving the worst for last.

"Treble is safe, friend Peter, because of you! You ssaved our Importance! You! You and dear friend Chloe Cary ssaved him!"

Great, I thought. But?

"But you died in the ssaving of sso many, dearest friend Peter. Your brother Tom's explosion took your livess. You and dearest friend Chloe. Sso sso sad!"

Oh, my god. Chloe? Dead? It was hard to process. My own death there? That was nothing. That me wasn't me. That me had never been me, had no connection to me. I couldn't feel anything for a me who wasn't me. Kait had suffered the same kind of death, and she was fine now. Back home now on Earth, safe and sound.

But Chloe. "Chloe is really dead?" I asked, trying to confirm things, understand them. Kait would be sad, too. Kait had really liked Chloe.

Hell. I loved her. Had loved her. And lost her forever, now.

"How did she die? Do you know?" I asked, and I sat back down into the hot spring.

He did the same thing, and seemed to listen for a few seconds before saying, "The two of you, together, were very brave, dearest friend Peter. You and Chloe Cary, sso sso brave. Your brother Tom had device in hiss hand, armed, ready. He needed to attach it to tower at water level on support leg, that wass all. From there, it would ignite, big explosion, and then all dissolvess—ssupport, deckss, tall tower all dissolve, tower crumbless, falls apart into esssential moleculess, wasshes away in water, ssinks to bottom of lake. Terrible!"

"But that didn't happen?"

"No! Very brave, my two friends! All in the water, you two and your brother Tom. Sswimming, fighting. And you sstopped him, device not attached to ssupport, tower doesn't fall, but, sso sso sorry, all three die in explosion."

I wasn't worried about me. No, I take that back. I was sorrowful that I'd died, but I had to admit that the me that I knew, sitting here in a hot spring on an alien planet with an alien overlord who professed to be my friend, was alive and aware and OK.

But Chloe. I'd loved that woman, and it was awful, terrible, that she was gone. I'd fallen very hard for her, not just in the time we'd been together but also in the time since then, thinking about her, remembering her. I'd really thought that somehow we'd be together again, somewhere and sometime. And we'd make love again, that slow delicious lovemaking that we'd had in my house at the beach in Florida, or maybe the sudden, passionate, frenetic lovemaking we'd had in her house in Malibu.

I hadn't seen her in more than a year my time, and nearly twice that long her time, and so it was hard to conjure up the look of her. And I didn't care. The look of her is where it had started, these feelings for Chloe. But it was all the rest—the shared background as athletes, maybe, leading to a public life filled with successes and failures. The conversations about Hollywood and politics and basketball and friends we knew and places we'd been. Remembering the smell of her on the sheets, the feel of the back of her neck, the taste of her. All of it, all that and more, had made her so real to me that it ached to think she was gone. My past was gone, and now my future.

And then Twoclicks gave me some hope. "You know, iss more complicated than that, friend Peter," he said, reading my mind again. Probably *really* reading my mind again. Who knew what technology was in me that I didn't know about? Who knew how private my own thoughts were?

"S'hudon needss Chloe," he said. "And S'hudon needss you. And S'hudon needss my son Treble."

"But she's dead. Gone."

"Is not quite sso, friend Peter. Chloe Traveled to get from our consulate in Loss Angeless to Niagara Fallss to meet with Treble."

Of course! Chloe, the original Chloe, was still there, in L.A.

But there were problems with that. The Travel tech was very secret; no Earthies could know of it. To keep the secret was worth dying for.

"Earth thinks she is dead. So how can any version of her still be alive? Everyone would know something is up. I'm sure there are rumors already, hints about this technology. Will this ruin the secret?"

"No, no, no, friend Peter," Twoclicks said. "To Earth sshe iss dead. Great mourning. I will show you funeral and ceremoniess and great ssorrow everywhere.

"But here, to uss, sshe is alive, and on the other Six there is great interest in you. Go to Harmony and Downtone and Melody and the otherss. Visit there. You will impress. You can explain humans. Lots of detailss. Dearest friend Chloe iss very smart, dear friend Peter! And that will help uss ssell productss. Whiskeyss from Irish villages! Beer from Czech Bohemia! Winess from Oregon valleys! All the rest, too. Handcrafted by Earthie hands! You can explain. You and Treble, and my dearest friend Chloe!"

Jesus, I thought. Twoclicks was babbling. Did that all mean something? "What are you saying?"

The answer was this: a scuffling sound, some pebbles falling as someone came down the path from the bluff above. Twoclicks had a huge smile on his face. He brought one of those spindly arms up out of the hot water and pointed up toward the bluff.

I turned to look. There were three of them. Treble led the way, smiling and skipping down the path, waving at me. And behind him, walking together, were Chloe and Heather.

We had our secrets, did Heather and I, old ones and new ones. But now, I thought, I could get past those. Heather waved as they reached the bottom of the path and stood there for a moment, looking our way. She'd been holding Chloe's hand, to steady her on the path, I supposed, but now they looked at each other and smiled and let go their hands and Chloe walked, then ran, toward me. I was out of the hot spring, had a towel wrapped around me as I headed her way.

"Peter!" she yelled, waving her hands. "Oh, Peter!"

And as I ran to her over that stony beach, I began to think it would all be all right. It was real, what we had, me and Chloe. I hadn't invented the whole thing. It was real and true and honest. I wouldn't be alone after all.

ACKNOWLEDGMENTS

Alien Day is the sequel to 2016's *Alien Morning,* a novel that was a finalist for the John W. Campbell Memorial Award for Best Science Fiction Novel of the year. Both novels emerged from a series of stories that I've published over the years, mostly in *Asimov's Science Fiction* magazine, so I owe a great debt to the late Gardner Dozois, who edited the magazine for many years and published several of the stories, and to Sheila Williams, who has edited the magazine since 2004 and has published more of them. In both cases, their editing advice greatly improved the stories that ran in that fine magazine and so ultimately led to improvements in this particular novel.

Special thanks to my fine first readers, Nick DiChario, Sue Rea, Samantha Chechele, Alan Smale, Robin Wilber, James Patrick Kelly, and Alexander Jablokov. Special thanks, too, to Dr. Joseph Springle, a primary-care physician who has been my dependable source for advice on matters medical in various stories and novels, including this one. Also, I workshopped excerpts from this novel at the annual Rio Hondo workshop run by author Walter Jon Williams and received excellent advice on improving the storytelling from all the participants in those workshops, but especially from my roommates at one of those workshops, editor and writer C. C. Finlay and writer Paolo Bacigalupi. Their advice sparked immediate improvements in the novel.

The novel is set on Earth and S'hudon, the alien homeworld. For the scenes on Earth, special thanks to our daughter, biologist Samantha Wilber, who spent months in Cape Town, South Africa, researching caracal cats and provided me with a wealth of information on Cape Town, the caracals, and the penguins who appear in the novel. My many friends in Ireland and Scotland will recognize some place-names that I have, in a few cases, moved around for purposes of storytelling, but I thank all those friends for the memories I have of matters Celtic, especially Michael and Kate O'Connor and all of Mike's friends at Hussey's pub in Killarney, and Alan Learmonth and Richard Lindsay, for guiding me in matters of Scottish pride, from the best pubs to the best football teams to the best music.

I was raised in the Midwest, though I have lived elsewhere for decades, but I paid homage to the Midwest in this novel, and especially to my old hometown of St. Louis. It was a delight sending the young S'hudonni princeling Treble on a trip to the zoo.

My family and I also lived for six years in the Buffalo/Niagara area of Western New York, and we greatly enjoyed the scenery, the people, and the towns of Lewiston and Youngstown, in particular. I've set the climax of the story there, paying my respects to the underappreciated Niagara Gorge, as well as to the famous Niagara Falls. I remain good friends with two people, in particular, from that area, James Ruggiero and Fran Sullivan, and I have combined their names into a heroic and brave boater in a crucial scene set near Youngstown.

For the scenes set in Hollywood, I am indebted to my friend Clark Perry, television writer extraordinaire, who talked me through what a visit might be like for an alien dignitary shown around by a top talent. My wife and I visited Los Angeles and the Hollywood area in January 2020, just before the COVID-19 crisis, and that, too, gave me some sense of where the S'hudonni consulate might be located and how to get there from one of the studios.

For those large portions of the book set on S'hudon, my research focused on red dwarf stars and the habitability of planets around those stars. The website centauri-dreams.org (and the book of the same name) and the article "ESO: Habitable Red Dwarf Planets Abundant," by writer Paul Gilster, from March 29, 2012, were key to my imaginings and to a great deal more research.

I am always indebted to my wife and first reader, the patient and brilliant finance professor and best friend, Robin Wilber, Ph.D. I am indebted, as well, to our adult children—Samantha, whose biology degree comes in handy for all sorts of stories where I need some help, including this novel; and my son, Richard Jr., a hardworking and adamantly independent Down syndrome young man who takes me on daily walks and brings me up to speed on how our favorite sports teams are faring.

I am most appreciative, too, that writer and editor Kevin J. Anderson, together with a talented team of graduate students in Kevin's Master's in Publishing program in the Graduate Program in Creative Writing at Western Colorado University bought my story "False Bay," which emerges from the *Alien Day* novel and which I put through several rounds of editing that, ultimately, greatly improved the material in the novel on Chloe Cary, kick-ass television and sweep star.

The sweep technology, which is as important to this novel as it was to *Alien Morning*, comes from a lifetime of journalism and journalism education and is my best guess at one of the new technologies we will have for news and entertainment within the next ten years.

For the material in both this novel and in *Alien Morning* that are set in Palo Alto, I owe special thanks to my sister, Cindy Wilber, who recently retired after more than twenty years as education coordinator at the Jasper Ridge Biological Preserve at Stanford University and has always been happy to show us around and talk about life in that most interesting town.

Finally, I am most appreciative of the expertise and friendship of my agent, Robert G. Diforio, of the D4EO Literary Agency, and I am deeply grateful for the editorial guidance and support of my editor, Robert Gleason, editor Robert Davis, production editor Jessica Katz, jacket designer Jess Kiley, and the rest of the staff at Tor/Forge.